PRAISE FOR ANNE GRACIE AND HER NOVELS

"The always terrific Anne Gracie outdoes herself with *Bride By Mistake* . . . Gracie created two great characters, a high-tension relationship and a wonderfully satisfying ending. Not to be missed!"
—Mary Jo Putney, *New York Times* bestselling author

"A fascinating twist on the girl-in-disguise plot . . . With its wildly romantic last chapter, this novel is a great antidote to the end of the summer." —Eloisa James, *New York Times* bestselling author

"With her signature superbly nuanced characters, subtle sense of wit and richly emotional writing, Gracie puts her distinctive stamp on a classic Regency plot." —*Chicago Tribune*

"Anne Gracie's writing dances that thin line between always familiar and always fresh . . . *The Accidental Wedding* is warm and sweet, tempered with bursts of piquancy and a dash or three of spice."
—*New York Journal of Books*

"Threaded with charm and humor . . . [An] action-rich, emotionally compelling story . . . It is sure to entice readers."
—*Library Journal* (starred review)

"Another [of] Ms. Gracie's character-rich, fiery tales filled with emotion and passion leavened by charm and wit."
—*Romance Reviews Today*

"The main characters are vibrant and complex . . . The author's skill as a storyteller makes this well worth reading." —*Kirkus Reviews*

THE
Summer Bride

ANNE GRACIE

BERKLEY SENSATION, NEW YORK

BERKLEY
SENSATION

An imprint of Penguin Random House LLC
375 Hudson Street, New York, New York 10014

THE SUMMER BRIDE

A Berkley Sensation Book / published by arrangement with the author

ISBN: 9780425283806

PUBLISHING HISTORY
Berkley Sensation mass-market edition / July 2016

PRINTED IN THE UNITED STATES OF AMERICA

10 9 8 7 6 5 4 3 2 1

Cover art by Judy York.
Cover design by George Long.

Penguin
Random
House

For Aunty Jean and Cousin Di,
with love.

With thanks to all the readers
who've followed the adventures of the Chance sisters,
and who wrote to me asking for Daisy's story.

And with thanks, as always to my writing friends
who are always there to listen and support and brainstorm.

Chapter One

It isn't what we say or think that defines us, but what we do.

—JANE AUSTEN, *SENSE & SENSIBILITY*

"I can make anyfing out of anyfing, but even I can't make a silk purse out of a bloomin' sow's ear!" Daisy Chance declared. "I was born in the gutter, raised in an 'orehouse and I got a gimpy leg. I don't look like a lady or speak like a lady and I ain't never gunna *be* a lady, so what's the point of—"

Lady Beatrice cut her off. "Nonsense! You can do anything you set your mind to!"

Daisy rolled her eyes. "Maybe, but I don't *want* to be a lady! I want to be a dressmaker—and not just any dressmaker. I aim to become the most fashionable modiste in London—fashion to the top nobs."

The old lady shrugged. "No reason why you can't be a modiste *and* a lady."

Daisy stared at the old lady incredulously. "You don't have no idea, do you? What it's gunna take—"

"Any idea. It's *any* idea."

Daisy rolled her eyes. "W*ork*, that's what it takes—hard work, never-endin' work. I'm workin' every hour God sends as it is, and even so I'm barely managin'. There ain't no time for me to prance around pretendin' to be a lady!"

"You *are* a lady!"

Daisy snorted, and Lady Beatrice went on, "Your entire nature declares it. Inside, you *are* a lady, Daisy—loyal, loving, honest, sensitive to others' needs—all we have to do is teach you to be ladylike on the outside as well!"

"Bugger that," said the budding lady. "Apart from the fact I ain't got *time* for all that, the thing is I don't *care* about it. And there's no point! All the lessons in the world ain't goin' to make me the kind of lady that Abby or Jane or Damaris is. They was born with lovely manners and a sweet way of speakin'—I was born in the gutter and brung up rough."

"*Brought* up not *brung*, and they *were* born not *was*. But that is immaterial—"

"No it's not. I've got a chance now—thanks to you and Abby and the girls—to make somef-some*th*ing of meself."

"Yes, a lady."

"No, a modiste, wiv a shop of me own. I want to *dress* fine ladies, not ape them."

Lady Beatrice drew herself up stiffly. "With me conducting your lessons, there is no question of *aping* anyone—and please do not use such a vulgar expression!"

"Yeah, well, I'm from the vulgar classes, me, and I call a spade a bloomin' spade, but if that's too blunt for you, I'll say it different—I ain't a lady and I don't like fakery."

"Says the girl living in my house under a false name," the old lady said with a sweetly sanctimonious air. "And presumably planning to open her business under that same false name."

Daisy gaped. "*You* can say that? You, who's told more lies about us than anyone? *Who* invented her own false half sister—and made her a bastard, eh? *Who* claimed us as her nieces when we weren't no such thing? *Who* made up the whole piece of nonsense about Venice? *Who*—" She broke off. The old lady was chuckling. She was proud of her lies.

Daisy said with dignity, "You know dam—perfectly well I only went along with the Chance surname for Abby and Jane's sake—they was in danger."

Lady Beatrice shrugged. "They *were*. Nevertheless, you still call yourself Daisy Chance instead of—what was your surname, anyway?"

"Smith. But that was just a surname somebody picked out of a hat. I'm a foundling, never known me mum or dad, so me real name is anyone's guess."

"You're getting off the point," Lady Beatrice said. "All the other gels will be gathering upstairs tomorrow afternoon and I want you there as well."

"I thought they wa—were finished with all that, now the Season has started."

The old lady waved her hand dismissively. "They require further polish. The gentle art of social intercourse— conversation, dancing and deportment—does not come naturally to all ladies, and Jane has a tendency to romp, rather than dance. So, you will come." It was an order, but there was the faintest note of uncertainty in her voice.

Daisy pounced on it. "No, I got too much work to do now to waste any more time on social flimflam." Daisy had found the lessons about conversation and deportment interesting enough, and she figured the curtsying might come in useful for her business, but that was enough. Besides, Lady Bea kept going on about her learning to dance, and that she down-right refused to do.

"An hour or two won't hurt."

"I can set a sleeve or finish a hem in an hour."

"Pfft!" The old lady dismissed the sleeve and the hem. "I want you there and you *shall* attend."

"Bad luck. I ain't comin'."

"I won't argue with you, Daisy. You *will* learn what I say you must! No niece of mine will leave this house knowing less than she ought."

Daisy glared at her. "But I ain't your niece and we both know it." The old lady was asking the impossible and she knew it, so why . . . .

The old lady glared back, stamping the floor with her cane. "Gels who live under my roof do as I tell them!"

"Or what?" Daisy demanded. There was a short, tense

silence, and she added half incredulously, "Are you *threatenin'* me? Tellin' me to do as you say or get out o' your house?"

The silence stretched. Daisy felt her stomach clench. Oh, gawd, her bloody temper . . . The old lady had every right to toss her back onto the streets . . .

Lady Beatrice subsided in her chair with a sigh. "Oh, don't be ridiculous, child. Of course I'm not. I might want to strangle you—and I'd be perfectly justified, stubborn wench that you are!—but you must know that I love you like a daughter—a stubborn, infuriating daughter who doesn't know what's good for her, mind—but then that's quite common in daughters, I'm told by women who have 'em. And nieces are clearly just as troublesome. *Some* of them," she added with a beady look.

Daisy started breathing again. Tears pricked at the back of her eyelids. She blinked them away. She never cried, but the old lady's declaration had shocked her. She knew the old girl was fond of her—Daisy was more than fond of her too—but to say, right out loud that she *loved* Daisy. *Like a daughter* . . .

Lady Beatrice continued, "But that doesn't mean I won't threaten, bully, cajole, blackmail and utterly insist on your doing some things you don't want to do." She gave Daisy a stern look. "Because that's what mothers and aunts do—*if* they have any sense."

She raised her lorgnette and fixed a horribly enlarged eye on Daisy. "So missy, you *will* attend this lesson—if I have to fetch Featherby and William to carry you there, kicking and screaming."

There was no point in continuing the argument, Daisy decided. They'd just go round and round, like two old boxers in a ring, making no progress and just getting tired. And upset. "All right, I'll think about it," she said in what she hoped was a convincing voice.

When the time came for the lesson, she'd lock her door. William and Featherby would hardly break it down.

The old lady graciously inclined her head. "I'm glad to see you're talking sense at last. You'll find these lessons invaluable."

"I still say you can't make a silk purse out of a—"

"Stop saying that, Daisy! If *you* are a sow's ear, what, pray, as your aunt, does that make *me*?"

Daisy's lips twitched as she fought a grin.

"Don't you *dare* say it, you atrocious gel!" Lady Beatrice threw a fan at her and missed. And then she started to chuckle. Daisy's own laughter exploded at the same time.

After a few minutes, Lady Beatrice lay back in her chair, wiping her eyes with a wisp of lace. "Dreadful, dreadful gel! I *refuse* to be the aunt of a sow's ear!"

"Can't choose your relatives," Daisy said with a grin. She picked up the fan, laid it on a side table and got up to leave.

"Nonsense! I do, all the time. It's perfectly simple to do, and a great deal more satisfactory—even when they're impossible." Lady Beatrice gave her a speculative look. "So, upstairs then, tomorrow afternoon at four."

"I'll see how me sewin's goin'." There might be some work she could take with her.

"Sewing, going," said Lady Beatrice, emphasizing the *g*'s. "Don't drop your *g*'s."

Daisy gave her a basilisk look. "That friend of yours, Sir Oswald Merridew—he drops his *g*'s all the time."

"Yes, but in an aristocratic, stylish manner."

"Then that's how I'll drop mine then," Daisy said with a grin.

Lady Beatrice threw her handkerchief at her. "Impossible gel!" But she was trying not to smile.

Daisy picked up the handkerchief and gave it back to her as she left. As she closed the door, the words *stubborn wench* floated after her.

Daisy tromped up the stairs, feeling shaken. Her bloomin' temper—she'd practically dared Lady Bea to chuck her out on the streets, and then where would she be? Back where she'd started, that's where—homeless and friendless and with barely two pennies to rub together.

Oh, Abby or Damaris would take her in, she knew that,

but she'd never been anyone's charity case, and she wasn't going to start now.

Besides, she loved Lady Bea and didn't like upsetting her. Even if the old lady did have this crazy notion of turning Daisy into a lady.

The trouble was, Daisy was so tired. She woke each morning in the wee small hours, tossing the same problems over and over like a butter churn in her head—the work she had to get through, the promises she'd made, the money she didn't have . . .

She'd given up on trying to get back to sleep. Instead she'd started getting up in the dark, giving thanks that Lady Bea's house was fitted with the wonder of gas lighting.

Better to work than worry.

But now here she was, snapping at the slightest provocation, losing her temper with the people she cared most about.

You must know that I love you like a daughter . . .

A lump came to her throat. No one had ever loved her like a daughter.

Nobody had ever loved Daisy at all—not until she'd met Abby and Damaris and Jane—not really. Oh, there had been declarations in her past, but they'd proved to be false. Men were liars and cheats—at least they were to a girl on her own with nothing to offer except herself.

And she'd thought Mrs. B. had cared about her like a daughter, but when the time came . . . Nah, Daisy had learned her lesson young: In this life, you were on your own.

But even when things had gotten so desperate with Abby and Jane, they hadn't dumped Damaris and Daisy—which would have been the practical thing to do, them not being related at all. Instead they'd vowed to stick even closer together and become as sisters.

Daisy still hadn't gotten over the wonder of that.

And then they'd moved in with Lady Beatrice—an earl's daughter, a real, proper blue-blooded toff, no matter what state she was in at the time—and she'd claimed them as her nieces.

Lady Beatrice was the best thing that had happened to any of them.

Still, the old lady had a maggot in her brain. A blind man

could tell Daisy would never make any kind of fine lady, even if she wanted to—which she bloomin' well didn't! But would the old girl listen?

Daisy had no illusions about herself. She was a little Cockney guttersnipe with a gimpy leg and a foul mouth—though she was working on the swearing and her grammar. But she loved beautiful clothes and—praise be!—she was good at making them.

She was going to *be* somebody, and she was going to do it all herself: *Daisy Chance, Dressmaker to the Toffs*, with a shop and a business all her own. That was her dream, and she was so hungry for it she could almost taste it.

She reached her workroom. When she first came to live with Lady Bea, it had been her bedchamber—the first time in her life she'd had a room all to herself—but gradually her sewing had taken it over and they'd pushed her bed into Jane's room and replaced it with a big, old table.

It was a large, spacious room, and on a clear day it was flooded with natural light. Light was precious for a seamstress. Now there were clothes and fabrics and bits of braid and lace draped everywhere.

Daisy loved stepping into this room—her cave of gorgeousness. Visible evidence of her dream coming true. *This* was what mattered. *This* was her future, not some mad idea of turning her into a bad imitation of a lady.

Daisy threaded her needle and picked up the dress she was working on. She had a long list of things to do. The Season had already started, but her work had only intensified. Two more ball gowns to finish off, luckily they weren't as fiddly as the one she'd made for Jane's first ball; and then three more morning dresses—gawd, but the gentry were big on visiting—and a new pelisse to cut out.

Jane's shepherdess costume for the masquerade next week hung by the door. Daisy had altered an old dress of Lady Bea's and it had come up a treat. Perfect for a wear-it-once costume. Saved her a heap of time.

But . . . so many orders, so many promises she'd made.

Oh, Lady Bea had lent Daisy Polly and Ginny, her maids,

to sew for her every afternoon. And Jane, Abby and Damaris knew about Daisy's dream and did whatever they could to help.

But Abby and Damaris were married ladies now, and Jane had made her come-out and was promised, if not officially betrothed, and it was her job now to attend as many social occasions as she could and establish herself as a member of the ton. All the girls had other responsibilities. And it was them wearing Daisy-made clothes to fancy society events that was the reason she had so many orders now, so she wasn't going to complain.

Daisy sewed every minute God sent—and more. But it still wasn't enough.

She'd tried putting her prices up, quoting ridiculous prices, just to put people off and slow things down a bit, but it only made some ladies more determined than ever to have one of Daisy's creations.

Rich people were mad. But that madness was going to make Daisy rich and famous.

Eventually.

If only she could make the clothes quicker. But how? She was barely scraping by as it was—she paid Polly and Ginny a bit whenever she could—on top of what Lady Bea paid them—but there was no extra money to employ anyone else.

Getting fabric was no problem—Max and Freddy, her brothers-in-law, owned a silk importing business—but things like lace and fancy bits and bobs cost money, and tradesmen wouldn't hand over the goods unless she paid.

And toffs might be rich, but they took forever to pay.

Round and around her thoughts went, turning the same problems over and over in her mind, and as always, the only solution Daisy could come up with was to work harder. And longer. And faster.

Her needle flew.

Some time later, a knock sounded on Daisy's door. She looked up and saw Lady Beatrice's butler, Featherby standing in the doorway.

"What?" She glowered suspiciously at him. "If you've come to drag me off—"

He looked faintly shocked. "I have no intention of dragging you anywhere, Miss Daisy. I just wanted a quiet word. May I come in?"

She sighed. "Come in then, Mr. F.—and don't call me Miss Daisy. Not when we're alone. I ain't forgotten—if everyone else in this bloomin' house has—how we all met—me, Abby, Jane, Damaris, and you and William."

"I haven't forgotten," Featherby said smoothly, shutting the door behind him. "I thought maybe you had."

She stared at him. "Whaddya mean? Of course I remember." She patted the seat beside her in invitation. "We was in the attic of that half-wrecked place that was going to be knocked down, and you and William was livin' downstairs."

Featherby seated himself with a reminiscent sigh. "All of us living on the brink of disaster."

"Yeah, but—"

"William was an ageing, broken-down prizefighter, getting pounded to mincemeat for a few shillings, and I was a disgraced former butler, dismissed without a character for drunkenness."

"Drunkenness?" Daisy gave him a surprised look. "But I've never seen you touch even a drop."

"Not now, I don't. But it was pure luck"—he smiled—"*chance*, if you will—that you girls needed our help that day. And that Lady Beatrice took William and myself in, as well as you girls." He gave her a long, steady look. "We're secure now—or as secure as any servant with an elderly employer can be—and we have no intention of risking our position."

Daisy narrowed her eyes. "Are you sayin' I'm threatening your security?"

"No, not at all," Featherby said smoothly. "But—and I say this on the strength of our previous acquaintanceship, and not as a butler—or not only as a butler—do as the old lady wants, Daisy."

"But it's stupid—"

"Do it anyway. It matters to her that she teach you all the things a lady needs to know."

Daisy rolled her eyes. How many more times did she have to say it. "But I ain't never gunna—"

"Do it anyway," Featherby repeated. "Because you love her. Because she loves you."

Daisy was silent a moment. Lots of talk of love flying around this morning. She wasn't used to it. Had no idea how to handle it.

She frowned, considering his words. She did love the old lady, she did. But . . . She gestured to the piles of garments in various stages of construction. "Look at all this, Featherby. I ain't got time to waste ladifying meself for no good reason."

"Make the time."

"And how does me work get done, eh?"

Featherby shrugged. "Find another way. You're talented and clever and resourceful. And you're young. You have your whole future ahead of you, Daisy." He lowered his voice for emphasis. "Lady Beatrice doesn't. She's old. And whatever her reason, this is what she wants for you."

"Did she send you up here to talk me into—?"

Featherby looked slightly affronted. "No, she has no idea. I sought you out as a friend, not as a butler."

Daisy believed him. She nodded, mollified.

Featherby waited a moment, then continued, "Lady Beatrice is the reason none of us is still living in a rundown slum, living from hand to mouth. She's the reason you have this rosy future you're working so hard for."

There was a long silence. "You're sayin' I owe her."

Featherby made a noncommittal gesture. "It's your decision."

Daisy heaved a sigh. "I know." She hesitated, rubbing a finger back and forth along the seam of her skirt, then muttered. "But I feel like such a fool, Mr. Featherby, clumpin' around practicing curtseys wiv me gammy leg, let alone trying to dance."

"I know," he said gently. A faint smile crossed his normally impassive features. "You should have heard William the first time he put on footman's livery."

Daisy looked up. "He didn't like it?"

Featherby's smile widened. "He loathed it. Swore he wasn't going to go around all trussed up like a Christmas goose."

Daisy laughed. Big, rough-hewn William wasn't the smoothest of footmen.

"But he grew accustomed to it, and he found a way to make the role his own," Featherby finished. "And so will you, Daisy. You can do anything you put your mind to."

Proving, Daisy thought, that he'd heard the whole argument between her and Lady Bea. Still, Featherby wasn't given to saying things he didn't mean. "You reckon so?"

"I know so. So, will you attend the lesson tomorrow?"

Daisy sighed. "You know I will. You've made me feel that big." She made a gesture with thumb and finger.

Featherby gave her an approving smile. "My dear, never think that I intended to diminish you in any way. You—all of you girls—have the biggest hearts in the world." He hesitated, then added in a voice that was slightly husky, "Lady Beatrice and your sisters are not the only ones who love you, you know. I never did have children . . ."

Daisy blinked and a lump formed in her throat. Featherby was such a perfect butler that it was easy to forget he was a man with his own private thoughts and feelings. She opened her mouth to say something, but he cleared his throat and surged to his feet, and suddenly he was no longer the kindly friend who'd just deprived her of the power of speech, but a very dignified butler whose face never expressed emotion of any kind.

He moved towards the door.

"Mr. Featherby."

He stopped and glanced back at her, one brow raised.

"Do you like bein' a butler?" She'd never wondered that before, had taken it for granted. But now she was curious.

For a second she thought he wasn't going to answer, but then he said, "Remember the situation when we first joined Lady Beatrice, the mess she was in, the disarray, the dirt, the chaos and discomfort?"

Daisy nodded. She did indeed.

The place was a pigsty and Lady Beatrice bedridden and helpless.

"Now, because of me, this household runs like the most perfect clockwork, seamlessly and invisibly." Then Featherby grinned, positively grinned. "Do I *like* being a butler, Daisy?" He swept her a bow that combined grace, dignity and a fair degree of triumph. "I love it! I am to butlerdom what you are to dressmaking—simply the best there is. In fact—though I hesitate to boast—I am regularly offered large . . . shall we say, *inducements*—I shall not call them *bribes*—to enter the employment of other ladies and gentlemen." He wrinkled his nose fastidiously.

Daisy's eyes widened. "What? You mean people are tryin' to steal you from Lady Bea? You're not tempted, are you?"

Featherby drew himself up proudly. "Not for one instant. William and I will never leave Lady Beatrice. Never! Not while I have breath in my body."

Daisy nodded. She felt like that too about the old lady.

"I'm glad we've reached an understanding, miss."

Daisy shrugged. She'd take her sewing with her to the lessons; she could sew as well as listen. "I ain't going to dance, though," she called after him just as the door was closing. "You won't get me on any blood—er, bloomin' dance floor!"

Chapter Two

*It is a truth universally acknowledged, that a single man
in possession of a good fortune, must be in want of a wife.*

—JANE AUSTEN, *PRIDE & PREJUDICE*

Patrick Flynn leapt lightly from the hired hackney carriage, instructed the driver to wait, and rang the doorbell of Lady Beatrice's home in Berkeley Square.

"Mornin', Featherby," he greeted the butler familiarly. When Flynn had first arrived in London, knowing only Max, Flynn's business partner and Lady Beatrice's nephew, the old lady had invited him to stay. He'd spent his first few weeks living here and it had set him on exactly the path he wanted.

"Miss Daisy ready, is she?" Flynn asked. It was still quite early in the morning, but he'd sent a note around the previous evening. They'd received word that one of his ships carrying a special cargo of silks was due to dock this morning. Since Daisy was making clothes for Max's wife, Abby and her other two sisters, Max wanted him to give Daisy first pick.

"Not quite, sir, but I'm sure she won't be long. In the meantime, I'll take your coat and hat, and if you would care to wait . . ."

Flynn did not care to wait, but he had no choice. Women were invariably late.

As the butler took Flynn's overcoat, his expression became

more than usually blank. Flynn smiled at Featherby's pained, feigned obliviousness, and stroked his waistcoat.

Featherby did not approve of Flynn's colorful waistcoats. He wasn't the only one. When Flynn took over Freddy Hyphen-Hyphen's bachelor apartments, he'd also taken on his valet, Tibbins. Tibbins frankly and openly despised the flamboyant waistcoats and tried at every opportunity to convince his master to get rid of them.

Flynn cared not the snap of his fingers for his valet's—or anyone else's—opinions. He had no love for the current English fashion for dressing a man like a wet weekend in Wales; Flynn liked a bit of color.

He'd entered London society with a view to finding a fine, fashionable lady to take to wife, and wiser and more fashionable heads—well, Freddy Hyphen-Hyphen, who was an elegant sprig—had persuaded him to dress more conventionally—for the moment, at any rate.

Today, not even such an arbiter of fashion as Hyphen-Hyphen could find fault with the immaculate buckskin breeches molded smoothly over Flynn's thighs, his highly polished black boots, his fine linen shirt with its high starched collar, the elegantly tied neckcloth and the perfectly tailored dark blue coat made for him by the very exclusive Weston, tailor to the fine gentlemen of the ton.

No, Flynn would have been complete to a shade—a very dull shade in his opinion—except for his waistcoat, which had not been made for him by any gentleman's tailor.

Today's waistcoat was a riot of snarling black and yellow embroidered Chinese tigers on a scarlet and blue silk background. Their eyes were tiny crystals that glinted green or red when he moved.

He had half a dozen of these vividly colored waistcoats, mostly made of Chinese or Indian embroideries and all made by Miss Daisy Chance, who charged Flynn an exorbitant price for the privilege—with a cheeky grin that all but admitted it was bare-faced robbery.

"Tell the lass to shake a leg, will you, Featherby?"

Featherby inclined a regal head. "I shall inform the young

lady, sir. In the meantime, Lady Beatrice would, I'm sure, be delighted to entertain you. She's in the front drawing room." With an imperious wave of his hand, Featherby indicated the room. "I will have tea brought in."

"Oh, but I haven't got t—"

But the butler had gone, damn him, disappearing through the green baize door that led to the servants' domain. With a sigh, Flynn made his way to the drawing room, already half regretting that he'd agreed to take Daisy with him.

It wasn't that Flynn minded Daisy's company—he liked the girl fine—it was just . . . he preferred to inspect his cargo on his own. It was a private little ritual he enjoyed each time one of his ships docked, meeting with the captain, going over the cargo manifest, then poking quietly through the various stores and bundles, the boxes and the exotically wrapped items, and deciding what he would do with them all.

It was a reminder of how far he'd come, a small, private . . . all right, yes, a small, private gloat.

Flynn grinned to himself. And maybe not always so small.

Trading was in his blood. He never knew in advance exactly what his captains might bring. Oh, there was the bread-and-butter cargo, silks and tea and spices and what-have-you, depending on where the ship had been trading, but he encouraged all his captains to keep an eye out for anything special and unusual.

Rich people were prepared to pay handsomely for the rare and exclusive.

And this particular ship was the *Derry Lass*, whose captain, McKenzie, traveled with his wife, Mai-Lin, who was a born trader on both sides of her heritage—the Scottish and the Chinese. She'd never yet failed to surprise him with some rare and beautiful item. And as well as silks, she had a nose for fine jade. Flynn collected jade.

Still, if he had to take an outsider along with him—and a female at that—Daisy was a good choice. She had an eye for quality, that girl, and a knack for knowing the kind of things that ladies—and therefore merchants—would snap up.

He knocked on the sitting room door and entered.

The dowager Lady Davenham, who preferred to be addressed as Lady Beatrice, the title she'd been born with, was seated on an overstuffed armchair, her skirts arranged around her like a queen's robes, leafing through the pages of an illustrated periodical in a bored fashion. She looked up and brightened.

"Mr. Flynn, my dear boy, come in, come in. Just the man I wanted to see. I am bored to death with the company of women! Oh, not my darling gels—you know me better than that—but morning callers—and when I heard the bell just now, I thought you must be one of them—though it is a ridiculously early time for morning calls and nobody with the slightest pretension to fashion would make a morning call before noon—though of course it's quite a different matter with a gentlemen caller, particularly a handsome one like yourself. You are welcome at any time."

She raised her lorgnette and raked her gaze over him, lingering over the fit of the buckskin breeches. "You look to be in fine fettle, dear boy. I do like those breeches. So many men just don't have the wherewithal to fill a pair of breeches properly."

Flynn hid a grin. He was pretty sure he knew what she meant by *wherewithal*. She was an outrageous old bird.

Finally she dragged her gaze up to his face and beamed up at him. "So, what brings you here—do you want some tea? Of course you do—just tug on that bellpull, will you and—oh, here are William and Featherby now with the tea. Perfect timing as usual, Featherby. Be seated, dear boy, there where I can see you." She gestured graciously.

Flynn sat.

The footman, William, set down the tea tray. Featherby poured while William put out a plate of dainty cakes and biscuits. As Featherby handed Flynn his teacup, he said, "Miss Daisy's compliments, sir. She's changing now and will be down in an instant."

Lady Beatrice's brows rose. "Will she indeed? That will make a change. You are honored, Mr. Flynn. The wretched gel hardly ever graces us with her company these days. Not for mere *social* occasions." She snorted.

"Oh? And why would that be?"

She waved a dismissive hand. "Sheer stubbornness."

The footman and butler withdrew. Lady Beatrice drank a mouthful of tea, picked up an iced pink almond cake and said, "Now, dear boy, tell me, how is your matrimonial quest proceeding?"

"Well enough, thank you, m'lady." He took a ginger biscuit, thought about dunking it in his cup of tea, reflected that the practice was frowned upon in elegant circles and crunched it down in two bites instead. He washed it down with a mouthful of tea. The ginger was good and spicy, the tea as weak as water. He preferred Indian tea, strong as it could come. Lady Beatrice invariably drank China.

She raised her lorgnette and said sharply, "*Well enough*? What does 'well enough' mean? Have you found a suitable young lady or not? Who have you met so far? How it is *going*?"

Flynn took another biscuit. "Excellent ginger nuts, m'lady. My compliments to your cook."

Lady Beatrice was forever trying to winkle information out of Flynn concerning his plans and any potential courtships he might be considering. Ever since she'd met him, the old lady had been dying to match him up—and he was grateful for her introductions. But he'd always steered his own course, and he preferred to keep his own counsel until he'd made a final decision.

His reluctance to discuss the matter in detail fair drove the old lady mad. And to be honest, Flynn quite enjoyed teasing her.

She eyed him narrowly. "Finding you've aimed rather too high, have you? I did warn you. A lowborn, uneducated sea captain, Irish—and Roman Catholic to boot!" She shook her head.

"Lapsed, m'lady, and though all you say is true, I don't believe I'm aimin' too high," Flynn said mildly. He was comfortable in his own skin and knew his own worth. "I'm also

rich—a self-made man with a fleet of ships and a tradin'
empire that spreads from here to the four corners of the earth."

Lady Beatrice sniffed. "Money acquired *in trade*."

Flynn grinned, undeceived by her disparaging tone. "Aye,
m'lady, lots of nasty vulgar money at me disposal which the
poor lass who consents to become me wife will have to help
me spend. 'Twill be a terrible burden for her, I'm thinkin'."

Lady Beatrice's finely painted lips twitched. "Undoubt-
edly. Modesty is not one of your virtues, is it Mr. Flynn."

Flynn shrugged. He'd never seen the point of hiding his
light under a bushel.

She picked up a dainty pastry bulging with cream and
nibbled on it thoughtfully. "Max and Freddy have introduced
you to a number of likely prospects, I know. As have I
myself. But the Season has only just begun. Don't give up
hope yet, dear boy, there are plenty of eligible gels—"

"Oh, I have me eye on a likely lass," he said unwarily.

He'd pretty much settled on Lady Elizabeth Compton, the
daughter of the Earl of Compton. Lady Elizabeth looked to
be everything he wanted in a wife—blue-blooded, pretty,
young but not too young, and as far as Flynn could tell, sweet-
natured. The only daughter of an impoverished earl, her father
had subtly indicated he had no objection to a jumped-up
lapsed Irish Catholic, as long as his fortune was fat enough,
and Flynn's was.

"Have you now?" Lady Beatrice leaned forward, her
aristocratic Roman nose practically quivering, like a hound
given the scent of a hare. "The finest young lady in London,
you told me you wanted. This gel is a lady I presume?"

"To her fingertips, with a pedigree as long as your arm."

"Who is she then? Do I know her?"

Flynn shook his head. "Nothing is settled yet."

"I know how to keep my mouth shut, if that's what's
worrying you," she said tartly.

"To be sure, ma'am," he said in a manner calculated to
soothe her ruffled feathers. "But I'm a wee bit superstitious
about speaking before any arrangements have been made.

Once things are settled, I promise you, you'll be the first to know. I'm truly grateful for the introduction."

"Oho!" Lady Beatrice set her teacup aside, raised her lorgnette and leaned forward. "So I introduced you to the gel, did I? Which one is it, then? Is it—"

"I don't intend to discuss it, m'lady," Flynn said firmly. He was grateful for the introductions to various members of the ton that Lady Beatrice and Max had made, but he had no intention of letting the old lady—well-meaning as she was—oversee his courtship. Or blab it around before he'd even spoken to the girl.

She took no notice and began reeling off names, her beady gaze, intensified by her lorgnette, focused intently on him. "Is it Miss Harrington? Or the Grainger gel—forgot her name—the pretty one, with the unfortunate hair? No? Then what about the Sherry gel—Marianne? A little long in the tooth, but still perfectly eligible. No? Hmm, let me think, who else have I introduced you to?"

Flynn could have sworn he hadn't moved a muscle, so how the devil did the old lady know it was none of the girls she'd listed? Freddy Hyphen-Hyphen claimed the old lady was some kind of mind-reading witch, and the rate she was going, a distraction was in order.

"It might be the daughter of a duke," he confided, "and that's all I'm going to say. I wouldn't want it to get out." He picked up a third ginger nut and chomped into it. Let the old girl muse on that little red herring.

"A *duke's* gel?" Her brow knotted. "Not many of those left on the shelf—and none that I know of coming out this season, either. She's made her come-out, this gel, has she?"

"Oh, yes." Flynn sipped his tea and kept a straight face.

"The only duke's gel that I can think of—the only unmarried one, that is—is Lady Pamela Girtle-Bute. But of course it couldn't possibly be her."

Flynn leaned forward with what he hoped was a guileless expression. "Why not?"

"Pammy Girtle-Bute?" The old lady snorted. "Frightful

gel! Long past her prayers and no wonder. No looks to speak of—a perfect barrel of a girl—and those teeth!! And a crashing bore, to boot. Carries on a conversation as if she's the only person in the room, can't shut her up—and loud. Even the deaf are deafened. Add to that her propensity for keeping pet rats—d'you know, she took one once to a ball—carried it in her reticule—wretched creature got out, of course—you should have heard the commotion! And the smell . . ." Lady Beatrice waved her hand in front of her nose. "No, a man would have to be more than desperate to choose Pammy Girtle-Bute."

"Oh." Flynn sipped his tea with a downcast air. "I'm sorry you think so."

The old lady stiffened. "You can't mean it! Not Pammy Girtle-Bute!"

He shrugged. "She *is* the daughter of a duke."

"But she's utterly atrocious! You can't possibly—"

"I don't want to discuss it," Flynn said virtuously.

"But you cannot—"

"Delicious ginger nuts," he said.

"There are plenty of gels almost as well born as Pammy Girtle-Bute, but a great deal more pleas—"

"As I said m'lady, I make me own choice." With the air of a man who has finished talking, Flynn perused the cake plate, decided a fourth ginger nut would be too much and selected a large pastry, oozing jam and bulging with cream.

He lifted the pastry high for a careful bite, partly to ensure he did not drip any of the cream, and partly to hide his expression from the old lady. It was a tricky operation, but when he lowered the pastry, it was to find the old lady scrutinizing him through her lorgnette with a severe expression.

"You are a wicked, wicked tease, Mr. Flynn!"

He finished the pastry and wiped his hands and mouth, wiping away—he hoped—any trace of a smile. "If you say so, m'lady."

"I do! You almost had me believing that appalling tale."

"Surely not, m'lady. And you so fly to the ways of the world."

She fixed him with a gimlet stare. "Don't try to butter

me up, you rogue! That atrocious tale could have caused me to have palpitations! *Palpitations*, I say!"

Flynn smiled. "Palpitations? Never say so m'lad—"

She thumped her cane on the floor. "I am a frail old woman and not to be lied to!"

"Ah, you're as strong as an—"

"If you say *ox* Mr. Flynn, I shall—I shall hit you!" She gripped her cane meaningfully.

He chuckled. "No need for violence, ma'am. I was goin' to say as strong as an er, an elf—yes, that's it, strong as an elf—a delicate, elegant, canny, ageless wee elf."

Lady Beatrice snorted. "You're a silver-tongued rogue and a shameless rascal, Mr. Flynn."

"If you say so, m'lady."

"I do. I can't imagine why I ever imagined that I liked you." She gave him a long baleful stare that did its best to look stern.

He gave her a slow grin. "Well, milady, that would no doubt be me irresistible Irish charm."

Her lips twitched. She pursed them ruthlessly back into an appearance of severity. "Irresistible Irish blarney, more like. Kissing that wretched stone or whatever it is that you Irish do."

"Now why would I bother to kiss the Blarney Stone when there are so much more enticin' things to kiss, milady?"

A reluctant chuckle escaped her. "You are quite, quite shameless." Then a cunning expression came into her eyes. She wagged a bony finger at him. "You're in need of a lesson, Mr. Flynn."

He quirked an eyebrow. "Am I indeed?"

"Yes, and you'll have it, tomorrow at four o'clock sharp." She pointed. "Upstairs." She regarded him with a pleased expression.

She couldn't possibly mean what he thought she meant. "What kind of lesson?" he asked warily.

"A dancing lesson, Mr. Flynn. Now don't argue—you'll oblige me in this. Wicked man that you are, you owe it to me for the Dreadful Fright you gave me."

She heaved herself to her feet, using her cane as a lever.

Flynn leaped forward to help her but she batted his hands away impatiently. "Four o'clock sharp, d'ye hear me?"

"But I know how to dance."

She gave a scornful snort. "Nonsense! You've been at sea most of your life—they don't dance the hornpipe at Almack's, you know!"

He opened his mouth to inform her that he might be a seaman, but he knew all the fashionable dances, but at that point Daisy arrived, buttoning her pelisse, a bonnet dangling by its strings from her arm. "Mornin', Flynn. Sorry to keep you waitin'."

Lady Beatrice leveled her lorgnette at Daisy. "You are dressed to go Out."

Daisy nodded. " 'S'right. I'm goin' somewhere with Mr. Flynn."

"Going somewhere? To where, pray tell?" When Daisy just grinned the old lady turned to Flynn. "You are honored, Mr. Flynn, honored, I say. The wretched gel has refused to accompany me anywhere of late! She refuses to make morning calls, turns her nose up at the most delightful events, and only occasionally will she even consent to walk in the park with the gels and me."

"Pooh, you hardly ever walk anyway." Daisy finished buttoning her pelisse, crammed her bonnet on and tied the strings. "You just sit in your carriage and take people up to gossip with. I ain't got time to waste on that sort of thing."

Flynn watched her tying the strings of her bonnet with no apparent care. The hat sat rakishly on her tousled brown locks, and yet the final effect was both stylish and flattering to her pale, angular, vivid little face. Her whole outfit was simple—plain with none of the frills and bits that other women seemed to like, but neat as a new pin, and somehow elegant. She was a tidy little package, young Daisy.

Daisy turned to Flynn, her eyes bright with anticipation. "Righto, Flynn, I'm ready."

"Mr. Flynn hasn't yet finished his tea," Lady Beatrice pointed out acidly, disregarding the fact that she had herself been on the point of leaving the room.

Daisy frowned at him. "Did you come to drink tea? I thought you was in a hurry to get to the docks."

"The docks?" Lady Beatrice repeated in a tone of faint horror. "You're going to *the docks*?"

"One of my ships has just arrived, m'lady—"

"And he's givin' me first pick of the loot," Daisy announced with glee. "Come on then, Flynn. No time to waste."

D aisy stepped outside, pulling on her gloves. She glanced at the leaden sky. "Brr, call this spring? Still bloomin' freezing!" Wisps of fog clung to the cold ground, a blanket of ethereal gray feathers. When she'd risen that morning and peered out of the window, the fog had been so thick the gas lamps in the street were barely visible, a mere glimmer in the dark.

Flynn had a hackney carriage waiting. The horses tossed their heads, snorting clouds of smoky breath in the chill air, and shifting restlessly, their hooves clattering on the cobbles.

Daisy climbed into the carriage, settled herself in the corner and grinned at Flynn as the carriage moved off with a jerk. "Thanks for askin' me along, Flynn."

He gave a shrug of acknowledgement. "It's no trouble. Thanks for not keepin' me waiting too long."

" 'S'all"—she broke the sentence with a huge yawn—"right."

He smiled. "Wishing you were still in bed, are you? Hope I didn't disturb your lie-in."

"Lie-in?" She made a scornful sound. "I been up since four."

"Four? In the *morning*? Good God, why?"

She shrugged. "I'm up at four most days. I don't have time to lie abed like a fine lady."

"Why on earth not?"

She shrugged. "Habit, mostly," she lied. "I get bored lyin' in bed 'til all hours."

He raised one dark, winged brow in a way that suggested he saw straight through that one, so she added, "I'd've thought you of all people would understand, Flynn. I'm building a business here, and so I'm working every hour God sends." And then a bit more.

"I see. Business is brisk, I take it."

"Certainly is." She forced a grin. "Can't hardly keep up with the orders." Couldn't keep up with them at all, if the truth be told, but she wasn't going to admit that to a soul.

"That's grand then. If you're so tired, grab a bit of kip. I'll wake you when we get there." He stretched out his long, booted legs, leaned back comfortably against the leather squabs and gazed out of the carriage window.

Daisy had no intention of dozing off when Flynn was right there beside her. She pretended to stare out of her window but watched him from the corner of her eye. He was one good-looking man, Flynn. His breeches fit nice and tight, his legs were long and powerful, and he smelled delicious—clean and manly, not like so many posh gents who drenched themselves in perfumes and smelled like a blooming flowerpot.

No, Flynn was all man. She fancied him rotten—always had, from the first day he'd come swaggering into Lady Bea's parlor, as brash and confident as if he owned the place. Those bold blue eyes of his had summed up every female in the room, a perfect invitation to sin.

From the very first he'd been danger wrapped in shades of masculine elegance—he'd just come from Freddy Monkton-Coombes's very exclusive tailor—all the while complaining about having to dress like a peahen—not a peacock—in drab colors. With a gold earring in his ear, like a bloomin' pirate. He was wearing it today; it glinted in the dim light.

He'd flirted with her that first day, just a bit—and she'd flirted back.

Daisy sighed. In the old days she'd have gone after him like a shot, but she'd turned respectable now, and so had Flynn.

He was planning to marry the finest young lady in London, and Daisy was starting up a business of her own. They were on different pathways, and a romp between the sheets wasn't on the cards for either of them. More's the pity.

Besides, Flynn was her friend, the first man she'd ever been friends—real friends—with. The men she'd known in the past were users—pimps, predators, thieves and swindlers—all crooks of some kind.

Flynn was different, and she wasn't going to risk spoiling their friendship with a bit of rumpy-pumpy, no matter how tempting it was. That sort of thing never lasted—and the breakup always ruined the friendship.

So it was look but don't touch.

She eyed his long, muscular thighs in their gleaming boots, and smiled to herself. Lucky he was such a treat to look at.

The carriage wended its way through the streets. She could tell when they arrived at the docks by the smell—dank, wet, stinky, salty river mud. She shivered.

"Cold?" Flynn asked her.

"Nah, just . . . that smell."

"Ah." The carriage pulled up and they climbed down. While Flynn paid the driver, Daisy looked around. The fog was still thick here, lying like a sullen, dirty pall over the Thames. Beneath it she could hear the lapping of water, and above it the *pip-pip-pip* of some seabird. She pulled her pelisse more tightly around her.

Half a dozen big boats were moored along the wharf, their hulls caressed by the swirling fog, their masts etched sharp and dark against the silvery sky.

"Which one's your boat?"

"Ship," Flynn corrected her. "Out there." He pointed to a distant shape, a ghost ship floating on fog. He put two fingers to his mouth and let out a long complicated-sounding whistle. From the depths of the fog, another whistle answered him.

Daisy frowned. "What's it doin' out there? I thought you said it was in port."

"It is. I always inspect the cargo before we moor the ship."

"Why? Wouldn't it be easier to do it on land?"

"Aye, but quicker to do it on board, while we're making arrangements for our men to unload and transfer the cargo to our own warehouses. I prefer to spend as little time on the docks as possible."

Daisy could understand that—she hated the river and the docks, but Flynn was a sailor. They were supposed to like the stink of the sea. "Why?" she asked.

"Thieves." Flynn sent out another whistle, shorter this time, then turned back to Daisy. "Gangs of thieves raid in the night—in the daytime, too, some of them—barefaced and brazen. And vicious. That's the reason for those fences and the ditches there." He gestured. "Not that you can see much in the fog. There's also private guards patrolling, but when it comes to valuable cargoes, I prefer to use me own men. Last week one of the gangs set fire to a warehouse, so I'm takin' no chances. The cargo isn't spending a moment longer here than necessary."

Daisy nodded. There were thieves everywhere. On the other hand . . . She eyed the expanse of water mistrustfully. Under the muffling blanket of fog, she could hear the lapping of water against piles. "So how do we get on board? Were you whistlin' to tell them to land the boat?"

"Ship—a boat is smaller. No, we'll go out in—yes, it's here." He strode towards the edge of the wharf, leaned over and spoke to someone Daisy couldn't see.

Daisy followed him and looked down. There bobbing away in the fog was a small rowboat with a man seated in it. "Go out in that little thing?" she exclaimed. "Not on your life!"

"It's perfectly safe," Flynn assured her.

"It bloody well isn't!" Daisy backed away. She'd nearly drowned once. Every time she smelled that stinky dank river smell, she remembered that panic, the sense of the waters closing over her head, of choking on the filthy stuff . . .

Flynn smiled, as if amused. "Don't worry, I won't let you fall in."

"You won't get the chance!"

"I thought you wanted first pick of the goods. If you don't . . ." He shrugged.

Daisy thought of all those gorgeous things hidden away in that big boat. *First pick* . . . She swallowed. "All right, but I'm warnin' you, Flynn, if that thing tips over—"

"It won't, and even if it did, I wouldn't let you drown. Unlike most seamen, I can swim like a fish, so you're perfectly safe with me." He held out his hand. With a deep breath, and hoping he couldn't feel how much she was shaking, Daisy took it. It was warm and strong.

The only way to get into the nasty little boat was by climbing down a wooden ladder built into the wharf.

"A gentleman would let you go first," Flynn said.

"Don't even think of it," Daisy told him. Modesty be buggered. "I ain't goin' nowhere unless you're there to break me fall."

With a soft chuckle, Flynn disappeared over the side, landing with a small thud in the boat. "Your turn, Miss Daisy." The little rowboat rocked and bobbed around madly. Flynn stood looking up at her, as calm as if he was on solid ground.

First pick of the goods . . . Taking a deep breath, Daisy turned her back on the river, hooked her skirts up a bit, and started down the ladder, one careful step at a time, hanging on for dear life.

Fog swirled around her, waves slapped nastily against the flimsy little boat and the weed-ridden piles of the wharf. Overhead, river birds shrieked like lost spirits. Daisy took a breath to settle her nerves . . . and the scent of the river closed over her.

She froze.

"Daisy?" Flynn's deep voice came from somewhere far away.

Daisy didn't move—couldn't move.

A pair of strong hands seized her by the waist. "Let go, I've got you."

But she couldn't.

He wrapped one brawny arm around her and with his other hand unclenched her frozen fingers, and *thud*! They landed in the little boat. It rocked wildly and she clutched at Flynn in fright.

"You're fine, lass." His voice was calm and deep and soothing. "Just sit down and be still now." He pressed her down onto a plank.

He said something to the man, then did something with a rope and pushed. The little boat left the wharf with a swish, and the man started rowing.

Flynn sat down beside Daisy. "It won't take but a moment to get to the ship." It was a bit of a squash, but the feel of his strong body beside her was a comfort. He'd said he could swim.

Shamed by her stupid panic, Daisy sat as still as she could, her back straight, her head held high. She held on tightly and, she hoped, inconspicuously. She was shaking like a leaf.

The oars splashed, the sailor pulled in a steady rhythm.

After a moment, Flynn said quietly, "I'm sorry, I didn't realize you really were frightened of the water."

Mortified by his quiet sympathy, Daisy mumbled, "It's nuffin'." She hated being such a coward.

And then because he seemed to be waiting, and because she felt so foolish, and because the salt-sour acrid smell of the river was half suffocating her she found herself muttering, "It's just . . . I nearly drowned once."

"What happened?"

"Bloke pushed me in. Thought it was funny, stupid bast—" Remembering she was trying to clean up her language, she broke off. "I can't swim. Lucky for me a riverman saw me go under. He pulled me out with a ruddy great hook, ripped me dress to bits." She grimaced. "He thought it was pretty funny too—said most of his catches were dead uns, but I was still wriggling." A shudder rippled through her as she remembered.

Flynn slid an arm around her waist. "Well, you're perfectly safe with me."

Daisy tried not to lean into him. Normally she would have shaken him off—she didn't need the temptation—but she was too grateful for the secure, solid feel of him. In any case, temptation was the last thing on her mind—she was too bloody scared.

As they slid smoothly through the water, the shape of the big ship slowly coalesced out of the fog. They traveled in silence, the sounds of the river echoing around them, made eerie by the fog and their lack of context. It was taking forever.

Beside her Flynn let out a little huff of amusement.

She turned her head and eyed him suspiciously. "What?"

"I'm thinkin' even if you did go in, you'd be in no danger of drowning." He added, "Wood floats."

"What?"

"You're as stiff as a board. Likely if you hit the water you'd float."

She narrowed her eyes at him. Then she elbowed him in the ribs. Hard.

"Ooff!" But he was laughing too. "That's better," he said. "And here we are at the ship."

The little boat bumped gently against the side of the ship. Overhead she could see the prow, with the figurehead of a carved and painted bare-breasted woman pointing from it. The name *Derry Lass* was painted in crisp gold-edged black letters.

A rope ladder hung down from the side of the ship. Daisy eyed it. Her stomach clenched. Climbing a fixed wooden ladder had been hard enough, but a rope one that would twist and swing, with the river beneath her . . .

"I can't—" she began.

"Ahoy there, *Derry Lass*!" Flynn called up. "Lady comin' aboard."

A couple of heads appeared above, then a rope with a canvas sling was lowered.

"Sit in that," Flynn said, helping her to her feet. "The lads will haul you up. It's perfectly safe—like a swing at the fairground. We use it for loading and unloading cargo— and ladies."

Anxiety scalded her throat, but she'd made a right ninny of herself once already this morning, so she swallowed her objections—and her fear—and allowed Flynn and the sailor to help settle her onto the strip of canvas.

"Ready?"

She nodded, clutching the ropes like grim death. Lordy, but she felt a fool.

"Take her away, lads," Flynn called up.

The ropes snapped taut, the canvas sling pulled tight around her bum, and "Lord lumme!" Suddenly she was swinging in the air, swaying over the water, her feet dangling and her skirts blowing.

"Keep still," Flynn instructed.

One of her shoes fell off.

"Caught it," he called up.

But Daisy wasn't worrying about her shoe. She was pulled high, and swung over the deck—a deck filled with a bunch of men and one woman, all gawking at the elegant sight she made—for all the world like a pudding dangling in a bloomin' pudding cloth. Talk about dignity.

Chapter Three

It is not time or opportunity that is to determine intimacy; it is disposition alone. Seven years would be insufficient to make some people acquainted with each other, and seven days are more than enough for others.

—JANE AUSTEN, *SENSE & SENSIBILITY*

Flynn shoved Daisy's shoe in his coat pocket and swiftly climbed the rope ladder. Captain McKenzie was waiting to greet him, along with what looked like the entire ship's crew neatly lined up.

Mrs. McKenzie—Mai-Lin—was also on deck, talking to Daisy who was shaking out her skirts, straightening her bonnet, and trying to look like she traveled by sling all the time. He repressed a grin. She was a game little thing.

"Captain Flynn, welcome aboard," McKenzie said with a salute that carried an echo of the royal navy, where he'd served for many years. The seamen lined up on the deck snapped to attention as well. It might be a privately owned trader, but McKenzie ran it with military efficiency.

Flynn felt a ripple of pride at the sight. This was his ship, one of many. He inclined his head to the assembled crew and McKenzie dismissed them to go about their work.

"McKenzie, Mai-Lin. You look ravishing, as always, Mai-Lin."

Flynn turned to Daisy, a small red leather slipper adorned

with a jaunty red and white rosette dangling from one finger. "Need help putting it on?" he said with a grin.

Daisy grabbed it, blushing furiously, and while Flynn bowed over Mai-Lin's gloved hand, she shoved her shoe back on.

"This is Miss Daisy Chance, Max's sister-in-law," Flynn said when she straightened.

The polite smiles of welcome on McKenzie's and Mai-Lin's faces instantly warmed. "Max's sister-in-law," Mai-Lin exclaimed delightedly. "We heard a rumor he'd married."

"Come to think of it she's also the sister-in-law of our silent partner, Hyphen-Hyphen." Flynn added with a mock apologetic look at Daisy, "I mean, of course, the honorable Frederick Monkton-Coombes."

"Welcome aboard the *Derry Lass*, Miss Chance," McKenzie said.

"I'm delighted to meet you," Mai-Lin added warmly. "You cannot imagine how good it is to meet another woman after months at sea with only men to talk to."

"Miss Chance has an interest in some of our cargo," Flynn told them. "She's a dressmaker."

"Oh." Mai-Lin eyed Daisy's dress with interest. "Did you make that?"

Daisy nodded, unable to keep the pride from her voice. "Dress and pelisse."

"They're both lovely—so elegant." Mai-Lin gave a rueful laugh. "I have no skills with a needle at all, unless it's to sew up a gash or a wound. But where are my manners— come along to the day cabin and we'll have tea."

"It's not a social call, Mai-Lin—" Flynn began.

"Tea," Daisy said firmly, "would be delightful, Mrs. McKenzie."

Flynn repressed a smile. Lady Beatrice to a T, only with a cockney accent.

The two ladies linked arms and headed for the captain's cabin. McKenzie gave Flynn a rueful look. "Sorry, sir. Mai-Lin's been pining for female company. Six months as the only woman on board . . ."

Flynn shook his head. "No matter." It was Daisy's time

he'd been thinking about, not his. These days he didn't have near enough to keep him busy.

McKenzie said, "Shall we go through the inventory while the ladies do whatever ladies do over tea and biscuits? If you tell me the kind of thing Miss Chance is interested in, I'll have the lads bring it up. No doubt Mai-Lin will have a few things to show you as well."

"I'm countin' on it," Flynn said. The two men went below decks.

An hour later Flynn had finished his examination of the accounts and of the inventory. Another excellent result. The profit on this shipment would be good—they wouldn't know the final result until the goods had been sold on, but he was very pleased.

"Right then, shall we join the ladies?" McKenzie asked. "And I'll tell the lads what to bring up for Miss Chance, shall I?"

"Best wait and let her tell them direct," Flynn said.

But when they approached the day cabin, it was obvious the process had already begun. The large central table that would seat a dozen men but was usually covered in maps and sea charts was piled high with colorful fabrics and embroideries. The two women were chattering nineteen to the dozen while several seamen stood by with resigned expressions, laden with rolls and folded lengths of fabric. Seeing Flynn and the captain, they straightened.

The ladies merely glanced up at the arrival of the men, then returned to poring over fabrics. Mai-Lin held up a bolt of glittering silver-embroidered green gauze for Daisy's inspection.

Daisy looked for all the world like a woman who'd wasted her time coming to the ship, that there was little of interest for her here. She fingered the delicate fabric, and draped it this way and that, all the time with a pained expression, then sighed and made a careless gesture, indicating the bolt should be added to the pile on the table. "I s'pose it'll do. Are you sure you ain't got anything better to show me, Mai-Lin?"

Mai-Lin turned away to tell one of the seamen to bring forward the blue silk next and in that moment Flynn glimpsed a fleeting expression of glee on Daisy's face as she surreptitiously stroked the green gauze, then turned back, ready to be bored with indifferent blue silk.

In a dramatic movement, Mai-Lin unrolled the first few yards of shimmering silk for Daisy's perusal, saying, "You will find no finer than this anywhere in the world—see how from one angle the color is the purest turquoise, and yet when you move it, in the folds it shimmers the palest gold. It would make a superb ball dress, would it not?"

Daisy's eyes gleamed, but she managed a seen-it-all-before kind of sigh.

"But perhaps, being English, you have little experience with true Oriental quality," Mai-Lin said sweetly.

"Mai-Lin you mustn't—" McKenzie began, but Flynn laid a hand on his arm, and shook his head. "Let's leave them to it," he murmured.

"But Mai-Lin—"

"Might just have met her equal. Shall we step outside and blow a cloud?"

As the men left the day cabin, Daisy was heard to say, "I s'pose I *might* be able to find some use for this bit of stuff."

Flynn smiled to himself. The haggling had already begun.

While the two men leaned peacefully against the rail, sampling a cigar from the selection McKenzie had acquired, the sound of battle could be heard drifting up from the day cabin.

"A guinea a yard for *that*? Do you think I come down in the last shower, Mai-Lin?

"Such ignorance of the quality of silk . . ."

McKenzie looked horrified, but Flynn chuckled softly. "Kindred spirits, they are, McKenzie, take my word for it."

Finally it was time to leave. The large parcel of fabrics was carried out by two seamen and carefully lowered into the small boat under Daisy's anxious eye. She seemed much more worried about the fabric than her own safety, and allowed herself to be lowered in the sling and rowed back to shore with a minimum of fuss—though she sat as stiffly as ever on the boat. This time, however, she didn't clutch the side of the boat, but the string handle attached to the parcel.

Flynn wondered which she'd expect him to save first in the event of a capsizing—herself or her precious parcel. He opened his mouth to share the observation with her, eyed her grim expression, and changed his mind. She was in no mood for jokes.

Once safely on shore however, Daisy turned to Flynn, her eyes glowing with excitement. "I got to thank you, Flynn," she said earnestly as he carried the huge parcel toward the waiting carriage. "I never dreamed of such gorgeous fabrics. I never seen anything like those ones that have two colors, depending on what angle you're lookin' at them. And some of that embroidery—it'd take me months—and it's so beautiful."

"Pleased with your acquisitions, are you, then?" Flynn asked as he packed the precious parcel into the carriage and held out his hand to help her up the steps.

"My bloomin' oath I am!" she said fervently.

As usual she pretended not to see his hand, but climbed in unassisted. He didn't know whether she just didn't like being touched, or whether it was because she didn't like any hint that she might need help climbing up, bad leg notwithstanding.

"That Mai-Lin is nice, ain't she?"

Flynn said dryly, "From the sounds of your bargaining, you were enemies sworn."

Daisy laughed. "Did you hear some of the things she said to me? Proper disdainful she was, callin' me ignorant, and unsophisticated and actin' like I didn't know nothing about the quality of good she was showin' me—Lady Bea couldn't've sounded more hoity-toity. Yeah, she can bargain like a proper little fishwife, can Mai-Lin." She grinned at Flynn. "But then, so can I!"

He chuckled. "I told McKenzie you were kindred spirits."

"Yeah, I liked her. She's going to look out for more materials for me on her next trip. Buttons and trimmings, too. We had a right good natter. I'm goin' to make her a dress and pelisse as well and she reckons she can get me some special embroideries."

But as the carriage rumbled through the busy London streets Daisy's bright spirits suddenly dimmed. She stared out of the window, chewing thoughtfully on her lip. The worried expression seemed to deepen the closer they came to Berkeley Square.

"Something bothering you, Daisy?" Flynn asked after a while.

For a few moments he wondered if she'd even heard him but, "I think I might have gotten a bit carried away," she said with a guilty look.

"What do you mean?"

"I was so excited by all them beautiful materials, I reckon it went to me head."

"I don't understand."

"I can't afford them, Flynn, and that's the truth. I can afford maybe about a quarter of what I've got there—if that." She nodded toward the parcel sitting on the seat opposite.

"Afford it?" Flynn exclaimed in surprise. "But you don't have to pay a penny. It's all taken care of."

She stiffened. "'All taken care of'? What do you mean? I'm not a charity case, you know, I'm—"

"Calm down, firebrand—nobody's callin' you a charity case. Didn't Max tell you?"

"Tell me what?"

"That it's all paid for—now don't jump down me throat," he said when she opened her mouth to argue. "Just let me finish—and then, if you don't like it, take it up with Abby and Damaris."

"Abby and Damaris? What's it got to do with them?"

He shrugged. "You're makin' clothes for them and Jane, aren't you? I suppose they want to make sure you have the right materials—and before you bite my nose off again, it's not going to cost either of them a penny, either—nor me. It'll all come out of Max and Freddy's share."

She glared at him, unconvinced. "So you're not paying for me?"

"Not a penny. Ask them, if you don't believe me. It's nothin' to do with me—I'm just your escort. Max and I arranged it all last night, when we heard the *Derry Lass* had been sighted. Mai-Lin is famous for finding extra special things."

She didn't look happy—pride was a strange and unpredictable thing—but he could see her turning over the idea in her mind. And then something else occurred to her. "But all that bargaining I did with Mai–Lin."

"You enjoyed it, didn't you? And so did she."

"But I bargained her prices down so low—oh, gawd, she'll think I'm a right royal skinflint."

Flynn stared at her a moment—who the hell would ever understand women? First she was crowing at getting the better of Mai-Lin in a bargain, now she was all guilty over that same bargain. He began to laugh.

Daisy scowled at him. "What's so bloomin' funny?"

But Flynn knew better than to explain. He gazed out of the carriage window for a moment, watching the buildings pass by, and then changed the subject. "The day has fined up a treat, now the fog has lifted. Goin' for a walk in the park this afternoon, are you?"

"Nope."

"Not even to look at the fashionable ladies and see what they're wearin'?"

She shook her head. "Got no time to waste. Too much work to do. Anyway, I've seen all the fashions I need to. I make me own styles."

There was a little pause. Even in the dim light of the carriage Flynn could see how pale and tired-looking Daisy was, now her excitement had passed. He'd noticed it earlier, but he'd put it down to her fear of the water. There were dark shadows beneath her eyes that never used to be there. "Lady Bea said that you never go out with her or the girls anymore."

"That's right. I ain't hunting for a husband. I got no time to waste on such things."

His brows rose. "You're not interested in marriage?"

"Nope."

"Not at all?"

"Nope."

"Why not?" In Flynn's experience, every girl wanted a husband.

"Oh, gawd, Flynn, don't you start."

He frowned. "Start what?"

"Lady Bea goes on at me all the time about it. Wants to turn me into a lady of leisure." She snorted.

Flynn couldn't see the objection. If Daisy were married she wouldn't be looking so worn out, she wouldn't be running herself ragged "sewing every hour God sends" for the gentry. And getting up at four in the morning.

"Don't you want children?" It was the main reason Flynn was intent on marrying; he wanted children most of all. To have a family again.

"Nope." She gave him a cheeky grin. "Unnatural, ain't I?"

He wasn't quite sure what to say, but she went on cheerily, "Never had nuffin' to do with kids, and babies scare me to death. Always screaming, puking or wetting themselves—and worse! And babies are so little and fragile . . . They die too easy." She grimaced. "So, no kids for me, thank you very much."

The carriage rattled over the cobbles. Flynn pondered her words. He'd never met a woman who didn't want kids— or at least pretend to want them. He wondered if it was to do with her illegitimacy. She'd never made any secret of being born "on the wrong side of the blanket." "How do you feel about your sisters havin' children?"

"That's different. I'll be just an aunt. Aunts can come and go. They're not responsible, not stuck with the kid forever."

"It won't worry you when Abby or Damaris start increasing?"

"Not a bit." She gave a soft smile. "Abby was born to be a mother. A baby to Abby would be heaven on a plate—or in a basket. She'll make a lovely mother, and so will Damaris. And Jane, too, when her time comes. Not me."

He thought about that for a moment. "So what's heaven on a plate to you?"

"To me?" She fell silent, then slid him a cautious glance.

"Go on." He was curious. He'd never met a woman like Daisy.

"Me own shop—one that I own meself—in the best part of town." She darted another glance at him and, encouraged by his interest, went on in a rush, "I want it to be all elegant and posh, wiv a big bay window and lots of light and velvet curtains and soft rugs on the floor so you can't even hear yourself walkin'. And inside I'll have gorgeous big gilt-framed looking glasses so people can look at themselves in beautiful clothes— my beautiful clothes—that I design and make myself, I mean. And they'll be ladies, real proper toffs, there to buy—"

The carriage hit a pothole and bumped roughly, and she grabbed the seat to steady herself. She glanced at Flynn, suddenly self-conscious. "You probably think it's stupid, a bit of foolish—"

"I don't," he said quietly. "I think it's a grand dream to have. One day I'll tell you a story about a boy who stood barefoot on the Dublin docks, gazin' out to sea, dreaming of havin' a ship of his own." He gave her a wry smile. "More than foolish some would say, considerin' I could barely even feed meself at the time, but—" He glanced outside as the carriage came to a halt. "Here you are back home, so I'll save that tale for another day."

He went to hand her down from the carriage but again, she rejected his help. He passed the big parcel of fabrics to William, the footman who'd appeared the moment the carriage had stopped.

Flynn watched as Daisy hurried up the front steps. He knew she was sewing dresses for the other girls, knew she was keen to make money, but until this morning he hadn't quite realized the scope of her ambition. Her own shop, in the best part of town.

He was glad now that he'd brought Daisy to the ship for the first look at the cargo. Not that he'd ever tell anyone about his private little ritual, but if he ever did, he thought this girl, with her soft voice, her rough accent and her dreaming eyes, might just understand . . . .

She knew what it was to stand in the gutter and look up at the stars.

He climbed into the carriage and gave the driver the address of the Earl of Compton. Time to make a morning call on Lady Elizabeth Compton.

Strictly speaking he was calling on Lord Compton—single gentlemen did not make morning calls on single ladies—but on Flynn's last two visits, after a few minutes' conversation in the library—nothing of any consequence—Lord Compton had taken him into the drawing room where his daughter and her chaperone were receiving guests. A few further minutes of conversation, then Lord Compton would make some excuse and depart, leaving Flynn with his daughter and her visitors.

It suited Flynn quite well. There was little chance of any personal conversation, but it was pleasant enough, and he was able to observe how Lady Elizabeth conducted herself in company.

Today there were three gentlemen—two youngish, one elderly—and half a dozen ladies of various ages; mamas and their eligible young daughters, Flynn gathered after Lord Compton had introduced them.

Lady Elizabeth greeted him with cool composure—perfectly friendly, of course, but reserved—and invited him to be seated. She never did show much emotion, but was always perfectly, immaculately polite to him. A perfect lady, in fact. Today she was dressed in pale yellow, her smooth fair hair drawn back in an elegant bun. She wasn't beautiful, but when she smiled she looked quite pretty.

She didn't often smile, though. She was in a difficult situation, poor girl—trying to look rich and serene, when Flynn—and probably the whole world—knew Lord Compton was deep in debt. No doubt once she realized Flynn would settle those debts, she'd smile more.

As he'd hoped, he'd arrived just in time for tea to be served. Flynn sat back in his chair, watching with satisfaction as Lady Elizabeth poured tea into dainty china cups and directed her footman to hand around small cakes and biscuits.

She'd served tea to her guests the first time Flynn had

visited her home, and as he'd watched the way she poured tea and handed around cups, he was struck by her elegance, her quiet competence as she ruled the tea table, ensuring each person had exactly what he wanted.

Something about the way she did it felt right, somehow. He remembered thinking at the time that it might be a sign.

He drank his tea—China tea, and weak as cat's p—water—and munched on some biscuits. Few of the ladies addressed him directly, but he gained more than his fair share of sideways looks, some approving, some curious and some downright disapproving. The two young gentlemen eyed him with lightly disguised hostility, and the old gentleman with a shrewdly cynical expression. He was some kind of uncle or cousin, Flynn knew. Probably knew exactly what was going on.

Flynn didn't give a toss for the opinions of any of them. They discussed the latest opera. He hadn't seen it. They discussed some poem by a fellow called Byron. Flynn hadn't read it.

He was bored. These society people thought themselves so sophisticated, but he doubted they'd ever even been out of England. Not that it mattered. He wasn't marrying them. He finished his tea.

After a polite interval he leaned forward and invited Lady Elizabeth to go for a drive in the park the following day. She accepted. He stood and took his leave, and the conversation died.

In the hallway he paused to take his hat and coat from a footman and he heard the buzz of speculation that followed his departure.

He smiled to himself. Toffs thrived on gossip. The invitation to drive had just confirmed his serious interest in Lady Elizabeth. He could almost hear what they were thinking, if not saying aloud in front of Lady Elizabeth: Whatever was the world coming to when a jumped-up Irishman of no background at all could openly court an English earl's daughter?

Lord Compton had indicated that Lady Elizabeth would welcome his suit, and that was enough for Flynn.

A few more of these morning visits, a few more park outings, a few more balls and routs and whatever else passed for an acceptable time to court a lady and he'd pop the question.

That evening Flynn joined Max and Freddy for dinner at their club—Whites, in St James Street. The ladies—all except Daisy—were attending some private musical evening; the men were escaping from it, citing business as an excuse.

Flynn was a guest, not a member of the club. Both Max and Freddy had offered to propose him, but Flynn had no intention of applying for membership just yet—at this stage he'd probably be blackballed in the election; all it took was one black ball among all the white balls in the secret ballot and his membership would be refused.

Flynn was too canny to allow that to happen. He'd play the long game—come as Max or Freddy's guest and let the other members get to know the jumped-up-*nouveau-riche*-Irishman gradually. And when the time came he'd ask the Earl of Compton to propose him—he'd be the earl's son-in-law by then, if all went to plan.

A waiter came and took their order, and the talk turned to their latest shipment. The transfer from the ship to their own warehouse had been successfully completed, and their man of affairs, Bartlett, was, according to Max, ecstatic about the potential profits. Bartlett was a minor partner in the company.

Their meals arrived—roast beef and Yorkshire pudding for Max, steak-and-kidney pudding for Flynn, and Dover sole and potatoes duchesse for Freddy. Conversation died as the men turned to the serious business of dinner.

Pudding followed, and then port and brandy were brought out.

"So, Flynn, how is the search for a wife progressing?" Max asked when the waiter had gone. "Anyone take your fancy yet?"

Flynn hesitated. He was a bit superstitious about discussing a deal before it was finalized.

"I might have found someone," he said cautiously. "I'll know more in a fortnight."

"A fortnight?"

"I've been invited to visit her home in the country," he said, deliberately vague.

"Anywhere in particular?"

"Kent."

Freddy and Max exchanged looks. "Hah! Lizzie Compton— I told you, Max," Freddy said triumphantly. "Laid a pony on it," he told Flynn. "Wish I'd laid a monkey, now."

"Dammit, you've been *betting* on me?"

"Why not?" Freddy added earnestly, "Not a public bet. Not in the club betting book or anything, just a small private wager between friends."

Flynn shook his head. Twenty-five pounds wasn't exactly a small bet, but he supposed it was better than five hundred. "Well, I'll thank you to keep mum about it. I don't want anyone to know—not your wives, not anyone—until everything is decided."

He turned to Freddy. "How the devil did you work it out anyway?"

"Not too difficult, given your requirements. And when you said Kent, it clinched it."

"How? There are dozens of eligible girls in Kent."

Freddy snorted. "You forget that until recently I was acquainted with every muffin on the marriage mart, know who they are and where they come from and what they want." He saw Flynn's expression and added hastily, "Not that I'm saying Lizzie Compton is a muffin, precisely. Very pleasant girl, I'm sure. Pretty enough little thing, but horribly—er, *delightfully* marriage-minded—which is exactly what you want, is it not, Flynn, dear fellow, so there—all working out perfectly." He took a large gulp of brandy.

Max leaned forward and said quietly, "I suppose you know that Compton is all but under the hatches. He'll be looking to you to tow him out of the River Tick."

Flynn nodded. "I didn't expect an earl's daughter to come cheap." He probably knew more about the earl's debts than most people; he'd investigated the man's situation thoroughly before he'd approached him.

It was another reason why he didn't want to discuss his marriage until it was settled. There were financial details to be hammered out before a final agreement was made between himself and Lord Compton. And the girl to court, of course.

Max frowned slightly, opened his mouth as if to say something, then shut it.

Flynn sipped his cognac. Max didn't approve? Too bad. It was different for Max; he might have been involved in trade along with Flynn, but being a lord, Max's position in society was assured; he could afford to marry for love—and had.

For someone like Flynn, marriage—especially marriage into a society family—was a business. The earl's crippling debts were the reason—the only reason—Flynn would be acceptable as a son-in-law.

Flynn had calculated the costs and decided he could afford them—all going to plan. All that was needed then was to propose to the girl. And for her to accept him. Her father had given him no reason to think she would not. "Lizzie knows her duty," he'd told Flynn.

Flynn didn't much like being thought of as a duty, but he was a practical man, and Lady Elizabeth Compton would suit his purposes perfectly. He didn't need hearts and flowers.

Besides, that was her father's view of things; he had yet to work out Lady Elizabeth's attitude.

Flynn was optimistic: He'd never had any trouble with women before.

Chapter Four

It is only by seeing women in their own homes, among
their own set, just as they always are, that you can form
any just judgment. Short of that, it is all guess and
luck—and will generally be ill-luck. How many a man
has committed himself on a short acquaintance, and
rued it all the rest of his life!

—JANE AUSTEN, *EMMA*

The next morning, Flynn received a package from Mai-Lin; a parcel tied with string. In her note she apologized for not giving this to him the day before, but she had been so enjoyably distracted by meeting the delightful Miss Daisy Chance, she'd quite forgotten.

Intrigued, Flynn pulled out a knife and cut the string. Removing several layers of thick brown paper, he found a lovely piece of embroidered silk satin wrapped around a carved mahogany box. Inside the felt-lined, purpose-built box was a pair of exquisitely carved jade vases, pale green, and so intricately carved they might have been made of wax. Each had its own especially made carved wooden stand.

He'd never seen anything quite so lovely. It was a matched pair, but each vase was unique; a simple classic lidded vase shape, seemingly set casually in among flowers, so that water irises grew up the side of one vase, and a sprig of blossom carelessly rested on the lid, as if fallen there by accident. The other vase had a vine twining up it, and a tiny bird fluttering in the branches, as if sipping nectar. And yet each vase was carved from a single piece of jade. The artistic skill involved . . . It quite took his breath away.

When he'd finished examining the vases, he replaced them carefully in their box, and set it aside; they would be displayed next in the fine home he intended to make, along with the other beautiful pieces he'd collected over the years. They were not for his bachelor lodgings.

He wondered whether Lady Elizabeth liked jade. Not that it mattered.

He wrote a quick note of thanks to Mai-Lin—she'd outdone herself this time—sealed the note, and picked up the piece of silk. A thought occurred to him, and he held the fabric up against his chest and glanced at his reflection in the looking-glass. Two vividly colored peacocks, their tails spread gorgeously, strutting their stuff . . .

Behind him, his valet sniffed. Flynn hid a grin. Tibbins's sniffs were a language all of their own.

"Shall I clear that rubbish away, sir?" Tibbins had already disposed of the brown paper. He reached for the fabric.

"Do you think there's enough fabric here for a waistcoat?" Flynn asked.

"No. Perhaps a small tea cloth," Tibbins said repressively. He reached for it. "Shall I—"

Flynn slipped it into his pocket. "I'll take it to Miss Daisy and see what she thinks."

"You'll pull Mr. Weston's elegant coat out of shape if you keep putting things in the pockets, sir."

Flynn shrugged. "It's my coat. And pockets are for putting things in."

Tibbins sniffed.

Flynn called in at Berkeley Square around eleven. "Morning, Featherby, Miss Daisy in?" he asked, when the butler answered the door.

Featherby gave him a dry look. "These days she's rarely out, sir."

"I'll just pop up to see her then, shall I? Got a bit of fabric I want to ask her about."

"Of course, sir." The household was well used to Flynn coming and going. He'd run tame in the house ever since he'd first arrived in England.

"May I prevail on you for a small favor, sir?"

Flynn paused. It wasn't like Featherby to ask for anything. "What is it?"

"I'll be sending up a pot of tea and some sandwiches in a few moments. I'd be grateful if you would encourage Miss Daisy to eat some of them."

Flynn frowned slightly. "Off her food, is she? Nothing wrong, I hope?"

"Oh, no, sir, just that she's been working so hard lately, she often forgets to eat."

Flynn nodded. "Leave it to me." He mounted the stairs in a thoughtful frame of mind. So Daisy was forgetting to eat, was she? And if she was up every day at four, she couldn't be getting much sleep.

At this rate the girl was going to make herself sick.

He knocked and entered, and found Daisy sitting cross-legged on the window seat, frowning over some intricate piece of sewing. "Flynn," she exclaimed. "What brings you here—no, give us a moment, me lap's full of these little beads and if I spill 'em . . ." She carefully tipped a stream of tiny glittering crystals into a jar, and screwed on the lid before getting to her feet.

She stretched. "Gawd, me bloomin' back—I been hunched over that dress for hours. But it's the best place for the light." She straightened and gave him a sunny smile. "So what do you want?"

Flynn pulled out the Chinese fabric. "Mai-Lin sent me this. It's not very big. But I was wonderin' if you could make it into a waistcoat. "

Daisy took it from him and examined it, caressing the fine fabric almost lovingly. "Beautiful piece of stuff, ain't it? It's small, but . . ." She draped the silk against Flynn's body, this way and that, eyeing it thoughtfully.

He took the opportunity for a closer examination while her attention was on the fabric. She was too pale, and looking somehow fragile. He frowned. Someone needed to be taking better care of her; it was clear she wasn't going to do it.

"Yeah, I reckon I can make it work. I'll have to pair it with some other fabric, just for the edges—here,"—she gestured—"and here." She glanced up at Flynn. "You got time to wait, while I work out a design and take some measurements?"

"Don't you have me measurements already?" He always found it a bit unsettling, having Daisy put her hands on him. A bit . . . arousing. There was nothing in it, of course—she wasn't doing anything his own tailor didn't do—but his body didn't react to his tailor the way it reacted to Daisy.

"Of course, but this will take a bit of fiddlin' and I want to be sure this embroidery is visible. Otherwise what's the point?"

Flynn pulled out his watch and consulted it. He was due to collect Lady Elizabeth in an hour. "Go ahead then," he told Daisy.

"Got somewhere to be, eh?"

"Taking a lady for a drive."

She grinned. "Not a duke's daughter who keeps rats I hope."

He chuckled. "You heard about that?"

"I certainly did." She picked up a pad of paper and started sketching a design. "So you got your eye on a real proper lady, eh?"

"I do." He couldn't hide his satisfaction.

"Courtin', then are you?"

"Just about."

"So tell me about her. What's she like?"

Flynn hesitated. Daisy slanted him a look from under her brows. "You don't think I'm going to blab to the old lady, do you? I know how to keep mum." Her pencil flew. "Besides, I didn't ask for a name—not that it'd mean anything to me anyway—I just wondered what she was like."

"Her family is a very old and noble one, related to half the aristocrats in the kingdom. She comes from Kent—that's where their principal house is, and where she grew up. She was educated at home—"

"Gawd, no, not something straight out of *Debrett's*, Flynn. What's *she* like? Herself, not her family."

Flynn had looked up Lady Elizabeth's family in *Debrett's*. It was only practical. But women weren't interested in such things. He thought about how to describe Lady Elizabeth. "Well, she's quite pretty. Young. Slender. Dainty. Light brown hair that curls a little." He paused, trying to think what else to say.

"Blue eyes?" She was laughing at him.

"How did you know?"

She snorted. "Just a guess."

Actually, now he came to think of it, he wasn't sure whether Lady Elizabeth's eyes were blue or green. Or maybe they were hazel, like Daisy's and changed color according to what she was wearing. Yes, that was probably it. Hazel.

She shook her head over her sketch, tore off the sheet and crumpled it up. "I didn't ask what she looked like, Flynn—I asked what she was *like*. What kind of a girl is she? Would I like her? Is she funny or serious? Has she got brothers and sisters? Has she got a temper? Does she like animals—that kind of thing."

Flynn considered that. "No sisters or brothers. And she's serious. As for whether you'd like her . . . I can't think of any reason why you wouldn't. She's a perfect lady—always polite."

"Politeness bein' what I look for in a friend," Daisy agreed sardonically. She kept sketching, but after a minute looked up. "That all you got?"

Flynn shrugged. "I don't know her very well. Yet."

At that moment, the footman, William, arrived with a tray containing a pot of tea, two cups, a plate of sandwiches and a dish of small cakes. He set the tray down, saying to Daisy, "Mr. Featherby says you're to eat and drink something, or he'll want to know the reason why."

"Gawd, old mother hen he is." Daisy rolled her eyes and put her sketch aside. "No need to fuss, William, I was gaspin' for a cuppa anyway." She turned to Flynn. "Want some tea, Flynn?"

Flynn was neither hungry nor thirsty, but he nodded.

Daisy set out the cups and poured a thin stream of dark fluid into the first one. Flynn leaned forward. "Is that Indian tea?"

She nodded. "Yeah, can't stand that cat's pi—that weak China stuff that Lady Bea likes. I like proper tea, good and strong and hot. Do you mind?"

"Not at all." Flynn watched as she poured, then reached for the sugar tongs.

"One lump or two?"

"Two," said Flynn. She handed him his cup and he stirred in the sugar then sipped the hot, strong brew with pleasure.

Daisy passed him the plate of sandwiches. Very fancy they were, too—small triangular sandwiches with their crusts cut off—chicken, and egg, and . . . "Am I mistaken or are they honey rolls?" he asked.

She nodded. "I expect so. Have one."

"You first."

She shook her head. "No, thanks. Not hungry."

"Oh." He sat back, the plate of sandwiches untouched.

"Eat," she urged him. "Featherby will be cross if we don't touch nothing."

He shrugged. "I can't eat unless you do. Not polite, is it?"

She rolled her eyes at him, and picked up a chicken sandwich. Flynn waited until she'd taken a bite, then took one himself.

"So," she said as they ate and drank, "you know practically nuffin' about this girl and yet you're plannin' to marry her."

"I do know her—sort of—I know her family, her background."

Her mouth was full of sandwich, so she just raised a skeptical eyebrow at him.

He found himself saying, "That's how they do things in the English upper classes. She's an earl's daughter."

Her brows climbed higher. "And that's why?" she said when she'd finished her sandwich. "Because she's the daughter of an earl?"

"Yes, dammit, that's why."

She said nothing, just dusted crumbs from her fingers but

the carefully blank expression on her face—so very unlike Daisy—prompted him to add, "And why shouldn't I marry an earl's daughter?"

"No reason at all." Her tone said quite the opposite.

He shoved the honey rolls in her direction, too annoyed to speak. She selected one, bit into it, chewed, swallowed, then said lightly, "I just never took you for a snob, Flynn."

"I'm not a snob."

She snorted. "Course you're not."

"I'm not."

"But you're marryin'—oh, excuse me, *considerin'* marryin' a girl you hardly know, simply because she's an earl's daughter."

"It's not because of that—or not only because of that." He tried to explain his feelings about wanting to marry the finest young lady in London but it came out a bit . . . tangled.

He hadn't gone far when she interrupted. "Lordy, you don't need to justify yourself to me, Flynn. I don't give a toss who you marry, as long as you're happy with her. I was just interested, that's all."

She started packing up the tea things and continued, "I don't care if you're a snob, anyway—I am one meself when it comes to me customers. I want toffs—proper, top-of-the-trees toffs—to come to my shop. They got taste, most of them, and they'll give me shop consequence, bring it into fashion, like. And it's the same with you—I get it: marryin' this earl's daughter will give you consequence."

"That's not it—" he began. But it was. He just hadn't thought of it in such bald terms.

"Marriage is different, though. If I was wanting to get hitched—which I ain't—I'd want to know more about the person I was marryin'. You're goin' to be stuck with them for life, so I'd want to know a lot more about them." She gave him a sideways glance, her eyes clear. "Manners and bein' pretty and ladylike and being related to posh people is important to you, I know, but . . . she's got to make you happy, Flynn."

Daisy set the tea tray aside and straightened with a laugh. "Hark at me, the expert on marriage, the girl who's never been married and ain't never goin' to be. Sorry, Flynn, it's none of my business, so I'll stop stickin' me bib in. Now about this waistcoat—what sort of buttons would you like? I reckon covered ones, don't you?"

O n his way to collect the phaeton he'd hired for Lady Elizabeth's drive, Flynn ruminated on the conversation with Daisy, mulling over the questions she'd stirred up.

What did he know about Lady Elizabeth herself, apart from the polite public face she showed him?

And was he really so shallow, choosing a wife solely on appearance and pedigree? There was more to his choice than that, he was sure, but he was forced to concede that there was some truth in Daisy's accusation.

It wasn't as if he thought members of the aristocracy were any better than ordinary folks. He didn't care the snap of his fingers for other people's opinions of him. It was just . . . Daisy's words came back to him.

Marrying this earl's daughter will give you consequence.

And why shouldn't he have consequence? Hadn't he earned it?

It wasn't snobbery. He'd made his fortune by seeking out the best of everything—he had an eye for quality, he liked fine things, and he saw no reason why that approach wouldn't work just as well in selecting a wife.

He collected the phaeton—a very smart equipage, black with gold trim, pulled by a high-bred pair of glossy matched bays—picked up the reins and eased into the busy London traffic.

The sun had come out and he felt very fine as he negotiated the streets of Mayfair. Preferring quality was not the same as being a snob. He had a plan, and he intended to stick with it. He'd always been a man of his word: he'd announced to the world that he wanted a highborn wife, and what he wanted, he went after, and got.

Invariably.

In a few weeks' time, if all went as planned—and why

would it not?—he'd be a betrothed man, and to the daughter of a blue-blooded English earl: Lady Elizabeth Compton, who was related to half the aristocracy of Great Britain. And he would be too, once he married her.

Not bad for a man who was once a barefoot wharf rat working the Dublin docks.

He caught that thought, pulled it out and examined it.

Dammit! He *was* a snob.

But just because Lady Elizabeth Compton was a highborn titled lady didn't mean she wasn't the right girl for Flynn. Daisy was right—he didn't know the girl well enough. Yet.

There was plenty of time to get to know her better, starting with this drive. He was glad now he'd chosen this earlier-than-fashionable time, because he'd seen how the toffs drove at the fashionable hour in Hyde Park—at a crawl, stopping to chat to people in other carriages, and to take friends up for five minutes and put them down again five minutes later.

This way he'd have Lady Elizabeth all to himself.

Besides which, at the hour for fashionable promenading he had an engagement for a lesson with Lady Beatrice—God help him.

So much for having Lady Elizabeth all to himself. She'd brought her maid with her, a grim-faced damsel of uncertain years who eyed Flynn with barely disguised contempt. It was clear she thought him not near good enough for her precious wean.

Flynn gave the woman a grin as he helped her into the little seat at the back of the phaeton. He quite enjoyed being disapproved of. It gave him something to work with.

There was no conversation of any significance on the way to Hyde Park: Flynn needed to concentrate on the traffic. Luckily the horses were well used to the chaos of London traffic because they didn't turn a hair, and trotted elegantly and smoothly along.

Lady Elizabeth sat beside him, her back straight as a little soldier's, and with about as much expression on her face.

She was shy, he told himself. It was the first time she'd been alone—or almost alone with him. And she might be a nervous passenger.

He set himself to relax her.

They discussed the weather—it was warming up, Lady Elizabeth observed. Flynn responded that, having lived a good part of the last ten years in tropical climes, he didn't yet find it warm.

Lady Elizabeth found nothing to add to that topic, not even a question about where he'd been, or what it had been like living in foreign climes.

Talk turned to the Season. "Are you planning to attend the masquerade ball next week, Mr. Flynn?"

"I am indeed. Lookin' forward to it. And I'll be wearin' a proper costume, not just a domino that some fellows—me friend Lord Davenham, for one—consider proper wear to a masquerade."

She didn't respond—was it shyness, nerves or lack of interest?—so he said, "What costume are you plannin' to wear, Lady Elizabeth?"

"Oh, that would be telling." But it was the closest he'd seen to a smile on her face, so he pursued that line of conversation.

They were still talking about costumes she had seen—or worn, he wasn't sure—at other masquerades as they swept through the wrought iron gates of the park.

"The spring flowers are starting to bloom," Lady Elizabeth observed. "Spring is such a happy season, is it not. And after the cold of the last year . . . "

At least the girl was trying. Flynn tried to think of something to say, so he asked her to tell him the names of all the flowers they could see, claiming he only knew about tropical blooms, which was a lie.

He knew nothing about flowers at all. Could name a rose. And a daisy. And a daffodil. He spotted one about to bloom and they admired it for a few minutes. Daffodils were, apparently, happy flowers.

They moved on. This kind of talk was getting him nowhere. What would he be able to tell Daisy—or anyone else—if she—or they—asked him what Lady Elizabeth was like? That she thought flowers and seasons were happy? And that she liked dressing up.

Time to be blunt.

"Has your father spoken to you about me, Lady Elizabeth?"

In the rear, the maid sniffed.

He felt rather than saw Lady Elizabeth's cautious sidelong glance. "Yes."

"So, you're clear about me intentions?"

She made a small sound in her throat and nodded.

"And you're happy to be courted—I'm not asking for an answer to the bigger question, mind—just that you're willin' to get to know me a bit better. With a view to—" He paused, considering the possibility of a breach-of-promise case, and demurred. "A view to seein' what might come of it."

There was a short silence. And a sniff from the back seat.

"Lady Elizabeth?" he prompted. "If you're not keen to go forward with this, now is the time to say so, before we've got in any deeper, and while there is nobody here to witness what you tell me."

From behind there came another meaningful sniff. Flynn recognized the Language of Sniffs, beloved of his valet. He added, "Unless your maid is a spy for your father, that is."

He heard an indignant gasp from behind. "Muir is my own maid," Lady Elizabeth said hastily. "She was my nurse and has been with me since I was a babe."

"And she don't tell tales on her lady, neither," came a grim voice from behind. Sniff.

Flynn smiled. "That's grand, then, so, what's your answer, Lady Elizabeth? Are you happy for me to continue with this court—with us visiting and going for drives and such until we both know our minds. Because if you don't want it, say so now. I won't hold it against you and I won't tell a soul. I prefer straight dealing."

She took her time answering. Considering how to say it, no doubt.

"Papa has made my duty clear to me, and I am willing

to . . . to go forward with this acquaintanceship," she said at last.

That told him. She was *willing*. Flynn was her *duty*. Flynn, with the moneybags to drag her father out of the debt he'd mired his family in.

Gambling, horses and women—that's what Flynn's investigations had shown Lord Compton had frittered a fortune away on. Flynn had no time for the man.

A man ought to ensure his family was protected from debt, not gamble his money—and their security—away on his own pleasures.

Compton was cold-bloodedly sacrificing his daughter in exchange for Flynn's fortune. And she would *do her duty*.

Still, he couldn't blame the girl for not responding any more warmly. In fact, given that they hardly knew each other—yet—he found her honesty quite appealing. She was mighty cold for a girl who'd just agreed to be courted, but he had no doubt he'd be able to warm her up.

He hadn't even kissed her yet.

Lord, but these English had it all arse about—marry the girl, *then* kiss her. And of course the bedding to follow.

He contemplated that prospect. Would she be *doing her duty* then?

Faith, but that would take the fun out of things.

They completed their circuit of the park, noting daffodils and snowdrops and other charming—and probably happy—flowers, and then Flynn turned the horses for home.

He hadn't made a lot of progress, but the air had been cleared between them, and he fancied she was easier in her manner with him than she had been when they started out.

Certainly her maid glared at him with slightly less severity as he helped her down. It was progress, of a sort.

"I wonder, Miss Muir, would you know my manservant, Tibbins? Ernest Tibbins?" he asked her.

The maid looked at him as if he was mad. "No, why would I?"

"It's just that you both seem to speak the same language,"

Flynn said. "Afternoon, ladies." He drove away with a faint smile on his face, leaving both females staring after him.

The drive hadn't gone quite as he expected, but he wasn't unhappy with the result.

He wasn't entirely happy, either.

The girl might be willing, but she could hardly be called eager.

Daisy's questions itched at him. Until she'd flung those questions at him, he'd never really questioned his desire to marry a highborn, titled lady. It had seemed perfectly reasonable.

But putting Daisy's questions together with Lady Elizabeth's response to him . . . well, it made a man think.

On the one hand, he'd always prided himself on not giving the snap of his fingers for what anyone thought of him. On the other, class was important. In every country he'd ever visited, society was arranged in layers, and it was always better to be on the top than on the bottom.

By marrying Lady Elizabeth, he'd be getting a wife with a fistful of aristocratic connections—and hopefully children. More than anything, Flynn wanted children.

He knew how he and Lord Compton would benefit, but what about Lady Elizabeth? What was she getting?

A husband, certainly, and a wealthy one at that. But she didn't know Flynn well enough to judge if he'd be a good husband to her or not. For all she knew he might be a wife-beater or a gambler and whoremonger, like her father.

No, marriage to Flynn was her *duty*. But what was her alternative?

Her home was entailed. Once her father died she'd be homeless, dependent on her cousin's charity. And she'd been on the marriage mart a couple of years already, so it was clear none of the other nobs wanted a dowerless girl, no matter how pretty-behaved and well-born.

There was no doubt in Flynn's mind that she'd accept his proposal, when he made it. The match was everything he'd claimed he wanted. Why then had this drive left a sour taste in his mouth?

His thoughts were far into the future as he guided the phaeton into the narrow mews that led to the stables. Marriage was for children, and he wanted his children to have every advantage. He didn't want them to suffer the way he had as a boy.

On the other hand, he didn't want to be raising a pack of little snobs who imagined the world owed them a living—and considered themselves superior to ordinary folk—simply because of who they were and who they were related to.

His fists knotted hard around the reins. No daughter of his would ever—ever!—be forced into marriage with a stranger for the sake of her father's debts.

He loosened his grip deliberately. There was no question of Lady Elizabeth being *forced*. He'd make sure of that. She might have limited choices, but there *were* choices.

She was stiff and awkward, but she didn't know him very well yet. She'd no doubt warm up a bit as she came to know him better. She might be thinking of duty, but Flynn could show her that duty could also be a pleasure.

If she ever gave him the chance.

He handed over the phaeton and horses to the care of the grooms and hurried off to Berkeley Square. Quarter to four. Almost time for his so-called lesson.

Chapter Five

*To be fond of dancing was a certain step
towards falling in love.*

—JANE AUSTEN, *PRIDE & PREJUDICE*

At five minutes to four, Featherby knocked on the door of Daisy's workroom. "Miss Daisy, it's almost time for Lady Beatrice's lesson."

Daisy scowled, but put the sleeve she'd been sewing aside. "I'll go, and I'll watch, but I ain't going to bloomin' well dance."

Featherby said nothing. He just held the door open for her, his expression bland.

Daisy picked up a dress that had the hem pinned, but wasn't yet sewn. Featherby eyed it but said nothing. He had a way of making things happen, just by . . . expecting.

She said, as if he'd argued, "I hate dancing. I'm no good at it."

She stomped her way up to the room that had been cleared for their lessons, entered and stopped dead. The carpet had been rolled back and all excess furniture had been removed, leaving only the piano and a few chairs arranged along one wall, but that wasn't what startled her.

As well as Lady Beatrice, Jane, Abby and Damaris, the elderly Frenchman Monsieur Lefarge who taught the various dance steps, and his cousin, Madame Bertrand, who played the piano, there were four gentlemen—a stranger, Max, Freddy and Mr. Flynn. Four.

"What the—?"

"The gels need more practice with actual gentlemen," Lady Beatrice declared. "So Monsieur Lefarge has brought another of his cousins to dance with Jane, and I invited dear Max and Freddy. And of course, Mr. Flynn is in need of lessons himself, having been at sea all his life."

"Not exactly," Flynn began. "And I did say I knew—"

But the old lady took no notice. "Abby and Damaris will dance with their husbands, unfashionable as it is, and Jane will dance with—"

"Flynn," said Daisy, seating herself and her sewing by the window.

"Nonsense! Jane is attending balls with the eyes of the world upon her. She needs further practice with someone who knows what he's doing. Monsieur Lefarge's cousin is an expert, Mr. Flynn is a rank beginner."

"I'm not, as a matter of—" Flynn began.

Lady Beatrice raised her lorgnette and eyed him with a beady expression. "I'm sure you perform the hornpipe delightfully, Mr. Flynn—and you must show us some day— but not today."

Max and Freddy stifled chuckles, not very successfully. Lady Beatrice gave them the kind of withering look that reduced grown men to schoolboy status. She continued, "Jane needs an expert to refine her steps, so she will dance with Monsieur Lefarge's cousin and Daisy, you will dance with Mr. Flynn."

Daisy looked up from her sewing "Who, me? But—"

"But what?" Lady Beatrice intoned. "Is this not a dance lesson? Did you not come of your own free will?" The old lady leveled her lorgnette at Daisy.

Featherby, who had been hovering, gave Daisy a Meaningful Look.

Daisy glowered. They were all ganging up on her. She looked at Flynn, who was wholly engaged in picking a piece of fluff off his coat sleeve. An invisible piece of fluff, the cowardly big rat.

"It'll be fun, Daisy," Jane said in a coaxing voice.

"You might find you enjoy it," Damaris added sympathetically.

Betrayed on all sides. Daisy looked at Abby, but Abby said nothing. She knew how Daisy felt about dancing, knew how she felt about her stupid leg. Daisy swallowed.

Flynn strolled across the room and held out his hand to her. "Come on, lass, there's nothing for it but to give in gracefully."

Gracefully? That was a laugh. There'd be nothing graceful about Daisy on the dance floor. And dancing with Flynn, of all people to make a fool of herself with. She didn't move.

"If you refuse me, the old lady will make me dance with the little old Frenchman. He's wearin' *rouge*!" Flynn said with a comical grimace. "You wouldn't do that to me, would you, Daisy? Not after I went out of me way to give you first pick of all those gorgeous fabrics." Laughter gleamed in his blue, blue eyes. He wasn't going to give up, she could see. He had no idea.

"Oh, all right, but it's blackmail." It wasn't. He was just bloody irresistible, damn the man. Scowling, Daisy dumped her sewing on the chair beside her and stomped grumpily onto the dance floor.

"Such a gracious acceptance, Miss Chance, I'm deeply flattered," Flynn murmured, his blue eyes dancing. He was enjoying this, the big rat.

"Stubble it, Flynn. I never asked for this."

"Me neither," he said. "I thought I was the only one pressed into this."

"Pressed?"

He shrugged. "The English navy has two kinds of seamen—volunteers and pressed men. Pressed men can kick forever and be miserable, or try to make the best of it. You can see which choice I'm makin'." He held out his hand.

Daisy sighed. He was right, blast him. Makin' a fuss never did nobody any good. Certainly not Daisy. Best to get the rotten

dance over and done with as quick as she could. And hope that
Flynn had to concentrate so hard on his own steps that he'd
never notice Daisy making a dog's breakfast out of it.

"We will start wis ze waltz," Monsieur Lefarge announced.
A wizened elderly Frenchman, he wore fashions reminiscent
of the previous century, including powder and rouge. "First ze
gentlemen bow, like zis,"—he demonstrated—"and ze ladies
zey curtsey like zis." Again he demonstrated and despite his
tight satin pantaloons he performed a graceful curtsey. "Ze
gentlemen place ze hands like so, and like so." He demonstrated, then checked they were all positioned correctly. "And
now, Clothilde, but slow, *s'il vous plaît.*"

Madame Bertrand played a chord. Daisy took a deep
breath and prepared to make a complete fool of herself. The
dance began.

"One-two-sree, one-two-sree, one-two-sree," Monsieur
chanted. Daisy could hear her own uneven steps, loud as
loud could be on the wooden floor, clump-two-clump,
clump-two-clump. Probably everybody else could hear too.
It was mortifying.

Flynn's big hand was warm on her waist. It was completely distracting. He tried to swing her around.

"Oy! Stop pullin'."

"I'm not pullin', I'm leading. It's what men are supposed
to do."

She snorted. She could smell his shaving soap, and the
fresh scent of well-laundered shirt. And Flynn. He always
smelled nice. Her own palms were sweaty. She wanted to
pull her hand out of his and wipe it, but there was no chance.

He moved forward and she stumbled backward. "Now
you're pushin'," she said.

"No, you're resisting." He seemed to find it all so amus-
ing. She got crosser and crosser.

"Mademoiselle Daisy, you must let ze gentleman lead."

Daisy scowled. "Bugger this. I can't bloomin' well dance
and I wish—"

"Stop fighting it, will you, girl," Flynn told her. "Just shut
your wee trap and let me lead."

Daisy wanted to kick him, but Lady Beatrice was watching, eagle-eyed.

Daisy tried to remember her steps. She stared at his waistcoat, scarlet, green and gold Chinese dragons on a black background. She'd made that waistcoat. She remembered every stitch.

"One-two-sree, one-two-sree . . ." the Frenchman chanted. His cousin twirled Jane daintily around. Jane floated like a gossamer fairy. A dainty gossamer fairy.

Daisy was more like an angry troll. "I hate this," she muttered. Clump-two-clump, clump-two-clump.

"Really? I'm havin' the most delightful time," said Flynn as he wrestled her into a turn. "Of course I've got the most charmin' and agreeable partner . . . "

She glanced suspiciously up at him.

His eyes laughed down at her. "And I never realized waltzing and wrestling had so much in common."

She tried to glower, but somehow a laugh escaped her.

"Good God!" he exclaimed in amazement. "It laughs?"

"I'll kick you if you're not careful." But her mouth kept trying to smile.

He chuckled. "If you'd only relax and let me lead you might even find you enjoyed it."

She snorted. "Chance would be a fine thing."

"Chance would be a fine thing, if only she would let me lead." After a few more tightly wrestled twirls he stopped. Was it over? Thank goodness.

Daisy tried to pull her hand free, but Flynn held onto it tight. "Madame Bertrand," he called, *"Encore une fois, mais plus vite, s'il vous plaît."*

"What did you say?" Daisy began, but the music began again.

"Now," Flynn said and taking her in a grip much closer than Monsieur Lefarge had showed them, he began to twirl her rapidly around the room. The music was twice as fast as before.

"What the 'ell—" Daisy tried to keep up. She tripped and almost fell. She clutched him tight. He took no notice, just kept twirling her around and around. She forgot all about remembering the steps; it was all she could do to stay on her feet. If he let go of her, she'd fall flat on her face, she was certain. Or her arse.

"You bastard! Let me g—oh, bloody 'ell!" as she stumbled again.

He grinned and kept dancing.

The minute this bloomin' dance finished she was going to kill him. She hung on grimly, certain that any minute she'd trip and sprawl across the floor, making a complete fool of herself.

Somehow, she didn't.

With one big, warm hand anchored firmly around her waist and the other holding her hand, he kept her steady, despite her uneven steps. He was strong. His big body was the anchor around which she swirled.

There was no chance of her falling, she realized gradually. She might trip, she might stumble, but Flynn wouldn't let her fall.

With that realization she relaxed a little, and suddenly the rhythm of the music started to make sense. She forgot about her leg, and her uneven steps and the clump-two-clump and whatever she was supposed to be doing; she just let him spin them around and around. And around.

Oh my gawd, so this was what it was like to dance. She was practically flying.

"That's better," he murmured. "See, when you stop fighting me, when you forget about your limp—"

She stumbled.

"Sorry, I shouldn't have—"

"Shut up! Just shut up!" she hissed furiously. But it was back to clump-two-clump.

They finished the dance in silence. Madame Bertrand played the final chord, and finally, finally Flynn let Daisy go. She stepped back, breathing heavily and, in an action she hadn't made since she was a small child, she wiped her sticky hands on her skirt.

He stared down at her, dismayed. "Daisy . . ."

She refused to meet his gaze.

"Sank your partners," Monsieur Lefarge instructed.

Flynn bowed and said in a low voice that only she could hear, "I didn't mean to . . . It was just . . . when you stopped thinkin' about yourself, and bein' self-conscious, you danced light as a fairy—"

But Daisy didn't want to listen to such rubbish. She knew it wasn't true. She bobbed him a curtsy, muttered her thanks and headed for her seat. The whole room could hear her clumping unevenly across the bare floorboards.

She glanced back at the other occupants of the room. Jane said something to Lady Beatrice and hurried away—no doubt to see to that blooming dog she'd adopted—Damaris and Freddy were laughing about something, Max and Abby were still entwined, murmuring softly to each other.

Only Flynn stood watching her, a slight frown darkening his brow.

She knew her face was red. She didn't care. She'd made a right bloomin' fool of herself. She felt like bursting into tears, but she never cried. Never.

She picked up her folded sewing, looked across at Lady Beatrice and raised her voice, saying, "I done the bloomin' lesson, so I 'ope you're satisfied. Now, I got work to do."

She marched from the room—didn't even slam the door—and hurried upstairs to her workroom, the place where she could be herself again: Daisy, who knew what she was good at, knew where she belonged—in her own little empire.

And not on any bloody dance floor.

After the dancing lesson Max invited Flynn to join him and Freddy for a drink—the girls were planning to take afternoon tea with Lady Beatrice and then there was something about dresses. Or costumes. Flynn gladly accepted.

He left ahead of the other two, and was making his way

down the stairs just as Jane came hurrying up, a furtive expression on her face.

"Miss Jane," he said politely and made to pass her on the stairs.

She hurriedly thrust something behind her, but not before he caught a glimpse of a small red leather shoe with a red and white rosette on the toe.

"Bringing Miss Daisy her slippers?"

"Oh, hush!" she exclaimed, looking around guiltily to see if anyone noticed. "She's not following you is she?"

"No, she stormed out ahead of me," he assured her. "She'll be in her workroom by now. Why, what's the problem?"

Jane showed him what she had been concealing, and said in a tragic voice, "My dog."

Only one shoe still bore a rosette—just. It hung by a thread. The other was chewed and bedraggled and utterly ruined. "Daisy's going to kill me. Or worse, my dog. But it's her own fault—she should never have left them out, tempting him with leather slippers! He's not used to living with people yet."

Voices sounded in the hallway above and Jane looked around frantically, as if seeking somewhere to hide the ruined slippers.

"Here, give them to me," Flynn said.

Jane thrust them into his hands and Flynn slipped a slipper into each coat pocket just as Max and Freddy appeared on the landing.

Jane murmured her thanks and hurried upstairs. Flynn hid a smile. Clearly he was expected to get rid of the evidence.

The two men joined him and, since it was a clear, cool day, they walked to Max's home, around the corner. Max took them to his library, where they settled into comfortable overstuffed leather armchairs.

He poured them each a drink. "I didn't expect you to be attending dance lessons, Flynn."

"Ah, well, apparently I need them; everyone knows all seamen can only dance the hornpipe." He leaned forward and added confidingly, "And did you know, they don't dance the hornpipe at Almack's? I was never so shocked in all my life." The others laughed.

"So you didn't tell her about all the balls and routs and parties you've danced at in various embassies and grand houses in the far-flung corners of the empire."

"She didn't give me the chance."

"So how did she twist your arm?" Freddy asked.

Flynn grinned. "Hornpipe issues aside, it was a punishment." He told them the story.

"Pammy Girtle-Brown!" Freddy shuddered. "Ghastly female! Not even a muffin, she's a . . . a stale Bath bun. That talks. And talks. And talks—all utter rubbish and at the top of her lungs. Spent a fortnight in her company at a house party once—snowed in—no chance of escape. *And* she keeps rats, lets 'em crawl over her body." He shuddered again and drained his glass. "Scarred me for life."

Max chuckled. "And Aunt Bea swallowed the tale?"

"For all of five minutes," Flynn said. "She was truly appalled. Claimed I'd almost given her palpitations."

"Serve you right then," Freddy told him. "Pammy Girtle-Brown! Give anyone palpitations!"

Max said, "I expect Aunt Bea wanted a partner for Daisy too—Abby says she's determined to make Daisy attend the lessons with all of them, no matter how much Daisy protests."

Flynn thought about Daisy protesting. He thought he understood at least some of her reluctance. "Do either of you know what's the matter with her foot?"

Freddy shook his head. "No idea."

"It's her leg, not her foot," Max said. "I'm not sure how it happened—some accident when she was a child, perhaps—but I think one leg is shorter than the other."

Flynn thought about the way Daisy moved and nodded. It made sense.

* * *

A few hours later Flynn left Max's house. He put on his coat and felt the shoes in his pockets. He ought to toss them away—they were no use to man or beast. He examined the well-chewed slippers. Well, maybe beast.

They'd been pretty shoes once. An idea came to him. He hesitated.

Oh, what the hell, why not?

So on the way home he stopped at a small backstreet shoemaker he knew of. He gave the man Daisy's ruined shoes and explained what he wanted. "Can you do it?" he asked the shoemaker.

The man assured him he could, and Flynn went on his way.

"A re you sure you won't come to the masquerade ball, Daisy?" Jane asked. "Lady Beatrice did get you an invitation, and it would be such fun, seeing all the wonderful costumes."

"No, thanks, lovey—not my style of thing at all." Daisy had too much work to do to go gallivanting. She straightened the blue satin bow on Jane's shepherdess costume. It had come up a treat, if she said so herself. Jane was nothing like any shepherdess Daisy had ever seen—not that she'd seen many in London—but she looked as pretty as a picture, which was the main point.

"Stubborn gel! It would do you good to get out of that poky little room and mingle with other people," Lady Beatrice declared.

"Can't," Daisy said. "No costume."

"Wear a domino," Lady Beatrice said. She looked magnificent as Good Queen Bess, in a purple and gold brocade and a gold ruff.

"You needn't stay long," Jane urged. "The ball is just around the corner. You could come for a bit, and then walk home."

"Look, stop worrying about me and go off and have your-selves a good time," Daisy urged them. She was sick of arguing. "I'm not in a party mood. I got a bit of work to do, then I'm for an early night." Below the front doorbell rang. "That'll be Abby and Max," she said. "Mustn't keep them waiting."

"Stubborn, stubborn gel," Lady Beatrice muttered and kissed Daisy on the cheek. "Make sure you do get a good night's sleep—you're starting to look frightfully pale and drawn!"

"I will," Daisy lied. She embraced Jane, followed them downstairs and waved them off in the carriage.

"Mad, isn't it, Featherby," she commented as he shut the door behind them, "goin' round the corner in the car-riage."

He gave her a mock-shocked look. "Good Queen Bess—walk? Unthinkable."

Daisy laughed. "You mean Lady Bea—walk? Unthink-able! Not when there's a carriage available." She hurried upstairs and returned to her workroom.

She was almost up-to-date on Jane's dresses—for the moment—and Lady Gelbart and old Mrs. Hartley-Peacock had been making anxious noises about wanting their bed gowns and jackets. The two old ladies were so desperate for them, they'd offered to pay Daisy double the price—in cash!—and she'd already quoted them a ridiculous price.

Cash in hand. She would work on those tonight.

Despite her weariness, Daisy grinned to herself as she picked up the first of the half-finished silk and lace confec-tions, in pink silk and creamy lace. She threaded her needle and got to work.

Who'd've thought that very first nightgown and bed jacket she'd made for Lady Bea would lead to a whole stack of orders from other rich old ladies of the ton?

And who would've believed the kind of thing she'd first made for the girls in the brothel would be so popular with respectable old ladies? But the naughtier they were, the better the old ducks liked them. These days Daisy was making them with real French lace and proper silk—all new—not bits cut from old dresses. She had to admit, silk felt beautiful against the skin.

But those years of picking apart old dresses for the fabric had taught her how to construct a garment—how to cut and shape clothing. She'd started off by using the pieces as a pattern, but soon learned to adjust and adapt them.

She'd always had ideas for clothes in her head.

And now she knew how to make them look exactly how she imagined. She loved that she could make a chubby girl look slim, or give a skinny girl a bit of added shape. She had a good eye for color too; the right color could make a woman look sallow or vibrant, make her eyes dull or sparkle. It was a source of never-ending fascination.

More and more orders were starting to come in—which was what she'd dreamed of. Why would she waste her time at a ball instead of getting something finished—something that she'd be paid actual money for?

Besides, why would she want to go to a ball and watch Flynn twirling around the room with the *dainty* Lady Elizabeth?

The ballroom was crammed to the gunwales, as the most successful ton affairs seemed to be. Flynn shouldered his way through the colorful throng, squeezing between a mermaid and a winged fellow dressed in a sheet, a coronet of leaves and precious little else—some sort of Greek or Roman god, Flynn presumed.

He spotted Damaris and Hyphen-Hyphen, both dressed in Chinese outfits, Freddy with a long mandarin mustache dropping down his chin.

"Got a bit of seaweed caught on your face," Flynn commented, reaching for it.

"Hands off, barbarian!" Freddy stepped back, and eyed him up and down. "Dammit, Flynn, you've forgotten to wear a costume." He turned to Damaris. "He's wearing exactly the same clothes I met him in."

Flynn grinned. Freddy knew perfectly well Flynn had commissioned this outfit especially for the ball. "Better than wearing your wife's dressing gown."

"Stop it, you two," Damaris said, laughing. "Mr. Flynn, you look wonderful—a most dashing and fearsome-looking pirate!"

Flynn tried to look modest, but he had to admit he was very pleased with his costume. He was dressed in tight red pants, gleaming thigh-high black boots, his dragon waistcoat, a frothy white shirt and a purple and gold brocade coat. On his head he wore a black headscarf with a white skull and crossbones on it, a mask that was a ragged strip of black velvet with two sinister eyeholes, and in his ear, his largest, shiniest gold earring. In a final touch, he'd thrust a cutlass through his black leather belt.

"And you look beautiful, Damaris. Much too lovely to be married to this ramshackle fellow." Her embroidered Chinese costume set off her slender elegance to perfection.

"Show a bit of respect, pirate—I'm a mandarin, you know, and pretty dashed important. I could have your head chopped off"—Freddy snapped his fingers—"like that! It would, I'm sure, be an improvement."

They were joined at that moment by Abby and Max, Jane and Lady Beatrice. They exchanged greetings and Lady Beatrice eyed Flynn with undisguised approval. "Now *this* is the kind of man I expected when Max first told me about his friend Captain Flynn—flamboyant, colorful and with more than a touch of pirate about him. A fine figure of a man, indeed." She peered at his cutlass—at least he hoped it was his cutlass. "I hope that thing's a fake. Don't want to cut the ladies' dresses to ribbons."

"Silver-painted cardboard, m'lady," Flynn assured her. "Got it from a theater company."

"Good." Her gaze raked him up and down again. "Daisy make that waistcoat, did she?" She poked his chest with the handle of her lorgnette.

Flynn nodded.

"Gel ought to be here to see it in its full glory."

"She's not here?" Damaris said, glancing around. "But I thought you'd arranged an invitation especially for her."

"Claims she's having an early night, but *I* know better." The old lady snorted. "Staying home to work, stubborn little creature. She's turning into a veritable troglodyte. Well, get along with you, children, the dancing is about to start. Off you go and find your partners."

Chapter Six

Flynn had engaged Lady Elizabeth for two dances—the first and the last waltz of the evening. He'd been too late to secure her for the supper dance, which would have ensured he could take her into supper and spend more time getting to know her. Still, he didn't mind.

He had no intention of dancing the last waltz with her. Instead he'd take her into the garden and kiss her. He'd been planning it ever since their drive in the park. Soften the girl up a bit. Show her that it didn't have to be all duty, that there could also be pleasure.

He damned well hoped there would be pleasure. He didn't want a dutiful marriage—he wanted something warmer, cozier. He didn't expect them to fall in love, but he did hope for affection, at the very least.

Not that the nobs acted exactly cozy—half the time husbands and wives seemed to have nothing to do with each other—though what happened in the bedroom was, no doubt, another thing entirely.

He glanced around the room. Masks, music, a bit of mystery;

it was an evening made for romance. A kiss or two in the moonlight, or in the shadows created by the colorful lanterns strung around the garden—that should set them on the right course.

In the meantime, he had no shortage of willing partners and had danced his way through a cotillion, the Sir Roger de Coverley and several other country dances while he was waiting for the first waltz.

He saw Lady Beatrice sitting watching the dancers. She noticed him, and beckoned him over.

"Been observing you, Mr. Flynn."

"Have you, milady? Like what you see, do you?"

Her eyes gleamed in appreciation—the old dear did love to flirt—but all she said was, "You acquit yourself quite creditably on the dance floor."

"Thank you, milady. That lesson you arranged for me seems to have done the trick."

She gave a snort of amusement. "Why did you not tell me you knew how to dance?"

Flynn smiled. "I never tell a lady what she doesn't wish to hear."

She snorted again. "That little habit—if it's true—is going to get you into a lot of trouble then." Her beady old eyes twinkled up at him. "I look forward to it."

"So do I, ma'am, so do I."

She laughed outright. "Get along with you then, you rogue. It's the waltz next, and you don't want to keep Lady Elizabeth waiting, do you?" She sighed and added, "If I were twenty years younger I'd cut her out."

"If I were twenty years older, ma'am, I'd—" he began gallantly, then blinked. "How did you know?"

"About Lady Elizabeth?" She gave him a dry look. "When will you realize, dear boy, that I *always* know *everything.*" She gave him a little push. "Now run along and dance with the gel."

Flynn chuckled to himself as he crossed the ballroom to where Lady Elizabeth was waiting. Hyphen-Hyphen was right—the old lady was a witch.

"Our waltz, Lady Elizabeth." He bowed and held out his hand.

She made no move to take his hand, just looked at it as if there was something wrong.

"What?" He glanced at his hand. He knew she didn't much like the look of his hands—you didn't do manual labor from childhood and end up with the smooth, pale hands of a gentleman. His hands were strong and capable. They might be marked with scars and nicks from a lifetime of hard physical work, but they were well scrubbed, and his nails were clean, neatly pared and lightly buffed.

He wasn't ashamed of his hands: They reflected who he was. And how far he'd come.

"Gloves, Mr. Flynn," she reminded him, flushing slightly.

"Oh, right." He pulled them out of his pocket, put them on and led her onto the dance floor.

The opening bars sounded and he took her in his arms. She was cool and graceful and composed. He smiled to himself, remembering the stiff, cross, spiky little hedgehog he'd waltzed with at Lady Bea's. Lady Elizabeth was the perfect partner, but somehow, the hedgehog had been more fun.

Still, he was here to court the lady. "You look very pretty this evening, Lady Elizabeth."

"Thank you, Mr. Flynn."

They twirled around.

He tried again. "You make a charmin' milkmaid."

"Thank you. There are several milkmaids here tonight, I noticed."

"Yes, but you're the prettiest."

There was a short silence. Below her mask she flushed a little.

"Are you enjoying the ball?"

"I am." She added, "I particularly enjoy all the costumes and the masks. It adds a pleasant air of intrigue to the evening."

"You know most of the people here well, I suppose."

"Oh yes. Almost everyone." She flushed again and Flynn remembered this was her third Season—no doubt her last, unless she found a husband. As it was, her father must have scraped up every favor owed him to finance this Season—going even further in debt in order to sell off his last asset—his daughter.

"So what do you think of my costume?" Flynn said easily.

An expression flickered across her face that he didn't quite understand. "It's very . . . colorful."

"Do you not like it?" he asked. "I don't mind if you don't. I'd rather you spoke your mind."

She hesitated. "It's just that it wasn't very . . . wise of you."

"Wise?"

"To remind people."

"Of what?"

"Your past."

He stared at her a moment, then laughed aloud. "Good God, girl, I was never a pirate. I'm a trader."

Her mouth tightened and she glanced around to see if they'd been overheard.

Flynn didn't give a damn who might be listening. "I was—I am—in partnership in a worldwide trading enterprise, along with Lord Davenham, Freddy Monkton-Coombes and another fellow you don't know."

"Yes but—" She broke off.

"Yes but what?"

She looked at him through the holes in her mask. "Lord Davenham and Mr. Monkton-Coombes are *gentlemen.*"

There was a long silence. They danced on. After a moment, Lady Elizabeth said in a bright tone, "That's a very interesting waistcoat. Are they sea-monsters or dragons?"

"Dragons," Flynn said shortly. Now she was trying to butter him up.

They finished the rest of the dance in silence. As he returned her to her seat, where her chaperone was waiting, she eyed him worriedly. "I hope I didn't offend you, Mr. Flynn. You did ask me to be truthful."

"I know." He forced a smile. "Teach me to be careful what I ask for, won't it?" She looked truly anxious, so he added, "Don't worry, lass—I've got a thick enough skin."

Her gaze dropped immediately to his hands.

His voice only grated a little as he said, "I'll see you after supper."

She smiled up at him, relieved. "Yes, the last waltz. I look forward to it."

After that Flynn wasn't much in the mood for dancing or talking. It wasn't the girl's fault—he *had* asked her to be truthful. And he *wasn't* a gentleman—he made no pretense to be one, so why had that comment irritated him so much?

He propped himself up against one of the columns that encircled the dance floor and sardonically eyed the colorful throng. A short fat bumblebee with fuzzy wings and bandy yellow legs danced by with a tall elderly fairy in floating draperies, followed by an elderly man in a toga dancing with a woman dressed as Cleopatra.

Dammit, Daisy ought to be here. Some of these costumes were fantastical and imaginative, and some downright ridiculous. Either way, she would have loved it.

D aisy heard the doorbell ringing below, but took no notice. It was late, almost eleven. Featherby would send whoever it was away. Everyone they knew would be at the masquerade ball.

A moment later Featherby knocked on her door. "Mr. Flynn is below, miss."

Daisy frowned. She'd thought Flynn was going to the ball as well. "Din't you tell him everyone was out?"

"He asked to speak to you, miss."

"Me? Whatever for?" Bemused, Daisy put her sewing aside, and stretched. It was probably time to finish up anyway. She'd been at it since before dawn. Her back ached and her eyes were sore.

A quick glance in the looking glass told her she looked as worn out as she felt. Flynn wouldn't care what she looked like—not that she wanted him to notice, but a girl had her pride. She tidied her hair, pinched a bit of color into her cheeks and went downstairs.

Flynn, dressed as a very colorful pirate, was seated in the drawing room. He rose as Daisy entered.

"Gawd, it's a bloomin' rainbow come to call," she exclaimed from the doorway. She raised her hand as if to shield her eyes, but under cover of her hand, she looked her fill. All those colors should have clashed, but somehow, he carried it off. He was a beautiful-looking man and the brash confidence with which he carried himself was downright irresistible.

"Very funny," Flynn said, smoothing down his coat with a satisfied expression. "Evenin', Daisy."

She grinned. "You shoulda been born in Lady Bea's time. The gents in her day were proper peacocks—wearin' silks and satins and brocades in all colors. Not like today, when evenin' dress for men is like . . . magpies—all black and white."

He laughed. "If I'd been born in Lady Bea's day she would have eaten me alive."

"Pooh, you'd handle her the same way as you do now—perfect," Daisy said as she seated herself.

Featherby had provided Flynn with a brandy, and a few moments later William appeared with a tray containing a teapot, a plate of finger sandwiches, and some of the little curd cakes she was so fond of. From the way Flynn's eyes lit up at the sight, he liked them too.

"I thought you were goin' to the masquerade with the others. You're dressed for it, right enough. Lost your invitation?"

"No, I was there earlier."

Daisy poured herself a cup of tea. "Want one?" He shook his head and raised his brandy glass.

"So what 'appened?"

He didn't answer, just picked up the plate of sandwiches and offered it to her.

Knowing he wouldn't eat unless she did, she took one. "Quarreled with your young lady, did you?"

He didn't meet her gaze, but said carelessly, "I've already danced once with Lady Elizabeth—that's her name: Lady Elizabeth Compton—and I promised her I'd be back for the last waltz of the evening. At these affairs you're only allowed two dances with the one girl." He took a sandwich and demolished it in two bites.

"So why are you here then, instead of dancing with some of those other girls?"

He sipped his brandy. "Lady Beatrice told me she'd arranged to have you invited, but that you refused because you had work to do."

"I do," Daisy said. "You of all people should understand that."

"I understand more than you think."

She narrowed her eyes at him. "What's that supposed to mean?"

"You're looking exhausted," he said bluntly.

"So what? Hard work never killed nobody. I'm startin' a business, remember?"

"I know, and that's why I decided to come tonight, when nobody else was here to overhear what I have to say."

Daisy gave him a flinty look. "What's it got to do with you?"

"Nothing. But I know a lot more about how to run a business than you do, and I have to tell you, you're goin' about it the wrong way."

Daisy stiffened. She set down her teacup with a clatter. "Well, thanks very much, Mr. Flynn, and now you've told me, you can get back to your bloody ball."

"Settle down, firebrand, I mean no insult."

"No? You tell me I'm doin' everything wrong—me, who's workin' my fingers to the bone every hour God sends, making beautiful clothes for Jane and the others—clothes that other ladies want to order—an' you expect me not to be angry? Bloody oath, I'm angry! What the hell would you know about ladies' clothin' anyway?"

"Nothing," Flynn said calmly. "You're excellent at designing and makin' clothes. But you said it yourself, woman—you're 'workin' your fingers to the bone every hour God sends.' And not goin' out. I haven't seen you at the park for weeks, and now I hear you turned down the opportunity to go to a ball—two balls if you count tonight—that the rest of the world would kill to attend. It's not like you, Daisy."

To her great chagrin, Daisy felt her eyes pricking with unshed tears. Only because her eyes were sore, she told herself. She blinked them fiercely away. "Yeah, well, I been *busy*."

"Tryin' to do it all yourself," Flynn agreed.

"And what's wrong with that?"

"Everythin'," Flynn said. "You can't expect to start a business by doin' all the work yourself."

"I don't, Mr. Know-it-all! Jane and Abby and Damaris all help out as much as they can, and Lady Bea lets two of her maids do some of the sewing in their spare time."

Flynn nodded. "And still, it's not enough. You've over-reached yourself, haven't you?"

"No, I bloody well have not."

Flynn grinned. "The swear words are flying tonight. Struck a nerve, haven't I?"

Daisy wanted to throw the teapot at him. How the hell did he know?

"What were you doin' before I got here tonight?"

"Sewin'," she muttered sullenly.

"Sewin' what?"

She glared at him. "Seams on a dress, though what it's got to do with you—"

"Could anyone else sew those seams?"

"Of course. But there ain't anyone—"

"And what is it that you do that nobody else can?"

She bristled. "Are you sayin' that anyone can do what I'm doin'?"

"Quite the opposite. Think, Daisy—what do you do in this business that nobody else can? Not Jane or Abby or Damaris or the maids—only you."

She rolled her eyes. It was obvious what she did that nobody else could. "I come up with the designs, of course."

"Exactly." He drained his glass and sat back in his chair. "Your trouble is, you're thinkin' too small."

Too small? She glared at him. "You're talkin' out yer arse, Flynn! There's nothin' small about wantin' to become the top modiste in London!"

"Nothing wrong with the ambition, no—it's the way

you're goin' about it that's too small. You need proper premises to work in—not your old bedroom—and you need to hire proper seamstresses to do the bulk of the work."

She snorted with bitter laughter. "Oh, yes, fine—proper premises and proper seamstresses. And what do I use for money, eh? Oh, of course"—she hit her forehead in a mocking gesture—"why don't I use all them bags of gold I keep lyin' around under my bed? They're only gatherin' dust."

"You need a partner."

"I bloody don't," she flashed. "Nobody's gettin' their mitts on my business." She'd lost everything twice in her life and she wasn't about to make it three times. Besides, she'd had enough of other people telling her what to do.

"Don't dismiss the idea before you know what I'm talking about. I'm talkin' about a silent partner."

"I could do wiv a bit of silence right now."

He ignored her. "Did I ever tell you about how Max and I got started with our trading company?" He didn't wait for her to respond, but continued. "We met on board ship. I'd been at sea for a few years by then an' had worked me way up to third mate. He was a gentleman passenger, just startin' out, aiming to become a trader. I had a few quid saved, he had barely a bean. But we had plans, both of us, or maybe I should call them dreams—big dreams." He looked at her. "Like you have."

Daisy waited, caught, despite herself.

"We decided to form a partnership—Max would use my savin's to acquire goods to trade, and then I'd sell them when me shop docked in England."

"Gawd, you were a trustin' soul, weren't you? Or maybe it was Max who was the trustin' one."

"There was trust on both sides. I trusted him with me savin's, he trusted me with the profit. Slowly we built up our profits—but they were slow. It wasn't until Hyphen-Hyphen's aunt died—"

"Damaris's Freddy—his aunt?"

Flynn nodded. "It might have been his great-aunt, I don't recall—but whoever she was, she left him a good-sized lump of cash. And instead of blowin' it all on high living, like most young gents would, he decided to invest in our dream—Max had written to him, you see—and he used the money to become our silent partner."

Daisy folded her arms, feigning disinterest. She was still cross with Flynn, but she wanted to know more. Why hadn't she heard about this from Damaris? Probably because Freddy never talked about such stuff as business to ladies. Nor did Max. Toffs didn't. "Go on," she said. "I'm listenin'."

"We used Hyphen-Hyphen's nest egg to launch ourselves in a big way—we amassed as much cargo as we could afford—choosing the kind of goods that we knew would make a good profit, and hired a ship. I captained it and sailed it to London. We risked everything on that first cargo, but the risk paid off.

"It was the start of our trading empire—and in case you don't know, 'cause I'm told it's vulgar to talk about this kind of thing in polite company, Flynn and Co. is one of the biggest private trading companies in the British Empire."

He paused a moment to let that sink in. "And it all started because Max and I took on a silent partner, who trusted us with his money." She didn't say anything, so he added, "And we all benefited—Max, me, Hyphen-Hyphen and Blake Ashton, the fourth partner. You haven't met him yet. He's still out east somewhere."

Daisy nibbled on a curd cake, turning over his story in her mind. "So what's the story of your success got to do with me and my dressmakin'?" She thought she understood, but she wasn't sure.

"If you took on a silent partner, you'd have enough money to rent a premises and hire some seamstresses. If you had enough people to do all the work, you could spend your time using your talent for designing, instead of sewing seams into the night. You could be meeting ladies of the ton and increasing orders that way, instead of living like a hermit. And you'd be producing more clothing. In other words, you could turn it into a proper business, instead of a backyard operation."

He painted an enticing picture all right: her own premises,

a team of seamstresses working under her direction. Herself, swannin' around the ton, minglin' with duchesses and takin' orders. Not that she wanted to mingle with duchesses. It was their money she wanted, not their company.

But Daisy knew a fairy tale when she heard it—they always sounded too good to be true. And there was always a hidden cost. "Did Freddy tell you what to do with his money?"

"No, though he did insist on being able to inspect the books. It's how he got interested in business, as a matter of fact. Turns out he had a talent for it."

"So if I took on a silent partner, he wouldn't be tellin' me what to do all the time? He'd stay out of me way?"

Flynn pursed his lips. "I wouldn't say that. Speakin' hypothetically, of course, if, say, the silent partner were a man like meself, he might want to make sure you knew how to keep account books properly, might want to offer an occasional bit of advice—"

"Nope. Not interested." Daisy stood abruptly, brushing crumbs from her fingers. "Thank you for visitin', Mr. Flynn. It's time to go back to Lady Liz now. She'll be wantin' her dance. Thank you for the story and the unwanted advice."

Flynn stood with a rueful expression on his face. "Don't be too hasty to dismiss the idea, Daisy. Just promise me you'll think about it."

"Oh, I will, you can be sure of that." She'd think about it, but that was all. She'd had enough of people taking over her things. All her life, whenever she'd managed to get something of her own, somebody—usually a man—always managed to grab it for himself.

And the law—damn it to hell and back—always favored the bloody man.

Twice in her life she'd lost everything. Never again.

She wasn't a trusting soul like Flynn had been. Or maybe it was Freddy who'd been the trusting soul. Whatever, Daisy wasn't big on trust anymore.

Last year, after working hard all her life, she'd ended up on the streets, homeless and almost broke—again—with only a small bundle of fabric scraps, leftovers and other people's discards. And that wasn't down to any man, but to Daisy's own . . . foolishness. Trusting the wrong person—again.

If it weren't for Abby and her sisters—and Lady Bea— she'd never have had the opportunity to try and make her dream come true.

All her life she'd been at somebody else's beck and call— everybody else's. She'd been the lowest of the low.

Now she had a chance—a real chance—to make something of herself, and she wasn't going to risk losing it. Not again.

And more than anything she wanted to be her own boss. She'd had a taste of freedom at Lady Beatrice's and it was in her blood now. She wasn't ever going back to being bossed around by other people, being told what to do and how to do it and when to do it.

No, she wanted to do this her way, and if she failed, she'd have only herself to blame.

She didn't mind the idea of a silent partner, but a male partner—even one like Flynn, who she liked and almost trusted—was a risk she couldn't afford to take. As far as most people were concerned, property—and a business was property—was a man's domain. If there was a dispute, well, the law was made by men for men. She had no illusions about that.

In any case, she'd bet her last penny that with the best will in the world, Flynn would never stay silent, never let her decide things for herself. He was a man too used to being in command.

Besides, she fancied him too much, and God help a girl who went into business with a man she fancied. Fruit, ripe for the picking.

"I'm thinkin' it might be pleasant for you and me to step out into the garden, and sit this one out," Flynn said, tucking Lady Elizabeth's arm into his. "It's very warm in here and you're looking a wee bit flushed."

"Oh, but—" She hung back. "It's a lovely idea, but I don't think we should. It's not quite . . . proper."

She turned a look of subtle entreaty on her chaperone, but her father, who was standing close by, said in a brusque voice, "Don't be missish girl—nothing's going to happen to you. Go on outside with Mr. Flynn."

"Yes, Papa," she said, her voice almost . . . defeated. As if her father was flinging her to the wolves.

Flynn gritted his teeth. For two pins he'd drop the whole idea and go home. He wasn't in the mood for this. He'd had enough female trouble this evening.

First Lady Elizabeth's tactlessness earlier in the evening, then Daisy, flinging back his offer of a silent partnership in his teeth, as if he'd mortally insulted her—stubborn little wench! And now this, a young lady he was courting acting as if an invitation to walk in the garden was tantamount to an offer of rape!

But once he'd charted a course, he followed it through to the end—unless there were shoals ahead, or some unseen obstacle. He'd planned to kiss Lady Elizabeth tonight and he'd damned well do it.

He led her into the garden. At first they simply strolled together, her arm tucked into his, enjoying the mild evening, and the colored lights that bathed the garden in reds and yellows and pinks and blues—and left the rest in shadows. Flynn had plans for those shadows.

The occasional murmur and giggle from a darkened corner showed he wasn't the only one making use of the garden for a spot of dalliance, though by comparison, his plans were relatively chaste. A couple of kisses, a bit of a cuddle, and then he'd see where they'd go from there.

It was his experience that women loosened up once the kissing started. He had no plans to seduce her though. No, he'd keep this fairly innocent. Schoolgirl stuff.

She was nervous. Normally a little on the quiet side, tonight she chattered nonstop about the gardens, the lights, the costumes, what she'd eaten for supper, what Flynn's plans were for the morrow . . .

Anything, he guessed, to fill the silence. And to prevent him from broaching any more personal topic.

They passed under an arch and came to a tiny, miraculously secluded courtyard.

He stopped. She stopped with a jerk and turned a pale, set face to him. He could feel the tension running through her. He smiled. "Relax, Lady Elizabeth. I'll not hurt you, lass."

She stiffened. Flynn drew her closer, put a finger under her chin, because she was trying to look away from him, and kissed her, softly at first, just lips on lips, brushing lightly. Warm, soft, gentle. Gathering her in.

She made no move to move closer, or indeed to move away. She just stood there stiffly in his embrace. As if ready to endure . . . whatever. She was trembling—and not in a good way.

Surely in this, her third Season, it couldn't be her first kiss.

Maybe it was. He was getting nothing from her. Nothing except resistance and . . . nerves.

He drew her closer, and deepened the kiss, gently parting her lips for the first light touch of his tongue—

"Splt!! Ugh!" She shoved him away and stumbled a few steps backward, wiping her mouth, revulsion in every movement. "What are you—?" She broke off, and eyed him anxiously. There was a short silence, then, "I'm sorry. I wasn't . . . prepared for . . ."

"Your first kiss?" Flynn asked.

She hesitated, then nodded. But she didn't meet his eye. A lie then. No matter.

He moved forward again, but she flinched. *Flinched.*

He dropped his arms and stepped back. He'd never made a girl flinch in his life. "I'll take you back inside."

He turned to leave but she clutched his sleeve. "No, you can't!"

He turned, frowning down at her. What was going on here?

"Sorry—I'm sorry, Mr. Flynn, it's just—" She gestured around the shadowy garden, lit by gaily colored lanterns. "Someone might see us . . ."

He shook his head. "Nobody can see us here. I think we both know what's happening here, Lady Elizabeth. I apologize. My mistake in thinkin' you were willin'."

"Oh, but I *am*! I *promise* you I am! I must—It is just—" She swallowed convulsively, her eyes stricken. "Please believe me, Mr. Flynn, I am willing. *Very* willing. When we are married, I will . . . It will be different. I will welcome your . . . attentions then."

I will do my duty then.

"I don't think so," Flynn said gently. "Don't worry, lass. There's no blame to you attached. "

"Oh, but there is. Please. Papa will—" She broke off, chewing her lip. On the verge of tears. "Please, you must believe me. Here—I will prove it." She grabbed him by the arms, stood on tiptoe and mashed her mouth up against his.

Flynn tried to turn it into a kiss, but it was a miserable failure, even worse than before. He tasted desperation and revulsion in equal measure. He'd never experienced anything like it.

He gently eased her away. She stood there, wringing her hands in agitation, waiting desperately for his reaction. Did she really imagine that could convince him?

He glanced around the garden to make sure they could not be overheard. He lowered his voice. "Is there someone else?"

"Someone else?" She started guiltily and scanned his face frantically. "No? Who do you mean. Have you heard something? Did Papa say—? Oh, please no."

"Hush, lass, there's no need to take on so. All I want to know is, is there another man you would prefer to marry? Someone your Papa doesn't approve of?" Someone with no money, in other words.

She shook her head. "No, there's no one I prefer to marry. No one, I promise you. Truly."

"Are you sure? Because if you tell me there is, I will help you."

Again she shook her head. "There is no one," she said dully. "I only wish there were." And then she realized what she'd said and her face crumpled. "Oh, I'm sorry, I did not mean—"

Flynn stared down at her. There was something else going on here, something he didn't understand, and he wanted to get to the bottom of it. "What do you mean?"

"Nothing, nothing at all." She practically gabbled the words. She clutched at his sleeves again. "Please, Mr. Flynn, I'm sorry, I didn't mean to insult you. I *am* willing, *more* than willing."

"No, you're not." He knew when a woman was interested and she was the very opposite. So why was she so anxious to convince him otherwise? He added in a soothing voice, "I'm not offended, Lady Elizabeth. Don't worry, I'll not be asking your father for your hand—"

"Oh, but you must, or else—" She broke off and looked away, chewing on her lip, clearly distressed.

"Or else what?"

For a few moments he was sure she wasn't going to say anything. She opened her mouth, closed it, opened it again, and finally whispered so softly he almost didn't catch it, "Lord Flensbury." She shuddered.

Flensbury? He'd never heard of the man. "Who is Lord—"

But at that moment, bells rang to signal that it was time for the unmasking, and the garden was suddenly filled with people, and squeals and laughter and exclamations and all chance of any private conversation was gone.

"I'll call on you at your home tomorrow morning," Flynn told her over the hubbub. "You can tell me all about it then."

Chapter Seven

*"I am afraid," replied Elinor, "that the pleasantness of an
employment does not always evince its propriety."*

—JANE AUSTEN, SENSE & SENSIBILITY

Flynn, normally a good sleeper, passed a restless night
but he woke with one clear resolve: He wasn't going to
marry Lady Elizabeth.

That debacle of a kiss last night—and her extraordinary
reaction—had convinced him. And with that decision firm
in his mind, it was as if a weight had been lifted from him.

As he shaved and dressed, he pondered his blindness.
He'd chosen the girl without knowing anything about her.
Fool! Like shopping for a wife in one of those fancy London
shops, giving it about as much thought as any simple purchase. What the hell had he been thinking?

He ate his breakfast in a pensive mood. If he hadn't been
so blinded by his ambition he would've seen it much earlier.
The girl didn't fancy him at all. She wasn't simply nervous
of him—she saw him as some kind of brute with the phy-
sique of a laborer and great ugly hands. Some kind of pirate.

She couldn't even bear him touching her with those
hands. *Gloves, Mr. Flynn.*

It was all about his money. And her future security.

Mind you, he was no better. Take away her family name

and connections, her title and her fancy manners and he wouldn't have given her a second look. She was pretty enough, but there wasn't a spark of attraction between them. Or even friendship. Twenty minutes in her company and he was ready to leave. Luckily that was the polite thing to do. But a lifetime of it . . .

He cleaned his teeth, brushed his hair and gave a cursory glance at his reflection in the looking glass. What the devil had he been thinking?

As Daisy had reminded him, marriage was for life. And now he thought about it with a clear mind, he realized he wanted a marriage like his own parents had—close and loving. His memories of them were hazy—just a child's recollections—but he remembered them talking and laughing and sometimes even fighting together, but always together, in good times and bad. Looking back, he realized they'd been friends as well as lovers.

He didn't want the kind of ton marriage where husband and wife came together as strangers, bred a couple of heirs and then turned elsewhere for love. Illicit love, and sometimes not even that. As long as it was discreet, it didn't seem to matter.

They weren't all like that, he knew. Max and Abby were deeply in love, and so were Damaris and Freddy.

But Jane was—if Daisy was correct—planning on marrying a dull and dreary little lord for exactly the same reason as Lady Elizabeth would marry Flynn—if he asked her. Wealth and security.

Which brought him to the topic of Lord Flensbury. Who the devil was he?

He picked up his hat and left his apartment. He was off to make a few morning calls. In the actual morning. Lady Elizabeth and her father first. Best to get it over and done with.

It was a fine spring morning, and Flynn decided to walk. He chose a route that wasn't the most direct, but the most interesting—to him. He liked walking past the shops, looking into the windows, seeing what people were buying. It paid to keep abreast of the market.

Nothing to do with putting off the dreaded interview with Lady Elizabeth.

One shop window contained a pretty little display, a table set for tea, with a large blue teapot, a pair of willow-patterned cups and a willow-patterned plate on which a variety of small cakes rested.

Seeing it, he stopped dead. And was suddenly a thousand miles and more than twenty years away. Mam serving up tea, pouring it hot and strong from her big blue teapot, her good tablecloth covering the battered old table—she'd embroidered it herself when she was a young girl, and woe betide the person—man or child—who spilled anything on that cloth.

Cakes were a rarity in the house he'd grown up in—they were too poor for that—but brown bread and butter and sometimes honey, or potato bread, or biscuits would be served on Mam's willow-patterned plate—the one with a chip out of the corner. It had been a wedding present, and Mam loved it.

A loudly cleared throat made it clear he was blocking the way. Flynn moved on, his mind still in the past. Flynn had been responsible for that chip in Mam's plate—an accident when he was just a wee lad—and he'd always intended to get Mam a new one.

He never had. By the time Flynn had earned enough to buy a plate, she was dead—they all were, his entire family, taken by the cholera. And Flynn was all alone.

He'd left Ireland shortly afterwards, gone away to sea and tried never to think of what he'd left behind, what he lost. He'd made it his habit to look forward, not back. The past was too painful.

Still, the cheerful little window display had reminded him of the good times; he hadn't thought of teatime at home for years. No matter how poor they'd been, Mam always got out the good tablecloth and had something tasty to eat sitting on that willow-patterned plate. And she sure as hell made sure that every kid was clean and neatly dressed and ready with their best manners, even if there was only family at the table. Because nobody was more important than family . . . .

He walked on, smiling to himself. It was a good memory. When he got a proper home, he'd buy his wife a blue teapot and a willow-patterned plate. It wouldn't mean anything to her, of course, but he'd see it and remember . . . .

A wife . . . Why the devil had he imagined it would be so easy and straightforward?

He'd been walking for some time, lost in thought, when an urchin running by swerved, nearly bumping into him. Startled, Flynn looked around and realized that somehow, he'd brought himself to Berkeley Square.

Might as well drop in on Daisy and see if she'd reconsidered his silent partner proposition.

Nothing to do with putting off an awkward and uncomfortable visit to Lady Elizabeth.

Lady Beatrice was not yet receiving, Featherby informed him, but Miss Daisy was up. Flynn hurried up the stairs. Daisy was exactly who he wanted to talk to—not just about his proposition, but about Lady Elizabeth.

He found he had a need for a sympathetic ear—a sympathetic female ear. Daisy was very easy to talk to.

"Did you give any thought to what I was talking about last night? Takin' me on as a silent partner, I mean."

"Yeah, I did and the answer's still no." Daisy had thought about it all night. It was a good idea—in theory. But she couldn't bring herself to put everything she'd worked for in someone else's hands. Particularly not a man's. Not again.

And particularly not Flynn's. Flynn, for all his good intentions, couldn't help but interfere and boss her around. Daisy had had people telling her what to do all her life, and she had no intention of letting anyone be the boss of her, ever again.

Freedom—being her own boss—was bloody lovely. Even if it was tough at times. She wouldn't give it up for quids.

"That's a bit shortsighted, don't you think?"

"No, I don't."

"You're struggling."

She lifted her shoulders indifferently and continued with her sewing. "Don't you worry yourself none about me, Flynn. I'm doin' all right. "

"No you're not—you're exhausting yourself, trying to do it all yourself."

The fact that he was right was annoying but she said in a calm enough voice, "Listen—a year ago I was nothing but a skivvy, a maidservant in a bro—a business establishment. I was waitin' on everybody—scrubbin' and mendin' and at everyone's beck and call at all hours of the day and night! Now look at me—I'm livin' in the poshest part of town, with the daughter of an earl who claims me as her niece and this"—she brandished a piece of fabric in his face—"this'll warm the shoulders of a duchess. I know I'm havin' trouble keeping up with orders—but that's better than havin' no customers at all, ain't it?"

"It'd be even better if you had some help," he said bluntly. "And if you took me on as a partner, you could afford it."

"I appreciate the offer, Flynn, truly I do, but . . . I just can't bring meself to hand over half of me business—any of it really—to somebody else." She wasn't going to explain her reasoning to Flynn. He'd want to know more, and she wasn't going down that path, thank you very much!

"You wouldn't be handing it over—you'd be taking on a silent partner."

"Yeah, and if I took you on as me so-called silent partner you'd stay out of me business, would you? You'd let me make all the decisions?"

He hesitated and she laughed. "'Course you wouldn't. You'd be interferin' all the time, tellin' me a better way to do things, tellin' me I'm doin' it wrong, that I'm thinkin' too small—any of this ring a bell, does it?"

He frowned, but didn't answer.

"See?" she said softly. "And you're not even me partner."

He acknowledged the truth of what she said with a wry gesture. "I know, I can't help stickin' me nose in. But I still reckon you're making a mistake."

"Maybe, but it's my mistake, ain't it?"

He regarded her with a troubled expression and she felt a prick of compunction. "Listen, I know you're tryin' to help, Flynn—and I'm not saying you're the same—but . . . I've trusted other people before—people I thought cared about me—and . . . well, let's just say it was a mistake, both times." A big mistake.

He gave her a shrewd look. "A man, both times?"

"What makes you think that?" Only once was a man, but she could feel herself blushing anyway, the way those blue eyes of his were looking at her. She broke eye contact and said briskly, "Doesn't matter who it was. Doesn't change the way I feel." And because he was still looking at her and making her feel guilty, she added, "Look, don't take it personal, Flynn. I learned the hard way that it's a bad idea to mix business with friendship."

He considered her words, then shrugged. "Fair enough. I won't bother you again, though if ever you change your mind—"

"I won't." She finished sewing a strip of lace onto Lady Gelbart's bed jacket, and glanced up at him.

He stood up, as if to leave, but instead started pacing restlessly around, touching this and that, absently picking things up—strips of braid, a piece of fur, garments in various states of assembly—and putting them down. She was sure he wasn't really noticing what he was doing.

He stopped, staring out of the window holding a newly finished nightgown that had been draped over the back of a chair—one of the fancy ones so popular with old ladies. He stood there frowning, his legs in their tight breeches and gleaming boots braced as if on the deck of a ship. Commanding the oceans . . .

She swallowed. He made quite a sight, staring out at nothing in particular, running the silky fabric through his fingers, seemingly lost in thought. For a full minute Daisy quite forgot to sew.

She ought to make some cheeky comment, break the silence, but the picture he made . . . the tall, strong figure, the delicate silk and netting nightgown sliding through those very masculine hands, hands marked by life, not softened by lotions and a life of ease and privilege . . . Her mouth dried.

"Oy—" Her voice croaked, and she cleared her throat. "I 'ope you got clean hands."

"What?" He glanced down and saw what he was holding. He held it up to the light—the fine silk was practically transparent, the netting and lace artfully placed to reveal . . . and conceal. A look of amusement spread across his face. He swung around to face her, holding it up against his chest.

The delicate feminine nightgown floated then settled with a sigh against his tough male body. "You wear this sort of thing, do you Daisy?" He quirked a dark eyebrow. Superbly confident in his own masculinity, a lurking challenge in those blue eyes of his, his gaze raked her.

To Daisy's annoyance, she felt herself blushing. The contrast between his big, hard body and the whisper-soft lacy garment was quite . . . erotic. She said in as brusque a tone as she could manage, "'Course not—it's for one of me customers."

He glanced at the frivolous, scandalous nightgown again and his brows rose. "You mean proper ladies wear this kind of thing?"

She nodded. "Yep. The properer they are, the more the ladies love 'em. Even old ladies love 'em." Truth be told, the old ladies loved them most of all.

"*Old* ladies?" He looked at the flimsy handful of silk and lace. "Old ladies wear something like *this*?"

She grinned, enjoying his surprise. "That's right. The old ducks can't get enough of them. That one's for the Honorable Mrs. Hartley-Peacock. She'll be wearin' it to bed tonight, I reckon."

He hastily put the nightgown down.

She chuckled. "And this 'un"—she held up the one she was finishing off—"is for Lady Gelbart. Both of them are as old as Lady Beatrice—in fact it was them seein' one I made for her that started it all. I've made dozens—all for the most respectable old ladies in the ton. And you wouldn't believe what they're prepared to pay." Flynn was the one person she knew who would understand that little gloat. It being vulgar to talk money.

"Good God. Respectable old ladies, eh? I never would have guessed."

She shrugged. "You never can tell what ladies are thinking."

"And isn't that God's own truth?" he said in such a different tone that Daisy looked up from her stitching. He wasn't looking in the least bit amused now.

"Something on your mind, Flynn?" There was a short silence. "Something happen last night after you left here?"

"You might say so. Or maybe it was what didn't happen." He sat down heavily.

Daisy threaded her needle, picked up another strip of lace and prepared to listen.

"I tell you, Daisy—I've never experienced anything like it in my life." Flynn was up again, pacing back and forth in front of her window seat like a big dark cat. "There was no spark at all. Nothing. It was like . . . like kissin' a fish."

"Mm-hmm." Daisy kept sewing. Did he think she *wanted* to hear all about his bloomin' love-life—in *detail*? Gawd, men were blind. And vain.

"Are you listenin'? Like kissing *a fish*!"

She shrugged. "Yeah, well, it happens."

"Not to me, it doesn't."

"Maybe." She didn't want to hear about Flynn kissing another girl, she really didn't. And his insistence on sharing every blooming detail with her was starting to irritate her.

He stopped in front of her, looming over her like a great grumpy bear. "What? What aren't you implyin'?"

She rolled her eyes. "Most men think they're God's gift to kissin'."

His eyes narrowed. "What's that supposed to mean?"

She smoothed the seam, checking it was all even, then tied off the thread and carefully snipped off the end. "*She* might not be the problem."

"What?"

He stood there, blue gaze burning into her, waiting for further explanation. Her temper flared, so she told him.

"Coulda been the way you kissed her. I mean, Jane's bloomin' mutt licks me fingers and toes all the time, and I hate it."

He stared at her, outraged. "It's hardly the same."

"No, but still . . ." She shook out the finished bed jacket. Perfect. Old Lady Gelbart would be delighted. She hopped off her seat and crossed the room. Two more orders completed.

"Are you sayin' I don't know how to kiss a girl?" he demanded in a silky tone that didn't deceive Daisy for a minute. His eyes were blue chips of anger.

She held up her hands in a peaceable gesture. "I'm not sayin' nuffin'. It's Lady Liz who gets to judge, not me." But she couldn't help adding, "And it sounds like she did."

He followed her across the room. "I damn well do know how to kiss."

"Sure you do." She folded the finished garments and placed them in the basket on the dresser, ready to be ironed, then packaged up for William to deliver.

"I'm good—bloody good if you want to know. I've never had any complaints before."

"I'm sure you haven't."

Flynn glared at her in frustration. Her tone made it clear that she thought the women in his past were simply too polite to complain. Which was so damn far from the truth it was a joke!

As he watched, she picked up another half-finished garment and headed back to take her seat in the window. It was a red rag to a bull. Her complacency, the attitude that her damned sewing was so much more important to her than anything he might have to say, drove him wild.

She was so blasted certain the fault lay with him. He clenched his fists, itching to shake the smugness out of her. She stepped around him, giving him a little half smile, obviously meant to soothe his injured masculine feelings. It was the last straw.

He grabbed her, swung her around and planted one on her.

"Oy! What the—mmmph!" She stiffened, resisting him

for a few seconds, then . . . with a small sigh, her mouth softened beneath his.

She parted her lips for him and heat, like embers from a fire, glowing and alive, rushed through him.

He pulled back, shocked, but didn't let go. Couldn't let go.

The instant explosion of . . . hunger . . . need . . . *arousal* stunned him, sent his head spinning. What had started in anger and frustration—a simple need to prove himself as a man—had spiraled instantly into something else.

He stared down at the woman in his arms. *Daisy?*

She blinked back up at him, her big hazel eyes wide and a little dazed, apparently as surprised as he was. Her mouth was damp, rosy, enticing.

He released her shoulders, sliding his hands up the slender column of her throat, his blunt fingers spearing through the softness of her hair as he cupped her head in his hands. She stood motionless, staring up at him, and he was drowning, drowning in her eyes.

His thumbs framed her delicate pixie face, and he heard the trembling intake of her breath as he stroked the silken skin of her jawline, and felt her pulse leap under his touch. A shudder ran through her and her eyes darkened.

His blood surged with possessive need, and he lowered his mouth to kiss her again, deeply, passionately, tasting her, exploring.

Her hands came up to grip his shoulders, and she pulled him closer, angling her head to deepen the kiss, to accept him, her small slender body pressed against his, twining against his as she returned kiss for kiss, making muffled little sounds that drove him wild with wanting.

When he pulled back a second time, his heart was hammering in his chest. He released her and stepped away, shakily, his body braced for action, fighting the arousal pounding through him.

They stared at each other, speechless. Shocked.

Daisy could make him feel like this? He'd always liked the girl, always enjoyed a light bit of flirtation with her . . . but . . . *this?*

Daisy seemed to be breathing just as hard. "Gawd, Flynn," she said at last. She staggered to the window seat and collapsed into it as if her knees were about to give way.

"I know." It had taken him just as much by surprise. Never in his life . . . He struggled to take in the enormity of what had just happened. *Daisy?*

Her sewing lay in a crumpled heap on the floor, forgotten. He should have felt triumphant—his point proved—but he was still too stunned.

"Well, that settles one thing," she said eventually.

"What?" He was still trying to come to terms with it.

"If you kissed Lady Liz like that—"

"I didn't." He'd never kissed *anyone* like that. In his *life.*

"Well, if you kissed her half as—"

"Not even half."

They stared at each other for a long moment, then she gave a shiver and made a visible effort to pull herself together. She collected her sewing and folded it neatly. She set it down on the window seat, smoothing it with hands he noted were trembling slightly, and said, not looking at him, "It's definitely not you, then. It's her."

Flynn didn't say a thing. He just stood there, looking down at her. *Daisy!* He could hardly come to terms with it.

"She's probably one of them Ladies of Llangollen." She pronounced the last word as if she was clearing her throat.

"Ladies of *what*?" What the hell were they talking about?

"Llangollen." More clearing of the throat. She looked at his face and laughed. "That's how the Welshies say it, anyway. I knew a Welsh girl once. The English say it as Lan-gollen."

"If you say so. And who or what are Ladies of Lan-whatsit?" He could hardly believe they were having some conversation about some blasted place in Wales. He just wanted to haul Daisy back into his arms and kiss her senseless.

"Llangollen. They're a couple of posh ladies who didn't want to get married—not to men, anyway—and so they run off and set up house together in Wales—in Llangollen. They're famous—haven't you heard of them? They're Irish."

"No." What did he care about—oh. Finally Flynn saw what she was getting at.

She shrugged. "Some women are that way inclined."

There was a short silence. "You mean, Lady Elizabeth is . . ."

She nodded. "Like them Ladies of Llangollen, maybe. Has to be, if you kissed her like that and she didn't like it."

"I told you, I didn't kiss her like that." He didn't want to talk about Lady Elizabeth, dammit. His mind was reeling. His body was thrumming with newfound awareness.

Daisy was his *friend.* He was supposed to feel *comfortable* with her—the only woman in London he could talk business with, the only lady he knew who didn't object to his occasional bad language. He *liked* her.

That kiss was supposed to demonstrate his expertise, not knock him sideways.

"I don't know that I've ever kissed anyone quite like that, Daisy." His voice sounded oddly hoarse. "Certainly I've never felt—"

She jumped up briskly. "Look, sorry to interrupt, Flynn, but one of me ladies is comin' in a few minutes and I got to get ready." She bustled around the room, tidying up like a small, efficient whirlwind, avoiding his gaze. "It's been nice chattin' with you, Flynn. Dunno what you can do about Lady Liz, but you'll sort it out. I got to get these things pressed and tidy the room. See yourself out, will ya?"

Flynn, watching her flit around the room, frowned. She was babbling. Trying to ignore what had just happened. Daisy—who confronted everything and everyone head-on.

So he wasn't the only one who'd been affected. Hah!

He'd leave now—he had his own doubts about this so-called appointment of hers, but he needed to sort out his feelings. And sort things out with Lady Elizabeth.

Daisy could pretend all she wanted—he'd be back. That kiss had stunned him, and he wasn't going to ignore it. He didn't know what it meant, didn't have any idea what he was going to do about it, but he was damned if he'd pretend it hadn't happened.

* * *

He let himself out of Daisy's workroom and met Lady Beatrice on the landing. "Flynn, dear boy, delightful to see you again so soon. Did you enjoy the masquerade ball last night?" She took his arm. "Visiting Daisy again, eh? Been seeing quite a bit of her lately, haven't you? I thought now the Season had started, and with your courtship of Lady Elizabeth, you wouldn't pop in quite so much." She cocked her head and added with a mischievous expression, "Not trying to seduce my Daisy, are you, Flynn, dear boy?"

He blinked. "What? No, I—" He swallowed.

She chuckled at his discomfiture. "No need to look so appalled—I'm not accusing you of anything. I have no idea where these notions come from. They just . . . pop into my head. But you wouldn't dream of compromising my dear gel, would you?" She smiled at him with a guileless expression.

"No, of course not, Lady Beatrice." Flynn felt like a boy caught with his hand in the cookie jar.

She patted his hand. "Of course not. You're a man of honor, I know, and I'm a foolish old lady. Walk me down the stairs, will you, dear boy? I am shattered, positively shattered—I'm too old to attend balls." She bore him along, chattering animatedly about the ball, sharing all the latest *on-dits*.

Flynn was the one who felt shattered. First the kiss, now the old lady seeming to read his mind—before he even knew it himself. *Not trying to seduce my Daisy, are you, dear boy?*

It was just a kiss for God's sake.

"Are you all right, my boy? You seem a trifle *distrait*." The old lady's question jolted him back to the present.

"My apologies, m'lady, I was woolgathering."

"Things not going too well with Lady Elizabeth, eh?"

Flynn stared at her. How did she do that? She was a witch, she must be. "Not exactly," he admitted. "But speaking of Lady Elizabeth, I have a question for you. What do you know about Lord Flensbury?"

* * *

The minute Flynn left, Daisy stopped fussing around. She dumped the armful of clothing she'd gathered, and collapsed into a chair. Her knees still felt all weak and wobbly. That kiss . . .

So she fancied him rotten—so what? She wouldn't dream of acting on it.

Gawd, if a woman acted on every fancy she had, she'd be ruined in a flash, and Daisy was too smart to let herself be ruined by a man.

He was flirting, that's all. The man was born to flirt. Those blue eyes of his were an invitation to sin—and enjoy it. And she had to admit, she enjoyed flirting back.

But they were just friends. She enjoyed talking to him, she liked making special waistcoats for him—and charging the earth for it—and talking with him about business and other things. He was good company, Flynn.

It had only ever been a bit of fun, nothing to take seriously. And it still was.

A kiss. She'd had dozens of kisses. Hundreds, maybe.

Nothing like that one.

Too bad. It didn't mean nothing. He'd only kissed her to prove a point about Lady Elizabeth, that's all. That fact that it had just about knocked her into next Tuesday was . . .

Was her own bloomin' fault. She shouldn't have stirred him up about it. Teasing him had been irresistible. But it had turned out to be dangerous.

The way he'd stared at her afterwards . . . as if he'd never seen her before. As if he could eat her up.

She'd have to nip that idea in the bud quick smart. She didn't want him getting ideas. He ought to know as well as she did that there was no future in it, only danger, especially for her—but men didn't always think of that. They had an itch, they scratched it. It was women who bore the consequences.

So if Flynn was making plans, if she'd read that gleam in his eye a'right, he was going to be one disappointed

Irishman, because Daisy wasn't interested in any kind of—what did the toffs call it? *Dalliance*, that was it. She wasn't having none of it.

She was a respectable woman. Now. She had a business to protect.

It was just a kiss, that's all.

Chapter Eight

The world is pretty much divided between the weak of mind & the strong, between those who can act & those who cannot, & it is the bounden duty of the capable to let no opportunity of being useful escape them.

—JANE AUSTEN, *SANDITON AND OTHER STORIES*

It wasn't far to Compton House—all the nobs lived fairly close together—but Flynn took his time getting there. He felt no responsibility to Lady Elizabeth and he was eager to get back to Daisy and explore his reaction to the kiss—their mutual reaction, if he was any judge.

But his conversation with Lady Bea on the subject of Lord Flensbury had disturbed him. The old lady had twigged to the significance of his question straight away. "So Flensbury is Compton's alternative choice, is he? Poor little Lizzie."

"Why? What's wrong with the man?"

"On the surface, perhaps nothing. Flensbury's is an old family, aristocratic and very well connected. And he's wealthy." She paused. "But he's also ancient—eighty if he's a day—and has gone through three wives that I know of without getting a son on any of them. Rumor has it he's looking for a fourth, a gel young enough to breed with. Determined to cut out his cousin—his heir—who he hates."

Eighty? And Lady Elizabeth was just two and twenty. Not to mention being a . . . Lady of Llangollen. Dammit, it was no better than a rape.

He must have made some kind of sound, for the old lady nodded and said, "Quite so. And Flensbury isn't the kind of man I'd want any of my gels to even meet, let alone marry, even if he were fifty years younger."

She curled her lip and added, "Unsavory practices. Nobody knows what the first three wives died of, but nobody doubts they're happier now."

She cocked her head and eyed Flynn shrewdly. "You're definitely not marrying Lizzie Compton, then?"

"Yes. We don't suit."

"And so her father will press her to take Flensbury. Poor little gel."

It hadn't been at all what Flynn wanted to hear. It was one thing for the girl not to wish to marry at all, but to be forced to wed an eighty-year-old . . . with unsavory practices.

Flynn swore and kicked a pebble along the street. He wished now he'd never heard of Flensbury, never asked Lady Bea about him. He didn't want to know. It had nothing to do with him.

The man sounded thoroughly unpleasant—appalling even—but he wasn't Flynn's problem. Any arrangement concerning Lord Flensbury was between Lady Elizabeth and her father. Lady Elizabeth was of age; nobody could force her to marry.

Except that she had no money of her own, and her father had made no provision for her future, so unless she married . . .

Flynn kicked another stone, hard. It *wasn't* his responsibility. *She* wasn't his responsibility. He had, perhaps, raised a few expectations, but she didn't want him, either—that kiss last night had proved it. And besides, he'd made no promises.

Her future was nothing to do with him. *Nothing.*

He reached the Compton house and rang the doorbell. He'd speak to Lady Elizabeth privately, tell her his decision, clear things with her father, then get the hell out of there.

The butler ushered him into Lady Elizabeth's drawing room just as she was pouring tea for a small handful of guests. As Flynn paused in the doorway, watching her graceful handling of the large teapot, something clicked.

That feeling he'd had the first time he'd seen her in her home, it wasn't some mysterious instinct telling him Lady Elizabeth was the girl for him. It was the teapot—an echo of memory of Mam and the tea table, a reminder of home and family and childhood security, before the cholera had shattered everything.

The symbol of family that he'd harbored in his mind—all unknowing—since he was a small boy.

If he hadn't walked past that shop this morning he might never have realized it. The last little thread tying him to Lady Elizabeth dissolved.

He took a seat and accepted a cup of tea. He'd wait out the other visitors and speak to her in private. Given her reaction to his kiss last night, she ought to be relieved.

He thought of Flensbury and swore silently.

It *wasn't* his problem.

"Please, I'm so sorry I was so silly last night. Can we try again?" They were seated in the garden, on a low bench next to some neglected roses. Lady Elizabeth's eyes were liquid with incipient tears. Her mouth wobbled. "I promise you, I'll do better. If you'll just give me another chance . . ."

Flynn sighed. It would make no difference. He had no desire to marry her now—less than no desire—but the sight of her trying to force an expression of eager willingness onto her face . . . He felt like a brute.

He shouldn't have come at all, should have just stayed away, let Lady Elizabeth and her father draw their own conclusions. But that would be the coward's way out. He had raised expectations—and not just in the girl and her father— he was well aware there had been talk and speculation among the ton. So he needed to face her like a man.

"Please, if we could just try kissing again, I promise I will not—"

"No, lass." He placed a comforting hand on her arm and before she could stop herself she recoiled, just a little.

Realizing what she'd done, she leaned toward him with a forced smile. "Sorry, you startled me."

But it wasn't that. It was his hands. *Gloves, Mr. Flynn.* Or maybe it was just because he was a man.

"Ah, lass, can't you see? You don't want me to touch you at all," he said gently. "If a man and a woman are to be married, there needs to be an attraction between them. You have to *want* to be touched."

She bit her lip. "I could try . . ."

He shook his head. "There's no point. It wouldn't be right for either of us."

"But if you don't marry me, it must be . . ." She shuddered. "Lord Flensbury. And that will be even worse—oh, I'm sorry, I didn't mean—"

"Why must you marry Flensbury?" Flynn asked bluntly. "I don't understand."

She stared at him as if he were lacking in wits. "Because of Papa's debts, of course. He's facing ruin."

"I know that. What I don't understand is why *your* happiness must be sacrificed for the sake of your father's debts."

"He's my father. It's my duty."

Flynn snorted. "It's your father's duty as a parent to take care of you, to provide for you—not to sell you off to the highest bidder like some kind of prize heifer."

A fat tear rolled down her cheek. Flynn watched helplessly, regretting his brutal honesty. He hated it when women wept. But it was time she faced the truth.

He tried a different tack. "What is your father doing to solve his debt problem?"

"I . . . I don't know."

"Well I do, and the answer is nothing—*nothing*! He hasn't reduced his expenditure, he hasn't adjusted his lavish way of life in the least, he's not even investigating how he could earn money. Worse, he's continuing to gamble and he's squandering a fortune on—on other things," he ended lamely. But he couldn't speak of Lord Compton's mistresses to his gently bred virgin daughter.

"I know," she said in a low voice. "His mistresses."

So she knew. "Then why on earth would you think you owe it to him to marry someone you find objectionable?"

She said in a resigned voice, "What else can I do? I must marry, and it's not as if there's anyone else I want to marry . . ."

"Isn't there someone, some friend or relative you could live with?"

She produced a handkerchief and dried her eyes carefully. "My aunt would take me in—my mother's sister. She and Papa have never got on." She folded up the handkerchief and looked at him hopelessly, as if that was that.

"Then why not go to her?"

"I can't. She lives in Italy. She eloped with an artist—he was Italian, and was employed to paint her betrothal portrait—but instead she ran off with him and was cast off by the family." As she explained her hands moved restlessly, pleating and repleating the handkerchief as if was the most important thing in the world to get each fold exact. He was sure she had no awareness she was even doing it. "She and Mama stayed secretly in touch, and after Mama died she wrote to me several times, inviting me to visit. Of course Papa wouldn't hear of it."

It was the perfect solution. Out of the country and off his conscience. "Then go to your aunt."

"How? I have no money."

"I'll give you the money."

"No!" She looked at him, shocked. "I couldn't possibly accept it."

"Why the hel—why on earth not?"

She gave him a clear look. "Strange as it may seem, Mr. Flynn, I do have a little pride left. Since I am not to marry you, I could not possibly accept your money."

"Make it a loan then."

"No. It's quite impossible." She was quite firm in her resolve.

Flynn stared at her in exasperation—and a slender thread of reluctant admiration. Her convoluted reasoning was quite mad, of course, but he could see she was operating from a position she thought was honorable. And far be it from him to deny the girl her pride. She had little enough left.

She said with dignity, "It is kind of you to be concerned, Mr. Flynn, but it is not your problem. *I* am not your problem."

It was exactly what he'd been telling himself all along, but it was even less convincing when she said it. She might believe it; *he* might even believe it, but he couldn't leave her in this mess. It wasn't of his making, but he'd contributed to it.

"I own a fleet of ships. I could arrange passage—"

"Thank you, but no. The subject is closed. I should not have been so indiscreet as to involve you in my private concerns." She rose and held out her hand. "Good-bye, Mr. Flynn. Thank you for being so honest with me. It has been a pleasure knowing you."

Flynn bowed over her hand. "It's been a pleasure and a privilege knowing you, Lady Elizabeth." He liked her a great deal better now—giving him this calm and dignified dismissal—than he had during any of their previous acquaintance.

Not that he'd changed his mind in the least. He was delighted to be off the hook.

But *she* wasn't off it, and that was the trouble.

"Daisy, Daisy." Gentle hands shook Daisy's shoulder.

"Wha—?" Daisy jerked awake with a start, her pulse pounding. It took her a moment to realize where she was—in her own bed. Alone. In the middle of the night. A pale shape bent over her. "Jane?"

"You're not ill, are you Daisy?"

Daisy blinked into the darkness. "No." Her nightgown was twisted high above her waist. She felt hot and sweaty—and it was a cold night.

"Oh, it must have been another bad dream then. Your legs were thrashing around and you were moaning and groaning so fearfully I was quite worried."

Daisy felt her face heating. Thank goodness it was dark

and Jane couldn't see her. Thrashing around? Moaning and groaning? It wasn't fear.

She thrust away the sensations—so real she could almost still feel them—of big, calloused hands stroking her, teasing, arousing her to distraction . . . She tried to shove her night-gown back down around her legs.

She was aching, acutely sensitive. Damp.

Jane plonked herself on the side of Daisy's bed. "Is something worrying you, Daisy dear? It's usually me who has the bad dreams, not you."

"No, it's nothing," Daisy muttered. "Don't worry—probably just the onion soup from last night. Go back to bed, Jane."

Jane hesitated. "Are you sure? Because this is the second night in a row you've had one, so it can't be the onion soup. If you want to talk about—"

"I'm sure. There's nothing to talk about, really. "

"Is it the business? Because if it is—"

"It's not. It's nothing—just a stupid dream. Now, go back to bed or you'll catch a chill."

Jane went, reluctantly. Daisy hunched her bedclothes around her and feigned sleep until Jane drifted back to sleep.

Stupid dream was right. Damn that Flynn.

She was sleeping worse than ever, and now it wasn't only business worries that kept her tossing and turning. *Thrashing around and moaning.*

He'd got her all stirred up with that blooming kiss. Twice now she'd woken up all hot and bothered, with her night-gown hitched up around her waist and her bedclothes in a twist. Hot and damp and . . . lust-ridden.

That one blasted kiss had knocked her endways. Given her a taste of the forbidden. Taken her feelings about Flynn from a harmless, secret fantasy and turned them into . . .

No! She wasn't goin' there.

Two days since that kiss and she hadn't seen hide nor hair of him—apart from in her dreams. If he had been interested, if that kiss had affected him half as much as it had affected her . . .

But from what the others said, he was still seeing Lady

Elizabeth. A woman who kissed like a fish, but who was a *lady*. A pretty, sweet-spoken *dainty* lady who no doubt danced like a thistledown fairy, not a clumping great Cockney clodhopper who swore like a trooper.

Not that she cared. She didn't want anyone. She had a business to build.

She checked that Jane was sleeping soundly, slipped out of bed and began to dress in the dark. It wasn't much earlier than she normally got up anyway, so she might as well get busy.

Maybe if she acted as if it didn't affect her one way or another, the . . . *feelings* would go away. That worked for most things. She was good at not wanting what she couldn't have, and one thing was clear in her mind, no matter which way she looked at him, she couldn't—and wouldn't—have Flynn.

"I don't understand why you wanted me to go with you to the park," Lady Elizabeth said. "Of course, it's very pleasant, but . . ." She darted him a cautious glance. "You haven't changed your mind, have you? About . . ."

"No," Flynn assured her. "But you don't mind if your father doesn't know that yet, do you?"

"Oh, no. In fact while Papa thinks we're still courting . . ."

"Exactly," said Flynn, patting her hand. He'd remembered to wear his gloves today. They strolled along, bowing to some, stopping to chat to others. Lady Elizabeth, of course, knew practically everyone.

Flynn didn't miss the silent glances exchanged. They'd love it when the news got out, damn their eyes. Not that he gave a snap of his fingers for their good opinion.

He watched the ton parading their wares in the park— their clothes, their style, their availability in some cases, and their unmarried daughters.

He glanced down at the woman on his arm, now so comfortable with him, because he no longer had expectations of her. He'd had a lucky escape there—only because he'd broken the rules of polite ton behavior, sneaking her outside to steal a kiss or two. Otherwise he'd never have known, not until he found himself shackled to a wife that couldn't bear his touch.

The thought of embarking on another search for a high-born wife depressed his spirits. They stopped to chat briefly to an acquaintance of Lady Elizabeth's, then moved on.

All these people had known each other practically from birth—they were related, or their families knew each other—had known each other for generations—or the men had attended boarding school together—it was a closed little group.

And they all, to a greater or lesser degree, cooperated in keeping outsiders out. Outsiders like him.

Oh, he could buy his way in and marry one of them. But he'd always be an outsider.

It hadn't bothered him before, and it didn't really bother him now—he'd been an outsider most of his life.

He had friends like Max and Ash, and now Freddy—real friends, not simply business partners. Friends and equals; he'd been friends with Max for years before he ever knew he was a lord.

Out there in the real world, it didn't matter. A man was judged by what he was made of, not who he was related to.

He watched the brightly clad fashionable throng, strutting and bowing and strolling, seeing and being seen. English society was like a birdcage, a big, comfortable, elegant birdcage with invisible wires. Those inside knew the unwritten rules and those on the outside could only enter with permission.

Trouble is, he was now far more aware of those unwritten rules than he was when he'd first set out to find a highborn wife, and he didn't much like them.

He strolled on, lending half an ear to Lady Elizabeth's bland and predictable chat, responding when required, Lady Elizabeth's dour maid, Muir, trailing grimly behind, giving Flynn silent dagger looks from the rear.

When he'd first arrived in London, he had this idea about fine ladies that they were delicate, innocent creatures, soft and gentle and in need of protection.

He needed that, somehow. He was in a position to protect

and care for a wife and children now, not like before . . . when he hadn't been able to help his family at all.

He cut off the painful thought. The past was the past. Nothing he could do about it now. He had a future and it was his to shape, as much as any man could shape the future.

Not only his future. He would protect Lady Elizabeth by not marrying her. Ironic, that.

He scanned the line of elegant carriages making their slow way around the park. No sign yet of Lady Beatrice. He hoped she hadn't forgotten the little agreement they'd made the day before. If she had, the whole point of this walk with Lady Elizabeth and her maid would be lost and the wretched business would drag on for another day.

Lady Beatrice's barouche approached. Finally. The instant she spotted him, the old lady poked her driver with her cane and the carriage slowed to a halt. She beckoned him over with an imperious wave.

He steered Lady Elizabeth through the gently milling throng of elegantly dressed ladies and gentlemen.

The old lady greeted them enthusiastically. "How do you do, my dears? Isn't it a lovely day—one might almost believe that spring really is here to stay! Flynn, my dear boy, I do like those boots. Lady Elizabeth, you've snagged the finest looking man here, so I fear I must punish you for it!"

Lady Elizabeth blushed rosily. "P-punish me, Lady Davenham?" She was invariably punctilious about using Lady Beatrice's correct form of address.

"I just set two of my gels down to stretch their legs"—she waved a vague hand, and Flynn saw Jane and Abby walking arm in arm some short distance away—"and I need someone to keep me company." The old lady patted the seat beside her invitingly. "Flynn, help Lady Elizabeth up."

"Thank you, it's very kind of you." Lady Elizabeth glanced back at her maid. "And Muir?"

"No, no, your maid can stay here and keep Mr. Flynn company. Can't leave the poor man stranded and all alone, like a shag on a rock, can we? Now come along up, my dear, you're holding up the traffic."

Flynn hid a smile as he helped Lady Elizabeth into the barouche. The old lady was a master manipulator. The carriage drove on and he turned to Muir. "Shall we sit over there while we're waiting for your mistress to return?"

Muir gave him a look of deep suspicion, but consented to accompany him to a bench some little distance away from the fashionable circuit.

"You're very loyal to your mistress, aren't you, Muir?" he said as they sat down.

"I am." She gave him a disdainful look. "So don't expect me to gossip about—"

"Far from it. Though," he added in a coaxing voice, "I would like to know a little about her aunt. The one who lives in Italy."

The maid sniffed. "Why would you want to know about her?"

Flynn gave her his best charming smile. "I'm trying to find out whether Lady Elizabeth's aunt in Italy is someone she could turn to."

Her eyes were chips of ice. "And why would you want to know that?"

"Because, you stubborn woman, I want to try and help the lass."

"And why—"

"Because as you no doubt know—if you're in your mistress's confidence—I'm not going to make her an offer, which means—she tells me—that her father will force her to marry Lord Flensbury. And before you ask why I care, I don't know, but I do. So, would this aunt in Italy take her in or not?"

There was a long pause while Muir thought about what he said. "She would," she said finally. "In a heartbeat. But there's no chance of—"

"Oh, look, Miss Muir," Flynn exclaimed. "You've dropped your purse."

Muir looked at the thick brown purse that had suddenly appeared at her feet. "That's not mine."

"Yes it is," Flynn said. "You dropped it just now."

"I didn't. I've never seen that purse before in my—"

Flynn picked it up and shoved it in her hands. "You

wouldn't want to lose it. That's the purse that contains the nest egg you inherited from your recently deceased cousin."

Muir stared at him.

"Or perhaps it's the sum you won in the lottery."

'But I never enter the lott—"

"I don't care *how* you got it—you're the one who has to convince your mistress. But five hundred pounds will get both of you to Italy in comfort and will support you for some time while you're there, assuming the aunt doesn't change her mind."

"Five hundred p . . ." Muir fumbled with the fastening of the purse and peered inside. Her lips moved silently as she counted the notes bundled inside. She counted them twice then looked at him in stunned disbelief.

"But why would you—"

"I told you, I don't want her misery on my conscience, and she's too proud to accept any help from me. Do you think you could convince her?"

For a long time she didn't respond. He couldn't see her expression; she was staring down at the purse that she now clutched tightly to her bosom. Finally she said in a low voice, "You would trust me to use this money—for *her*? What would stop me from agreeing now and running off with it, leaving Lady Elizabeth to her fate? Five hundred pounds— it's a fortune for the likes of me."

"I know." Flynn was well aware of the temptation. A lady's maid might earn fifteen pounds in a year, and he was damned sure Lord Compton wouldn't be paying Muir anywhere near that. "I'm gambling on what my instinct tells me."

"And what does your instinct say about me?" she asked in a low voice.

"That you love your mistress and would do anything to help her."

Her fingers tightened over the purse, and she sniffed, but it was quite a different kind of sniff. Flynn realized she was crying. He pulled out his handkerchief and handed it to her.

"Thank you, sir, oh, thank you," she whispered.

"No need to mention this to anyone," he said gruffly. He hated it when women cried. "I don't care what story you tell your mistress, just get her out of the country and away from that pathetic excuse for a father."

"I will sir, oh, I *promise* you, I will," Muir vowed. "And thank you! A thousand times, thank y—"

"There's Lady Beatrice's carriage. Now put that purse somewhere safe and let us go and meet your mistress." He stood up, relieved to be able to put an end to it.

Chapter Nine

*"Seldom, very seldom, does complete truth belong to any
human disclosure; seldom can it happen that something
is not a little disguised or a little mistaken."*

—JANE AUSTEN, EMMA

Flynn attended a party the following night—the first one
he'd attended where Lady Elizabeth wasn't present. She'd
cried off with a headache or some such thing, and he couldn't
say he wasn't sorry not to have to see her here tonight.

He was starting his search for a wife all over again.

He leaned against a doorway and surveyed the throng of
pretty damsels with a jaundiced eye. The whole Lady Elizabeth experience had made him more than a touch cynical.

One of these young ladies might one day become his
wife.

The thought no longer delighted him quite the way it
once had.

Polite society . . . He snorted. The politeness was about
as thin as a layer of silk. Deception was more like it.

They smiled, they flirted, they welcomed, but it was his
money they wanted, not Flynn. Him they would tolerate, or
try to. Behind those smiles was often a layer of hidden contempt for his blunt ways, his battered hands, his history.

He'd always known that his fortune was what would
make him acceptable, but now he was more aware of the

subtle arrogance of aristocratic superiority—bred in blood and bone, and he didn't much like it.

Lord Compton had gambled away his fortune and was ready to sell his only child into virtual slavery so he could continue his hedonistic lifestyle unchecked, and yet he—and the rest of polite society—considered himself vastly superior to a man like Flynn.

Flynn used to think it would be a fine thing to get himself a fine, dainty, ladylike, highborn wife. A sign of everything he'd achieved. For a canny man he'd been damned naive.

It was like looking into a sweet shop and longing for a particular sweet that had caught your fancy. You couldn't afford it, but it was all you dreamed off. You knew if you could only get it, it would taste sublime.

And so you worked and you saved, and you finally had the money. You stepped into the shop, and with pride laid your money down on the counter—and the sweet was yours. And when you bit into it, it tasted of . . . nothing.

The delicious appearance was all for show.

Once bitten twice shy. Serve him right for letting ambition blind him. He'd proved he could marry an earl's daughter—and where had that got him?

He would choose more wisely next time.

He wasn't interested in a girl who only wanted him for his money, he didn't want someone who'd always think herself superior to him, simply because of her birth. And he sure as hell didn't want a girl who'd marry him out of duty, and then have to *force* herself to the marriage bed.

What he wanted was . . .

Aye, that was the question. What *did* he want?

He thought of the sweet response that Daisy had given him, the intoxication of a simple kiss.

He looked around the room. Girls in white dresses swirled around the dance floor, women in low-cut gowns swished by, giving him sultry, come-hither looks.

There was nothing for him here.

He made his excuses to the hostess of the party and walked back to his lodgings. There was nothing for him there either. He felt unaccountably lonely, which was ridiculous. He'd been alone most of his life and now here he was, in the most sophisticated city in the world, with society at his fingertips, and friends—good friends. He had no reason to feel lonely.

Maybe he should get himself a mistress.

He'd barely arrived home when there was a pounding on the door. It was almost midnight—strange time for a visitor. Flynn had given Tibbins the evening off, so he answered the door himself.

Lord Compton practically fell into the room. "She's bolted! The filly's bolted, dammit!"

"You've lost a horse?" Feigning ignorance, Flynn gave him a look of mild enquiry. "What do you imagine I can do about it?"

Lord Compton missed the sarcasm. "Not a horse, you fool. The little slut's eloped! Heading for the border at this very moment with some dammed milksop I've never heard of—a Mr. Felix Something-or-other. Not a penny to his name, I'll be bound."

"Are you referring to Lady Elizabeth?" Flynn said coldly. A man ought to speak more respectfully of his own daughter.

"Of course I am—who else would it be?" Lord Compton stood glaring at Flynn, his fists clenching and unclenching. "Well, don't just stand there, you fool! Go after them!"

"I don't think so." He didn't for a moment believe Lady Elizabeth had eloped with a man. Her maid, yes. And he doubted she was on the way to Scotland, but he couldn't be sure.

"Dammit, did you not understand me, man—she's bolted. Left you standing high and dry. Made a complete fool of us both! Little bitch left me a note—see?" He waved a piece of paper at Flynn.

Flynn took it and retreated into the sitting room to read it in the better light there. Lord Compton followed. "Cunning little cow expected me home tomorrow evening but I came home early. Cards not running my way."

Flynn read the note and hid a smile. Lady Elizabeth, according to the note, had eloped supposedly to Gretna with a Mr. Felix Rome. *Felix* meaning happiness; it wasn't hard to guess the significance of *Rome*.

"Brandy, Lord Compton?" Flynn handed the letter back to Lord Compton who tossed it impatiently aside. It floated to the floor.

"No, I don't want a blasted brandy! Are you going to let her get away?"

Flynn shrugged. "She's made her choice."

"No, blast you, she has not! According to the servants, she only left a few hours ago, so we can still catch her. I'll drag her back and get her to the altar as planned."

Flynn arched a brow. "Against her will?"

"The gel doesn't know what's good for her."

"No, she doesn't know what's good for *you*," Flynn said with delicate emphasis.

Compton ignored him. "The fellow she's bolted with must have tricked her. Wants her for her fortune, I'll be bound."

Flynn raised his eyebrow. "In for a disappointment then, isn't he?"

Lord Compton flushed. "I'll catch her, stop this nonsense. Get a special license and you can marry her out of hand. A good bedding will soon tame her." The man was vile.

"I'm not going to marry your daughter. Understand me? *Not*."

Lord Compton's jaw dropped. "But you have to. I've got debts, man! Bailiffs only holding off bec—" He broke off, realizing it was not the most tactful approach, and tried another tack. In a coaxing voice, he said, "Flynn, you're a good fellow. You've got to help me. I can't have my little gel ruinin' herself with some damned unknown. My curricle's downstairs, we can make the Great North Road in no time."

"No."

"Dammit, then I'll fetch her myself." Compton headed for the front door. "Flensbury will still have her. He won't mind damaged goods."

He was worse than vile. Flynn opened a door. "This way, Lord Compton."

Compton started through it, then stopped. "What the—"
Flynn gave him a shove, slammed the door and locked it.
The earl hammered on the door, yelling and swearing.

Flynn returned to the sitting room and finished his brandy.
An excellent drop. He picked up Lady Elizabeth's note and
smiled as he dropped it in the fire. Rome, eh? Good for her.
But he didn't want her father out there searching for her. He
might learn that she wasn't headed for Scotland after all.

The least Flynn could do was give the girl a good head start.

The front door opened and his valet, Tibbins, entered, saying, "Good evening, sir. How was your—" He broke off, staring at the closet door from which sporadic furious pounding
and a stream of abuse was coming. He glanced at Flynn. "Sir,
there appears to be someone in . . ." He indicated the closet.

"Yes, I know," Flynn said. "Pack me an overnight bag,
will you?"

"But, sir, what on earth is going on?"

"I'm spending the night at a hotel."

"But . . ." Tibbins indicated the commotion coming from
the closet.

"Exactly," Flynn said. "I won't get a wink of sleep with that
racket."

"But who *is* it, sir? He's roaring like a wild beast."

"Close enough. It's a wild earl." He grinned at his valet's
expression. "A furious, frustrated and desperately enraged earl."

"An *earl*?" Tibbins' eyes almost popped. "But shouldn't
I—?" He tentatively pointed towards the closet.

Flynn put out an arm. "Not on your life! I'll be off as soon
as you can get my bag packed. You can stay the night here or
elsewhere, as you wish, but you will not release him until
eight o'clock tomorrow morning. Understood, Tibbins?"

Tibbins cast a miserable eye at the closet door and was
rewarded by a volley of thumps and yells. "But sir, he's an
earl."

"Yes, but a very nasty one. And up to his neck in debt,"
he added, knowing Tibbins's priorities.

Tibbins looked shocked. "In debt, you say?"

"Bailiffs on his doorstep, he told me so himself. He's to

stay locked in there all night—at least until eight o'clock
tomorrow morning, do you understand me?"

Tibbins swallowed. "Very good, sir."

"And if I hear he's been let out one minute sooner . . ."

Tibbins sighed. "You won't, sir."

Flynn gave his man a sovereign. "Good man. Now go
and pack my bag—and one for yourself if you like. You
won't sleep with that racket going on. Grillons Hotel is
reputed to be very comfortable. You can come with me."

Tibbins glanced at the roaring rattling closet and made
up his mind. "Very good, sir."

D aisy always looked forward to Lady Beatrice's literary
society days—she loved having stories read aloud to
her. She could read well now, thanks to Abby and the girls
teaching her, but she couldn't sew and read at the same time,
and by the time she fell into bed at night, she was too tired
to read.

At the literary society she got to sew and listen to a story.
And talk to people as well during the breaks. These days it
was just about the only outside company she got.

Today though, she was feeling a bit . . . on edge, wondering whether Flynn would turn up or not. He often attended
and usually it was a pleasure to see him.

Since that kiss, however, she felt stupidly self-conscious
and awkward at the prospect of seeing him. Which was
ridiculous, she told herself crossly. He was just Flynn, the
same as ever he was.

She had no problem with fancying a man—it was only
natural, after all—and she had to admit that she fancied the
pants off Flynn. She had from the start.

And why shouldn't she? He was a gorgeous chunk of man-
hood, handsome in that Irish way with thick black hair with a
hint of curl, and bold blue eyes that knew how to flirt and how
to laugh—a combination she'd always had a weakness for.

Her whole body tingled in remembrance. In different
circumstances she might act on it, fancy his tight pants right

off him—and his shirt and smalls, too—but it wasn't going to happen.

He was still courting Lady Elizabeth, and if he looked at Daisy in any way, it would be as a bit on the side. And she wasn't going to be second best, not for anyone.

Not that the question would even come up. She was respectable now.

He probably wouldn't even come today. Now that the Season had well and truly begun, there were plenty of other events to attract a man.

She gathered her things together. Lady Beatrice had decreed that it did not *do* to be seen sewing a hem or a seam or—heaven forbid—some kind of undergarment, so today Daisy was embroidering forget-me-nots on a pair of tiny puffed sleeves that would go on the latest dress she was making for Jane.

But she fiddled around, delaying her arrival—not thinking about Flynn—and by the time she arrived the room was more than half-filled and Daisy's usual place—beside Lady Beatrice—was now taken by the bloke who was unofficially engaged to Jane—Lord Comb-it-up—and his aunt.

Daisy didn't mind. She found another seat behind a couple of large ladies with enormous hats. As long as she could hear the girls reading she didn't need to see them.

Abby, Damaris and Jane did the readings. The three girls were the big attraction—them and the good stories they chose. Abby read the best, Damaris was a close second, and while Jane was a bit stiff and wooden when she read—she didn't do nearly the thrilling voices that Abby and Damaris did—she was the most beautiful. And still unmarried.

Daisy settled herself with her sewing basket at her feet and the sewing in her lap. She smiled and nodded, as various people greeted her. She knew most people here but made no move to circulate or join in any conversation. It was enough that she was here, accepted as belonging. Some days she wanted to pinch herself at the thought that she was on nodding and smiling terms—cool as you please—with half the toffs of England.

So she preferred to sit back and watch, looking at what the various ladies were wearing, and imagining how she'd dress them differently. It was always an improvement—in her mind, anyway.

Featherby rang a little bell to signal the start of the first reading and people hurried to be seated. Daisy waited for the reading to begin.

Still no sign of Flynn. He wasn't coming, then. Good. That would make things easier.

A hush fell over the room, and Abby began to read aloud: "Harriet Smith was the natural daughter of somebody. Somebody had placed her, several years back, at Mrs. Goddard's school, and somebody had lately raised her from the condition of scholar to that of parlour-boarder. This was all that was generally known of her history. She had no visible friends but what had been acquired at Highbury, and was now just returned from a long visit in the country to some young ladies who had been at school there with her."

Daisy bent to her embroidery. She was enjoying this story. *Natural daughter* meant that like Daisy, this Harriet girl was someone's bastard. The gentry set great store by legitimacy, and Daisy could see where this story was leading—Harriet would want what she couldn't have and that would be her undoing. It always was.

A few moments into the reading, there was a small stir at the door and an immediate buzz of surreptitious conversation. A late arrival. Heads turned toward the door with critical expressions. People in London would talk right through opera and plays, but woe betide anyone who interrupted when Abby was reading.

Flynn stood in the doorway like a bold buccaneer, quite indifferent to the indignant looks he was getting. As if he blooming-well owned the place. Arrogant, but in a way that made her toes curl deliciously.

He made a fine sight, with tight buckskin breeches molded to his long, powerful thighs. Boots and buckskins suited some men and not others: Flynn was made for them. And he certainly knew how to fill a coat—those lovely big shoulders and strong arms owed nothing to padding, she knew.

Her body remembered the feel of them only too well.

He made no move to find a seat. He surveyed the crowd in a leisurely manner, looking for someone and Daisy was pretty sure she knew who. Her whole body tightened, alert to his presence.

Hidden behind the large ladies with even larger hats, she looked her fill. She wasn't the only woman secretly ogling him either. Half the people in the audience were murmuring and whispering: a few were crossly shushing the talkers and waiting for Abby to resume reading, the remainder—the majority of females there—were gazing at Flynn with barely disguised lust.

She couldn't blame them. There was something irresistible about a man who was ever-so-slightly untamed, the promise of all that simmering uninhibited masculinity unleashed in bed . . . Confident and capable and unashamed. Masculine to the tips of his big calloused hands, and not shy about showing it.

Those hands would know their way around a woman's body too. As for how he could kiss . . . She gave a little shiver, just thinking about it.

The buzz continued, low and furtive, rippling through the room. Daisy frowned. Flynn always drew people's attention, but this was different.

A murmured exchange between two ladies behind her caught her ear. "The cheek of him, showing his face here today."

"Shameless! Quite shameless!"

What was shameless about it? Daisy wondered. Flynn often attended the literary society. She tried to remember who was sitting behind her, but the gossips were severely hushed and Abby continued reading: "She particularly led Harriet to talk more of Mr. Martin, and there was evidently no dislike to it. Harriet was very ready to speak of the share he had had in their moonlight walks and merry evening games; and dwelt a good deal upon his being so very good-humoured and obliging. He had gone three miles round one day in order to bring her some walnuts, because she had said how fond she was of them, and in everything else he was so very obliging."

A romance. Daisy tried to forget about the odd reaction to Flynn's entrance and concentrate on the story. She did love a good romance. She hoped this one would end happily, but that Emma, she was trouble . . .

Her mind wandered. What did those women know about Flynn that was so bad?

Apparently undisturbed by the attention his arrival had received, Flynn found himself a seat and settled back to listen. Daisy knew the moment he'd spotted her; she felt his gaze like a touch on her face, warm and unmistakable.

Her cheeks warmed but she bent over her embroidery and didn't look up.

In the first break, tea and wine and little cakes were handed around. People were free to talk and the two ladies behind her resumed their exchange.

"Lord Compton is said to be furious . . ."

Lord Compton? Daisy pricked up her ears and leaned back to listen.

". . . Lizzie Compton . . . eloping in the dead of night . . . Nobody knows, my dear. Some nobody . . . the Scottish border . . ."

Lady Liz had *eloped*? Which meant that Flynn was . . . Daisy almost tipped her chair back to hear the last part.

"Publicly jilted," the lady behind her said, a trace of malicious glee in her voice. "Or as good as. The whole world knew he was on the verge of a declaration."

"Lord Compton blames the Irishman . . . crude fellow . . . no idea how to handle a lady . . ."

"More suited to the stable than the drawing room, although . . ." They tittered, knowingly.

Daisy couldn't believe her ears. Flynn, publicly jilted? Lady Liz had eloped? If so she was furious on Flynn's behalf. If Lady Liz had done a bunk, she was the one in the wrong, not Flynn. He had every right to show his face wherever he wanted.

Daisy was on the verge of turning around to defend him when one of the ladies exclaimed, "Oh, don't look now, Letty, he's approaching! Such a deliciously untamed brute."

Daisy looked up to see Flynn prowling towards her, apparently unfazed by the gossip that surrounded him. He had to know about it, surely.

Before he could reach her, Lady Gelbart swept up, saying, "Daisy, my dear, I want you to meet Mrs. Foster, whose late husband was a distant relative of my late husband's. She has an ardent desire to meet you."

Daisy blinked and scrambled politely to her feet. *"Me?* You wanted to meet me? Whatever for?" And then remembered to make her how-de-dos.

Lady Gelbart's companion was youngish—about thirty-five, Daisy guessed—and very elegant, dressed in what looked like the latest French fashions, simply but superbly cut, in shades of lilac edged smartly in black. In mourning? Or did she just know that lilac suited her pale skin and dark hair perfectly?

Lady Gelbart laughed. "My fault, I'm afraid, my dear. She was visiting me when your beautiful"—she glanced around and lowered her voice discreetly— *"garments* were delivered, and I could not *wait* to open the parcel. So now she's mad for some for herself."

Flynn arrived at the point and the conversation abruptly came to a halt.

"Daisy," he began.

"Ah, Mr. Flynn." The old lady turned. "I am so sorry to hear of your troubles."

Daisy swallowed. She wanted to say something too but she didn't trust her tongue. It was nice that Lady Gelbart was so open and straightforward. Daisy hoped that the nasty gossips behind her were getting a lesson in manners.

He inclined his head. "Please don't be concerned on my account, Lady Gelbart. Lady Elizabeth made the right choice for her, and I wish her all the happiness in the world."

The old lady patted his arm. "So gracious, dear boy, such generosity of spirit. I can quite see why Bea is so fond of you."

She glanced across the room and added, "I would talk more, but I think Bea is trying to catch your attention."

He followed her gaze to where Lady Beatrice was indeed waving imperiously, a silent command for him to join her. He gave Daisy a rueful glance. "Ladies." His bow took in all three of them, then he left.

Old Lady Gelbart watched him go and sighed. "Lizzie Compton is a fool. Such a charming young man, and he wears those buckskins so well. Most men don't look quite so fine, especially from the rear."

He did have a lovely bum, Daisy acknowledged. Firm and masculine and well-shaped. Not that she was interested, she reminded herself firmly.

She turned back to Mrs. Foster, who, interestingly, hadn't eyed Flynn at all. "So, Mrs. Foster, you liked what I made for Lady Gelbart?"

Mrs. Foster nodded and said in a low, musical voice, "Indeed I do. They're quite exquisite and delightfully . . . naughty. I would like to order a set for myself, if that's possible. Lady Gelbart told me you didn't have a business premises, and I'm not yet on calling terms with Lady Beatrice. I did leave a card the other day, but—"

"So I brought her with me to the literary society instead," Lady Gelbart said. "Knew you'd be here."

"I'm finding it quite delightful," Mrs. Foster said. "What fun to have books read aloud to you, and how clever to turn the occasion into a party."

Lady Gelbart spotted another crony, and patted Mrs. Foster's arm, saying, "I'll leave you to work things out with Daisy, my dear."

Which left Daisy in a position to quote Mrs. Foster an even higher price than Lady Gelbart had paid. She really shouldn't take on any more work, but if it was a cash payment . . .

It was. Mrs. Foster agreed to her price without a blink and they made an appointment for her to come and be measured and discuss the design and fabric the following day. And she would bring cash. She preferred to pay up front, she said, and Daisy wasn't going to argue.

Daisy was thrilled with her new customer. She was happy to be making things for the old ladies, of course—a sale was a sale—but it wouldn't do her business any good if she got a reputation for catering only to old ladies and young girls— married women were the ones with money. Mrs. Foster might be a widow, but she was still quite young, good-looking, very fashionable and best of all, she was quite obviously rich.

The arrangements made, Mrs. Foster then confessed she was new to London, that she'd lived abroad for the last ten years with her husband, who had died just over a year ago. She was now emerging from the seclusion of her widow-hood, and knew almost nobody, so she ended up spending the rest of the literary society meeting sitting with Daisy.

In the breaks they talked fashion—for all her widowhood, Mrs. Foster was very up-to-date. Daisy was dying to know all about Lady Liz's elopement, but she'd find out eventually, and in the meantime she enjoyed their discussion enormously.

And for whatever reason—because he thought she was having a private female conversation? Or because he didn't want to talk about being jilted?—Flynn didn't come near Daisy at all for the rest of the afternoon.

Which was good, she told herself. Perhaps they could get back to normal now. Although whenever she'd glanced at Flynn, he'd been watching her. With a look in his eyes she didn't trust.

He didn't look at all like a recently jilted man. He didn't act the least bit humiliated. It was a big disappointment for the gossips.

Chapter Ten

Surprises are foolish things. The pleasure is not
enhanced, and the inconvenience is often considerable.

—JANE AUSTEN, *EMMA*

The literary society meeting was over. The last good-byes drifted up from the front hall. Daisy sat in the deserted drawing room finishing off the last little bit of the second sleeve.

Flynn had left earlier; Lady Beatrice had commandeered his help with the stairs. Daisy hadn't spoken to him at all. He hadn't come near her since that first brief exchange. She wasn't sure whether she was pleased or annoyed.

Pleased, she told herself. Though she would have liked to know more about Lady Liz eloping. Oh, she'd had an earful about it this afternoon, but she didn't trust the gossips. She wanted it from the horse's mouth.

Although he might have been the last to know.

She finished embroidering the last tiny cluster of for-get-me-nots on the sleeve—the final one would be done after the sleeve was attached to the dress—tucked the needle into the fabric and wound the remaining silk thread around the needle to hold it in place.

A sound from the doorway distracted her. She looked up. Flynn stood leaning against the doorjamb, watching her.

Her heart started thumping. How long had he been there?

He smiled at her, warm and knowing and shamelessly wicked, and it was as if the large spacious room had suddenly been drained of air.

She tried to look uninterested, to nod calmly and return to her embroidery, all cool and dignified, but her mouth was fighting that idea, wanting to smile back at him.

Get a hold of yourself, girl, she told herself. *This one ain't for you.*

She'd thought about it all through the readings, had hardly taken the story in for thinking about him and what she'd learned. He might not be going to marry Lady Liz, but he'd soon be chasing after some other fine lady to marry—one who wasn't such a cold fish.

Daisy would still be his bit on the side, and she wasn't interested in that. Besides, she couldn't risk it. Building her business was her number one priority, and if she was going to deal with the ton, she had to live by their rules. They might turn a blind eye to a discreet liaison between a lady and a lord, but a shopkeeper didn't have the same freedom.

Nobody would allow his wife and daughters to buy clothes from a dressmaker who wasn't respectable beyond reproach. So whatever that glint in Flynn's eye meant, as far as Daisy was concerned, it wasn't going to happen.

Feigning indifference she picked up her basket and rose as if to leave. "Thought you'd left already."

He prowled towards her. "Forgot something."

"What?" She looked around, but could see nothing left behind.

"This." He took two long steps and hauled her into his arms. One brawny arm wrapped around her waist, lifting her right off her feet in a possessive manner that thrilled her to her toes.

She tried to resist. "Oy, what—"

But his mouth possessed hers—no hesitation, no careful seeking of approval, no attempt to seduce or entice—he just took from her what he wanted. And he wanted everything. He devoured, he plundered, he took greedily, hungrily, with an intense concentrated energy that simply shattered her.

Because he gave back as much as he took. More.

Daisy thrilled to it. Her body thrummed with pleasure, mind-numbing, bone-dissolving, toe-curling hot waves of pleasure that collected and gathered in the pit of her stomach, creating an ache there, an empty hollowness that was almost painful in its need to be filled.

Finally he let her body slide slowly back to earth, letting her feel the hard thrust of his arousal, bold and unashamed against her belly. He stood holding her against him—truth to tell she was leaning against him, she could barely stand without his support.

His big hand cradled the nape of her neck, his thumb stroking the soft skin there, all tender and careful, as if she was a baby bird—and didn't that turn her into an even bigger puddle of mush, dammit.

He gave a big sigh. "Ah, Daisy, me girl . . ." He cupped her chin and gave her another quick kiss—a hard, possessive branding that rocked her to her bones—then released her and stepped back.

Daisy staggered back, panting. She was barely able to stand, her knees like soft noodles, her senses in a daze. His eyes were stormy dark like she imagined the sea would look, though she'd never seen the sea. They skimmed lightly over her body, taking in her flushed face—going by how hot she felt, she must be bright red—the hard points of her aching nipples, and the heaving of her chest.

His gaze returned to her mouth. She felt it almost like a touch. She ran her tongue over her lips—they felt swollen and tender—and he tensed, then shook his head, muttering, "No, not yet."

Yet? As if it was just a matter of time. His choice, whenever it suited him.

It brought her to her senses. She scrambled for some level of composure, managed to find her voice. "What do you mean 'not yet'?"

She wiped her mouth with her sleeve, deliberately, as if she could somehow wipe away the last few minutes, wipe away the imprint of his kisses, doing her best to look unaffected. "There ain't going to *be* anything else—I don't care if you've been jilted—there'll be no more of this, this kissin' and . . . and whatever—you hear me?"

One dark silky brow rose, a lazy, confident, *knowing* challenge. "Tryin' to tell me you don't want it?"

She lifted her chin. "That's right, I *don't* want it."

He gave a soft, deep huff of laughter. "Liar."

"I don't tell lies." Daisy picked up the basket she'd dropped when he'd grabbed her.

"Liar. You like it—don't try to deny it."

Stung, she retorted—because she didn't tell lies—"I never said I didn't *like* it. I said I didn't *want* it. And I don't."

He gave a slow, masculine smile, one that completely discounted what she'd told him. "Darlin', you can't tell me you like it, and expect me to walk away. You do want it, you're just in a flutter. "

"I'm not! I'm—"

"And I don't blame you. I feel it too. But if you want to play hard-to-get, that's fine by me. I enjoy a good chase."

Daisy clenched her fists. "You're not listening to me, you big—"

"That's right, I'm not." He grinned and ran a lazy finger down her cheek. She wanted to smack it away, but somehow she couldn't make herself move. He added, "That first time we kissed took us both by surprise, I know. So I wanted to check."

"You wanted to—?"

"Check, yes." He seemed oblivious of her growing indignation. Seemed, in fact, pretty damned pleased with himself. "Test the waters. See if it was an accident, a . . . a collision of anger and surprise and . . . sensation. So I decided to kiss you again—it's the only reason I came to the literary society—and see how it compared to that first time. Find out if it was the same."

She couldn't help herself. "And was it?" She silently cursed herself for encouraging him, but her mouth dried as she waited for his answer.

"No." His blue eyes burned into her. He paused—deliberately, the swine, knowing she was hanging on his words—then said, "It was even better."

She fought against the wash of pleasure his words had caused, knowing he'd felt the same. But it had to stop. She told him so.

Again he ignored her. "No need to be nervous about it, lass. It's perfectly natural for a man and a woman to feel this way."

"I'm not bloody *nervous*, you great—"

"Of course you're not." It was clear he didn't believe her. "But you'll get used to it. Now, I can't stay around and chat. I've got an appointment."

She watched him leave, anger, frustration and the lingering remnants of intense arousal warring in her brain and body. An appointment? Who with? She'd watched him at the literary society, talking to this lady and that.

Charming them.

Watching them flirt and blush and simper.

As if it didn't bother him in the least that he'd just been jilted. It didn't seem to bother the ladies either.

If he thought he was going to dangle after her at the same time as he was pursuing some other fine lady . . . pick her up and put her down at whim, whenever he felt like it . . . scramble her brains whenever he felt like it . . .

She hurried after him and caught him at the top of the stairs.

"Oy! Listen, you great Irish lummox—I mean it when I say that it's not going to happen again, all right? From now on, you don't touch me. You don't kiss me, you don't pick me up or, or stroke my cheek—I said stop it!" she snapped, dodging back and swatting at his hand as he stroked her cheek with a thick Irish finger. "None of that lovey-dovey stuff—you know what I mean."

He grinned, a flash of white teeth. "What 'lovey-dovey stuff'—you'll have to be more specific. Give me an example, a demonstration perhaps." The big rat was enjoying this.

"You know exactly what I mean." She poked him in the chest. "Just behave yourself, all right."

He quirked a brow at her. "Or?"

"Or . . ." She cast around for inspiration. "Or I'll push you down the stairs."

He spread his arms wide in invitation. "You can do whatever you want with me, Daisy darlin'. I'm all yours."

She eyed him, fuming. For two pins she *would* shove him down the stairs. But she wasn't the violent type. She was more ladylike these days. Lady Beatrice's lessons had rubbed off on her.

His grin was triumphant. "See, you couldn't hurt me if you tried."

She punched him in the stomach. Hard.

"Oof!" He doubled over, then swore softly under his breath.

"That'll teach you to take me serious!" She picked up her basket and stormed off.

A low chuckle followed her. She clenched her fists. And winced.

"And you make all these marvelous garments from this one small room, Miss Chance?" Mrs. Foster wandered around Daisy's workroom, examining everything with apparent fascination.

Daisy wasn't too sure about her calling the room *small*—it was bigger than any room Daisy had ever had—but she accepted the compliment as it was intended.

Mrs. Foster bent to examine the beading on the bodice of a dress. "Superb! And you do it all by yourself? I can't believe it."

"A couple of Lady Beatrice's maids help out from time to time, and me sisters do as much as they can to help too."

"But two of them are married, aren't they? And the third one has just commenced her first Season, so they must be quite busy." It was an astute observation. She cocked her head and eyed a half-finished dress pinned to a dummy form. "The drapery on this is simply wonderful."

Daisy glowed at the praise. She'd worked hard to get that effect.

She'd taken Mrs. Foster's measurements, and they'd decided on the fabric—red silk with black lace—and the cut—low and exceedingly naughty. "I've been a widow for a year," Mrs. Foster said with a twinkle, "but my husband was ill for a long time before that. I'm not sure that I'll actually *do* anything, but I want to feel like a desirable woman again, and these deliciously wicked garments will do the trick, I just know it."

Usually after measuring up a customer and taking the order, Daisy called for tea and cakes, and then that was that—she didn't have either the time or the inclination to sit chatting. But it was different with Mrs. Foster and long after the tea had been served and the little iced cakes eaten, the two women stayed talking.

Mrs. Foster seemed genuinely fascinated by the whole process, and particularly with Daisy's plan to one day open a shop of her own.

"How wonderful to have such a clear direction for your life," she commented. "After my husband died, I realized that I'd built my entire life around him, and around the expectation that we'd have children. But we never were blessed that way, and so . . ." She spread her hands in a helpless gesture. "Here I am, with neither a husband or children, and no idea what to do with myself."

Daisy hesitated. It wasn't really polite to ask personal questions, but Mrs. Foster had already shared so much. "You don't aim to marry again, then?" She'd assumed that was the lady's reason for coming to London.

"I don't know. Perhaps. If I meet the right man. But he would have to be exceptional—I've found I like being an independent and wealthy widow, with only myself to please. Marriage would change all that." She made a rueful gesture. "In any case most men aren't interested in a woman my age—not for marriage, at any rate. Besides, I'm not sure I want to devote the rest of my life to a man—exceptional or not. "

She rose. "Now, I must leave. I've taken up far too much of your time, I'm sure, but it's been so delightful chatting with you, Miss Chance."

"I've enjoyed it too, Mrs. Foster," Daisy assured her—and it was true. "I'll have your things ready next week, I hope. Where shall I send them?"

"I'm staying at the Clarendon." Of course. The smartest hotel in London.

Daisy usually let Featherby show customers out, but today she personally escorted Mrs. Foster to the front door and bid her a warm good-bye. It wasn't because she was a wealthy customer either; she had the oddest feeling that despite their obvious differences, Mrs. Foster could become a friend.

Flynn called the next day and was shown straight up to her workroom. That would have to stop, Daisy decided. She couldn't have him popping in whenever he felt like it. He was too distracting. Too big. Too charming.

And too damned arrogant.

That thump she'd given him didn't seem to make a ha'porth of difference. He still marched in here, bold as brass with that smile of his, and the gleam in his eye that she didn't trust an inch.

And had to fight to resist.

"So, you never did tell me about Lady Liz running off with someone—" she began.

"I brought you a present." He held out a parcel to her.

"A present?" She stared at the lumpy, clumsily man-wrapped, brown paper parcel. "You got me a present?" Her teacup started rattling on its saucer. She put it down.

"Take it."

She eyed it uncertainly then shook her head. "I don't want presents from you, Flynn." Presents would turn their friend-ship into something . . . different.

"You don't know what it is, yet." He thrust it into her hands and sat back. "Open it and see." There was an eager half smile on his face. His blue, blue eyes gleamed with anticipation.

Blast the man. Nobody ever gave her presents. Why did he have to do something like this? A romantic gesture . . . And he'd wrapped it himself.

With fingers that were suddenly clumsy, she undid the string and opened the parcel. And stared at the contents, frowning. "*Shoes*?" They looked a bit like the shoes that had mysteriously disappeared—her favorite red ones with the rosettes. These were red too and had rosettes, only . . .

She picked up the right one and examined it carefully. And felt ever-so-slightly sick.

Flynn said, "Beautifully made, aren't they? I thought of it after we danced that time. Go on, try them on—I think you'll find it makes a difference. I knew a man once who— oh, just try them on, Daisy—you'll see."

With him standing over her, urging her on, grinning like a fool, there was nothing else for it. She sat down, and with shaking hands pulled off her old shoes and put on the shoes he'd brought her. They were a perfect fit, slipping onto her feet as if they'd been made for her.

As they most obviously and humiliatingly had.

"Stand up."

Daisy stood up.

"Now walk around the room a bit."

Daisy took a few steps around the room.

"See the difference?" Flynn was clearly delighted.

She forced herself to nod. She couldn't bring herself to say a word.

"Well, what do you think?" The big stupid Irishman stood back grinning. So bloody pleased with himself. Mr. Oblivious.

She wanted to hit him. Her first—and probably her only present from him, and it was . . . this. She held herself in as tight as she could.

He saw her expression and frowned. "Daisy . . ." he began uncertainly.

"Thanks, Flynn," she managed to get out. "You have to leave now. I—I got an appointment in a few minutes." She walked smoothly to the door in the new, cleverly made red leather shoes with the jaunty little rosettes on the toes, and opened it. Snowflake, the cat, came slinking in, dripping white hairs everywhere, no doubt, and she didn't even care.

"Don't you like them?"

"Very clever workmanship, thank you," she said and, trying for a jaunty, careless tone, added, "Good-bye." She held the door open for him. And waited.

With a puzzled expression he walked toward the door. "It might take a while to get used to them. Keep wearing them. You'll come to love them, I promise."

Flynn walked slowly down the stairs, perplexed by Daisy's reaction. That hadn't gone the way he'd hoped it would, and he wasn't quite sure why. The shoes themselves were perfect—soft red leather with rosettes, just like the ones she'd lost—she didn't know about the dog, of course. And beautifully made.

You could hardly tell they were different.

And when she'd walked in them, you couldn't tell she had a bad leg, hardly at all. It was just as he'd hoped.

But she'd gone strangely quiet. He couldn't even tell whether she liked them or not. That wasn't like Daisy at all—she generally let you know exactly what she thought—and in no uncertain terms.

Maybe she wasn't used to getting presents. She was still annoyed with him telling her she was running her business the wrong way—she now made a point of not discussing business with him. He smiled to himself. That would keep.

And she was cross about him kissing her—but God, a couple of kisses and he was hard and aching and it was all he could do to keep mastery over himself when he was with her.

She'd warned him off, but he wasn't going to be taken in by that little piece of feminine bravado. He snorted. *She liked it but she didn't want it?* What sort of female logic was that?

He reached the bottom of the stairs. Maybe he'd pushed

her too far too fast. He had a tendency to do that when he wanted something badly, and he wanted Daisy very badly. He was on fire for her.

He'd planned to talk to her about it today, but she'd clammed up after he'd given her the shoes. And kicked him out with a lame excuse.

He nodded to Featherby as the butler let him out. Life had been so much simpler on a ship, with nobody but men to deal with, and any storms on the horizon were just thunder and lightning, wind and giant waves. Reading women was so much harder.

With hands that were shaking, Daisy closed the door carefully behind him, waited until she was sure he was gone, then pulled off the hateful shoes and flung them as hard and as far as she could at the wall. The right shoe made a loud clunking noise as it hit. As it would, being heavier than the other.

I thought of it after we danced that time.

For her that dance—for a few minutes anyway—had been the one time she'd felt as if she was truly dancing, floating in Flynn's arms as she'd never in her life floated. A few moments of magic.

Despite her better judgement, knowing it was stupid and pointless, knowing nothing was going to come of it anyway, she'd allowed herself to dream, just a little. Because there had been no romance ever in her lonely life.

Tupping, yes. Romance, no.

So, even knowing there was no point, she'd let herself dream of those few precious moments, reliving them again and again. Building stupid bloody castles in the air. Just to have and remember.

While he'd been hatching a plan to make her look less of a cripple, buying her a shoe with a built-up sole.

A single tear trickled down her cheek. Daisy scrubbed it fiercely away. This—this was what she was letting herself in for if she weakened towards Flynn—foolish, impossible, painful reality.

The cat twined around her ankles. She picked it up and cradled it to her chest, sinking her fingers into his soft fur. "I'm not even going to think about him anymore, Snowflake. My business is the most important thing in my life, not a stupid big oblivious Irishman."

Snowflake purred and butted Daisy under the chin. She sat in the window seat, the cat in her arms.

The business might send her broke, but it wouldn't break her heart. Only people could do that.

Flynn called on Daisy the following day. He'd been thinking about her odd reaction to the shoes. Ladies weren't supposed to accept personal items as gifts from gentlemen not related to them. Had he offended her by presuming too much?

It didn't seem like Daisy, but she had been getting an earful of what constituted proper ladylike behavior from Lady Beatrice, he knew.

He was just about to head up the stairs to her workroom when—"Mr. Flynn, where do you think you're going?" Lady Beatrice, leaning heavily on her ebony cane, eyed him beadily from the doorway of the downstairs drawing room.

"Up to see Daisy." He pointed.

"You may see her in here," the old lady declared majestically. "Featherby, too! And fetch Daisy down here. About time that girl emerged from that room of hers for a change! And tell Jane to come as well."

"She's out walking the dog, m'lady," Featherby told her.

"Dratted beast. But at least one of my gels is getting some fresh air and exercise. Well, come along, Mr. Flynn," she commanded. "I don't stand around waiting for men all day, you know."

Flynn hid a smile and gave her his arm. The old lady was clearly in A Mood. He escorted her into the front drawing room, sat her down and set out to coax her into a better frame of mind. By the time Daisy joined them the old lady was chuckling and telling him he was a wicked fellow.

He rose as Daisy entered. She wasn't wearing the shoes. But he told himself that she would hardly wear them in her sewing room or even around the house.

"You didn't mind me giving you that little present, did you?" he asked after they'd gone through the usual politenesses.

Daisy gave a brief indifferent shrug.

He glanced at Lady Beatrice, who narrowed her eyes curiously, but said nothing. Apparently Daisy hadn't told Lady Beatrice about the shoes.

"Have you worn them outside yet?"

"No."

He frowned. "Are they not comfortable? You might need to wear them in—"

"They fit."

"Of course they fit," Flynn said. "I gave the shoemaker your old—"

Her eyes narrowed. "So that's where my red shoes went—my favorite shoes—you stole them!"

He didn't respond; he had an innocent dog to protect— well, not innocent at all—but he had promised Miss Jane he'd get rid of the evidence.

She took his silence as guilt. "I don't suppose it occurred to you to return them to me afterwards, did it? My *favorite* shoes."

"I'm afraid not. They weren't in a fit state . . ."

"No," she said bitterly. "I expect the cobbler had to pick them apart to make those . . other *things*."

He frowned. Other *things?* "Don't you like them?" He glanced at her feet. "Have you . . . have you worn them at all?"

"No." She stood up.

"But—"

"Oh, don't worry, I'll make sure to wear them if ever I go out in public with you, Mr. Flynn. I wouldn't want you to embarrass yourself by bein' seen walkin' wiv a *cripple*."

Flynn shot to his feet. "Daisy, no! I didn't mean—"

But she was gone. Flynn went to follow her but found his way barred by Lady Beatrice's ebony stick. "Let her go, dear boy. She's upset."

"I can see that. But I didn't mean—I didn't think she'd take it that way . . ." He went to step around her but this time the ebony stick didn't just block his way, it rapped him smartly on the shins. Luckily he was wearing boots.

"Stop right there! I don't know what this is all about, but if she doesn't want to talk to you, she doesn't have to. The gel has a right to be alone if she wants to," the old lady said with magnificent indifference to the way she'd dragged Daisy out of her workroom earlier. "Now take yourself off and work out a way to mend this. I'll see you at the next literary society meeting." She jingled a little bell.

Flynn stared at her blankly and swore under his breath. As if he cared about the blasted literary society. Daisy thought he was *embarrassed* by her limp. He'd *hurt* her. Beyond that, nothing else mattered.

But Featherby arrived with his hat and coat and a moment later Flynn found himself out on the street, wondering how the hell he'd gotten it so damned wrong. And how the hell he was going to make it up to her.

He took a few steps and heard the sound of a window opening above him. Out of habit he glanced up; he'd lived in places where all kinds of revolting things were routinely tossed from high windows.

A couple of missiles came flying out. He ducked and, one after another, two shoes bounded onto the pavement. Red shoes with little rosettes on the toe. One of them bounced into the gutter.

Flynn stared at them a second. Damn her, he wasn't blasted well going anywhere. He was going to sort this out here and now! He picked up the wretched shoes, stuffed them in his pocket and marched back up to the house.

"Out of my way, Featherby!" he growled, quite prepared to knock the butler down if necessary.

Featherby took one look at his face and stepped aside.

Flynn barreled up the stairs two at a time. He reached Daisy's door and flung it open without knocking. "Daisy."

She turned to face him, her piquant little face tear-stained and woebegone. It ripped his heart apart.

"What?" she snarled. Ah, that was his girl. Down, but not out—never out.

He closed the door behind him and, on an afterthought, locked it.

"Oy! What do you think you're doin—?"

"I'm going to have this out with you, dammit!—once and for all."

She snorted and planted her hands on her hips in a militant, come-on-then fashion. "Are you now?"

He pulled the shoes out, brandished them, tossed them aside and stalked towards her. "You daft wee eedjit. You think I got you those damned shoes because I was embarrassed at the way you walk?"

She glared at him. "Well, what else—"

"I got them because of the way you were dancing."

"So? What's the diff—"

"Not because you were *limping*—but because *you* were so damned embarrassed and self-conscious."

"I bloody was *not*!"

"You bloody well *were*. I knew the minute you forgot about your blasted limp—you floated, girl, floated in my arms, and it was . . ." He swallowed. "It was just the two of us, you and me, and the music, floating."

She made a scornful-sounding snort, but it was all bluff—his little scrapper trying to tough it out. Her eyes were shiny with tears.

"And then I said something stupid about not thinking about your leg, and you immediately went all stiff and wooden and clumsy in me arms—but it was *me* who was the clumsy eedjit then, Daisy, me who was the fool."

She hunched an indifferent shoulder as if he were stating the obvious.

"I just thought . . . I knew a man at sea who had one leg shorter than the other, and this Chinese cobbler made him a pair of boots with the heel built up. And when he put them on, damn me if he didn't walk the same as everyone else. And it was easier on his leg, he said—not so many aches and pains."

She gave an impatient-sounding sigh and glanced at the window with an expression of boredom. The jury was still out. But at least she was listening and hadn't tossed him out yet. Or punched him.

"So I thought, if your limp worried you that much, I'd get you a pair of shoes you could dance in and not worry." His voice lowered. "Because you were made to dance, you know that, don't you, girl? Like a fairy in me arms, you were that day."

Her mouth quivered and she turned abruptly as if to stare out of the window. He thought he glimpsed a tear rolling down one silken cheek, but she made a quick little movement with her hand and it was gone.

He grabbed her by the shoulders and turned her back to face him. "Listen to me, Miss Daisy Bloody-Stubborn Chance—I don't care if you *never* wear those blasted shoes. I couldn't care *less* that you limp!"

She stared up at him and swallowed, her eyes wide, wet and beautiful.

He continued, his voice low and intense. "I wouldn't care if you had a wooden leg—or two wooden legs and a great damned hook instead of a hand! It's *you* I want—you." He cradled her face between his hands. "I want you any way I can get you, Daisy—limping, dancing, punching—even biting and scratching."

He could feel her softening, and took a risk, lowering his voice to a deep seductive murmur. "And now I come to think of it, I wouldn't mind a bit of biting and scratching, come to think about it. If you're in the mood for it."

There was a long silence. He braced himself for a punch or a kick.

She gave a little huff, half of laughter, half of tears, and he pulled her against him. "I'm sorry I hurt your feelings, Daisy-girl," he said in a low voice. "I'm a big stupid clumsy eedjit. Will you forgive me?"

She looked up at him for a long moment then gave a trembly little sigh. "Bastard," she whispered. She shook her head as if mourning his hopelessness and thumped him in the chest with a small fist.

But it was a half-hearted thump at best—he barely felt it.

"Bastard," she whispered again. She reached up, drew his head down and kissed him.

Chapter Eleven

She was feeling, thinking, trembling about
everything; agitated, happy, miserable, infinitely
obliged, absolutely angry.

JANE AUSTEN, MANSFIELD PARK

He tasted salt tears, anger, and the sweet, hot, honey taste that was Daisy. Wild honey, with a tang of spice.

With a little moan she opened for him. The sound fired his blood. Heat rushed through him, hot rum and cinnamon on a tropical night.

She kissed him open-mouthed, enticing, teasing, lavishing him with the kind of generosity that characterized her spirit—she was all or nothing, his Daisy. Loving or fighting, she threw herself into it whole-heartedly.

He gathered her in, deepening the kisses, his hands roaming over her, learning her, caressing her curves through the layers of clothing. Her body softened against his, pliant and welcoming.

She sagged against him and grabbed his arms and Flynn felt a jolt of masculine satisfaction, knowing it was his kisses that had caused her knees to weaken.

"Come here, sweetheart," he murmured. He gripped her by the waist and lifted her, intending to seat her on the nearby table.

Instead her legs came up and wound around his hips, gripping him tightly, pulling him into the curve of her body—and
all the time kissing him, her mouth, her tongue, her hands
eager. Hungry. Making muffled little sounds that purely drove
him wild.

His head was spinning, his whole body tight, throbbing,
aching with the force of his desire. Summoning all his powers
of control, he staggered to the table, her legs locked around
him, her tongue tangling fiercely, hungrily with his.

One-handed he swept to one side the delicate fabrics spread
over the table and sat her on the edge of the table. He made to
move back, to ease the urgent throbbing of his groin, but she
gripped him by the hair and pulled him back towards her. Her
legs tightened around his hips, pulling him even harder against
the enticing cradle of her thighs.

He groaned. *Hard* was the word. Had she not noticed
his cock-stand, hard and aching, straining against the fall
of his breeches?

His every instinct screamed at him to lay her back across
the table, flip up her skirts and plunge into her sweetness,
deep and hard. Riding her long. Possessing. Claiming.

But this was Daisy. An unmarried girl. He had to take it
slow. Even if it killed him. She obviously had no idea she
was driving him wild with her kisses.

He caressed her breasts through the layers of her clothing,
feeling the small hard points thrusting against the fabric, just
as his cock thrust against his breeches. He rubbed the tips of
the nipples with his thumbs and she moaned and wiggled
against him, planting moist kisses along his jawline.

And the occasional nip, which sent him almost to the point
of explosion.

He reached one hand around behind her and found the
laces at her back. He tugged, hoping luck was with him. It
was. Her neckline loosened, just enough for him to ease it
down and slide a hand in. His fingers brushed over small,
warm, silken-skinned breasts, and he marveled at the softness
of her as he teased the hard little nubbins of desire and heard

her moan as she pushed herself against him, rubbing up against his hand like a little cat.

He loosened the laces further and pulled the neckline down. His mouth dried as he released her small pert breasts, the berry-dark nipples pouting for his attention. "God, you're beautiful," he muttered thickly and bent to take one rosy nipple into his mouth.

She arched and squirmed and grabbed at his shirt.

He slid his palm down to her ankle, then stroked steadily upward. He half expected her to stop him at that point—it would kill him, but he was almost at the point of no return, and he'd had no intention of going this far in the first place.

Not yet.

The inside skin of her thighs was as soft and silky as the rest of her, and he smoothed and stroked and caressed, moving ever higher toward his goal, expecting her any moment to pull back and clamp her knees together.

Instead she gave a little wriggle and almost a purr of approval.

His palm encountered a nest of soft curls. "I do like an old-fashioned girl," he murmured, his fingers stroking through the curls. The sweet musky smell of her filled his nostrils. He inhaled deeply.

She pulled back and frowned at him. "What d'ya mean, old-fashioned?" It came out in a rasp, breathy and indignant.

His fingers caressed her knowingly. "No drawers."

"Oh." She shivered at his touch. "Never got in the habit. Only toffs wear 'em. Too pricey for o-o-ordinary folks—ohhh." Her breath hitched and she clutched his shoulders. "Do that again."

She was slick and slippery and he stroked deep between the hot sleek folds of her flesh, reveling in the way she quivered beneath his touch, her eyes closed, rocking and gasping and pushing herself against him.

He bent to her breasts, sucking on the hard little berries, first one, then the other, and she clutched his hair with both hands holding him against her. Between her thighs his fingers moved, stroking and caressing. His thumb grazed the small sensitive nubbin and he felt the spasms start deep within her. She flung herself back, giving in to the waves of pleasure with a high, thin cry.

He was ready to explode himself. He hadn't planned to take it this far. He hadn't planned it at all. Flynn battled with his conscience. Not to mention his desperately straining body. But she was open and eager and ready for him. One-handed he reached for the fall of his breeches and began to unbutton.

At that moment, someone started knocking urgently on the door. "Daisy! Daisy, is everything all right?"

"Oh, gawd, it's Jane!" Daisy blinked, the muzzy, unfocussed look fading from her eyes. She sat up and hastily started pulling down her skirts, which were still around her waist. She hopped off the table. Her knees buckled and she grabbed him for support.

"I'm fine, Jane," she called. "Just . . . knocked something over."

"But I heard you cry out. Are you hurt?" Jane rattled the handle of the door. "Is this door *locked?*"

"Nah, you know I never lock it. It's probably just stuck." She patted her hair and clothing into place and checked Flynn's appearance. He finished buttoning his waistcoat and tried to straighten his neckcloth. And did his best to will away his cock-stand.

She reached up and finger-combed his hair into place, which didn't help. "Ready?"

He nodded. "Don't worry, if there's any danger of scandal, I'll ma—" He bit off the rest of the sentence, shocked at what had been about to come out of his mouth.

She paused, gave him an odd look, then marched to the door. "Don't be daft, Flynn. There's not going to be any scandal."

Flynn watched her, stunned at what he'd almost committed himself to. Marry Daisy? The thought hadn't even crossed his mind before this. He'd only said it because of what Lady Bea had said earlier, and because Jane was banging frantically on the door and it still could be a scandal.

And when you were caught seducing—or as good as seducing—a respectable girl, that's what followed. Marriage.

"Here we go . . ." Daisy rattled the door to cover the sound of the turning key and swung it open.

Jane practically fell into the room. Daisy caught and steadied her. Featherby stood in the doorway peering cautiously in. His gaze took in Flynn's slight dishevelment, his position behind the table—the cock-stand was almost under control now—and Daisy's mussed hair, flushed face and kiss-reddened mouth. He gave Flynn a hard look, his expression rather like a stuffed owl's.

Flynn gave a slight shake of his head. He was a good egg, Featherby. He wouldn't give them away. But Lord, what had he been thinking of to let things go so far? In the old lady's house.

Not thinking at all.

"Oh! Mr. Flynn!" Jane exclaimed. "I didn't realize you were—"

"He was having' a fittin' of his latest waistcoat," Daisy said. She grabbed a piece of fabric, folded it and started busily tidying up the table.

"But I heard you make such a loud—"

"Tripped over Snowflake. Knocked something over and stubbed me toe. Hurt like you wouldn't believe."

"What did you knock over?" Jane asked, looking around.

"Dunno—Flynn must've picked it up. I didn't notice. I'm fine, Jane, don't worry." She turned to Featherby. "Show Mr. Flynn out will you, Featherby? We're finished here." She hadn't so much as glanced at Flynn since she'd told him not to be daft.

"Of course, come with me, Mr. Flynn," Featherby said smoothly.

"I'm not finished with you yet, Daisy," he growled.

Finally she met his gaze. "Oh, yes, you are. Good-bye, Mr. Flynn."

Featherby preceded him down the stairs, stiff-legged as an offended cat. Flynn took no notice. He was still thinking about what he'd almost blurted out. An offer of marriage.

He swallowed, thinking about it. She was right—it hadn't turned into a scandal—luckily only Jane and Featherby had been at the door. But if it had been someone else, Lady Beatrice, or one of Daisy's customers . . .

He would have done the honorable thing and married the girl. Of course he would. A scandal could ruin Daisy's reputation—and her business. He was a man of honor, and Daisy was his friend. He wouldn't do that to her.

Luckily he wouldn't have to.

At the bottom of the stairs Featherby turned. "I'm disappointed in you, Mr. Flynn. You've been an honored guest in this house. Lady Beatrice trusted you."

"Nothing happened." It came out as a growl.

The butler fixed him with a gimlet look. "Miss Jane in her innocence might not have understood the significance of those sounds, but I certainly did. I blame myself for trusting you in the first place. I should never have given you the opportunity."

"It won't happen again," Flynn told him curtly. It wouldn't either. He'd let things get out of control. He'd only meant to kiss her. To apologize, make up for hurting her feelings.

Some apology. He'd almost ruined the girl. In her own home.

"It most certainly won't." Featherby passed Flynn his coat. "There will be no more private fittings or conversations with Miss Daisy in her workroom. I'll send a maid to sit with her at all times you are in the house. Better still, you can talk to her in Lady Beatrice's presence, in the drawing room."

Flynn gritted his teeth as he shrugged himself into his coat. The implication that he couldn't be trusted with Daisy, that he had to be *watched*, was infuriating. And for a *butler* of all people to be raking him over the coals was, dammit, it was . . .

Entirely justified, dammit.

"Good day, Mr. Flynn." Featherby handed Flynn his hat. Flynn crammed it on his head and without a word strode off.

*　*　*

Daisy hustled Jane out of the room as well, pleading the pressure of work, which was true, but the minute the door was shut—and she resisted the temptation to lock it again—she collapsed on her window seat.

Her body was still reverberating on the inside from Flynn's . . . attentions. *The little death*, the Frenchies called it. She'd never really believed in it, 'til now; the girls at the brothel used to fake it—said it made the men feel good.

But she'd never experienced it, even though Flynn was the third lover she'd had—if you could call him a lover when they hadn't actually done it.

He hadn't even come himself. She ought to feel a bit guilty about that, but it was hard to feel guilty when really, she felt . . . she felt . . . wonderful.

She curled up in her window-seat, her own private eyrie, but though she tried to retrieve those delicious loose floating feelings, Flynn's cut-off words niggled at her. *Don't worry, if there's any danger of scandal, I'll ma—*

Ma—what? All she could think of was *marry you*. She was sure that's what had hovered on the tip of his tongue, before he'd thought better of it.

Flynn, the man who wanted to marry the finest lady in London? Marry *her*?

No, that couldn't be right. He hadn't even gotten under her skirts—not properly. But what if he imagined she was some kind of sheltered innocent, like Lady Liz, or Jane? The kind of lady who expected a marriage proposal to follow after a kiss? A respectable virgin with a pure reputation? He might think he had to marry her then.

It was how the nobs saw things—especially if you got caught. She grinned, thinking of their close shave.

If Jane hadn't come busting in, they would have gone all the way. And if they had, Flynn would have realized she wasn't a virgin, and marriage wouldn't even have crossed his mind.

The red shoes lay tipped on their side on the floor. She

picked them up. She wasn't ever going to wear them. She should toss them away. If it hadn't been for these shoes she never would have . . .

Never would have heard him say: *It's* you *I want—you . . . any way I can get you.*

And she would never have known what bliss was to be had in Flynn's arms.

I don't care if you never wear those blasted shoes. I couldn't care less that you limp! She felt her face crumple.

She looked down at the shoes and found she was hugging them to her breast. She tried to swallow the surge of . . . of *feelings* that welled up in her throat. It was a quarrel that got out of hand, that's all.

She shoved the shoes in the back of the wardrobe and closed the door. She wouldn't wear them, but she couldn't bring herself to throw them away. They'd always remind her of Flynn.

Who'd have thought that just by kissing and touching you could experience . . . *that*?

What the man could do with his mouth and tongue . . . Her nipples were tender and tight and the rest of her was jelly-soft and feeling just as sweet. She knew now why it was called making love.

Those big hands of his, deft and knowing, playing her like a blooming violin. Just thinking about his touch sent a flurry of little echoes, warm ripples that pooled in her belly, a clenching deep inside her.

What would it be like to go all the way with him? It had to be even better.

But it wasn't going to happen ever again. She couldn't let it happen.

It was all just a mistake anyway. A stupid quarrel that got out of hand.

Flynn was still in a filthy mood that evening. He wrestled with his neckcloth while Tibbins hovered, watching Flynn's efforts with a pained expression. But Flynn was a grown man and could dress himself, dammit, so he'd waved the valet off.

He'd been invited to a ball tonight, and dancing and doing the pretty to a bunch of toffs was the last thing he wanted to do.

But what he wanted to do—which was take Daisy to bed—wasn't blasted well possible.

Lady Elizabeth was neatly off the scene, even her father had left town—no doubt fleeing his creditors—and Flynn needed to refocus his attention on the process of finding himself a wife.

But he couldn't get Daisy out of his mind.

It was lust, that was the problem—unfulfilled desire, clouding his judgement. What he needed was a woman—any woman—in his bed. And that alone was a good enough reason for attending this blasted ball.

Since he'd come to London, he'd been remarkably restrained as far as women were concerned. It didn't seem right to him to be courting one woman and tupping another at the same time, so he'd remained more or less celibate—and therein lay his problem.

Frustration interfered with a man's ability to think clearly, which was why he was going to the blasted ball.

From the start of the Season—and before—he'd had more invitations than he could count; some subtle, some blatant. Married women, widows, all ages, all shapes. He preferred widows; he was no saint, but he had no desire to come between a man and his wife. And he was not the kind of man who seduced innocents.

Apart from Daisy.

He flung his fourth mangled neckcloth aside. "Dammit, Tibbins, you tie the blasted thing!"

With an expression of unbearable smugness Tibbins stepped smoothly into the breach with a new starched neckcloth.

Flynn felt like strangling him with it. He wouldn't have to put up with this kind of behavior on a ship! Valets and butlers telling him what to do!

But he knew the real source of his fury. And the solution.

He'd go to the ball, find some willing woman and ride her until they were both senseless. And then he'd get his life back on track.

*   *   *

Three hours later, he found himself leaning against a fluted plaster column, glowering at the colorful throng of ladies and gentlemen, dancing, laughing, flirting, conversing—all so damned jolly, blast them.

He'd danced with a dozen different ladies so far—all pretty, some quite beautiful. Some were lively conversationalists, several were perfectly charming. Discreet—and not-so-discreet—invitations had flowed like wine.

Not one of them had interested him.

There was only one woman he wanted to bed, and she wasn't here. She was probably home alone, working her fingers to the bone, sewing a naughty silk nightdress for some old lady. Getting worn down and exhausted, but refusing all help, stubborn little fool.

He looked over to where Freddy and Damaris were dancing—so unfashionable for a husband and wife to live in each other's pockets, but did they care? Abby and Max too. They were sitting this one out together, quietly and companionably, Max's arm resting protectively along the back of Abby's chair. Abby was looking a bit tired, but when she turned her head and looked up at her husband, she glowed.

For some reason it made him think of Mam, when she was tired or dispirited. Da would put his arm around her, and she'd look up at him and smile, and it was as if a candle had lit up inside her.

Watching Abby smile up at Max, seeing how proud and protective his friend was of his wife, it was like an ache in his chest.

Would he ever find a woman who'd look at him like that, a woman who was everything to him, like Mam had been to Da, like Abby was to Max, and Damaris to Freddy?

He eyed the younger ladies, the unmarried ones.

A waiter sailed past him bearing a tray full of wineglasses. Flynn snagged one, drained it—and nearly choked. Ratafia. Sickly sweet stuff.

Several ladies drifted by, trying to catch his eye, sending inviting smiles. He pretended not to see.

He asked another waiter for something stronger. Champagne was all that was on offer. He tossed it down. All bubbles. No body.

He wasn't in the mood for this, wasn't prepared to be some bored lady's entertainment for the night, had no desire to be a pawn in some married couple's fencing match.

The ton did a grand job of marrying off their children for money, position and land. And while some married for love, and some arranged marriages prospered, most left behind them a wake of bored, unhappy, shallow, sometimes desperate women.

The men were all right—most men were tomcats at heart. But the women . . . Most women, as he understood it, wanted love. And trapped in a loveless marriage, they turned to distraction, and affairs. Titillation. Danger. The thrill of the forbidden.

And that was what was on offer to Flynn tonight.

He sighed and straightened. A fine gloomy mood he was in tonight, to be sure. He wasn't fit for man nor beast, and certainly not for a woman.

He needed a drink, a proper drink, not a bit of froth and bubble.

Or Daisy.

He took himself home, tossed back a brandy and flung himself on his bed. He closed his eyes and tried to sleep. But despite the brandy, he was wide awake. All he could think about was Daisy.

Just the thought of her made him aroused and aching.

He forced himself to ignore the demands of his body and tried to distract himself by listing the qualities he would look for in a wife, a more personal list this time. He'd learned from his mistakes. He needed to know the girl he married, needed to like her—hopefully he would even come to love her. And she, him. Because children needed to be brought up in a home with love.

Now, as he lay on his bed, drifts of childhood came back to him, little things he hadn't thought of in years. For so many years he'd tried to block out the memories. He'd always felt he should have done more, that somehow, he should have been able to save them.

But he'd been a boy, just a boy.

He remembered the day he'd knocked Mam's willow-patterned plate over, and how she'd scolded him for his carelessness in chipping it, playing ball inside the house. And how after the scolding she'd hugged him, saying," You're just like your father—boys will be boys." And she'd laughed as Da had grabbed her around the waist for a quick kiss and cuddle before taking the boys and the ball outside.

They were always kissing and cuddling, his parents.

After the accident, it was never quite the same. His father, always such a strong and vigorous man, hated the helpless creature he'd become, dependent on his wife and children for everything. But Mam's love had never wavered and looking back, Flynn could see now, that had kept Da sane.

One of his last memories of them was a few days before he left home to try to find work. He hadn't told them yet of his plans to save them all—that he was going to Dublin to find a job and make his fortune. Twelve years old, God help him.

His little sister Mary-Kate had brought her wee doll to Da to be mended. And Da, who couldn't do much else but lie there, mended it, and then made them all laugh as he made the doll talk and give cheek to Mam and to Mary-Kate.

It fair broke Mam's heart, seeing Da so helpless, but she never let him see it, just laughed along with little Mary-Kate. Afterwards Flynn had seen her turn away to wipe a tear. It broke his heart too seeing Da like that.

His parents' love had been the bedrock of his childhood. So often he'd woken in the night, a bad dream perhaps, or some more real worry—they were desperate times. He'd lie in the bed he shared with his little brothers, listening to the soft murmur of voices as his parents talked over the day, made plans for the morrow. He couldn't make out the words, but the soft exchange in the darkness soothed him and lulled him back to sleep. They might talk of everyday things, but he could feel the love between them.

That was the kind of marriage he wanted; companionship and love and mutual support. Partners in life, no matter what life brought them.

A friend who was also a lover . . .

A lover . . . His body ached for fulfillment.

He opened his eyes and sat up, staring into the darkness. *A friend who was also a lover?*

He was a blind great eedjit!

He'd been going about this whole business arse about.

Why the hell was he looking for a highborn lady, when the woman of his heart was right there under his nose, giving him cheek and keeping him awake with lust half the night?

Chapter Twelve

*Know your own happiness. Want for nothing
but patience—or give it a more fascinating name:
Call it hope.*

—JANE AUSTEN, *SENSE AND SENSIBILITY*

Flowers started arriving in the Berkeley Square house the next day. The first bunch was small, a little posy of sweet-smelling violets tied up with ribbons, and a single white daisy in the center.

"Who could have sent them?" Jane wondered aloud. There was a card with them, plain white, though of good quality, and clearly addressed to Miss Daisy Chance, but there was no other name attached, no sign of a sender.

Daisy shrugged. "A happy customer maybe?" She had a suspicion, but surely he wouldn't do something so . . . so *daft*.

The next day pink roses arrived, again with a single white daisy in the center.

"Aren't they lovely?" Jane rhapsodized as she brought them upstairs to Daisy's workroom. "You can't claim these are from a customer—not with that daisy at the heart. So romantic."

Daisy sniffed. "What's romantic about a daisy? Pretty common flower if you ask me."

"It's symbolic—he's saying there's only one Daisy. That you're unique."

"How do you know it's a him?"

"Well of course it's a man—who else would send you flowers?"

"And here's another one," Featherby said from the door. He carried a bunch of pale yellow primroses. Daisy didn't even have to look to see whether there was a daisy in the middle—she knew it would be there.

"So who is it, Daisy?"

"No idea."

Jane laughed. "Have you been meeting some gentleman in secret?"

"No, that would be you, wouldn't it, Jane?" Daisy knew all about Jane and her accidental-on-purpose meetings with a certain gypsy in the park.

Jane flushed and gave a guilty glance at Featherby, who busied himself arranging flowers and pretended not to hear.

And as she'd intended, the question nipped Jane's open speculation in the bud and she left Daisy in peace.

But who the hell was sending her flowers? She couldn't think of anyone except Flynn. She knew Featherby had told Flynn off good and proper—he'd told Daisy off as well, and made her feel like a worm. She'd known a bit of scandal would be ruinous to her business, but she hadn't thought how the old lady would feel. Especially after all those proper-lady lessons.

But if one bunch of flowers was an apology, two was . . . well, she couldn't imagine, and she didn't even want to know what three might mean. And as for the single white daisy in the middle of each bunch . . .

It looked like—it couldn't possibly be, but it did look like he was courting her. After telling the world he was going to marry the finest lady in London.

And that was ridiculous. As if he would turn from courting a fine aristocratic lady like Lady Liz to someone like Daisy Chance. In a pig's eye he would!

* * *

"Mrs. Foster to see you, Miss Daisy," Featherby said later that afternoon and stepped back to let Mrs. Foster in.

Daisy looked at her in dismay. "Oh, but I haven't finished—"

"I know it's far too early for my night wear to be ready, but I didn't come about that. I hope you'll forgive me for barging in like this," Mrs. Foster said, pulling off her gloves. "But I've been thinking." Her eyes were sparkling with excitement.

"Oh?" Daisy couldn't imagine what about.

Mrs. Foster waited until Featherby had left, then seated herself and said, "I think I told you that my husband died a little over a year ago."

Daisy nodded.

"And that I've been trying to think what to do with the rest of my life."

Again, Daisy nodded.

"He left me very well off, you know," Mrs. Foster said diffidently. "And to add to that, an elderly aunt died recently and left me a substantial nest egg."

Some people have all the luck, Daisy thought. And instantly felt guilty. Mrs. Foster was now without family—that mattered more than money.

"And I've been thinking, the nest egg—well, it's like free money, isn't it?"

"Mmm." Daisy made a polite noise. In her experience there was no such thing as free money. But what did she know?

Mrs. Foster continued, "And so I thought I should do something special with it—something different and exciting."

"A holiday?"

"Better! I thought I might invest it."

"You mean like in building canals and mines and, and steam engines and things," Daisy said, hoping to sound intelligent.

"Heavens, no—nothing so dreary. I want to invest in you."

Daisy blinked. "In *me*?"

Mrs. Foster nodded. "In your shop."

Daisy stared at her, then shook her head. "I don't know what you mean. How could you invest in my shop? I haven't even got one yet."

"I know. This would enable you to buy one. It's not a small nest egg, Daisy. It could make all the difference in the world to you and your business."

She named a sum that made Daisy blink. That much, and she was calling it *free money*? It was too good to be true. "If you mean like a loan—no, thanks. I don't believe in borrowin' money."

It was the best way she knew to court certain doom. In Daisy's experience people got beaten up—or worse—if they couldn't pay a loan back, and far from helping them out over a bad patch . . . Well, let's just say it never turned out well.

"No, it's not a loan, it would be an investment. My husband was in business, and when he became ill, I learned— oh, you have no idea how much I learned! I'll tell you all about it one day. But for you, my proposal would work like this: I give you the money, you use it to secure the premises— the shop—and to purchase and install fittings and equipment, and to employ seamstresses—that kind of thing. And in return, I get a share of the profits."

It all sounded so easy. Daisy didn't trust it. "What if there ain't any profits? What if I go bust?"

"Then I lose my investment." She gave Daisy a confident smile. "But you won't fail. I have tremendous faith in you and your designs, Miss Chance."

Daisy wasn't sure about it at all. "I don't think—"

"You would own fifty-one percent of the business, and you would control everything. I would just be your silent partner."

A silent partner? She remembered what Flynn had said about silent partners. Freddy had used an inheritance from an aunt to become a silent partner with Max and Flynn and their other friend, and it had helped get their company started. And look at them now—they were all rich.

Mrs. Foster added, "Of course we would have it all written down in a legal agreement—for your protection and mine."

"I dunno," Daisy said after a long pause. "I'll have to think about it." It sounded too good to be true. There had to be a catch.

"Of course." Mrs. Foster rose, pulling on her gloves. "Think about it, get some advice from your family and friends, and let me know. I'm sure you'll make the right decision." She smiled at Daisy and clapped her hands together girlishly. "I must confess, I find the whole idea of going into the fashion business monstrously exciting."

Daisy gave her a tentative smile in return. Exciting? Yes—and bloody terrifying.

Flynn made a morning call on Lady Beatrice the following afternoon, all very formal and correct. The first Daisy knew of it was when Featherby told her Lady Beatrice desired her presence in the drawing room. He wouldn't explain why, merely held the door for her, waiting in a bland yet implacable manner.

With a sigh, Daisy tidied herself and made her way to the drawing room.

On the threshold she stopped. And blinked. Seated on tapestry-covered gilt-edged chairs sat the usual collection of old ladies—and Flynn, a dainty teacup in his big fist, sipping pale China tea with lemon as if it was nectar of the gods.

She frowned. Flynn hated China tea.

He rose and bowed, greeting her politely as if he hadn't had her skirts up around her ears only a few days earlier. Almost a week. He waited until she was seated before seating himself. He looked very pleased with himself.

She wanted to ask him about the flowers, but she couldn't— not in this company. Thank goodness Jane was off walking her dog and wasn't here to bring it up. The old ducks loved any hint of a mystery, and add in a sniff of potential romance—and flowers were romantic—and they'd be all over it, and then Lady Beatrice would want to know what was what—and then there'd be hell to pay.

"Tea, Daisy, my dear?" Lady Beatrice asked, and without waiting, Featherby poured a cup and handed it to her.

She looked up to thank him, but instead intercepted a silent exchange between him and Flynn. Featherby gave Flynn a meaningful look—Daisy had no idea what about. Flynn, however, seemed to know. He inclined his head at Featherby, then smiled at Daisy.

Daisy frowned. Whatever that look meant, she didn't trust it.

Lady Beatrice's gaze went from Daisy to Flynn and back a dozen times. Her cronies exchanged glances and did the same.

Daisy felt like a blooming butterfly skewered on a pin. What the hell was Flynn playing at?

For the next twenty minutes Flynn chatted and charmed and had the old ladies falling over themselves with delight. He hadn't said a word to Daisy that was the slightest bit out of place, but by the time he left she was thoroughly bewildered.

That evening the four girls gathered around the fire in Jane and Daisy's bedchamber. Max and Freddy and Flynn had gone off to watch a mill—a boxing match—and since Lady Beatrice wanted an early night and had retired to her bedchamber, Abby and Damaris seized the opportunity for an informal supper of hot chocolate and toast and crumpets in front of the fire.

It was a reminder of old times, before Abby and Damaris were married—even before they'd met Lady Beatrice—when their lives had been so difficult, and they'd decided to band together and become "sisters of the heart"—just to survive.

Daisy loved these gatherings, just the four of them, and no manners or proper behavior to worry about, where they would just talk and talk. And eat. And talk.

Damaris and Daisy sat on the bed, sewing. Abby and Jane toasted bread and crumpets while the three cats supervised. At least Jane hadn't brought the blooming dog in as well.

Daisy gazed into the fire, mesmerized by the dancing flames. She should have been thinking about Mrs. Foster's amazing offer, but instead she hadn't been able to get Flynn out of her mind. What was he up to?

"Daisy? *Daisy*?"

She jumped, startled out of her reverie. "What?"

"What about the daisy?" Damaris asked.

Daisy glanced at the vases of flowers that graced the bedchamber. Those single daisies . . . they got to her.

"I took 'em out, why?"

"Took them out? Whatever for?" Damaris frowned over the dress she'd just finished hemming. "I just offered to embroider this one for you, but if you don't want them anymore . . ."

Daisy felt herself flushing. "Sorry, I was thinkin' of something else. I didn't mean the dresses."

Jane looked up. "I thought you were doing forget-me-nots on that dress, not daisies."

"Haven't you noticed?" Damaris said to Jane. "Daisy embroiders a little daisy inside the neck of each garment she makes. Just a tiny one, in white chain stitch with a French knot or two in yellow for the center."

"Does she?" Jane scrambled up, leaving Abby to mind the food, and hurried to her wardrobe and started examining her dresses. "Oh look! You're right," she exclaimed. "It's in this one—and this—and this—and—"

"It's in all of 'em," Daisy said, to stop Jane exclaiming over every blooming thing.

"How pretty. But why bother to embroider something where nobody can see it?"

She hunched her shoulders in embarrassment. "It's nothin', just . . ."

"She's signing her work, aren't you, Daisy?" Damaris said softly. "Like an artist or a craftsman."

Daisy nodded. Damaris's matter-of-fact acceptance gave her the confidence to explain. "Painters sign their paintings, and the men that made those chairs of Lady Bea's—they put their mark on their work, and—"

"And I sign my china and my paintings," Damaris added.

Daisy nodded. "That's what gave me the idea. So I thought . . . why not? It only takes a moment. You probably think it's a bit stup—"

"I think it's a lovely idea, Daisy," Abby assured her warmly. "It makes your clothes even more personal and special."

"Oh, yes, I think so too," Jane agreed. "And how lucky that you're called Daisy, instead of Annabel or Gwendolyn—imagine embroidering that." They all laughed.

"Do any of you know anything about silent partners?" Daisy asked. "In business I mean."

Damaris shook her head, "Not really. All I know is that Freddy was one in Max's company."

"Flynn's company," Daisy corrected her. It was called Flynn and Co., after all.

"Max never talks business with me," Abby said.

Jane, who was still standing beside the wardrobe, gave a little scream. "The toast, Abby!" She dived toward the toasting fork, where a slice of thick-cut bread was smoking badly.

Abby removed the charred toast from the fire, examined it, decided it was beyond saving and dropped it in the coal scuttle. "Come along everyone, it's time we ate."

It was a feast. A cloth was spread on the hearth rug, laid with dishes containing butter, honey, several kinds of jam, marmalade, fresh cream, cheeses, goose liver pâté, even anchovy paste, though why Cook had sent up anchovy paste when none of them liked it—apart from the cats—was a mystery.

"Max, no! You can't have it." Abby pushed Max the cat away. It was the third or fourth time she'd had to stop a cat from raiding the food.

"Put them bloomin' cats outside," Daisy said, not for the first time. "They'll knock something over in a minute."

"Poor little kitties, we're tempting you with all these lovely smelling dishes, aren't we?" Jane crooned as she collected the butter, the pâté and the pot of anchovies and put them on a small side table.

Daisy rolled her eyes. As if cats couldn't jump. She was as fond of the cats as any of them, but she wanted to eat in peace. She folded her sewing and before she joined the others on the hearth rug, made a small detour, scooping up three half-grown cats and depositing them outside in the hall before she returned to the fire and sat down. She answered Jane's accusing look with, "They can come in afterwards and polish off the scraps, but I'm not picking cats out of me supper all night. I want to relax."

A large pot of thick, sweet chocolate had been sitting in the grate, keeping hot. Using a cloth pad to hold the handle, Damaris carefully poured it into cups while Jane and Abby buttered toast and crumpets and handed them around.

"Oooh, this is lovely," Daisy said, crunching into a slice of toast oozing with melted butter and tangy orange marmalade. Damaris was eating toast and strawberry jam topped with thick whipped cream and Jane was eating crumpets dripping with honey. "I can't think of anything nicer for supper. Who invented toast, do you reckon? They must have been a genius."

She glanced at the others, all busily tucking in, and her eyes widened. "Abby, what the *'ell* are you eating? Is that *anchovy paste*? With *cream*? Washed down with hot *chocolate*?"

Abby gave a rueful glance at her slice of toast, slathered with anchovy paste and topped with cream. She glanced at Jane and gave a little shrug. "I suppose there's no use trying to keep it a secret any longer. Jane knows, and Max, of course, and I was going to tell you both when Lady Bea was with us but"—she gave a tremulous little smile—"I'm going to have a baby."

Damaris jumped up and hugged Abby. "Oh, Abby, I'm so thrilled for you!" And for the next few minutes it was all hugs and congratulations and "When is the baby due?" and "What did Max say?"

Of course Daisy hugged and smiled and congratulated Abby too. She knew how much Abby wanted children. Abby would make a wonderful mother and Max a good father.

But it was a little strange, all the same. For the first time in Daisy's life she'd seen someone who was thrilled—really, truly, honestly *thrilled* at the prospect of having a baby.

Her experience was the opposite. Everyone she'd ever

known had treated pregnancy as a disaster, a fate to be avoided at all costs. Some girls who fell pregnant—and wasn't that a telling phrase?—even risked their lives going to the old women in the back alleys.

A baby was a problem to be solved—not celebrated.

Some of the girls had loved their babies, it was true, but they still gave them away. Even some of the married ones.

And if the baby died—as quite a few did—there was grief in some of the girls, to be sure, but also a measure of relief. God's will and all that. And the babe was soon forgotten, or at least never spoken of again.

Even Daisy's own mother had given her away. Or sold her. She wasn't sure. But she hadn't wanted her.

Daisy looked at Abby, so glowing and happy and proud and excited. She couldn't imagine what it would be like to feel that way.

As for the baby, what would it be like to come into the world being wanted and loved and cared for? Part of a ready-made, loving, protective family.

Daisy couldn't imagine it.

Chapter Thirteen

I have not the pleasure of understanding you.

—JANE AUSTEN, *PRIDE AND PREJUDICE*

Flowers continued to be delivered, each posy with a daisy in the center of the arrangement. And for the following three afternoons, Flynn made a very correct morning call. Daisy was summoned to the drawing room each time.

By the second visit, she was bristling with suspicion. It couldn't possibly be what it looked like. He wouldn't do that to her.

By the end of the third visit she was simmering with impotent fury.

He was pretending to court her. And everyone except Daisy was fooled by his act.

It had reached the stage where Featherby and William had had to bring in more chairs, as more of Lady Beatrice's cronies kept coming, all twittering with excitement because Something Was Going On.

They watched Flynn and Daisy's interactions with the avidity of spectators at the court, or a play—why, Daisy had no idea, because with that audience, she and Flynn could only speak of the most commonplace things.

Her frustration grew. She had no opportunity to speak to

Flynn alone, to ask him what the hell he was playing at. He, however, seemed perfectly comfortable with the attention, and entertained the room with charming anecdotes and tales of his adventures. The old ladies adored him.

Daisy wanted to smack him.

It was probably some scheme to get himself out of Featherby's black books, and it had worked too. Featherby had unbent to such an extent that he was regarding Flynn with a benevolent expression, and Lady Beatrice was positively beaming at Flynn when he rose to take his leave. But why did he have to involve Daisy?

There was a hushed intake of breath from the gathered ladies as he took Daisy's hand to bow over it, and a long sigh when he released it.

Daisy could have boxed his ears.

The moment he left she stomped upstairs in a temper. She didn't for one moment believe he was courting her. And the next time she saw him alone, she'd tell him.

She knew what he wanted—a nice, tame, sweet-spoken little wife, a perfect lady who'd be an ornament to his home, popping out babies and playing Lady Bountiful to the poor, attending balls and dancing 'til dawn in his arms.

Well, that wasn't her, and Flynn blooming well knew it. He was playing some deep game and she didn't like it one little bit, so he could just stop sending her flowers and looking at her like she was a . . . a cream-filled cake that he was waiting to have for his tea.

Whatever it was, she wouldn't go along with it.

She had other plans for her life.

It was some kind of game. He couldn't possibly be serious.

Finally, finally after days of the dreariest good behavior, gallons of weak tea and hours of insipid conversation with a gaggle of old ladies hanging off his every word and glance, Featherby allowed Flynn upstairs to talk to Daisy on her own.

"Leave the door open," he called after Flynn as he took the stairs two at a time.

He was anxious to see her. Desperate, in fact.

She didn't even greet him. "What are you playin' at, Flynn?"

No polite society hypocrisy here—straight out with the question. Ah, but she was a breath of fresh air, his Daisy. "Playin' at? What do you mean? I've come to vis—"

"Stop jokin' around. You know what I mean. Sendin' me flowers—I know it's you so don't bother to deny it. And all those bloomin' morning visits—what are they about?"

He hid a smile. She was spoiling for a fight. Not that he minded. "Something botherin' you, sweetheart? I thought you liked flowers."

"Don't call me that! I'm not your sweetheart!"

"Something botherin' you, my little hedgehog?"

She tried to glare at him some more, but her lips gave her away and a laugh escaped her. She put her work down and gave a sigh. "Gawd, Flynn, you're enough to drive a girl to drink. What am I goin' to do with you?"

He grinned. "I can think of a few things."

She shook her head. "No." She held up her palms as if to hold him off, though he wasn't anywhere close enough to touch her. Yet. "None of that nonsense. I told you before, it's got to stop."

"What's got to stop?"

"This . . ." She groped for a word. "This charade."

He frowned. "It's not a charade."

"I'm talking about the impression you've been givin' Lady Bea and her friends. And Featherby. They think you're *courting* me, Flynn."

"I am."

She blinked, then shook her head. "Stop jokin' around. I'm serious."

"So am I. I want you, Daisy."

She paled. Her eyes were liquid, luminous as she searched his face to read the truth in it. Her mouth opened, then shut. Flynn just waited.

There was a long silence. She bit her lip, and slowly the color flushed back into her cheeks as she mastered herself. Again, she shook her head. "Flattered as I am—"

"*Flattered?*" He could hear the *but* coming already. Dammit!

She narrowed her eyes at him. "Yes, flattered—now are you going to let me finish?"

That was his girl—knock her down and she came up swinging. "Go ahead."

"Right, as I was sayin', I'm flattered you want me—and I'll admit that I'm attracted to you too—"

"Then if—"

"Oy! Will you bloody listen?"

"Go on." Not flirting, then. She was serious.

"I admit, I do fancy you, and in different circumstances, I might . . ." He leaned forward, but she continued, "But I ain't. I ain't going to let it go any further."

"Why not?"

"I can't afford it."

"Afford?" He frowned.

"With me business only just gettin' started I can't afford even the slightest hint of scandal or improper behavior. I'm not like those ton ladies, where everyone is prepared to turn a blind eye to their goin's-on, as long as they're discreet. If it got out that I had a fancy man, it would be the ruination of—"

"'Fancy man'?" Flynn said indignantly. "I'm no fancy man! Do you think I'm tryin' to give you a slip on the shoulder or somethin'? Dammit, Daisy—you ought to know me better than that! I'm not the kind of man to trifle with the affections of an innocent girl!"

She gave him a sharp look. Her mouth opened, as if she was about to say something, but she shut it again.

He continued, "I'm talking marriage, girl."

"*Marriage?*" Her jaw dropped.

He nodded. "You, me and a preacher. Marriage." He waited.

She stared at him for a long moment, then sighed. "I thought that's what you were goin' to say the other day—when Jane and Featherby caught us at it. Don't worry, I'm not going to hold you to it."

"Hold me to i—"

"It was my fault—all my fault—so you don't need to go being all honorable and—"

"I'm not being honorable! Dammit, Daisy, I mean it! I want to marry you."

"No, you don't."

"Don't tell me what I want or don't want," he snapped, annoyed at her calm contradiction. "You don't like it when I argue with you like that—"

"Yeah, but with me it's true. You're just feeling . . ."

"Feeling what?" He prompted after a moment. "Go on, tell me what you think I'm feeling."

"Guilty about gettin' under me skirts that way."

He shook his head. "I don't feel the slightest bit guilty about it. All I feel is regret that Jane came home when she did and that we didn't get to finish."

"And we never will."

He smiled. "I don't give up so easy, Daisy love. And when I want something enough, I usually get it. And I want you, be assured of that." He took a few steps towards her, planning to kiss her into compliance, to reassure her.

She skittered back out of reach, tripped on a cat and almost fell. Flynn dived forward and caught her arm, steadying her.

"Are you all r—"

She shook off his hold and scooped up the cat. "The one room in the house where she's not allowed so she tries to sneak in all the time." She held it against her breast, stroking it. But it was a defense.

"I don't blame her."

She put the cat out, closed the door and leaned against it, eyeing him with a troubled expression.

"I don't know why you've suddenly got this daft notion to marry me, Flynn, but it's crazy. You came to London tellin' the world you wanted to marry a fine fancy highborn lady—and now you're offering for me? It doesn't make sense. Is it because Lady Liz jilted you?"

"She didn't jilt me."

"But everyone says—"

"That's the story everyone believes. But—and this is for your ears only, Daisy—she didn't elope with anyone. I think you're right about her bein' a lady of Langwhatsit—she's gone to live with an aunt in Italy."

He watched her face, pausing to let it sink in. "The elopement story was to keep her father off her trail so she could make a clean getaway. If I didn't marry her—and I'd told her that I wasn't going to—he was plannin' to marry her off to a ghastly old ruin for the sake of his debts." He snorted. "Some father, eh?"

Her wide hazel eyes scanned his face earnestly. "So you're not upset?"

He shook his head. "I helped arrange it."

"Oh." She frowned. "But that still doesn't explain why you're asking someone like me. There are plenty of fine unmarried highborn girls out there."

"I know. But I've changed me mind. I don't want to marry a toff's daughter—I want you. And before you say anything, I'm not askin' 'someone like you'—I'm asking *you*. And there's no one like you. You're one of a kind, Daisy Chance."

Which was the message he'd been trying to send her with those flowers. But it seemed his girl didn't understand the language of flowers. Or maybe she did and just didn't like it. She still had that troubled, mulish look on her face.

"So I'm asking you to marry me. What do you say?"

He could see before she even opened her mouth that he wasn't going to like her answer.

She twisted a bit of material between nervous fingers. "Well, those were real nice words, Flynn, and I'm truly flattered. And I'm sorry, but it still ain't going to happen. I'm the last girl you should marry."

"Why would you say such a thing? Explain it to me, Daisy, so I can understand."

For a long moment he thought she wasn't going to respond. But she gave a sigh and said, "All right, but you're not going to like it."

He shrugged. "I haven't liked anything you've said so far, so what have I got to lose?"

Daisy seated herself in her window seat, tucking her feet under her, and gestured him to a chair halfway across the room. He took the chair and moved it closer, close enough for him to reach out and touch her. Typical Flynn—never did what she asked.

Why couldn't he simply accept her no and leave her alone? It was hard enough for her to push him away without him fighting it.

She took a deep breath—she wasn't looking forward to this. "A few moments ago you called me an innocent girl. I'm not. I'm a bastard, a—"

"I know. You told me the first day we met you were born on the wrong side of the blanket."

"Let me finish, Flynn," she said quietly. He waited. "I'm a bastard, a foundling—even my own mum didn't want me. And before I come to live with Lady Bea and the girls, I didn't live a respectable life."

"Me neither. Some of the things I did when I was a lad tryin' to survive on me own." He shrugged. "You do what you can to stay alive. I won't judge you, Daisy."

All right, so she was going to have to lay it on the line here. "I haven't finished yet. I'm not a virgin."

There was a short silence, then he shrugged. "Neither am I."

She gritted her teeth. He wasn't taking her seriously. "Yeah, well, I doubt you lived in a brothel most of your life."

That rocked him. "A *brothel*?"

She nodded. She was tempted to leave it there, let him draw his own conclusions, but pride, and something in the way he was looking at her—with compassion rather than judgement or disgust—made her continue. "It's not what you think—I never did sell me body. I was a maidservant, scrubbin' and cleanin' and doin' whatever needed doin'. At the beck and call of the girls and their customers." She let that sink in and added, "But I ain't no innocent. And I ain't no virgin."

"But—" He frowned, trying to piece it all together.

"Abby and Damaris and Jane ain't really me sisters. I met Abby in the street." She was quite prepared to tell Flynn the worst about her own life, but the other girls' stories were theirs to tell, and private from everybody except their husbands and Lady Bea.

"And through Abby you met Jane and Damaris, I see. What an incredible coincidence, running into your half sister like that. How did you know? You don't look alike."

She looked up and gave him a piercing look. "You'll keep this private, won't you?"

"Of course."

"We're not half sisters at all. I am a bastard—at least I assume my mum and dad never married, whoever they were—but I'm a foundling. The girls are no relation to me at all."

"No relation *at all*?"

"Nope."

"Then how did a chance meeting in the street turn into . . . all this." He spread his hands, indicating the grand house she was now living in.

"I was homeless. I'd just run away from the brothel. Mrs. B., the owner, had decided to retire and she gave it over to her son Mort. He was a nasty piece of work, Mort, and the place . . . changed. It weren't safe for me no more." She shivered recalling how she'd been told by one of the girls that Mort had promised Daisy to a man who liked beating up girls, and who fancied himself a crippled little maidy.

"And Abby?"

"Abby took me in."

"Took you in? A stranger she'd just met on the street? Didn't she know about the brothel?"

"She knew. She's got a heart as big as Hyde Park, has Abby." She swallowed. There was more to the story, but she wasn't going to tell him about Jane and Damaris being kidnapped and sold to Mort. She'd helped them escape and because of that Abby had taken her in.

And called her sister, through thick and thin.

"And then when we came here to live with Lady Bea, Abby brought me with her."

"And Lady Beatrice?"

"Knows all about me. I told you, I don't tell lies, and I wasn't goin' to lie to a helpless old lady."

Flynn snorted. "Nothing helpless about her that I can see."

"She was helpless then, believe me," Daisy said softly, remembering the state they'd found the old lady in. "She'd been sick." And neglected and abused by her pigs of servants, but she wasn't going to talk about that either—the old lady had her pride and those dark and desperate days were long past.

"So that's it, me scandalous past. I've had two lovers before y—" She broke off. Calling Flynn her lover wouldn't be smart.

He swooped in on it. "Before me, which makes it third time lucky."

"You ain't my lover, Flynn," she said quietly.

He gave a slow, sleepy-eyed smile. "I beg to differ." His gaze dropped to her chest where her blasted nipples were probably sitting up beggin' him to take notice.

She folded her arms. "Look, apart from all that, I can't be your wife. I'm not any kind of lady, I don't know how to run a house or be a hostess to grand people—"

"I've seen you—"

"You've seen me pour 'em cups of tea and talk to them—yeah. Not hold a ball or plan a dinner party or organize a *soirée* or a Venetian breakfast—whatever that is. I don't know the first thing about how to run a household. And I could never bring meself to play Lady Bountiful to your poor folk."

He frowned. "What poor folk?"

"The ones on your estate."

"Oh, those ones." He nodded.

"See, Abby and Jane and Damaris could. They've never been one of the poor."

"But—"

"Oh I know they had nothin' and no one and were in danger of starvation—we all were." His brows shot up in surprise, and she realized she hadn't told him that bit.

"And that's for your ears only, so don't blab about it. Their poverty was just accidental, anyway. They fell into it. It's not the same as being born poor, like me—the real proper poor, I mean."

"Why? Poverty is poverty no matter who you are."

"No, it's not." She thought about how to explain. "For

some folks, poverty is a . . . is an attitude. If you think you're poor, you'll always be poor, and even if you get rich, some little part of you always remembers bein' poor, and still feels poor inside. Abby and Damaris and Jane—they had posh parents and fell into poverty by accident—so they'd be good at playin' Lady Bountiful. Though Jane, I reckon, still feels poor inside at times . . ."

She shook her head. She'd gotten off the track. "But I could never play Lady Bountiful, taking baskets of food and clothes . . . and stuff like that to the poor—the real poor— people like me, I mean. It'd feel all wrong. As if I was lording it over them or summat. You got to be born to do that kind of thing, I reckon."

There was a long silence. "I see," he said at last.

"So you understand me point of view?"

He nodded. "I do."

"So you see now why I'm the wrong sort of girl for you?"

"No."

"What? But I just explained—"

"You've explained why you don't want to play Lady Bountiful. And that you were born into poverty. In that, I reckon we're well matched. I was poor—real proper poor— too, and I have that little corner in me. It's a kind of hunger, that's always there, reminding you. Haunting you."

She nodded. That was it, all right.

"But as for Lady Bountiful, I don't have any poor who need visiting or baskets of food. I don't have any poor at all. At the moment my 'estate' is a set of rented rooms in St James that was once occupied by Freddy Hyphen-Hyphen, and the only other inhabitant is my valet, Tibbins."

"But—"

"It's true I want a big house—you must have heard me talk about it a dozen times—but I have no plans for a large country estate with tenants—poor or otherwise. I might buy a house in the country—maybe somewhere near Max's place, looking out over the sea—but my main home will be in London."

He added, "Of course, you could always take baskets of food to Tibbins, though I don't know how he'd—"

"You're laughing at me!"

He smiled. "Just a little. You're inventing reasons, sweetheart. Nothing you've told me has changed my mind in the least. All of those things you've mentioned you could learn if you put half a mind to it. Running a household must be a damn sight easier than running a business, but the prospect of that doesn't bother you at all."

And that was the nub of it.

"Yeah, I probably could—if I wanted to." She took a deep breath. "But the thing is, Flynn, I don't want to. I don't want to be anyone's wife. It's not you. I like you, Flynn, like you a lot, in fact—"

"In fact?" he prompted.

She shook her head. "The point is, if I was goin' to marry anyone, it'd probably be you."

"Only probably?" He leaned forward but she held up her hands to ward him off. His eyes were so very blue, it took every bit of strength she had to say what she knew she had to say.

"I told you before, I don't want a husband. I don't want to have kids. I got plans for me life—plans that don't include marriage. So . . ."—she swallowed and forced the rest out. "I thank you for the offer. I'm very honored you asked me, but I'm sorry, the answer's no."

There was a long silence. Then he took a deep breath and stood up. "I suppose I'd better take myself off, then."

"Sorry, Flynn," she said again. She felt terrible. It was the worst thing in the world, being told someone didn't want you. Especially since she did.

She wanted Flynn something fierce.

She just didn't want to be a wife.

He turned. "I might have lost the first round, but I'm not yet ready to throw in the towel." He gave her a swift smile. "I'll be back. I don't give up that easy, Daisy-girl."

He let himself quietly out of her room, closing the door after him with a soft click.

Flynn walked slowly downstairs. He didn't understand. He was a good catch, if he said so himself. Hell, he was a great catch: fit, strong, rich, lusty, with all his own teeth and hair.

Women liked him—ladies of Langwhatsit aside—and he'd had plenty of invitations to prove it. But he didn't go messing around in anyone's marriage bed—he didn't hold with infidelity. He'd be a good and faithful husband, he knew.

He knew in his bones, in his blood that Daisy fancied him as much as he fancied her.

So why was it so apparently unthinkable? So bloody *daft*?

She'd given him a string of reasons, none of which prevented them from marrying, as far as he was concerned. He didn't care about her past, it was her future he cared about—her future with him.

So what was wrong with the girl?

Featherby stood waiting in the hall. He'd known Flynn's intention—it was why he'd let him see Daisy alone. He didn't say anything—it was not a butler's place to ask—but a faint lifting of his brow was enough.

"She turned me down," Flynn told him.

Featherby's brows shot up. "You did ask her to marry you, didn't you, sir? I mean, she knew what you were offering?"

Flynn nodded. "She knew. I was more than clear. She called it a 'daft notion.'"

Featherby stared at him. "What maggot's got into her head now?" he murmured half to himself.

"I don't know," Flynn said. "But I aim to find out."

Daisy waited until she was sure Flynn was gone. Then she burst into tears.

He hadn't been bothered by her lack of virginity, her job in the brothel—anything.

But he needed a different sort of woman to run his home and have his kids. He might think he wanted Daisy now, while he was hot for her body—and who was the fool who'd kissed him and started that? Who'd led him on? Who'd wrapped her legs shamelessly around his waist and let him do whatever he wanted? She'd wanted it too.

But once the heat wore off he'd be wondering why he'd married her, and comparing her to the kind of proper lady he could have had.

She knew she'd be found wanting.

She wasn't the marrying kind. She wanted to be a famous dressmaker patronized by rich folks, not a wife and a mother—that was for other women, not her. She'd never wanted kids, never dreamed of having them, the way Abby and the other two did.

Even Lady Bea felt her life had been blighted by not being able to have a child of her own. Not Daisy.

Flynn wanted a quiverful of kids.

Refusing him was the right thing for both of them, she knew.

But oh, how it hurt to have to tell him no.

There was a sweetness in the man that she'd never encountered in any man before, especially not a man who was also tough and strong and masculine. And gorgeous.

And rich.

And gorgeous.

If she'd been born different . . . No there was no use going down that pathway. Some things in life you could have and others it was best not to even think about.

A short time later Featherby brought up a tea tray. Daisy, who at his knock had snatched up some sewing to give the impression she was working, set it aside, hoping he wouldn't notice her red-rimmed eyes. Or if he did, that he wouldn't ask about them.

He glanced at her once, then fussed about quietly, setting out little cakes and a pot and teacup. Strong India tea, just the way she liked it. Her favorite cakes. Not saying a thing.

He knew. Featherby always knew.

He bowed himself out and closed the door carefully behind him. The same way Flynn had.

I'll be back. I don't give up that easy, Daisy-girl.

More tears came then. She blinked them away. She poured

her tea and as she stirred in the sugar she found herself staring at the sugar lumps piled up in their little silver dish.

She was like one of these lumps of sugar—all hard and like a rock . . . until you dropped it in a cup of hot tea. Then watch it soften and melt and fall apart.

But sometimes, there was a little core of hardness that refused to dissolve, no matter how hard you stirred it.

She had to be that hard little lump from now on.

Else she'd lose herself.

Chapter Fourteen

It was, perhaps, one of those cases in which advice is good
or bad only as the event decides.

—JANE AUSTEN, PERSUASION

Lady Beatrice had summoned them all to dine that
evening—just a family dinner before they went off to
attend their various engagements: Max and Abby and
Freddy and Damaris were going to the theater, and Lady
Bea was taking Jane to a *soirée musicale*—which was like
a concert, only in somebody's home.

Daisy had been to a few *soirées* in the early days of living
with Lady Bea. They were all right if the people playing or
singing were talented, but sometimes they weren't.

Lady Bea, who was utterly thrilled by what she called
Abby's delicate situation and sometimes her *interesting
condition* and occasionally *the impending happy event*—
apparently proper ladies didn't say *pregnant*, or *up the duff*
or *having a bun in the oven*—was using it as an excuse to
gather her gels around her more frequently than ever.

Tonight it particularly suited Daisy; she'd thought long
and hard about Mrs. Foster's offer, and now she was ready
to talk to Max and Freddy about silent partners and what
they did or didn't do.

Luckily, Flynn hadn't been included in the dinner invitation. She wasn't sure why, but she suspected Featherby had said something to Lady Bea.

It would have been impossible trying to talk to him with the whole family looking on. And she didn't want him to know about any silent partner possibility, yet. He'd be hurt that she'd rather accept help from a stranger than from a friend.

He didn't understand: She was trying to protect him, trying to protect their friendship. If they even had a friendship now.

She pushed it out of her mind and tried to concentrate on the matter at hand: the silent partnership.

She liked both her brothers-in-law. Freddy was fun and easy to talk to, but she was a little in awe of Max; he was graver and more thoughtful. Very much head-of-the-family. Tonight Freddy was seated beside her, which made things easier.

"Freddy," she said after the first course had been removed and while the dishes for the second were being brought out. "Can you tell me a bit about what happened when you became a silent partner in Flynn and Co.?"

"Daisy, my dear gel," Lady Beatrice interrupted. "One does not talk about such vulgar topics at the dinner table."

"I'm not being vulgar," Daisy explained. "I'm asking about business."

"Which is a vulgar topic," the old lady said. "Anything to do with money is. Abby dear, tell me more about this play you are attending tonight. Who did you say is performing?"

Daisy rolled her eyes. The list of things a lady wasn't allowed to say was never-ending. She was bloody glad she wasn't going to be one—she'd never be able to open her mouth.

As Abby talked about the play, Freddy leaned towards Daisy and murmured, "After dinner. Meet you in the front parlor. Explain then."

Daisy grinned. "Thanks, Freddy."

* * *

"But why do you need to know all this?" Max asked. He had come with Freddy, and the two of them had spent the last fifteen minutes being peppered with questions about how Freddy had come to be a silent partner in Flynn and Co. and how the partnership had worked.

"I've been thinking about taking on a silent partner meself," Daisy told him. "Get the money I need to open a shop."

"We'll fund you," Max said. "You should have mentioned it sooner."

"Yes, of course," Freddy said. "Or if you don't want Max and me, the girls would love to invest in your business, I'm sure. In fact, come to think of it, didn't Damaris ask you about it a while back?"

"Yeah, she did, and I turned her down." Daisy turned to Max. "And thanks for offering, Max. I appreciate it, I really do, but I don't want to involve family."

He frowned. "But that's what family is for."

"Not for me it isn't," she said firmly. If it all went belly-up she didn't want her family involved. She'd only just gotten herself a family and she valued it too much—valued them too much to risk them in any way.

This way it was only money. Money came and money went.

Of herself and her ability to make beautiful clothes, she was confident. The ability to manage bigger amounts of money, and employ staff? And attracting the right sort of customers? And making sure they paid their bills? In those areas she was still to be tested.

"Ask Flynn, then," Freddy said. "He'd be in it like a shot. Always has an eye out for a good investment."

"No, not friends neither. I don't ask people for favors."

Freddy snorted. "You're too stiff-necked for your own good, young Daisy. Business is all about trading favors."

She shook her head. "I don't like owing people. And I won't take charity."

Max said dryly, "Freddy and I already have ample evidence of your pride and self-reliance. In some cases that's admirable, but—"

"The thing is, I've got someone who's interested. She's not a friend—more a customer, and an acquaintance—and she's got a nest egg, an inheritance from an aunt, just like you had, Freddy, and she's interested in what she calls 'investing.' So I thought I'd ask for your advice."

"What do you know of this woman?" Max asked.

"Not much. She's a widow—her husband was related to Lady Gelbart's husband. Lady Gelbart introduced us—she brought her to the literary society. Mrs. Foster—that's her name—said her husband left her very well off. She called the inheritance *free money* and wants to . . . I dunno, play at being a businesswoman, I suppose."

She liked Mrs. Foster, and she'd do her damnedest to make the business a success, but this way it wasn't personal. Only money.

She gave a silent snort. Hark at her thinking *only money* as if it grew on trees.

Max and Freddy exchanged glances. "How much does this woman want you to put up?"

"Nothing. She said she'd give me the money to get everything set up." She told them how much Mrs. Foster was willing to invest and they exchanged glances a second time. "She said we'd have to get papers drawn up, to protect both our interests, but that I'd own fifty-one percent of the business." She sat back. "So what I want to know from you two is, what's the catch?"

There was a long silence, finally Freddy shook his head. "Can't see one myself—not from what you've told us."

Max nodded. "It will all depend on the paperwork—the legal agreement she mentioned. Get Bartlett, our man of business, to arrange it. He's one hundred percent trustworthy, and he'll make sure there are no nasty hidden clauses to catch you out."

He added, "And don't look like that. You're not the only

one who worries about the family, you know. I accept that
you don't want us involved, but I won't have Abby worrying—"

"Or Damaris," Freddy interjected.

"That's right," Max continued. "You're our sister too and
we protect what's ours."

He fished his card case from his pocket, scribbled something on the back of a card, and handed it to her. "Give
Bartlett that. It will ensure his full cooperation. And when
the paperwork is drafted, bring a copy to me before you sign
anything."

"I'll look at it too." Freddy rose from his seat. "And that's
not a favor, Daisy-girl—that's what brothers-in-law are for."

Things moved very quickly after that. Max arranged for
Bartlett to call on Daisy the very next day—he didn't
think it suitable for Daisy to go to Bartlett's place of work,
which was the headquarters of Flynn and Co.

Daisy wasn't so sure about that—she would have liked
to see inside the offices of a worldwide trading operation—
but of course, she wasn't about to argue. Max was doing her
a favor, after all.

But it did cross her mind that Flynn wouldn't be so stuffy
about it.

She hadn't breathed a word of any of it to Flynn. She
didn't want to tell him until everything was finalized, and
that would depend on whether the silent partnership with
Mrs. Foster went ahead or not.

True to his word, he'd been back, and back, visiting her
as frequently as ever. Not to pester her, which she couldn't
have borne, but because he told her, "I don't aim to lose my
best friend over this."

Best friend. She felt a glow at his words.

"But don't think I'm givin' up," he'd added. "I'll ask you
just once, every day, in case you change your mind."

She wouldn't, but she was glad to know she'd be able to
keep seeing him. Even though it hurt. And even though she
wanted him fiercer than ever.

But it couldn't be. When it came to Flynn, it was look but don't touch.

Bartlett called on Daisy first thing in the morning—Lady Beatrice wasn't even awake. He talked to her about the partnership, what she wanted out of it, how she wanted to run her business and took her through every angle and permutation, peppering her with questions until she was quite dizzy.

He told her he'd call on Mrs. Foster's legal man next. "But don't look so worried, Miss Chance," he said as he tucked his meticulous and copious notes into a leather-bound folder. "We'll protect your interests. It all looks quite straightforward, but I'll make sure everything's tied up nice and tight." He smiled. "I must say, it's quite a change to be in on a business enterprise at the beginning. I look forward to watching your business grow."

"From your mouth to God's ears," Daisy said fervently. "Thanks, Mr. Bartlett."

He paused at the door. "Will you be wanting any assistance with finding a suitable premises? Because if you were, I'd be delighted to assist you."

She hesitated, not wanting to ask for too much.

He added, "I found this house for Lady Beatrice, and I also found the property that's Lord and Lady Davenham's London residence. Property is something of an interest of mine, so if you'd like . . ."

"It's very kind of you, Mr. Bartlett, but I dunno." Bartlett might be good at finding posh houses for rich folks, but a shop was a different matter altogether.

"What if I take a look at what's currently on offer and send you a list of possibilities? You could waste a lot of time, otherwise."

Daisy considered it. It would cost her extra, no doubt, but if it saved her time . . . "Won't it take you away from your work—your proper work, I mean? I wouldn't want to get you in trouble or nothing."

Bartlett smiled. "It won't get me into trouble—Lord Davenham himself suggested it. Besides, I have assistants who can deal with whatever comes up. Believe me, I'd enjoy the change."

"Then thanks, Mr. Bartlett, I'll take you up on that. Let me know what I need to do."

"I'll stay in touch."

"And Mr. Bartlett, would you mind not mentioning any of this to Mr. Flynn? I'd like to keep it a secret for a little while." Bartlett looked a bit uncomfortable—Flynn was his employer after all—so she added, "I'd like it to be a surprise."

Bartlett gave a short, clipped bow. "Trust me."

Within a few days, the silent partner agreement between Daisy and Mrs. Foster had been hammered out, the documents signed by both parties and a business account opened at the bank Bartlett recommended. Since it was the one that also dealt with Flynn and Co., Daisy was happy to go along with it.

Truth to tell, it was all rather intimidating. She'd hardly understood a word of the legal papers, outlined on thick legal paper, embossed and witnessed and sealed with red wax. And the sums involved were frightening to say the least. And the speed with which it all took place, it quite took her breath away.

But Bartlett explained everything in words she could understand, and at the end of it all . . . she owned a business. Money in the bank and all.

Bartlett had even arranged for one of his assistants—who turned out to be his nephew—to set up proper books and show Daisy how to keep track of money in and money out. It was a far cry from her stash under the floorboards in the attic at Mrs. B.'s. And different again from the bank account she'd opened under Max's guidance six months ago, when he'd learned she kept her money under her mattress.

So now she was ready to start. She'd prefer to hire seamstresses first—Flynn had been right the night of the masquerade ball when he pointed out to her that anyone could do the sewing, and that her talent was in design.

She'd have to interview women and see samples of what they could do but before that she needed to find suitable premises. She could imagine Lady Beatrice's face if Daisy arranged for a stream of seamstresses to line up for interviews outside the Berkeley Square house. It was bad enough that Lady Beatrice's own friends came to call for fittings.

She couldn't wait to get a shop.

She felt a bit guilty, keeping all these exciting developments from Flynn, especially since Bartlett was helping her so much and Bartlett worked for Flynn. But he also worked for Max and Freddy, which made her feel a bit better.

And with the best intentions in the world, Flynn would want to stick his bib in. He'd want to help and advise, and he'd end up taking over—just to help her, not meaning anything by it—and she didn't want that. This was hers, her very own business. Daisy Chance, who'd never owned anything.

So she wasn't going to tell him until she had all her ducks in a row.

"I've got a phaeton waiting downstairs," Flynn said a few days after Daisy had signed the papers. "I've come to take you for a drive."

"Sorry, Flynn, no time."

He made an exasperated sound. "Look at you—you're all worn out from workin' long hours, sewing your fingers to the bone and worryin'." He cupped her cheek and his voice softened. "You're gettin' thinner by the minute and you're as pale as paper. It's a beautiful sunny day—the kind of day you Londoners hardly ever see, so let's not waste it. Come for a drive in the park with me, just for an hour, and we'll put some roses back in your cheeks."

She shook her head. "Thanks, but I got to finish this."

"Then marry me and let me take you away from all this."

She smiled. "I don't want to be taken away from all this." Gawd no, not when she'd just signed a partnership agreement with Mrs. Foster and her dream was finally going to come true.

Her own shop. She could barely believe it. Not so long ago, all she owned in this world was a bundle of fabric scraps.

"But I want to take care of you."

She shook her head, charmed in spite of herself. "I can take care of meself, Flynn," she said gently. "Please, try and get it into that head of yours that I'm all wrong for you. Go away and find a nice, ladylike girl who *wants* to be pampered and cared for and live without a worry in the world. That kind of life would bore me stupid." Not to mention intimidate the life out of her.

"I don't want a nice ladylike girl," Flynn said. "I want you." He frowned. "That came out wrong."

She laughed. "It's all right, I know what you mean but really, I'm gettin' sick of hearin' this same old song. I've given you me answer, and if you're going to harp on about it, I'm goin' to have to ban you from my workroom."

"You wouldn't do that."

"Try me."

It wasn't him harping on marriage that was the problem, she acknowledged privately. It was him, coming around all the time, making her laugh, telling her stories, bringing her little things—even though she told him not to. Charming her.

And looking so blooming manly and handsome—and making no secret of how much he wanted her—it was killing her to resist.

He was slowly wearing her down.

She caught herself missing him when he went away— even for a few days—found herself looking forward to his visits—they were almost daily now.

The reason she was looking so tired wasn't only because of her long working hours, nor the nerves and excitement connected with the partnership. As much as anything it was dreams. Dreams of Flynn in her bed. Making her all hot and melty and . . . *bothered*.

It wasn't Flynn she didn't want; it was marriage.

"All right, I promise you I won't bring it up again—"

"Good."

"—today. You have to allow me at least one proposal a day." And before she knew what he was about he leaned in and gave her a swift but very thorough kiss.

Somehow, he managed to kiss her on every single visit. She tried to stay alert for it, to watch for it and prevent him, but . . . maybe she wasn't as vigilant as she ought to be. They were kisses to dream on.

He melted her bones every blooming time, and he knew it, the big rat.

Looking quite pleased with himself, he sat down opposite her, crossing his long-booted legs. "Now, what shall we talk about today?"

And that was another reason she couldn't bring herself to ban him from visiting her. He was quite happy to sit and talk to her for hours on end. It didn't slow her work down at all, and it was so good to have the company. Jane was busier than ever trying to juggle a gypsy and a lord—that couldn't end well, that was for sure—and now the Season had commenced, the house was always filled with company, which kept the maids busy 'til all hours.

Daisy knew how hard maids worked; she didn't want to make more work for them.

"I know," Flynn continued. "Tell me about how you found your sisters. Or did they find you? I didn't realize until the other day that it was such a recent event."

At that moment, Featherby knocked at the door. "Note for you, Miss Daisy. Hand delivered a moment ago." He presented it to her on a silver platter. "The, er"—he glanced at Flynn—"the sender said it was quite urgent you open it at once."

The note was sealed with a wafer and addressed to her in a cramped hand she recognized. Bartlett. Daisy opened it.

Suitable premises available for private inspection before noon today. Urge you not delay. Property on market tomorrow, and is of quality and price to be snapped up immediately.

The address was listed at the bottom. It was a street off Piccadilly—an excellent location. Daisy glanced at the clock. It was eleven already.

She put her sewing aside and stood up. "Sorry, Flynn, we'll have to talk another time. I've got to go out. Featherby, can you get me a hackney cab, please?"

Flynn rose, frowning. "What's this? You're going out? Now?"

"Yes." She grabbed her pelisse off the hook behind the door and shrugged into it.

"And yet you were too busy to go out with me."

"This is different." She crammed a bonnet on her head. No time to fuss about appearance.

"Is it?" He waited, but she wasn't going to explain.

"Sorry about this, Flynn, but I really do have to go. I'll see you later." And she hurried down the stairs.

Flynn followed.

"Any sign of that cab?" she asked Featherby.

"William is out in the street endeavoring to secure one."

She waited. And waited. Flynn received his hat and coat from Featherby.

Daisy paced back and forth in the entry hall, watching Featherby who was watching William. He would be hard to miss, William, but there seemed to be no cabs in the vicinity. She glanced at the hall clock. Quarter past eleven.

"It's urgent, is it?" Flynn said dryly. "Because as it happens I have a phaeton outside, waiting. I was intending to take you for a pleasant drive, but if we're rushing to a death bed . . ."

Daisy glanced at Featherby, who looked outside, then shook his head.

"All right then, thanks, Flynn." She was treating him badly, she knew. She gave him the address and he helped her into the carriage—lifting her, without warning, into it with his bare hands around her waist.

She didn't mind at all. It was lovely to be treated as if you were delicate and featherlight, even if you weren't.

"Lady Bea would smack you for that," Daisy said as he climbed in after her.

He grinned. "I know, but it's worth it."

She laughed.

"So, what's this place you need to get to in such a hurry?"

No point keeping it a secret now, so she told him everything, about Mrs. Foster and the silent partnership, about Max and Freddy, and about Bartlett and why they were going to this address.

He listened in silence and the more she told him the guiltier she felt, keeping it from him. It had been his suggestion, after all, that had begun it all. She'd thought she was protecting herself from his interference, but now it just felt . . . mean.

But not a word of reproach passed his lips.

And that made her feel worse than ever.

The shop wasn't quite what Daisy expected; for a start it wasn't for sale, but for lease—a five-year lease with an option to renew for another five years. In all other respects it was perfect. It even had gas connected, which meant light for working in during the dark of winter as well as heat.

"A lease isn't a bad idea," Flynn murmured in her ear. "Why tie up all your capital in a building?"

Because she wanted to *own* something. Something that belonged to her.

"If you lease the place, you could afford more staff and materials, produce more, sell more, and in five years, if you need to expand, you can."

She could see his point. She was glad now she'd invited Flynn to inspect the building with her. He'd offered to wait outside, but she felt mean enough without adding to it. "No, come in with me," she'd told him. "I'd be glad of another opinion."

To tell the truth, she was more than a little nervous. She'd never spent so much money in her life—never *had* so much money. The sums were quite frightening for a girl who'd earned a few guineas a year plus board and bed.

Gibbins, the agent, was a small dapper man, with an accent that started off as *quaite refained*, but once he realized he was talking to an Irishman and a Cockney, his East End origins became more apparent and his attitude slightly superior.

The more patronizing he became the less nervous Daisy got. She soon realized he'd discounted her completely; as far as Gibbins was concerned she might as well have been wallpaper.

From the beginning, he addressed himself entirely to Flynn.

To Flynn's credit he did nothing to encourage it—apart from looking big and impressive and beautiful, which she supposed he couldn't help. He hardly spoke a word, left it all to Daisy. As he should.

The agent's affectations didn't bother Daisy, but when throughout the inspection he continued to address himself exclusively to Flynn—when *she* was the one asking all the questions—she finally saw red.

She poked him in the ribs. "Oy, mate! *I'm* the one you're doin' business with, not him. And I'm standing over here."

Gibbins frowned and looked at Flynn for confirmation—which made Daisy even madder.

Flynn shrugged. "I'm just the driver."

Gibbins pursed his lips. "Do you mean to say the property would be leased by *a woman*?" He was still talking to Flynn. Daisy would have clipped him over the ear, except she really liked this building. The more she saw the more she wanted it.

Flynn's eyes hardened. "A lady, yes."

"And I'm *still* standin' over here," Daisy said, poking Gibbins in the back.

He turned stiffly. "But I understood . . . My communication was with a Mr. Bartlett."

"That is correct. My man of affairs," Daisy declared loftily.

Flynn had a sudden attack of coughing and turned his back. Daisy ignored him. To Mr. Gibbins she said, "Now, are we going to do business or does my man Bartlett have to tell the owner that you refused a good offer because you was too stiff-necked to deal with a woman?"

Gibbins looked unhappy. "I don't know . . . Don't you have a husband who can sign for you?"

Flynn shifted restlessly. Daisy was sure he was going to say something, tell Gibbins he was going to marry her or something. She narrowed her eyes at him in a silent death threat if he said so much as a word, then said to Gibbins, "No, I bloomin' well don't have a husband. I do however have a very healthy bank account. Now are you going to hiver-haver around like a kid in a sweetshop, or will you give me the lease?"

Gibbins was outraged by her plainspeaking, but after a moment he nodded. "It's very irregular, but I suppose so." He produced some papers.

Daisy hesitated—she wanted to sign them straight away, secure the shop immediately, but documents like these could contain legal traps for the unwary, and she knew she wouldn't understand the terminology. She took the documents. "I'll have Bartlett look through these, then I'll sign them and send them back. In the meantime I will take the keys." She held out her hand imperiously.

Gibbins hesitated.

"Big mistake if you don't," Flynn murmured.

Gibbins glanced at Flynn, looked at Daisy's face and meekly handed over the keys.

Daisy's fist closed over them. She held her breath, looking disdainful and imperious, until the odious little man had gone. She locked the door after him in case he changed his mind, then expelled her breath in a gust of relief. She turned to Flynn. "I got it, Flynn. I got me a shop!"

"You were brilliant, handled him perfectly," he said and seized her around the waist and twirled her around until she was dizzy and laughing. He let her slide slowly down his body, devouring her with his eyes.

A sudden tension filled the air. He lowered his mouth to hers, but after a brief brush of lips she twisted away, out of his arms, too full of excitement—too nervous and on edge—to let it go any further.

"Come on," she said, panting a little. "Let's look at it again."

"Haven't you already been over it with a fine-tooth comb?"

"Yes, but I had that horrible little man distracting me, and—I got a shop, Flynn!—I want to go over it all again now it's mine. Decide what I'm going to do with it." She was too excited to stand still.

With a rueful smile he followed her through each room again.

The shop—her very own place!—for the next five years, at least—was narrow, but it stood three stories high. The ground floor consisted of two sections, a more formal shop area with a gorgeous bay window, and a back section that was well-lit and spacious but a bit grubby and worn.

"Nothing a bit of paint and elbow grease won't fix," she declared. "I'll get curtains for that bay window—velvet, I reckon. Green. Or maybe ivory. And the same to screen off the back area. And a nice thick carpet on the floor. And some elegant chairs. And a huge big looking glass with gold edging. Maybe two."

The next floor up had big windows on two sides—the building was set on a corner block—perfect for a working area. Light was crucial for seamstresses. Of course some of them would take their work home, but most would be working here.

The back entrance led straight onto the stairs—there were two sets, one at the rear, that served the entire building, and one that just led to the first floor. "One for toffs and one for the rest of us," Daisy crowed.

The top floor would be used for storage, and for a place for her to work. She could already see the big table she'd place under the middle window. And a desk in the corner for the accounts and order books.

"I don't remember seein' this." It looked like a cupboard

but when she opened it, she found a narrow set of stairs. "Where do you reckon it goes to?"

The stairs led into a long, low attic room that ran the entire length of the building. Six windows were set into the sloping roof. They were dirty and didn't let in much light, but that was easily fixed. The room was dusty, but dry. Soap and water and a bit of elbow grease would make it a useful addition to their storage area. She glanced at the windows. Maybe even a working area.

At one end was an old bed, no mattress, just a bed-head, four legs and a frame of sagging ropes. In the middle was a long table that could be used for pattern drafting and cutting out. A couple of broken old chairs lay tumbled in a corner.

"Oh, look at this." A door at the end led out onto the roof. "You can see half of London from here," she breathed. "Look, Flynn—that's my kingdom out there. Ain't it beautiful?"

"Beautiful," he murmured and there was something in his tone that made her look around. He wasn't looking at the view at all. He was looking at Daisy.

"I'm that glad you came with me, Flynn," she said softly. "Thanks for being here, and for sticking up for me."

"I'm glad too," he said. "I needed to see my rival."

"Rival?" she frowned, puzzled. "What do you mean?"

"This." He gestured to the shop, his gaze not leaving her face. "This is what's keeping us apart, isn't it? What you want instead of me."

There was a long silence. The breeze picked up. Below her she could hear the rumble of the city, the cooing of pigeons. "It's not like that," she said at last.

"Isn't it?" There was a thread of bitterness in his voice.

And it was partly true, she couldn't deny it—but only partly. Gazing up into those blue, blue eyes, for once not gleaming with wickedness and laughter and arrogance, all her resolutions fell away.

It was marriage she was rejecting, not Flynn. Flynn she wanted with a burning hunger. And right now, with excitement coursing through her veins, on the doorstep of her dream coming true, she needed to show him, share this moment with him. Love him.

She stepped forward and placed her palms on his chest, feeling the strength and the warmth beneath her fingers. "I do want you, Flynn. I want you something fierce." And she pulled his head down to show him exactly how much.

Chapter Fifteen

*"Do come now," said he . . . , "pray come, you must come,
I declare you shall come."*

—JANE AUSTEN, *SENSE AND SENSIBILITY*

The moment she tasted him she realized how much she'd craved the taste of him, hot, masculine, dark and addictive. Her dreams were nothing to this.

Lord, but the man could kiss. The slow, deliberate slide of his tongue over hers melted her bones, stole the breath from her body.

She thrust her fingers into the thickness of his black hair and held him close, angling her mouth to explore him deeper. He moaned and his arms tightened around her.

Without breaking the kiss he lifted her and carried her to the table, setting her on it. Her legs opened and she wrapped them around his hips, pulling him hard against her.

She released his mouth and, panting, leaned back a moment just to look at him. His eyes were dark as the darkest night, midnight blue and yet somehow . . . hot. She reached for the buttons of his waistcoat just as he reached for the fastenings of her dress.

Their hands clashed and they laughed, and then the laughter died and she was feverishly undoing his waistcoat, undoing his elegantly knotted neckcloth and dropping it to one side. She reached into the opening of his shirt, desperate to feel him, skin to skin. Best quality linen but the neck was too narrow.

She ran her hands over him, enjoying the feel of his hard strength beneath the smooth fabric. Her fingers encountered his small masculine nipples, raised hard and wanting. She lowered her head and sucked one through the fabric of his shirt.

"God, lass, you're killin' me," he moaned. "Don't stop."

She shifted her attention to the other one, biting it gently and smiled as he groaned again, throwing his head back. He pulled away from her a little, and without thought her thighs tightened around him. She wasn't ready to let him go yet.

He felt it and gave her a swift smile. "Don't worry, I'm not goin' anywhere." He pulled the shirt off over his head and tossed it aside. It floated to the dusty floor unnoticed.

Daisy couldn't drag her eyes from him. Golden skinned with a sprinkling of dark hair across his broad chest, he was all hard, muscular man. "Gawd, Flynn, you're gorgeous." She traced the line of his chest with a finger.

"Men aren't gorgeous," he said but she could see he was pleased by the compliment.

"You are." She lifted her bum and wriggled and squirmed, tugging at her skirts.

"What are you doin'?" he moaned, his hips still locked between her thighs. "God, but you're killin' me, Daisy-girl."

"Sauce for the gander," she muttered.

"Callin' me a gand—" His words died as she pulled her dress up and over her head and dropped it on the table beside her. His gaze burned into her.

Her chemise was thin, fine cambric, perfectly plain and unadorned, but delicate enough to see through. She wore nothing underneath; her nipples would be visible. She could feel them hard and throbbing, eager for his touch.

"Now if we're talkin' beauty here . . ." He bent and, cupping her breast in one hand, he took one aching nipple in his mouth, sucking it through the fabric, and it was her turn to arch and moan. She clutched at his hair, kissing whatever part of him she could, her hands roaming over him, learning the feel of him.

Now her hands moved lower.

"We ought to—" The words died, strangled in his throat as her palm settled over the fall of his breeches, cupping him. Hard as he was, he hardened more under her touch. She rubbed her hand over his thrusting cock-stand, exploring the shape of him through the soft, supple doeskin.

"Don't," he groaned, pulling back. "I'll explode."

She made a sound, half laughter, half gasp. "That's the idea, ain't it?"

There was no breath of hesitation in her. She unfastened the fall of his breeches with fingers that were oddly clumsy. She wanted him—now.

She released him—he was a big boy, her Flynn. Her hand closed around the thickness of him.

He made a harsh sound, and she glanced at his face.

She could feel the tension in him—he was straining for control. She stroked down the length of him, light and delicate like thistledown, and he hardened even more beneath her touch. He was hard and soft—the skin softer than the finest doeskin, hard and hot beneath. She stroked him again, firmer this time, and watched as his eyes burned blacker and the tension in him mounted.

In both of them.

He was playing the gentleman, she realized dimly—letting her control how far and how fast. His body was shaking with the tension of it.

"It's you who's killin' me, Flynn," she whispered against the hot skin of his chest, because how could you not love a man like this? And yet she couldn't let herself. It could only ever be this. It had to be.

Enough waiting. He was drawn as tight as a bowstring, she was wet and throbbing, aching for him. Her thighs trembled with the wanting. And she was drowning in his sea-dark eyes.

She positioned him, feeling the hot, blunt tip nudging at her entrance. He needed no further sign. He surged into her, a long smooth possession that shuddered through her gloriously and she arched her back, thrusting her hips up to receive him.

He moved, thrusting, pulling back, thrusting . . . over and over . . . Her body welcomed him, hot and tight, gripping him like a glove, feeling so right, so good. Shudders started deep within her as she arched and clenched around him.

His fingers touched her where they were joined and she screamed and bit down on his shoulder. And shattered around him. Dimly she felt him come, as she floated away in a hot gush of ecstasy . . . and oblivion.

Daisy lay back across the table, one arm behind her head, the other resting on Flynn's bare chest. He was sprawled beside her.

She stretched and winced. "Ooh, we got to stop making love on tables."

He rolled over and stroked a finger up her bare thigh. "They have their charms—chiefly convenience—but you're right. From now on we'll make love in our bed. Comfort and convenience."

She sat up and looked at him. "'Our bed'? There is no our bed."

"When we're married, I mean."

She sighed. "We're not gettin' married, Flynn."

He sat up, frowning. "We damn well are."

"No, we're not."

He gave her a baffled, angry look. "What the hell was this about then?" He gestured to the table, their scattered clothes.

"Not marriage, that's for sure." She jumped off the table, straightened her chemise and picked up her dress.

He grabbed her and pulled her around to face him. "You said you wanted me—wanted me 'something fierce.' So what the hell are you playin' at—blowin' hot and cold?"

She shook off his grip and started pulling her clothes back on. "I do want you, you big Irish lout—haven't I just proved it?"

"Then—"

"I just don't want to get married. Especially now." She

picked his shirt up off the floor, shook it out and handed it to him. "Put your shirt on. It's distracting."

He ignored her. "Why especially now?"

"I've got even more to lose." She gestured to her surroundings.

"What the hell are you on about? What have you got to lose? If you marry me, you'll be a rich woman."

She shook her head. "Nope. If I marry you, everything I own will belong to you. That's the law."

"So? What difference would that make?"

Daisy gave him an exasperated look. Could he really not see? One of the girls at the brothel had been born rich. She married a handsome feller, but it turned out he was only after her money. He sold her home, took the lot and dumped her, leaving her penniless.

There was nothing she could do about it. It was the law: the moment she was married, her husband owned everything. She'd even gone to a magistrate. He'd tut-tutted and been very sympathetic, but the law was the law he'd told her, and there was nothing he could do.

That was how the poor girl ended up earning a living on her back in the brothel—through marriage.

Daisy suspected it was also the reason Mrs. Foster wasn't looking for another husband. Why would she, when life as a rich widow was ever so much more secure?

She looked at Flynn, who'd finally put his shirt on and buttoned his breeches and was much less distracting. "What if it was reversed?" she asked him. "What if everything you owned—all your ships and everything—got handed over to me. You wouldn't even have a say in what I did with it—not legally. Would you marry me under those circumstances?"

He hesitated.

"See?" she said softly. "That's how I feel too."

"I'd still marry you," he said.

She laughed. "You would not."

"I would. I'd trust you to do the right thing and give me my company back. It's not about legal rights, Daisy-love—it's about trust."

She bit her lip. "Ah, well then, that's me problem. I dunno if I can."

His hands froze in the middle of knotting his neckcloth. He was making a right mess of it too. "You wouldn't trust *me*?"

"Here, let me." She pushed him back to sit on the table, undid the neckcloth, shook it out, and snapped it straight to take the worst of the wrinkles out of it, running it back and forth over her bent knee.

He watched in silence, his eyes boring into her. She stepped between his spread thighs, and looped the narrow strip of muslin around his neck, trying not to be aware of how close he was. She could smell the scent of his body, enticing and masculine, feel the heat from his powerful thighs. The smooth friction of his jaw, dark with recently shaved whiskers. The feel of those whiskers on her skin was delicious.

For two pins she'd push him back and have her way with him again.

But that would solve nothing. Probably make it worse. There was a stiffness in him now that had nothing to do with arousal and everything to do with being offended. She'd trampled on his pride enough today.

She tucked the ends in and stepped back.

"Finished?"

She nodded. "It's not perfect, but it'll do."

"Thank you. Now you were about to explain to me why you wouldn't trust me."

"Well, I probably *would* trust you."

The stiffness eased slightly. Then he saw her expression and frowned. "But?"

She shrugged. "I'm a fool like that. I trust too easy. I been taken for a ride twice in me life, and lost everything both times by people I trusted." She shook her head. "I don't have no judgement when it comes to trusting people, not when me . . . not when feelings are involved."

"Feelings, eh?" He shifted closer.

She stepped back. "Yeah, feelings and I ain't saying any more, so don't push. It's hard enough as it is."

"It's certainly hard enough," he murmured, lowering his gaze.

She followed his glance to the fall of his breeches and laughed. "You're quick off the mark, ain't you? But I reckon it's a bad idea. You'll only start talking about marriage again."

He pulled her against him for a swift, hard kiss. "Count on it, darlin'. But not today. A proposal a day, remember? And we're done for today."

And because the man kissed like a dream, and she was already half melted and aroused—and because she was a weak-willed woman who had not a single bone in her body that could resist him—she rolled back on the table with him, and made love like there was no tomorrow.

Because the way things were going, there might not be, not for her and Flynn. If he kept going like this, she might have to stop seeing him altogether. It would half kill her, but she could see no solution to their problem.

He wanted marriage and she didn't. End of story.

Afterward they lay sated and boneless. Flynn was the first one to stir. The table was hard and uncomfortable. He pulled his clothing into place, gathered Daisy into his arms and carried her out to the place on the roof that overlooked the city. He settled her against his chest and they sat in silence looking out over the huge pulsing city.

Below them carts rumbled by, a picman called his wares, urchins shrieked, a dog barked—the sounds floated up, seeming to come from miles away.

It felt like they were sitting on top of the world.

"These two people who betrayed your trust so badly," Flynn said after a while. "Who were they? Men?"

Daisy shook her head. "Only one was a man—though I dunno that I'd call him a man. More of a worm, really. Artie Bell his name was." She was silent a while, reflecting, then she said, "I was sixteen and ripe for the plucking. He broke my heart and robbed me blind, the swine." She sighed. "I didn't have much but he took all me savings, everything I'd saved since I was a kid, every penny I'd ever earned. Not just the money neither—me few precious bits and pieces, some of them not valuable—just things that were precious to me."

The breeze was picking up. Flynn adjusted his position, and pulled his coat around her.

"A couple of bits of jewellery, a brooch one of the girls gave me when she left to get married—some of them did, you know. And a silver button that had fallen off the coat of one of the gentlemen. I offered to sew it back for him, but he told me to keep it, that he'd get a new coat." She glanced up at Flynn. "Who'd get a new coat instead of sewin' on a button? But that's toffs for you."

"How did he find your stash—this Artie, I mean?"

"Dunno. I had it hidden under a floorboard in the little attic room that I shared with one of the other maids. I dunno how he found it—I never showed it to nobody, not a soul— but the day he was gone so was me stash. Cleaned right out, every blessed thing—even the dust."

"Had you quarreled?"

"No, he just . . . disappeared. I was such a fool. Young love." She snorted. "Turned out he had a wife or two and kids by three more girls. He was a charmer, that Artie. A complete, cheatin' low-life rat."

"What happened to him?"

She lifted a shoulder. "Dunno. Come to a bad end, I hope."

He pulled her closer against him. "Who was the other one? The other person who broke your trust. Another lover?"

She made a bitter sound. "Wasn't a bloke that's for sure. But just as low."

"A woman? Who?"

She shook her head. "Doesn't matter any more. Water under the bridge."

But it mattered to Flynn. If he were to change his stubborn little wench's mind and convince her to marry him, he had to understand why she was so unable to trust him.

But right now she was stirring in his arms, stretching and

muttering about getting back to work. It would keep for another day. He'd made progress today.

This morning all he'd wanted was to take her for a drive. Now they'd made love—twice. She was a tough little nut to be sure, but sweet and clean and decent and loving, and he wanted her more now than ever.

He was a man who understood the long game, and he relished a challenge.

The next few weeks passed in a frenzy of activity for Daisy. She had taken the girls and Lady Bea to inspect her shop and Mrs. Foster as well, as her silent partner. They all had a fine time making suggestions, particularly for the decoration of the front part.

Pale green and cream with touches of pink was the final color choice—cream wallpaper with an embossed design, and shades of green for the curtains and furniture, and a few touches of pink, including pink light-shades, which Daisy claimed would give a more flattering light.

Mrs. Foster was hesitant to offer suggestions at first. "I'm supposed to be a silent partner, Daisy dear"—they were on first name terms these days—"so I don't think I should."

Daisy grinned. "I don't mind. I'll tell you if you get too bossy." She sobered a little. "It's your money I'm spending and it's the first time I've done anything like this. It's been me dream for so long, but I always thought me first shop would be a barrow down Petticoat Lane or one of the markets, not something as posh as this."

Louisa Foster was a little bit posh, but also surprisingly practical and Daisy felt more comfortable having someone to share the decision-making with.

Flynn too was very helpful and interested, but Daisy was a little wary of asking his advice—he had a tendency to take things over, did Flynn.

Although . . . She thought of that first time in the attic, making love on the table. He hadn't taken over then. He'd held back, letting her take the lead—and it wasn't easy— she'd felt how tense and tight-strung he was with the effort of holding back for her, waiting until she was ready. Not many men would do that.

The second time he'd taken her swift and hard and not quite so careful, letting himself go—a little bit rough, a little bit wild, but not quite out of control. A bold buccaneer kind of bedding that had driven her to the heights and over. She'd loved every minute of it, and her body had tingled and purred for ages afterwards.

She hadn't known it could be like that. Bloody glorious.

She was twenty-two or -three, or thereabouts—an experienced woman who thought she knew everything there was to know about tupping, but Flynn had shown her she didn't know as much as she thought.

She knew about techniques and positions—the girls at Mrs. B's were quite frank about that side of things, but it was all for the men's pleasure, not theirs. Women had to pleasure themselves, they said, because men wouldn't bother.

Flynn had seen to Daisy's pleasure every single time. He was a rare one, all right.

Being pleasured like that, the first time slow and careful, treating her like something precious, or the second time, taking her lusty and vigorous—he could take her any way he liked and she'd like it. But it stirred up feelings in her, feelings she didn't want to have.

He was going to break her heart, Flynn was.

When he finally understood that she'd never marry him, when he turned around and married the nice, genteel highborn lady he'd always wanted, it was going to kill her.

She'd survive, she told herself. Life was full of ups and downs and one thing she'd learned: She was a survivor.

Most days now she spent at the shop, supervising workmen—Bartlett had negotiated with the agent for a complete refit, bless him—interviewing women who could sew and embroider, getting in equipment and supplies, and getting things up and running.

She dealt with the upper floors first—making them fit for

her women to work in was her first priority. She had the walls
scrubbed, sealed and painted and the floorboards sanded and
polished to a satin smoothness—no sharp splinters or nails
would be left sticking up to catch her precious fabrics on. The
tables and benches too, she had cleaned and repolished.

Next was the attic. The big table that she and Flynn had
made love on—twice—was too big to take downstairs. It must
have been put together on site. Daisy decided to make the attic
her own area and use the table for plans and drafting. It was
light and airy and she loved the view from the roof.

She had it partitioned into two rooms, one three times the
size of the other. She had the big one lined with shelving and
storage cupboards. The small room contained the door to the
roof space. She had the whole attic painted and furnished and
installed a French enamel stove for winter warmth.

Louisa Foster's suggestion, those stoves—they were
clean and the fire was fully enclosed so there would be no
danger of flying sparks or hot coals or smoke escaping. Best
of all, they were wonderfully warming, Louisa said—she
found English houses so cold.

Daisy took her word for it and had one installed on each
floor. Women couldn't sew with cold fingers. Besides, as well
as being useful, they were elegant, unusual and French—toffs
loved things like that—especially if they were French.

By the time it came to decorating the ground floor area,
Daisy's fledgling business was up and running. She had half a
dozen women working for her and the orders she'd been losing
sleep over were all fulfilled, and more were coming in already.

Once work commenced on the ground floor, Lady Beatrice took to visiting every few days. After the first visit, she
had her own chair brought down, and sat enthroned in the
middle of things, impervious to hints that she was in the
way, with Featherby standing by in case she needed something. William was in Wales.

She watched the workmen like a hawk, raising her lorgnette, and aiming her ebony cane to point out that they'd
missed a bit. Daisy's big rough workmen trod lightly around
her, trying not to swear.

"It's a bit like workin' with the queen watching," one of them told Daisy.

"Why do you keep comin' back?" Daisy asked the old lady. "I thought you said talkin' business was vulgar."

"It is. At the dinner table and on all other social occasions it does not *do* to exhibit a vulgar interest in money and the making of it. A lady does not even acknowledge that such a thing exists. That is men's affair."

"Bugger that," Daisy said. "Yeah, sorry, I know I'm supposed to be stoppin' swearin'—but it's only you and me here. So if it's so bloomin' vulgar, how come you keep dropping in here every second day? I didn't think it'd be the kind of thing you'd be interested in at all, with all this dust and noise and big rough men clompin' around."

"No, dear gel, but it helps keep my mind off Jane's nonsense." Jane had taken William and Polly and gone gallivanting off to Wales. On a wild goose chase, Daisy reckoned.

"Besides," the old lady added, "I do like to watch men exerting themselves to please a woman. I find it quite refreshing. Quite"—She raised her lorgnette to eye a young worker who'd had the temerity to remove his shirt and was working in a string vest, his muscles gleaming with sweat—"Stimulating."

The ladies of the literary society were also curious about Daisy's new venture. They questioned her and Louisa about it endlessly during the breaks. They'd never known anyone who'd owned a shop, even though they shopped all the time.

Shopkeepers were beneath them and they'd never given them a thought. A few of the ladies were disdainful, it was true, but they'd never approved of Lady Beatrice including Daisy in all her activities—one had by-blows in the family, of course—men would be men—but one needn't acknowledge them, let alone include them in society events.

"Pish tush to that nonsense," Lady Beatrice had said— and Daisy agreed.

Most of the ladies, though—especially Lady Beatrice's particular friends—were excited and almost maternal on Daisy's behalf. Somehow, despite her lowly origins and common accent and the occasional bad language that still slipped out, Daisy had become their pet.

They were also fascinated by Louisa's involvement as a silent partner. You could see them considering it was something they might like to do—posh ladies never had enough to do, and were always mad for some new novelty. And for the moment Daisy's shop was it.

This level of interest wouldn't last, and Daisy was determined to make the most of it.

"Would it be vulgar to have a bit of a party at my shop the day I open it?" she asked Lady Bea one evening after dinner.

Lady Beatrice considered it. "Depends what you mean to do. How vulgar?"

"I mean invite people to the shop, give 'em wine and little cakes. And have Abby and the girls dressin' up, wearin' clothes I made and showin' them off."

Lady Beatrice's mouth pulled down. "My gels dressing up? I don't think—"

"A ladies-only party," Daisy said hurriedly, knowing the old lady wouldn't like men staring at the girls. "And only people we know. Like the literary society, only with clothes instead of books."

"No men?"

"Nope. Ladies only, and an invited guest list." Something a little bit exclusive and different. If they'd come, that is.

"Hmm." The old lady swung her lorgnette thoughtfully. "Let me think on it."

"What are you going to name the shop?" Mrs. Foster asked. She, Abby and Damaris stood outside the newly refurbished premises, contemplating the display in the front window. Currently it was elegant and discreet— Daisy thought a bit too discreet—just a single long white satin glove and a length of silk draped over an elegant black wrought-iron stand, but Damaris loved it. The shop was due to open the following week.

"Not sure yet," Daisy said. The name of the shop had been a frequent subject for discussion in the last few weeks.

"I thought just *Daisy Chance, Ladies' Fashions.* Lady Bea reckons it should be *Miss Chance, Mantua-maker*—only mantua-makers make court dresses and I don't, so I don't like it." Mantuas were old fashioned in Daisy's opinion.

"What about something French?" Mrs. Foster suggested.

"*Marguerite* is French for Daisy," Abby said.

"That's pretty," Damaris agreed. "And you could have a daisy—like this." She pulled out a small pad of paper and a pencil—she was never without one—drew something on it, and handed it to Daisy.

Daisy admired the sketch. It was a simple stylized daisy, elegant and stylish. "That's beautiful, Damaris. You're so clever. How you make something come alive with a few quick lines . . . But I ain't giving it a French name. I know it's all the rage, but I ain't French, and I ain't going to pretend I am."

"Neither are—" Mrs. Foster began.

Daisy cut her off. She'd already had this out with Lady Beatrice, who'd also favored a French name. "I know a lot of dressmakers pretend they're French, but it makes them look stupid, I reckon. Everyone knows they're faking it, and people just look down their noses when you pretend to be something you ain't.

"I don't mind fixing up me grammar, but I'll be bugg— I'll be blowed if I adopt any kind of accent—French or fake la-di-da." She glanced at Abby. "Like that Mrs. Pillburn-Smyth, who dresses nice and acts ladylike and elegant, and says things like 'How naice and how delaightful and how fraffly vulgah'—trying to sound like one of the nobs, but she ain't, and all the genuine nobs laugh at her behind her back—I've seen 'em, Abby, and you have too."

Abby nodded. "I know."

"I don't care if they don't like me accent or me name," Daisy said. "Me clothes are gorgeous! I make a woman *feel* like a woman—even if she *is* a lady—and if they want that, they'll come to me, not some pretend Frenchwoman or someone who sounds la-di-da but ain't."

The others laughed. "That's right," Abby agreed. "But you still need a name for your shop."

"How about just calling it *Chance* with a daisy beside it," Damaris suggested. She drew another quick sketch and showed them.

"I like it," Mrs. Foster said after a moment. "Elegant, discreet and a little intriguing."

Abby smiled. "A chance to be beautiful for everyone who shops here." Referring to the way she'd originally chosen the Chance surname.

Daisy thought about it, then nodded. "I like it too. *Chance* it is. With Damaris's daisy. In gold lettering—just here." She pointed. "Perfect."

Chapter Sixteen

It would be mortifying to the feelings of many ladies,
could they be made to understand how little the heart of
man is affected by what is costly or new in their attire.

—JANE AUSTEN, *NORTHANGER ABBEY*

It was the day of the opening. They'd decided on an afternoon party, so that the ladies who attended would then go on in the evening to their various social events and talk of Daisy's shop—that was the plan anyway.

The moment Lady Beatrice had decided to approve the party, she'd taken over all the arrangements, having elegant invitations made and sent out, inviting people herself, rather than making Daisy the hostess. "More difficult for them to refuse if it's me—besides, they're dying to see the place and this'll give them an excuse."

Featherby had taken on the practical aspects of the arrangements and had waved Daisy away, telling her to leave it all to him. He was enjoying himself, she saw, so she didn't argue. She had enough to do herself.

Abby, Damaris and Louisa Foster were all wearing Daisy-made outfits, and since it was ladies only, Louisa had talked Daisy into making a display of her gorgeous nightwear, not to be modeled in person—that would be too risqué—but on a dummy.

Daisy was reluctant at first; the nightwear was just a sideline. But Mrs. Foster had persisted, and when Abby and Damaris heard, they concurred.

"Remember how happy you made Lady Beatrice with that first lovely pink bed jacket you made her?" Abby prompted. "And how all her friends wanted one? They were your first orders, and helped get you started."

"And before you say they were for old ladies, remember how we first met?" Louisa reminded her.

Damaris added her mite, saying, "I loved wearing the nightgown you made me on my wedding night," and Abby nodded in agreement.

Daisy gave in.

When she came to arrange the nightwear, she couldn't decide which ones to show—she had a few finished and ready—so she ended up making quite a display, using a number of different dummies draped in sheer pink silk, the better to display the flimsy, naughty nightgowns and sumptuous bed jackets.

The only one unimpressed with the party arrangements was Flynn, who was put out that it was ladies only. "Why can't I come?" he asked for the umpteenth time.

"Because you're a man," Daisy retorted.

"Glad you finally noticed." He gave her a slow grin that made her insides melt.

"You can come and have a look after it's all over then," Daisy said with a little shiver of anticipation. She had plans for later.

Flynn made his presence felt anyway, sending several large bunches of red roses, each one with a single daisy at the center. Daisy set them in vases around the shop. The sweet rose fragrance was wonderful.

This time she left the daisies in place, because they were her shop's symbol. No one else knew who they were from, or the private meaning of the daisies. They were her own secret delight.

She'd given her employees the day off, and Featherby

and his minions took over the upstairs rooms, laying out trays of delicious-looking cakes and savories, dozens of glasses and crates of champagne.

"French champagne?" Daisy exclaimed. "I can't be wasting money on—"

"You don't expect the old lady to offer her guests anything less than the best, now do you?" Featherby told her. "Besides, she's paying. She insisted. 'Tell that stiff-necked gel of mine not to argue,' she said."

So Daisy didn't argue. She was thrilled. French champagne at an afternoon shop opening—that should get people talking about her shop all right.

Abby and Damaris arrived shortly afterwards. "It's so exciting, Daisy!" Abby said. "Everything looks wonderful. I wish Jane were here, she will be so sorry to have missed this, but . . ." She shook her head. Jane was still in Wales. "We brought you a little gift. It's from Damaris and me— and Jane too."

Damaris handed Daisy a small box. "It's just something small, but we hope it will be useful."

Inside the box were visiting cards, elegantly engraved in silver on a pale green card, with a daisy embossed and painted white with a gold center—just like the daisy on the window of the shop. The lettering said *Daisy Chance* and gave the name and address of the shop underneath.

"They're gorgeous," Daisy said. "But . . . I don't go visiting."

"No, but if you leave these in a dish—or better still have Featherby hand them around—ladies will take them," Damaris said.

"They're so pretty," Abby added, "and it might remind some ladies to patronize your shop."

Lady Beatrice was the next to arrive. Featherby had arranged a number of chairs to be brought in for the occasion, including the old lady's favorite chair. She seated herself in it and said to Daisy, who was pacing around like a trapped cat, "Don't look so anxious, gel—they'll come. I've never yet held a party that wasn't a crush and I don't intend to start now. Have a glass of champagne if your nerves are getting to you."

The words were barely out of the old lady's mouth when the first carriages arrived, stopping to drop their aristocratic female passengers off in twos and threes, then moving on to make way for the next. The ground floor soon filled with ladies, exclaiming and admiring, chattering and sipping champagne.

Abby, Jane and Louisa Foster's dresses were all admired, but the garments that got the most attention were the nightwear displayed in the back room. Daisy was flooded with enquiries.

"Cash only," she told them bluntly, and then to soften the blow added, "They're a very exclusive line and in short supply. French lace, you see."

A few ladies primmed up their mouths and stalked away, offended, but the word *exclusive* did its job and a number of ladies gave her orders, promising to send their maids with the money the following day.

"What are you doing?" Louisa hissed when she found out what Daisy was telling people.

"Starting as I mean to go on," Daisy said. "Nobs are famous for not paying their bills. So I'm lettin' them know upfront that it's pay or nothing."

"They won't put up with it."

Daisy grinned. "Twenty-two orders so far, and their maids are bringin' the money around tomorrow. I told 'em cash down or I won't start."

Louisa stared at her, then started to laugh. "You're an original, all right."

The last of the guests had left, Featherby and his minions had tidied away the party detritus, and Lady Beatrice, along with Abby and Damaris, was ready to leave.

"Are you coming, Daisy?"

"No, I've got things to do."

The old lady raised her lorgnette. "What things?"

Daisy gestured to the workroom behind. "I need to take

down this display and get things set up for me girls to start work again in the morning."

"We'll stay back and help," Abby offered.

"You'll do nothing of the sort," Daisy told her. "You're carryin', and you're dog tired, as anyone can see."

"Then I will—" Damaris began.

"No, you all get along home—it's easier to do it meself. And you know, it's been such a grand day, I don't want it to end. So I'll just take me time and enjoy meself here a little bit longer. In me own little empire."

Lady Beatrice frowned. "But how will you get home? Shall I send a carriage? And leave one of the footmen here?"

Daisy gave the old lady a dry look. "I got meself all around London—the worst parts of London at that—all me life without a footman or a carriage, and I can manage now, thanks all the same." They'd had this argument a million times; Daisy wasn't a sheltered society maiden and had no intention of becoming one. Might as well stick a London sparrow in a golden cage.

"But—"

"Stop fussin' now." She leaned forward and kissed the old lady on the cheek. "I'll be home later, so don't you worry. You're going to the opera tonight, ain't you?"

"Yes, but—"

"Then go home, have your nap and get all dressed up and gorgeous for Covent Garden. I'll be tucked up in bed and snorin' me head off before the second act even starts."

Lady Beatrice sniffed, but consented to depart, muttering something about stubborn gels.

Daisy locked the front door after her and hurried around, tidying up. She'd just started to dismantle the nightwear display when the knock she was expecting came at the back door. She hurried to open it.

"How'd it go?" Flynn asked.

She gave him a triumphant grin. "Twenty-eight orders! And almost all the little cards Damaris and Abby gave me have gone—and there were a hundred there when we started. This is all that's left—ain't they pretty?" She showed him the cards.

"Well done then." He watched as she dismantled the nightwear display. "You know, I reckon it was a mistake restricting the event to ladies only."

"Why?"

He nodded towards the last dummy, draped in an enticing black silk-and-lace affair. "If men saw that they'd become your best customers. Only not perhaps if they were with their wives."

Daisy gave him a thoughtful look. "You might have something there." Perhaps another shop, in a different part of town. Under a different name . . .

"Now, what was it you wanted me for?" Flynn said. "To get me all hot and bothered looking at that?"

She hid a grin. He wasn't so far off. "Come upstairs—there's something I want to show you." She almost laughed out loud, hearing herself say it. Gawd, she sounded like one of the girls at Mrs. B.'s. She was ridiculously nervous.

He followed her up to the attic, admiring the changes she'd made. "But why partition that end off? Isn't that where the roof door is?"

She opened the door to the smaller of the rooms and stepped inside.

He stopped dead in the doorway. "A bed?"

She nodded. She'd had the old bed refurbished, the rope framework restrung and tightened, and bought two new mattresses, one stuffed with wool and the top one with feathers. It was all made up now, ready for them, a soft crimson blanket spread over crisp white sheets and downy pillows.

It was a cool afternoon and clouding over, so she'd shut the door onto the roof, and then as an afterthought, placed lighted candles all around the room. The room was bathed in warm, soft candlelight.

She swallowed, her mouth suddenly dry. "I know I said I wouldn't be your mistress, Flynn, but . . . I've changed me mind."

"About marryin' me?"

She shook her head. "About bein' your mistress. I know it's risky, but this is as private as it can get, so if we're careful . . ."

He gave her a hard look. "I want more from you than just bed, Daisy."

"I know. But I ain't any kind of a wife, so this is all I can offer you." She drew back the bedclothes and was annoyed to realize her hands were shaking.

He didn't move. His eyes were hard and unreadable. The angles and planes of his face were shadowy in the candlelight. His mouth, his beautiful, clever mouth was set in a firm, unmoving line, his lips pressed tight.

Oh lordy, he was goin' to turn her down. She felt herself shriveling inside with the mortification of it, and made herself shrug and say in a careless, it-don't-matter-to-me voice, "Of course, if you're not interested . . ."

"I'm interested, dammit." He pulled her hard against him, cupped her jaw in one big hand and kissed the living daylights out of her.

She thought she knew what to expect but each time with Flynn was different. His kiss was almost savage at first, his mouth possessing her, his tongue plundering, hard, almost angry. Her blood rose in response to the barely leashed violence in him and her body thrilled to each rough, feverish caress.

And then quite suddenly he broke off, and simply wrapped her in his arms, holding her close, breathing heavily, like a man who'd run a mile.

"God help me," he muttered, and then he started kissing her again, this time lavishing her throat, jawline, her eyelids with feather soft caresses, as if she was some delicate piece of china or jade from one of his collections.

She melted.

It was the hardest thing of all to resist about Flynn, the way he could go from an almost out-of-control lust for her, to this, treating her so delicate and sweet, making her feel so special . . . cherished.

No one had ever cherished her.

She pushed open his coat and started to unbutton his waistcoat but he stopped her with a rough gesture, trapping her hands behind her. "No, not this time." His blue eyes burned into her. "First I'm going to peel you naked as an egg, Daisy Chance. And then I'll have my way with you. And then—maybe—I'll let you near my buttons."

True to his word he peeled each item of clothing from her, one by one, with agonizing slowness, her spencer, her dress, kneeling to remove her slippers, sliding his hands under her chemise to undo the ties that held her stockings, then rolling them down one by one, his big warm hands smoothing down her legs. After each stocking he planted a slow deliberate kiss in the arch of her foot, making her toes curl and sending shivers up and down her spine.

When she was down to her chemise, he sat back on his knees—her own had given way by then and she was sitting on the bed—and just looked at her. He bent forward and took one aching nipple delicately between his teeth, rolling his tongue against it, and then biting lightly, delicately. She gasped as a bolt of fire shot through her.

He smiled and moved his attentions to the other breast. With each caress, her breath hitched in a series of gasps. She leaned back, clutching the bedclothes in her fists as he laved and sucked and nibbled at her through the fine cambric of the chemise.

He rose and with a single sweep her chemise was gone and she was bare as an egg while he was fully clothed.

He sat back on his heels and simply looked at her, and she felt herself blush, because experienced woman or not, she'd never been stark naked before a man, not like this. She tensed. She wasn't much to look at she knew, little as she was, with no curves to speak of, and slight, small breasts, but the way he was looking at her . . . as if he could eat her up. As if she was . . .

"Beautiful," he murmured and bent and kissed her. Oh, those kisses . . .

Wherever his mouth touched, heat followed. Need built within her and she reached to pull off his coat, but was firmly restrained. He kissed her again, then moved to lavish attention on her breasts, teasing the nipples to aching, almost painful hardness, scraping lightly across them with teeth, and his whisker-roughened jaw.

His mouth closed over one and he soothed with his tongue and then sucked, and she almost screamed and came off the bed as a lightning flash shot straight from her breast to deep in her belly.

And then he was kissing her mouth again, his tongue tangling with hers, moving in a rhythm that was a promise of things to come. Drugging. Addictive. And all the time his hands moved over her, caressing, arousing, slow and sure and possessive.

She must have said something, because he murmured, "Like my kisses, do you?" and started to kiss his way down her body, along her throat, over her breasts, down over the softness of her belly and then he parted her thighs, and kissed the soft inner skin of her knees.

There was a pause as he simply looked at her there. She squeezed her eyes shut, trying not to feel self-conscious. He leaned slowly forward until his mouth was only a hairs-breadth away from her. His warm breath stirred the curls there, and she wanted to move, but didn't dare.

And then—"Flynn!" Her eyes flew open wide.

He pressed his face between her thighs and just breathed her in. Thank God she'd bathed that morning. She'd heard of this, of course, but no man she'd ever heard of would do it. They wanted it the other way, the girl's mouth on them.

She could hardly breathe for waiting.

He started on her . . . licking and tasting her like . . . like a cream-filled pastry, slow, luscious sweeps of his tongue, eating her up in small nibbles and nips, and ohhh . . .

Her world dissolved. There was just this moment, this bed, this man . . . and his beautiful, talented mouth.

She tasted of wine, the sea and a hint of roses, a musky sweet-salty taste that fired his blood and was Daisy, essence of Daisy. Wine and fire and spicy, salt-dark female.

He found the tiny nubbin between the creamy folds and circled it with his tongue, giving it the same treatment as he'd given her nipples earlier.

Her breath caught on a series of rising hitches. She arched beneath him and he felt her thighs begin to tremble. He slid a finger inside her and took her to climax, then as she lay, loose and soft and sleepy-sweet with passion well spent, he stripped off his clothing.

She watched him with appreciative eyes.

"I never knew a man could be so beautiful, Flynn," she murmured and ran a lazy hand down his spine when he sat on the side of the bed to pull off his boots.

He turned and looked at her. "Beautiful?" He snorted. "Men aren't beautiful. If you want to see beautiful, look in a mirror, girl."

It was Daisy's turn to snort.

He didn't bother trying to argue. She didn't see, didn't understand how special, how precious, how beautiful she was. He could spin words with the best of them, but words would never convince her. A lifetime of experience, a lifetime of being unwanted and used and let down was more powerful than any words he could give her. He'd just have to show her, over and over. And hope that eventually she'd trust him—and herself—enough to say yes.

He'd almost lost his temper when she'd first shown him that little room, so carefully constructed to hide away an illicit affair. He didn't want an affair, illicit or not—he wanted to build a life with her, raise a family. He wanted to have her walking openly on his arm, to show her off—*this is my wife!*— to stroll in the park, to sit down at the table, to be announced as they entered a ballroom, as Mr. and Mrs. Patrick Flynn.

When she'd first shown him the room, so carefully and lovingly prepared, her eyes glowing with shyness and uncertainty in the candlelight, the frustration had almost boiled over. He'd wanted to seize her, throw her over his shoulder in the most primitive fashion and drag her off to some . . . some cave where he'd make love to her until she understood finally where she belonged. Who she belonged to.

But she was so sweet and brave, tough on the outside and yet so vulnerable, and true—she hadn't led him on, hadn't promised him anything, but was offering him a priceless gift—herself, and at some risk—and he'd managed to leash the wild man within him.

Now she lay watching him with eyes soft and dark with the remnants of spent passion and a hint of growing arousal. She was giving him all she thought she had to give. It was up to him to show her she was wrong, that there was so much more—for both of them.

He made love to her then, intent, focused. She was ready, more than ready for him. He entered her with one smooth, slow thrust. Her hips rose eagerly to meet him. She held him tight, like a slick hot glove, her legs locked around him.

He paused, buried deep within her, his senses flooded with her scent, her taste, the silken soft heat of her, then loosened the wild man within him, taking her a little bit rough and a little bit wild.

She clutched at his shoulders, thrusting her hips with each movement, tightening her grip to bring him deeper, pulling him in, holding him hard, scratching, biting, bucking, kissing. The muffled noises she made fired his blood as the age-old rhythm caught them both.

He took her fast and hard, sweaty and slick and glorious.

His blood thundering and roaring for release, he felt her climax begin and heard himself give a triumphant shout as he shattered deep within her. And slid into oblivion.

He came to himself some time later. Daisy still slept, pale, sweet and vulnerable, her cheek pressed against his chest, her palm loosely curled over his heart, her legs still twined around him. He pulled the bedcovers over them and tucked her more closely against his body.

He wanted to spend the whole night with her here, where the outside world didn't intrude. But she would stir soon, muttering about getting back to work, or having to get home to Lady Bea or dinner or some other damned thing.

Above them the slanted roof window let in the last of the cool grey evening light. A spatter of tiny raindrops heralded the change of weather. But inside their tiny attic room all was golden, warm, cozy. Daisy slept on, her breath warm little huffs against his skin, her small, soft body curled trustfully against him.

Half a loaf was better than no loaf at all, his mother used to say.

But sometimes all it did was make you realize how hungry you really were.

In the following weeks Daisy's life passed in a flurry of activity. Dream-of-a-lifetime or not, it wasn't all beer and skittles. It was harder than she'd expected, forming a group of women into a team.

In the first week she had to sack one girl for nicking things, and another smelled so bad the rest of the girls complained. It turned out that she and her family lived in one room in a slum dwelling and the poor girl had only one dress to her name, and no place to wash, let alone money to buy soap. But she could sew like a dream.

Daisy immediately provided her with some lovely rose-scented soap, hot water, privacy and two complete changes of clothes and the problem was solved. Though of course then all the other girls wanted rose-scented soap as well.

Still, she now had the best-smelling seamstresses in London.

Then there were the accounts. Bartlett's nephew, Edgar, came three days a week to do the books, pay bills and write out invoices—he had an elegant hand, much nicer than Daisy's—but there was still a lot of paperwork, and Daisy struggled.

"Would you like me to do that?" Louisa Foster said one day when she visited and found Daisy swearing over an account. "I used to keep the books for my husband in his later years. I quite enjoyed it."

"*Enjoyed* it?" Daisy stared at her. "You *want* to do this? Are you sure?"

"Positive. I'm rather bored, if you want to know the truth. The Season is all very interesting and enjoyable, but time does hang heavy on my hands, I confess. So if you don't mind . . ."

"Mind? I'd love you to do the rotten things." And within the week, Louisa had taken over all the paper administration, leaving Daisy to handle the staff, design the clothes, and deal with customers.

Customers were the hardest. Daisy was perfectly comfortable doing fittings and discussing designs with clients, and she was good at selling. But there were times when she was "less than tactful" as Louisa put it—*not takin' shit from snooty bitches* was Daisy's version—and after a couple of weeks, Daisy realized she needed an assistant.

She interviewed a few and tried out several women, but none of them suited—they either put on false airs and the kind of pseudo-gentility that made Daisy want to strangle them, or groveled to the customers in a way that made her want to smack them.

Louisa Foster would be perfect—she'd helped out a couple of times—but she didn't want to work full-time. And besides, it would be awkward, waiting on ladies she knew socially.

In the end, Daisy found the solution right under her nose.

Polly the maid, back from Wales with Jane, was so interested in the shop she couldn't keep away—even visiting on her afternoon off. Daisy was frantic that day—there were several customers waiting, getting impatient.

Polly took in the situation at a glance and stepped in, soothing and placating and showing the ladies some of the new designs, quite as if she'd worked there forever. Her handling of the rich difficult ladies couldn't be bettered—she'd spent a lifetime doing it, after all—and at the end of the afternoon Daisy offered her a job, much to Lady Beatrice's disgust.

"Poaching my maids now are you, missie? Next you'll want Featherby and the clothes off my back."

"I made that dress of yours for you, and no, I don't want it back," Daisy retorted. "And I couldn't pinch Featherby from you if I tried. He's already turned down handsome offers from half the nobs in London!"

Lady Beatrice's eyes almost popped. "He has? Good heavens! And he refused? Well, well . . . I must increase his wages."

The launching of her business was endlessly exciting and challenging, but the thing Daisy most looked forward to in her week was making love with Flynn in stolen moments after all her workers had gone home.

He was completely discreet, making the arrangements by dint of a handwritten message delivered by a servant. *Needed, best quality gentleman's glove. Do you stock?*

And she would send a reply, depending on her situation, quoting a price that was code for a time. He would wait until her girls had left and the shop locked up, enter by the back door and go quietly up the back stairs.

She claimed pressure of work as the excuse for her lateness in returning to Berkeley Square, and Lady Beatrice, though clearly not happy with the situation, said nothing about it. Thankfully, planning Jane's wedding was taking up most of the old lady's attention.

The evenings were getting longer and warmer, and it was heavenly to lie in bed after making blissful love with Flynn, looking out over the rooftops of London, and talking. They never ran out of things to talk about.

She was learning more about her big Irishman—not just the things he could do with his hands and mouth and tongue, and what he liked her to do to him—but about his life before he came to London.

He was a born storyteller and was happy to tell endless tales of the Far East, exotic islands, strange and fascinating— and sometimes horrifying—peoples that existed in far-flung lands, though she wasn't sure whether the story of his narrow escape from the cannibals was real or made up.

He talked of how he first met Max—they were shipmates, and didn't like each other initially—and how their friendship developed into something that changed both their lives. Max taught him how to read and write and do sums on paper— Flynn had always done them in his head—and Flynn taught Max the ways of the sea, and about the foreign places they visited. They were new to Max, but not to Flynn. The two men were much the same age, but Flynn had been at sea since he was twelve, whereas Max sailed for the first time at eighteen. "We taught each other the necessities of life—'tis a grand thing indeed to be able to read and write—and I taught him how to fight like a pirate, not like a gentleman."

"Did you fight pirates?" Daisy was wide-eyed, imagining it all.

He laughed. "We fought lots of people, but it depends what you mean by pirates. Some of the worst pirates I've met look like respectable gentlemen."

She snorted. "And some wear earrings to prove it." She eyed his earring sourly. She'd never liked him wearing it, made him look common, she reckoned, but Lady Bea liked it, and so did Flynn, so the blooming earring stayed.

"I know why you wear that thing," she said. "It's to get up their noses."

"Whose noses?"

"The toffs. You dress like a toff but you wear that"—she jerked her chin towards his earring—"to let them know you're nobody's tame tabby cat, to let them know you don't give a toss whether they accept you or not. That you play by your own rules."

He fingered his earring fondly and grinned down at her. "Clever little puss, aren't you? Come to think of it, Miss Daisy Chance, you're somewhat of a pirate yourself, the price you charge me for those waistcoats. Don't I even get a discount now you have a shop and workers?"

"Nobody's makin' you pay me prices—go elsewhere if you like. But it's worth it at half the price—I mean double—"

"My point exactly."

They both laughed and that led to another round of making love, this time filled with teasing and banter and laughter. Nothing was ever routine with Flynn. She wasn't just becoming addicted to his lovemaking, she craved his company almost as much, and his stories.

He told her how he first became a trader and later taught

Max how to bargain, and how to spot unusual items that would resell well elsewhere. "You're a magpie, you'll understand," he told her one evening.

She stiffened. "Who are you callin' a magpie? Noisy rotten birds. And they swoop."

He laughed. "Settle down, hedgehog, it wasn't an insult. I'm one too."

"Oh?" She waited, unconvinced.

"When I first went to sea, whenever we landed, the other seamen headed for the whorehouses and spent what they had on women and drink and gambling. Not me. I liked to pick through the markets and little shops in the Orient, collectin' anything that took me fancy. Later I'd sell them on in some place where people had never seen such things. Turned out I was good at buyin' and sellin'—and the rest is history." He smiled. "See, we're magpies, you and me—we have an eye for the unusual. Makes us a good match."

She avoided that one. She usually changed the subject when he brought up marriage. But she loved hearing his stories, learning about his life, picturing him as a young seaman, poking through the markets. And showing young Max the ropes.

Rarely if ever did he mention Ireland, or why he left it, only that he was never going back there. "There's nothing for me there," he'd say whenever she pushed to know more, and then he'd change the subject, usually with some funny story.

Then one evening when the air was soft and warm with the promise of summer and they were sitting on the roof, Daisy snuggled up against him, his arm around her, watching the sights below, Flynn stiffened.

She followed his gaze to a woman pushing a cart containing a man who looked to have lost both legs. Behind came five ragged little children, following like a string of bedraggled ducklings, each one smaller than the last. The littlest one was being carried by a girl not much bigger.

Flynn stared for a moment, then with a muttered oath, put Daisy aside and abruptly stood.

"What is it?" she asked, but he left without a word.

She saw him a few minutes later, crossing the road and talking to the man and woman. He passed them something and the woman started weeping.

He left them as abruptly as he arrived and a moment later he returned, seized Daisy, pulled her onto the bed and made love to her with a focused intensity—all without a word—giving her climax after climax before pouring himself into her with a groan that sounded so pain-filled it tore at her heart.

Afterwards he lay with his head pillowed on her breast, silent and withdrawn. She lay stroking the thick dark hair from his face—he needed a haircut—listening to him breathe, hearing the distant sounds of the city coming in through the open door.

It caught him like that sometimes, afterwards, left him bleak and silent and withdrawn. Lost. She felt at the same time closer to him and more distant. He never would talk about it, and most of the time she was content to accept it.

Not this time. "Who were they?" she asked finally.

For a long time she thought he wasn't going to answer—nothing new there—but then he sighed. "No one—just one of the many poor bastards tossed on the scrap heap, and their whole family with them."

"Did you know them?"

"No. But in a way, I did . . ." And then he told her about his father, who worked with horses when Flynn was a boy. He'd had a real way with them, like magic, it was, until the day he was kicked in the spine and never walked again. He told her how his mam had slaved to keep them all—five kids there were—fed and warm, and how it was always a losing battle.

The rich man who his dad had worked for was sorry about the accident, but said it was God's will, and nothing he could do. He'd given Mam a few pounds one day and the next day his agent came with the news they had to leave the cottage they'd lived in all their lives. The cottage was for able-bodied workers and their families, not useless cripples.

"Me mam found us a couple of rooms in a hovel, and after a bit I left home to look for work in Dublin."

"How old were you?"

"Twelve. I was the eldest, so it was down to me. No jobs in Dublin for a skinny kid, so I became a wharf rat, sent home whatever I could every week through the parish priest—just a few coppers here and there. Not enough. Never enough."

Daisy smoothed his hair back. "You did your best."

He shook his head. "After about a year I went home— something wasn't right, I felt it in me bones, even though the messages came through from Mam the same as ever." His voice was bitter. "Neither me mam nor I could read or write, you see, so it was the priest writin' the messages . . . They didn't sound like Mam at all."

She waited, holding him, stroking him, feeling the tension, the anguish in him.

"Turned out they'd all perished of the cholera—every last one of them, Mam, Da, Moira, Mary-Kate, Paul, Rory and wee Caitlin. They'd been dead and buried for months."

The raw pain in his voice shattered her. "And no one had told you?"

He shook his head. "The priest had kept taking me money and making up the messages from Mam—he said he was using it for the good of others but I could smell the drink on his breath." He swore again. "So I hit him. A mortal sin that is, I reckon."

There was a long silence. He wasn't finished yet, she could feel from the tightness in his body.

"I couldn't even find a grave—they were all tossed in a pit—buried with strangers, dozens of people all together. 'A cholera outbreak in the slums, you see, boy. Nothing else to do.'"

"Oh, Flynn." She hugged him tight, wishing she could ease his pain. No wonder he said there was nothing for him in Ireland. Just bitterness and grief. And the unreasonable guilt of a thirteen-year-old boy who blamed himself for failing to save his family.

"So I left, walked back to Dublin, down to the docks and sailed away on the first ship that would take me."

"And you never went back?"

"Never. There's nothing for me there. I'll make meself a new life, a good life here, and you'll be part of it, won't you, Daisy-girl?"

He meant a new family. Daisy felt the guilt twist inside her. He'd get no family from her. She ought to cut him loose to find a nice girl who'd give him one, but she couldn't give him up. Not yet. Not when she'd just found him. Selfish she was, she knew it.

"What did you give those people in the street?" She gestured to the window.

"Nothin' much, just a bit of money to feed the wee ones—that little girl carrying the tiny one—our Mary-Kate used to carry wee Caitlin just like that, and her no bigger than a flea herself." His eyes had a faraway expression that told her he was seeing his little sisters in his mind. "And I told them to see Bartlett. I gave them a note for him. He'll find something for the man to do. Just because his legs are gone doesn't make him any less of a man."

"You're a good man, Patrick Flynn," she whispered, feeling tears prickling at the back of her eyes. She tightened her hold on him.

He turned in her arms and proceeded to make slow, intense, tender love to her, and Daisy found herself tearing up again with the feelings that swelled within her, too full to be contained.

"What's this?" he said, wiping away a tear with one finger.

"Nothing, just . . . sometimes the feelings get . . . too much."

"Then marry me and we'll have a bunch of little feelings together."

She almost burst out howling at the tender way he said it. Instead she forced herself to say, "Ah, Flynn, why keep asking me? You know I won't marry you. This is lovely but it's not going to last. You got to start looking for a nice girl to wed."

"I know. I've found one."

"What?" Her eyes widened. Not already, surely? She wasn't ready to lose him yet.

"Jealous are we?" He gave a soft laugh. "No need, me girl's right here." He kissed her. And the sweetness of that nearly broke her heart too.

Chapter Seventeen

"'How hard it is in some cases to be believed!'

'And how impossible in others!'"

—JANE AUSTEN, *PRIDE AND PREJUDICE*

Flynn called at Berkeley Square one Sunday afternoon, intending to invite the ladies—Daisy in particular—for a drive, but when Featherby opened the door he held up a finger saying, "Miss Daisy's in the front drawing room with a . . . a *person*. Someone she knew, from *before*." The way he said "*person*" and "*before*" spoke volumes. He gave Flynn a meaningful look.

"Someone from the brothel, you mean?"

Featherby nodded, looking relieved that Flynn knew about the brothel. "The Abbess herself, I think. I didn't like to leave Miss Daisy alone with her, but she insisted."

"Does she need me?"

"Not at the moment, but she might. Best to just listen." The two men tiptoed to where the drawing room door stood slightly ajar. Flynn glanced at Featherby with a raised brow. No accident that that door wasn't properly closed.

Featherby shrugged, as if to say *How else could I keep an eye on things?*

Flynn bent his year to the door and listened.

"Yeah, I know I owe you," Daisy was saying. "You picked

me up and took me in when I needed it—I know all that, and I'm grateful. But gawd knows I've paid you back for it a hundred times over—I worked for years for you for no pay—just a tip every now and then from one of the gentlemen."

There was a muttered response that Flynn didn't catch. He and Featherby edged closer.

Daisy continued, "And I'd still be workin' for you if you hadn't gone off and left me—and all the other girls—in your bloody son's evil hands."

"I couldn't help that," the other woman said. "He was my son, and—"

"And a vicious bloody thug wiv women—and don't try to kid me that you never knew it because you and I both know you never let him near your girls while you was running the brothel!"

Flynn wished he could see. He must have made some kind of frustrated noise, because Featherby silently indicated the slight gap between the door and the hinge. Flynn pressed his eye to the gap.

He couldn't see Daisy, but he had a good view of the Abbess. She was a raddled dame of sixty or more, elaborately dressed in a low-cut dress of satin and lace, her face and well-displayed bosom powdered and rouged. Her hair was elaborately curled and dyed a garish yellow, augmented with clusters of false curls.

"But what else could I do? He was my s—"

"You coulda *warned* us, coulda said you wanted to retire and was gunna hand everything over to Mort. Coulda given us a *choice*." Flynn wished he could see Daisy's face.

She stormed on, "But no, you ups and disappeared and the first we know of it there was locks on all the doors and we was *prisoners*. And Mort's bringin' in all the nasty customers—the ones who like hurtin' girls—and then he's kidnappin' girls and buyin' them off ships because he can't get nobody to work for him."

"I didn't know nothing about that," the woman whined. "And I'm that sorry, Daise. But I don't want to talk about the past. I miss you something terrible." She gave Daisy a pitiful look that sat uneasily on her well-painted, rather hard features.

Daisy snorted. "In a pig's eye, you do!" There was a short silence, then she continued in a quieter voice, "You were the closest thing I had to a mother, Mrs. B.—you know that? When I was little, I used to pretend you *were* me mother. I thought I'd live with you all me life and look after you in your old age, like a good daughter does." Her voice hardened. "But then you left me with Mort, and he was lining me up for a customer who had a fancy to beat up a little crippled maidservant, so I don't reckon I owe you nothing at all."

"But you *are* like a daughter—"

"Don't give me that! I *coulda* been a daughter to you but, like me real mother, you threw me away. And I reckon *she* might have been desperate, but *you* sure as hell weren't."

The helpless look faded from Mrs. B.'s face, and there was the face of a tough old Abbess who'd spent a lifetime running a brothel in the rough end of London.

"So, you reckon you belong here, do you?" she sneered. "With your posh old dame and your la-di-da friends. Does the old lady know you're just pretendin' to be her long-lost niece? What'll she say when she finds out you're no relation, a bastard brat from the stews, a brothel-raised skivvy who's spent her life at the beck and call of whores? And you can't even read or write."

"Lady Beatrice knows all about me." Daisy's voice sounded calm, but Flynn knew better. His girl was all stirred up, and no wonder. "I never did tell lies, you oughta know that. And I can read and write now. Me sisters taught me."

"Sisters my foot!" Mrs. B. snorted. "I never realized you was such a fool, Daisy. I dunno what their game is, but they'll use you while it suits them—you're a good little dressmaker, I'll give you that. But a hint of scandal and they'll drop you like a hotcake."

"No, you're the one who dropped me when I was no more use to you. And now you've found something out about me—maybe that I got a shop now—and so you're back, sniffin' around for what you can get."

Mrs. B. shrugged. "I keep me ear to the ground."

"No, you keep your nose in the gutter, where it's always been."

Mrs. B leaned forward and made a performance of looking Daisy up and down. She snorted. "So you reckon you're some kind of lady now, do you, Daisy Smith—born in the gutter, raised in a gutter, crippled and ignorant?" Her voice dripped scorn.

Flynn's fists were clenched. He'd never yet harmed a woman, but he could happily strangle this one.

"Wake up to yerself, girl! You'll never make any kind of lady. Come back to your own kind, where you belong."

"I belong here."

"Pshaw! Aping the toffs like a little dressed-up monkey is more like it." She shook her head, setting the false yellow curls bouncing. "You ain't no gentry-mort and you never will be. Lady Muck and her friends must be havin' a right laugh at you behind their elegant gloves, watchin' you trying to ape your betters, hobblin' along behind them, always trying to keep up. Take you to dances, do they?" And she laughed, a cruel laugh.

He couldn't see Daisy's face, but he knew her well enough to know that the picture the vicious old harpy was painting would be cutting very close to the bone. In some areas his Daisy was wonderfully confident, but in social matters . . .

He was about to burst in and send the old witch packing, but a hand gripped him by the arm, long nails digging into him. He turned, ready to shake Featherby's grip off, and froze. He and Featherby weren't the only ones listening at the door.

He opened his mouth to say something but Lady Beatrice smacked him with her lorgnette and shook her head, then silently waved him out of the way so she could hear better. Her eyes were cold and glittering.

Daisy bristled at Mrs. B.'s words. Lady Beatrice might be trying to turn Daisy into a lady—against all the odds—but she wasn't laughing at her. And neither were her friends. At that thought something shifted inside her and the hackles raised by Mrs. B.'s taunts settled.

"She ain't laughing," Daisy said calmly. "She loves me and I love her. And I love me sisters and they love me too."

Mrs. B. opened her mouth to scoff, but Daisy continued, "And I've learned from Lady Beatrice that being a lady isn't about being born in a big fancy house with a silver spoon in your mouth, or talking like a toff, or even acting posh. It's about how you treat other people, being careful of their feelings, and about having self-respect. And being kind."

"Pshaw!"

Daisy lifted her chin. "I might've been gutter-born and gutter-bred, but the gutter ain't goin' to tell me who I am. I'm Daisy Chance now. I've been given a chance to make something better of meself—and by God I'm going to take it!"

"Brava, my dear gel! And so you shall!" Lady Beatrice swept into the room, clapping. And oh, gawd, Flynn was with her. How much had he heard?

Lady Beatrice raised her lorgnette and raked it slowly over Mrs. B. who'd stood up when she entered. "And who might this be?"

Daisy knew at once she'd been listening at the door.

"Lady Beatrice, this is Mrs. B., my former . . . employer."

Lady Beatrice curled her lip. "The brrrrothel keeper?" She raised her lorgnette again and peered at the other woman in much the same way as she might inspect a rather nasty insect.

Shock battled with awe on Mrs. B.'s face—she'd probably never met a real titled lady before, and she hadn't believed Daisy that Lady Bea knew. "Yes I am, yer ladyship, well I was, but I—"

"You may be seated." Lady Beatrice gestured for Daisy to sit on the *chaise longue*. Flynn sat beside her. She gave Daisy a look as if to say *sit and don't say a word* then turned back to Mrs. B. "You were saying?"

"I was going to say, yer ladyship—very gracious of you, an' I'm sorry to bother you—but young Daisy 'ere owes me."

A finely plucked and pencilled brow rose disdainfully. "She

does?" Lady Beatrice turned to Daisy. "Is this correct, my dear? Do you owe this"—she grimaced distastefully—"this *person* money?"

"No, I bloody do not! She's a bloomin' bloodsucker, out for what she can get."

"A blood. Sucker," Lady Beatrice repeated. "You don't mean she's trying to *blackmail* you, do you, Daisy dear? Because that would surely be a crime, would it not?" She gave Mrs. B. a smile as innocent as a newborn lamb.

"I ain't tryin' to blackmail nobody," Mrs. B said hurriedly. "And if you thought that Daisy, well, ye're mistaken. Good heavens, a body tries to talk about old times and you call 'em a bloodsucker. Young people today, me lady—so quick to misjudge."

She eyed Lady Beatrice shrewdly. Daisy caught the look. The cunning old bitch hadn't missed the *Daisy dear*. "The thing is, yer ladyship, by rights, young Daisy here belongs to me."

"I bloody do not!" Daisy flashed, ready to jump up and argue. Flynn's hand found hers and squeezed. She glanced at him, read the message in his eyes and subsided—reluctantly, because she didn't like the way Mrs. B. was trying to wrap Lady Bea around her finger.

"Oh dear me, does she really?" Lady Beatrice said distressfully, giving an imitation of as fluffy an old dame as ever trod the boards. "I wouldn't want to be accused of theft. Are you sure she belongs to you, Mrs., er, Bcc?"

Daisy shifted restlessly. What the hell was the old lady playing at? It almost looked like she was ready to hand Daisy over.

Mrs. B. sensed it, too. She leaned forward and in a confiding tone said, "She does indeed, yer ladyship. I picked her up out of the gutters when she was just a nipper. Paid good money for her, I did."

"I see." Lady Beatrice nodded thoughtfully. "And do you have a receipt?"

Mrs. B. looked a little taken aback by the matter-of-fact response. "Um. Er . . . Yes, yes, I do. Not on me, of course."

"But you can produce such a document—viz, that you purchased one Daisy Smith—"

"—*viz?*"

"—however many years ago."

"Twelve years ago, maybe fifteen, me lady. I disemember the exact date—but yes, I can produce a paper sayin' that she's mine, all legal and proper." Mrs. B. gave Daisy a sly look. She'd get one forged in an instant.

"Excellent. We shall need it as evidence."

Mrs. B. frowned. "*Evidence?*"

Lady Beatrice nodded. "For the court case."

"*Court case?* Let's not be so hasty, me lady. I don't want no court ca—"

"Oh, but it must go to court." Lady Beatrice smiled. "You cannot be hanged without a trial, you know."

"*Hanged?*" It came out as a squawk. "What do you mean, hanged?"

"Slavery is against the law, my good woman—and what a misnomer that is! But I can't very well call you *you ghastly harridan*—though on second thoughts—"

"I ain't *got* no slaves!"

Both finely plucked and pencilled brows rose. "You just claimed to have bought and paid for my niece, Daisy. And that is slavery."

"No, no, me lady, you don't understand. It's just an expression, just a—"

"You rang, my lady?" Featherby intoned from the door. Daisy blinked. No one had rung anything.

"Ah, Featherby, just the man we need. This *person* claims to have purchased my niece, Daisy."

Featherby gave a start of artistic horror. "Surely *not*, my lady! Why that would be *slavery,* which is a *hanging* offense, I believe!" Daisy pressed her lips firmly together, fighting a smile. Featherby had been listening at the door too.

Mrs. B. clutched her throat. "No, no—it's all a misunderstanding, an 'orrible misunders—"

"Unless, of course, it was when Miss Daisy was a mere child," Featherby added, as if in afterthought. He paused and looked at Mrs. B. who seized on the excuse thankfully.

"Yes, yes, she were a child, not quite ten, weren't you Daisy, me love?"

"In which case," Featherby continued smoothly, "to the charge of slavery would be added the procurement of a child for immoral purposes—also a hanging offense."

"No! I never—Daisy, tell him I never—" But Daisy had stuffed her fist in her mouth and with her face pressed against Flynn's shoulder, couldn't say a word.

"*Can* a person be hanged twice, Featherby?" Lady Beatrice asked.

"Not as far as I know, milady—once usually docs the trick. The hangman is very efficient, I believe."

Mrs. B. moaned. "But I never—you ask Daisy, she'll tell you. I never made her—"

Lady Beatrice raised her lorgnette. "You *were* the proprietress of a brothel at the time, were you not? An Abbess, I believe they call it."

"Well, yeah, I was, but—"

Featherby shrugged magnificently. "In which case it would make no difference, milady. Either way she will swing."

Mrs. B. shook her head, the yellow curls frantic. "No, no, I tell you, it's all a misund—"

"Featherby, will you fetch William, please," Lady Beatrice said.

"I'm here, milady." William stepped into the room. They must all have been out in the hall, listening, Daisy realized.

Mrs. B.'s eyes widened. William was huge, a former boxer, with an oft-broken nose and two cauliflower ears. He looked at Mrs. B. and flexed his enormous hands—incongruous and strangely sinister in their white footman's gloves. "So you reckon you bought and paid for our Daisy, do yer, missus? Then I reckon you and me are going to take a little walk together." He gave her a mirthless smile. "Down to Bow Street."

"No no no!" Mrs. B. leaped to her feet and looked around wildly. "It's all a mistake. I never seen that girl in me life—me eyes ain't what they used to be." She peered at Daisy. "Is that dark hair? No, my girl was a redhead—pure ginger. Miss Chance? Never heard of her. I was looking for a Miss Smith but seems I was misinformed—sorry to have troubled—melady—" She bobbed a hasty curtsey and scuttled from the room like a hen in a hailstorm.

"Show her out, Featherby," Lady Beatrice began, but the front door slammed even as she spoke. There was a short silence.

Lady Beatrice dusted off her hands. "A rout, I believe. Featherby, champagne if you please—and five glasses. You and William were splendid. Daisy dear, you may remove your fist from your mouth now—not at all ladylike, my dear, though a reasonable tactic under the circumstances."

And then the laughter started.

"**D**id she really buy you when you were a child?" Flynn asked the following evening. He and Daisy lay in bed in their little attic room, watching a storm approaching on the horizon. It was the first chance they'd had to talk privately. They'd just finished making love.

Daisy nodded. There was still a part of her that couldn't stop wondering why, why Mrs. B. had left her behind like a worn-out pair of old shoes. She'd wanted to hear that Mort had insisted, that someone had forced Mrs. B. to abandon Daisy. She'd wanted to be given a reason.

Which was stupid. There was no reason. Daisy hadn't mattered to Mrs. B. at all—that was obvious. Daisy was the one who cared—not Mrs. B.

It was always the same.

"From your parents?"

"Nah, I told you, I'm a foundling. I was . . ." She hesitated. Best to spit it all out now. "She bought me from a child brothel."

"A *what*?" He sat up on one elbow and stared at her.

"It's all right, I was never touched." She grimaced. "As soon as they took me inside I knew what sort of place it was." She saw his expression and added, "When you grow up like me, you learn about such places young, and I wasn't goin' to have none of it. They locked me in a room, but I escaped up the chimney—lucky it was summer—and got onto the roof. I was climbing down when I slipped and landed on the cobblestones, *splat*! at Mrs. B.'s feet. Broke me leg and all."

"She was the—"

"No, she wasn't the one. To do her credit, Mrs. B. was always dead against usin' young 'uns in brothels."

Flynn made a skeptical sound.

"No, it's true. I know what you thought of her, and you're not wrong. She's a hard woman, selfish and ruthless, and tough as old boots, but she's not all bad, and she was good to me back then. She picked me up and took me home, never mind the mess I was in—"

"Mess?"

"I broke me leg remember? Mrs. B. paid the brothel owner a shilling—"

"A shilling?" he echoed indignantly. He wasn't sure whether he was insulted by the small sum or outraged that she was sold at all. A bit of both, he supposed.

Daisy shrugged. "Well, I wasn't worth nothing to him with a broken leg, and it pays to keep in good with your neighbors. She got a bloke to set me leg and bandage it up—even gave me some laudanum for the pain—'orrible stuff it was too. And then she put me on a bench in the corner of the kitchen, handed me a needle, thread and a pile of mending and set me to work. I sat there and sewed until me leg healed."

Only it didn't heal, not properly, Flynn knew.

"Lovely it was in the kitchen, always warm and plenty of company—and food!—you never seen such food. They made it for the gentlemen, you see. I never went hungry again. And that's how I learned to sew—I'd never so much as touched a needle before that, but by the time I could walk again, I'd found I didn't just like sewing, I was good at it. All the girls started bringing me their clothes to fix and to make over as well, so you see, if none of that had happened, I wouldn't be where I am today." She smiled and added, "I'm pretty lucky, I reckon."

"Lucky?" How the hell could she tell a story like that and conclude she was *lucky*?

She leaned forward and kissed him. "I ended up here, didn't I? Above me very own shop, with a lovely man in me bed and the best view in the world. I got food in me belly, a home to go to, sisters and an old lady who care about me, and friends—good friends. What more could I want?"

He looked at her sunny, open expression, and couldn't bring himself to say a word. Her wants were so simple. He wanted so much more. He kissed her instead.

Children didn't even figure in her consciousness. And why would they, with the experiences she'd had? Abandoned as a wee babe, nobody to care for her, passed around like an unwanted parcel until a raddled old harridan had scooped a broken child from the cobblestones and exploited her for years without pay—and in her ignorance and vulnerability, Daisy had mistaken that for the care of a mother.

His arms tightened around her. He wished she could have met Mam.

"Well, Daisy, you'll be next!" Jane exclaimed.

"Who me? What?" Daisy jerked upright, startled from a bit of a daze. Or was it a doze? She was right knackered. It was the evening before Jane's wedding, and the girls were having their last girls' nursery supper. In the weeks leading up to it she'd been working so hard to get everything perfect, she'd almost fallen asleep.

"Next to what?" she asked again.

"To fall in love and get married of course, silly," Jane said. "Weren't you listening?"

"Here, have some toast." Damaris passed Daisy a slice of hot, perfectly toasted bread.

"It's you who don't listen, Jane," Daisy retorted, buttering the toast. "I ain't never gettin' married. How many times have you heard me say so?"

Jane laughed. "Yes, but that's the way of the Chance sisters."

Daisy slanted her a skeptical glance. "What way is that then?"

"Our way. See, first there was darling Abby, governessing along, looking after everybody else, certain she'd never even have a chance to get married, let alone have a child of her own." Jane hugged her sister. "Now look at her—could you get anyone more in love than her and Max? And just look at that lovely expectant mother happy glow."

Abby laughed, a little embarrassed. "Oh, it's just the firelight," she murmured, but it wasn't. She did glow. Daisy had never seen her look so beautiful. Abby had always been elegant, rather than beautiful, but now . . .

Jane continued, "And then dearest Damaris—who was utterly adamant that she wasn't ever going to marry. All she wanted was a little cottage and some hens—remember?"

"And I do have my lovely little cottage and hens." Damaris deftly slid a slice of hot toast onto a plate and passed it to Jane.

"You also have darling Freddy who completely and utterly dotes on you." Jane laughed as Damaris blushed rosily.

"And then there's me . . ." Jane heaved a big happy sigh and smiled into the glowing coals of the fire. Her toast sat ignored on her lap. Abby retrieved it and buttered it for her. "I was so determined not to fall in love, to make a practical marriage."

Jane turned to Daisy. "You told me I'd fall for the most unsuitable man in London, remember? And I did. My darling, darling Zachary . . ." She gave a little wriggle of delight. "So you see, Daisy dearest, it's your fate. You'll be next. Chance girls always get what they deserve, and you deserve the best."

"I've got the best," Daisy said. "The best shop in London. Now eat your toast."

"Ohh, I'm not hungry," Jane declared airily. "Not for toast." Her dreamy look made it clear what she was hungry for, and it wasn't any kind of food.

"Well, I am." Abby took the toast she'd buttered for Jane. "It's dreadful. I'm always hungry and I fall asleep at the most inopportune times."

"You're increasing—it's natural," Damaris pointed out.

Daisy, who'd opened her mouth to admit that she felt exactly the same lately, closed it. She thought back, doing a calculation in her head. She looked at Abby, sleepy and rounded, fertile and glowing and happy.

Bloody hell.

Chapter Eighteen

Her mind was all disorder. The past, present, future,
every thing was terrible.

—JANE AUSTEN, *MANSFIELD PARK*

*U*p *the duff.*
 Supper was over, Abby and Damaris had gone home to their loving husbands and Jane had gone to bed to try to sleep—there was no way she would, she was too keyed up—and dream or daydream of her husband-to-be.

Daisy, too, was keyed up, but for a very different reason. She'd made an excuse and gone to her workroom, leaving Jane in bed. She needed to be alone, to think.

Up the bloody duff.

She *couldn't* be. She counted back the months. When had she had her last rags?

She was weeks overdue. She counted twice to be sure, but dammit, she'd missed two months. And her breasts had been so tender lately. She'd thought it was because of Flynn's attentions to them.

How the hell had it happened? She'd been so careful, using the methods the girls used at the brothel to keep from falling pregnant. She'd used them every single time . . . Except for . . .

Damn! The table. That first time with Flynn, on the table. She hadn't expected that, hadn't prepared for it, had taken care of things afterward, but it must have been too late. Like closing the stable door after the bloody horse had escaped.

She swore a blue streak.

She hadn't even noticed missing her rags, what with the shop and all—people did miss sometimes, when life was busy and worrisome. But it wasn't excitement or worry—it was carelessness, stupid bloody carelessness on her part.

What the hell was she going to do now?

One thing was clear. She wasn't going to tell Flynn. He'd whip her off to a church before you could blink and she'd be married.

Married, up the duff, and Flynn would own her shop, her lovely shop. And she'd have to become a lady, a proper lady, with all the trimmings, because that's what he wanted in a wife. A gracious, elegant, dignified ladylike wife.

Which was as far from Daisy as you could get.

She'd be hopeless at it, but she'd have to smile and act the lady and pretend to herself and everyone that she hadn't ruined his life.

No, she wasn't going to tell Flynn.

There were lots of things to do with unwanted babies. There were the old women down the back alleys with their knitting needles. Daisy shivered. She wasn't going there.

She could have the baby and give it away, like her mother did. She didn't have to wrap it in rags and leave it beside the gutter, as Daisy was—or at least that's what she'd been told. There were other choices.

The Foundling Hospital—Captain Coram's—they'd take a baby if the mother was respectable—"of good character." Nobody Daisy knew had managed to get a babe accepted.

Even if they did get in, a babe wasn't necessarily safe. Coram's took newborns—nothing over twelve months, and farmed the babes out to wet nurses in the country. Some of the blokes that hung around the brothel made a bit on the side, taking the babies from Coram's—supposedly to deliver them to the wet nurse—but some of them had been "lost" on the way. Babies died easy—everyone knew that.

And even if they survived that, she'd seen some Coram's

foundlings once, had never forgotten their well-scrubbed faces, their drab, neat, ugly clothing, as they walked in tidy lines to church, two by two. Not a smile to be seen among them, poor little things. A grim, dutiful, well-disciplined life, all planned out for them. No joy in it at all.

She put her hand over her still-flat stomach. "Don't worry, baby," she whispered, "I won't send you there."

And oh, gawd, what was she doing, talking to the baby already as if it was a person? That was the worst thing to do. Girls who did that never were the same after giving the baby away. Turned to blue ruin. Or opium.

She wasn't like those girls—she wasn't. She had a family now, and a shop. She wasn't poor and desperate and friendless. Her baby would be all right.

She could have the babe in secret and farm it out, somewhere nice and safe. With people who would take good care of it. Make it feel wanted. As if it belonged.

A baby needed to know it was wanted. And loved.

Was there such a place? How would she find it?

Lady Beatrice would help her. "She's lovely, Lady Bea," she told her stomach. "She'll make sure you go to a nice home somewhere." She broke off. She was doing it again. It had to stop.

She would go to bed now, try to sleep, talk to Lady Bea in the morn—no, it was Jane's wedding day. She'd have to wait until after. There was plenty of time. She was only a month or two along. She patted her stomach. "Not like you're goin' anywhere, are you?"

Jane's wedding went off a treat. Jane of course looked stunningly beautiful and glowed with happiness. She, her four attendants and Lady Beatrice all wore Daisy-made— excuse me, House of Chance—clothes and looked gorgeous, if Daisy did say so herself. Some of the guests also wore Daisy's dresses.

She couldn't have been prouder if she was the mother of the bride.

She placed her hand on her stomach. Unfortunate thought.

"Got a bellyache?" Flynn murmured in her ear. He was a groomsman, looking dashing and handsome—and for once, not colorful—all in black and white and silver gray. Freddy must have prevailed.

"No, I'm all right." She avoided his gaze.

"Just that it's the third or fourth time today I've seen you do that."

"No, it's just that woman's perfume, it's making me feel a bit sick." It was true too. "Excuse me, Flynn. Gotta go, need the . . . um." She hurried away. It wasn't ladylike to mention the privy.

She'd been trying to avoid Flynn all day. It was hard with both of them being in the wedding party, but she'd managed. He'd asked her earlier if something was the matter and she'd hissed, "Gotta be discreet, remember?" and moved away, leaving him frowning after her.

It was as if he knew something was up. But he couldn't. He was just being Flynn, taking care of her, acting as if she was some fragile . . . lady.

What the hell was she going to do when they all went down the country to Jane's new home? There was some kind of celebration there for May Day. They were all going—the whole family. Even Lady Beatrice had consented to visit the countryside, which she loathed. Flynn was going too, apparently. It would be even harder to avoid him at a house party.

But somehow she had to manage it because she was a rotten liar and if he kept asking her if something was wrong, she'd end up blabbing.

And that would ruin his life. And hers.

The wedding was over, Jane had left on her honeymoon and the house on Berkeley Square was very quiet. Lady Beatrice, declaring herself utterly exhausted, went early to bed. Daisy brooded about her problem. Maybe she wouldn't go to the country. Maybe she'd tell everyone she had to stay for the shop.

Jane would be so hurt if Daisy didn't come to Jane's first party as a new bride in her new home.

But if Daisy did go, there would be the problem of Flynn. She walked slowly up to bed, tossing the same fruitless thoughts around in her head. And stopped. Was that a light under Lady Beatrice's door?

She knocked softly in case the old lady had fallen asleep with the light on.

"Come," a stately voice answered.

Daisy poked her head around the door. "Are you awake?"

"What is it, child?' Lady Beatrice was sitting up in bed against a mound of pillows and wearing one of Daisy's bed jackets, the first one she'd ever made her, pink and ruffled and feminine. She patted the bed in invitation.

Daisy entered the room and climbed onto the bed. "Can't sleep?"

"Too much excitement," the old lady agreed. "Wasn't Jane a picture? And that husband of hers, so hands—" She broke off, frowning. "What is it, child?" she said in quite a different voice.

Daisy knotted her fingers together. They were shaking. Girls got chucked out in the streets for falling pregnant. Chucked out of their own families. Lady Bea, for all she claimed her as a niece, was no relation at all.

"Spit it out, gel."

Daisy took a deep breath. "I'm increasing." '

Lady Beatrice peered at her and shook her head. "Nonsense. You're not fat in the least."

"No, I'm *increasing*. You know, *in a delicate condition*." She couldn't bring herself to say *expecting a happy event* because it was a bloody disaster. Nor could she bear to say *in the family way*. She gestured with her hands, making a mound over her stomach.

Lady Beatrice frowned. "Good Gad, you mean you're *pregnant*? No need to beat around the bush."

Daisy rolled her eyes. She was never going to get the hang of being a lady. "Yeah, all right then, I'm up the bloody duff!"

"Don't be vulgar. And what does Mr. Flynn have to say about your condition?"

Daisy gasped. "How did you know it was him?"

Lady Beatrice snorted, as if it was too obvious for words. "So what are you going to do?"

"I don't know."

The old lady frowned. "You mean he won't marry you?"

"Oh yeah, he would—if he knew about it. But I ain't telling him."

"Why ever not? Put him to the test, gel, tell him about the baby and give him the opportunity to do the decent thing."

Daisy glowered at her. "He's been askin' me to marry him every bloomin' day for weeks."

"Without even knowing about the child? Good for him. There's your answer then. There can be no recriminations that you've trapped the dear man. Tell him the good news, and we'll start the wedding preparations at once. Good heavens—four weddings in one year! I shall be thoroughly exhausted!" she said in utter delight.

Daisy didn't move. She sat silently on the bed tracing the design on the satin coverlet with her forefinger.

Lady Beatrice raised her lorgnette. "Out with it, gel, what's the problem?"

"I ain't goin' to marry him," she muttered. "I can't."

The old lady gave her a sharp look. "You're not already married are you? Because if you are—"

"I ain't married. I just . . . can't."

"Why not? What's the sticking point? "

Daisy shrugged.

"A shrug won't do this time, my dear," the old lady said. "Come on, explain to an old woman so that I can understand— why can't you marry a man who is handsome, rich, madly in love with you—oh, and whose baby you happen to be carrying?"

"Because I can't, that's why."

"Oh, well, that clears it up wonderfully." The handle of her lorgnette tapped impatiently.

"It's me shop," Daisy said at last. "It's been me dream

for so long—all me life since I first picked up a needle and thread and sewed me first dress."

The old lady's stare bored into her. "That's it? A *shop* is preventing you from marrying the finest man I've met in a long time?"

Daisy hunched a shoulder. "It's been all I ever worked for, all I ever dreamed of. And if I marry him, I lose it. That's the law."

"Pfft!"

'It's true—"

"Pffffft! And piffle! A shop is a *thing*. It can be bought or sold—or even burned down!" Daisy crossed her fingers to avert bad luck. The old lady continued, "A shop can't talk to you, or argue, or offer comfort or encouragement. A shop can't love you."

Daisy bit her lip. She didn't need love. She'd done just fine in her life without it.

"You can't choose between a shop and a person."

"Yes I can." Trouble was, there were two persons, not one. Flynn and the baby.

The old lady pursed her lips and eyed her thoughtfully. "And what of Mr. Flynn? Will you deny him even the knowledge of the child?"

"What he doesn't know can't hurt him," Daisy muttered, but that wasn't true. How many hours had she spent in her life wondering about her mother, her father, what had happened? And why? Dreaming up all sorts of stories to account for why they had to abandon her.

Sometimes what you didn't know was an unhealed wound that quietly festered.

There was a long silence. Outside the wind whistled around the eaves. Lady Beatrice shifted, pulling her bed-clothes around her. "And the babe?"

Daisy's mouth trembled. "I don't know," she whispered. "I thought I could give her away, but . . ."

"Oh, it's a her now, is it?"

Daisy nodded. She didn't know how it had happened, but somehow the baby had become a person to her, a little girl with dark curly hair and big blue eyes like her daddy, and she couldn't, she just couldn't give her away to be raised by strangers who might not care for her properly, might not love her.

"I thought there might be some . . . some way we could keep her with us. Here."

"Did you just? Raise your little bastard in my house? Society would love that, I'm sure. They'd flock to your shop then, wouldn't they?"

Daisy flinched at the hard truths flung at her in a hard voice. She looked up, wounded. She'd hoped the old lady would help her, somehow make it all right.

Lady Beatrice gave an unrepentant shrug. "Nasty word isn't it? But that's what you'll make of her if you don't marry Mr. Flynn—a little bastard. You know what that's like, don't you, Daisy—to be a bastard. I don't imagine it's very nice."

Daisy had no answer to that. Even in the lowest gutters of London, a bastard was the lowest of the low.

"I know, but what else can I do?" Her face crumpled.

"Oh, come here, dearest gel." Lady Beatrice held out her arms and Daisy fell into them, sobbing.

"I hate this—I never cry," Daisy said on a hiccup some time later.

"I know. Abby's the same. I am told women in your condition are more subject to tears. I wouldn't know." The old lady stroked a straggle of damp hair back from Daisy's temple and handed her a wisp of lace. Daisy blotted her eyes with it.

"Feeling better? A good cry can do you the world of good, they say. As good as a—well, what I hope you experienced with Mr. Flynn—though that's nonsense of course. Those who say it have obviously never had a good man in their bed, I say. It simply doesn't compare. And it does make a mess of your face—crying I mean, not the other."

Daisy gave a shaky laugh. The old girl did love to shock.

She smiled and patted Daisy's hand. "Now go and wash your face and take yourself off to bed, young lady and think about what you're going to do."

Daisy blinked at her. "But I thought . . . I mean, you love telling people what to do."

"I do. But in this case you don't need my advice."

"Yes, I do."

The old lady shook her head. "Only you can decide this—you will be the one who will have to live with whatever decision you make. You and the babe and Mr. Flynn. But first you have to work out what it is you're so afraid of."

"Afraid?"

She nodded. "Yes, afraid. Daisy Chance, my brave little gel who confronts the world head-on, who kicked a large and appallingly nasty cook on the first day we met, is afraid."

Daisy bit her lip. She wanted to deny it, but she couldn't. She was afraid of the future, afraid for the baby. But a girl had her pride, so she managed to retort in something of her usual manner, "What am I afraid of, then?"

"I don't know, dearest gel," the old lady said softly. "Whatever the source of your fear, it is buried deep inside you. Look inside your heart, child, for what you truly want. And then ask yourself what you're so afraid of. Because until you know what it is—and confront it—you'll be forever running, and never knowing why."

She couldn't decide, she couldn't decide, she couldn't decide. It was bloody impossible.

Daisy turned over in bed for the hundredth time and thumped her pillow also for the hundredth time. She could blame the bed they were in the country, at Jane's new home, and sleeping in a strange bed was always tricky the first few nights. But it wasn't the bed.

Nor was her sleeplessness the fault of the strange, unnerving sounds that came out of the night. Those screams, like a person being tortured, were foxes, apparently. Mating. So foxes screamed too. And then there were owls . . .

She hated the country. Full of creepy-crawlies. Good thing they'd be going back to London in a couple of days. She couldn't wait.

But the country and the foxes weren't keeping her awake. Her thoughts went round and round.

Lady Bea was wrong about her being afraid. She'd thought about it and the only thing that frightened Daisy was the future of her baby. And that was frightened *for*, not frightened *of*.

It was just deciding what to do that was keeping her up.

It was obvious what she should do. She would keep the baby, raise her herself, and if Lady Bea didn't want her in the house, Daisy would move out. She'd find a small house, maybe even just a set of rooms at first, and pay someone to look after the baby during the day while she was at the shop.

She could do the whole thing discreetly. If she did it properly, her customers would never even know.

Hiding away her baby like she was ashamed of her.

She turned over and thumbed the pillow again.

Bastard. It was an ugly term. It'd hang over her daughter the whole of her life.

Daisy had embraced her own bastardy—told everyone from the start that she was born on the "wrong side of the blanket." But that was because she had no choice—she *was* a bastard, and as different from her "sisters" as chalk from cheese. "Wrong side of the blanket" explained everything.

Most families, most high-society families had a bastard or two tucked away. A few of the higher-ups, who didn't care what others thought, acknowledged their bastards; most hid them away like a dirty little secret.

Like Harriet in that book *Emma*—she never knew who she was really. Just that "somebody" had paid for her upkeep and education. She was a posh version of Daisy. Unwanted. Dumped, only in a nice genteel school instead of the gutter.

Daisy pressed her palms over her stomach. It was a simple choice: marry Flynn, lose her shop, make her child legitimate—and secure for life, because Flynn was rich. And because he'd love this little girl to bits.

Or give birth to a bastard and raise her as a dirty little secret.

No choice at all, really.

Why then was it so bloody hard to make up her mind?

She'd have to have a talk—no, something more serious— a *discussion* with Flynn, but that shouldn't be too hard, surely? He'd be pleased, she knew—he'd made no secret of wanting kids. And she liked Flynn, she really did. And he liked her. Even if she wasn't the kind of girl he'd always dreamed of marrying. The complete opposite, in fact.

He'd already asked her to marry him a dozen times or more, though she was sure that was just him being noble. He still thought her a decent girl, even after she'd told him everything about the brothel and all. So he'd be noble now and marry her and the baby. And pretend it was exactly what he'd wanted all along. Because that was Flynn.

It should be simple. But it bloody well wasn't.

Was it the shop? She didn't know. She loved her shop, but Lady Bea was right—when it came down to a choice between being her own boss and having her lovely shop and becoming a famous fashionable dressmaker—or giving this little one the kind of life she deserved, it was no choice.

She could lose the shop. It would be hard, after all she'd done to make it happen, but she'd proved to herself she could do it—be a success. Once they were married, Flynn would own it. But he'd be fair about it. He might let her continue dropping in there—she could probably design the clothes, if not run the shop. He might even give the shop back to her. He did say she should trust him.

But married men expected their wives to stay home, to run the household, and raise the children. Be a wife. Be a lady. Be a hostess.

She wouldn't much like it, she wouldn't be much good at it, not at first, but she supposed she could learn.

She shivered. She had to bite the bullet. She had to tell Flynn. Tomorrow.

All day she'd put off talking to him. Avoiding being alone with him. Dreading the talk she knew she had to have. The *conversation*.

He knew something was up too. He was watching her like a hawk. Like an owl. Like one of those blooming foxes. She was ready to scream herself—only not for the same reason.

And now, to make things worse, all the others—all the young people—had gone outside—in couples. Because it was a lovely warm night for a change, and a full moon. Romantic.

The only ones left in the sitting room were old people—and Flynn and Daisy.

He looked at her with the sort of brooding dark look that made her shiver. If there weren't no baby, no *discussion* to be had, she'd be out there with him like a shot, enjoying the moonlight. Acting like foxes.

Instead she avoided his gaze.

"Well," Lady Beatrice said, "are you two going or staying?"

"Stayin'." Daisy picked up a pack of cards and started to shuffle them—badly. Her hands were shaking. "The country gives me the creeps at night. Anyone for cards?"

Flynn gave her a long, dry look and rose to his feet. "I might as well walk the dog, then. Come on Caesar or Rose Petal or whatever your name is, we can bay at the moon together." He stepped through the French windows, with Jane's ugly dog snuffling happily beside him.

Lady Beatrice watched him leave. "Waste of a fine man like that, leaving him to bay at a full moon—alone—with a dog!" she informed the room in general. She turned to Daisy, lorgnette raised and said in a low voice, "Haven't you talked to that boy yet?"

Daisy shrugged.

The old lady snorted. "So you're still afraid, still running."

Daisy looked at her. "No. I ain't afraid. But since you mention it, I might as well get it over with." She stomped outside. "Oy, Flynn, wait for me."

Chapter Nineteen

*What one means one day, you know, one may not mean
the next. Circumstances change, opinions alter.*

—JANE AUSTEN, NORTHANGER ABBEY

The country was a horrible place at night. Downright creepy. Bushes shivered, trees creaked, their leaves whispering and slithering. Creatures lurked in, behind and under all of it. And the moon might be full and bright, a big fat golden ball up in the sky, but it turned everything to shadows. Moving, shifting, creepy shadows.

Give her a dark London alley any day.

Daisy heard a horrible snuffling sound, turned, saw a tall shadow move and almost jumped out of her skin.

"Gawd, Flynn, you and that dog gave me such a start." She hurried forward and grabbed hold of his arm. Damn. She hadn't intended to be so friendly—she'd planned a calm, rational *discussion*.

"Changed your mind about joining me, sweetheart?" And before she could say anything, he was kissing her.

And dammit, she was kissing him back, as if she had no blooming willpower of her own. Oh, how she'd missed this, missed him, and it was only a few days. It just felt like weeks.

His hand moved to cup her breast and the twinge of sensitivity there was enough to recall her to her senses. She wasn't here for a bit of a kiss and cuddle under the moon—there was a *discussion* to be had.

She wriggled out of his embrace. And immediately felt the chill of the night surround her.

"Something wrong, Daisy?" She couldn't see his face. It was in shadow.

She took a deep breath. "Did you mean it about wanting to marry me?"

"Yes." Not a shred of hesitation.

"You still want to?"

"Yes. What's all this about, Daisy? You've been acting like a cat with wet paws ever since your sister's wedding."

"Are you sure? About marrying me, I mean." She wished she could see his face, see what he was thinking, but he was just a tall dark silhouette.

"Yes I'm sure, dammit. Why?"

She swallowed. "I'm havin' a baby." For a long moment he didn't say anything—there was just the sound of things scuttling in the bushes, or maybe it was the dog. So she added to make it clear, "*We're* havin' a baby."

"Are you sure?"

She nodded, scanning the shadowed face desperately, trying to read his expression in the darkness.

And then she saw a flash of white teeth. There was a loud *whoop!* and she was seized in a pair of strong arms and twirled around and he was hugging and kissing her, so happy, so excited.

She felt quite sick. And not from the twirling.

Eventually he put her down, and somehow, in the darkness, found a bench for them to sit on. He sat and pulled her onto his knees, tucking her against his chest. She was grateful for his warmth. The moonlight lit his face now and she was glad, because it meant hers was in shadow, and he wouldn't be able to see how she felt.

"When's it due?"

She hadn't even counted. "I'm not sure. I think around Christmas."

"Christmas? That's grand. A Christmas baby." He hugged her, rocking her slightly, saying nothing for a few minutes. She waited for the next question.

It took a while to come. "How—I mean, I'm desperate glad about the baby, of course—you can't know how I feel at this moment, Daisy-girl"—but his voice broke a little and his arms tightened around her—"but I assumed you were doing something to prevent . . ."

"I was. But not . . . the first time."

"Ah, the table, was it?" He bent and kissed her. "What kind of a weddin' do you want? Quick and quiet or big and splashy?"

"What would you like?"

"Big and splashy for preference, but maybe since this little one is comin' along"—he caressed her belly lightly—"we'd better make it quick and splashy. Do you think you could manage that? You'll be wanting to make yourself a beautiful dress, I know."

"I can manage it." She was almost in tears. He was so generous, so accepting, such a good, dear, noble man. You'd think from the way he was reacting that this was exactly what he'd always dreamed of. And maybe the baby was.

But dreaming of a wife like Daisy? Never.

"Are you all right, love? Only you seem a bit quiet."

"Just a bit tired," she said.

He smiled. "That'll be the baby." He sounded so satisfied, so happy. She felt a tear roll down her cheek and surreptitiously scrubbed it away.

"I think I'd like to go inside now. It's cold. You wouldn't know summer is around the corner, would you?"

"Are we telling people yet?" he asked.

She shook her head. "Not yet—not until I start to show. I've only told Lady Bea so far—well I had to tell someone," she added, seeing his face fall a little. Guilt stirred. The father ought to be the first to know.

He shifted her in his arms so he could see her face, and in a quiet voice asked, "Are you all right about this wedding, Daisy?" He waited. "I mean, you've refused me every other time, so I know you're only marrying me for the babe. And that's fine and dandy by me, in case you're worryin' about it. But are *you* all right about it?"

She forced a smile. "Yeah, I'm happy about it, Flynn, don't worry."

"Is it the shop? Because you know I'll give it right back to you, the minute we're married."

"It's not the shop. I'm just a bit tired and, you know"—she touched her belly—"feelin' a bit sick."

It wasn't quite a lie. She did feel sick, only it wasn't the babe making her feel sick. It was herself.

" So you told him," Lady Beatrice observed. She and Daisy were in her carriage, returning to London.

"Yes, I told him."

"And? Ouch! My dratted bones will never be the same!" she added as the carriage bumped over another set of potholes. It was a very well sprung carriage, but the road was in a bad state. "Jane and her party. Why people wish to live in this godforsaken wilderness is beyond me! So what did he say?"

"We're going to get married."

"Excellent. When?"

Daisy shrugged. "Soon, I suppose. Before I start to show."

The old lady snorted. "Contain your enthusiasm, will you?"

Daisy sighed.

There was a long silence. They jolted along for a while, and then hit a smooth patch of road. "You didn't look in your heart, did you?"

Daisy shrugged.

"Then why all the gloom? If I have to sit here, looking at that miserable Friday face all the way to London I'll want to shoot myself before we get there."

Daisy sighed. "He put such a lovely face on it when I told him. He's thrilled about the baby and is acting all pleased and happy about the wedding."

"Acting?"

She looked up. "Well, he's bound to be disappointed, ain't he? I mean, I'm nothing like the kind of wife he wanted, but he's pretending as if he couldn't be more pleased." She felt her face crumpling and fought the urge to weep her heart out.

The old lady watched her with shrewd old eyes. "There are worse things in life than disappointment."

Daisy said nothing.

"I disappointed my husband by being unable to give him a son—or any child at all." She sighed. "His disappointment was nothing to mine, of course. I grieved for years." Lost in thought, the old lady stared unseeing at the countryside slipping past the window, then added, "He never loved me, you know."

Daisy moved from her seat, which faced backward, to sit beside the old lady. She slipped her fingers into the gnarled old hand and squeezed. "He was a fool then." Lady Bea was filled with love. Look at the way she'd lavished it on the four of them, who were no relation to her.

Lady Bea gave her a smile. "There are worse things than disappointment. But I think you do Mr. Flynn an injustice. He's always struck me as a man who knows exactly what he wants, and apparently he wants you."

"But I'm not a lady and he always said—"

"Oh, for Heaven's sake! It's all the fault of that harridan who raised you. Have a bit of faith in yourself gel—or if you can't, have faith in Flynn. He's the kind of man you can rely on—but that's half your problem—you don't like relying on other people, do you? Another thing to blame on that dreadful woman. Have you talked to him about your worries?"

"What's the point? He'll only lie to save me feelings."

"Says the girl who isn't afraid. Have you asked yourself why that is—why you think he's lying to you, and why you're afraid to tell him how you feel?"

Daisy knew why he was lying—because he was so noble and decent and good and kind, and not the sort of man who hurt women's feelings. Look at how he'd treated Lady Elizabeth. If he'd ended up married to her he would have put on exactly the same face, Daisy was sure.

He would never let on Daisy was a disappointment. The thought of living with that for the rest of her life was like a knife in her breast.

"Might it be that he loves you?"

Daisy shook her head. He couldn't. He'd never said so, though there had been plenty of opportunities. He'd only turned to Daisy because she was there—and available— after he'd been disappointed by Lady Elizabeth. And because he thought he'd seduced her.

"Might it be that you love him?"

Daisy bit her lip. Of course she loved him. How could she not? And loving him as she did, she knew she was the last person he should marry.

But the babe had changed everything.

The wedding was set for the first of June—the first day of summer. Lady Beatrice refused to countenance a hasty marriage by special license—they would have the banns called, like decent people. Nobody would accuse her nieces of needing to get married in a rush—even if they did. And when the baby was born, if people counted the months— well, that would only be those with vulgar, commonplace minds, and there was no need to take any notice of that sort of person. What business was it of theirs, anyway?

In any case, the first of June was the earliest date that St. George's Hanover Square, Lady Beatrice's local parish church, was free for a large wedding. Lady Beatrice and Featherby had thrown themselves into the arrangements with gusto. All Daisy had to do was design the dresses for herself and the girls, and have them made up. And turn up on the day.

Flynn only had to turn up. She hadn't seen a lot of Flynn since they'd returned to London—only in company, crowded company at that. He'd turned up to the house but she'd been "out." He'd sent notes but she'd replied saying she was "busy with the wedding arrangements" which was a big fat lie. He'd even sent messages to the shop, asking about "gloves," but she'd returned them, saying there were none available.

She didn't want to face him. She was feeling worse and worse about this wedding.

I know you're only marrying me for the babe.

She thought about it all the time, that conversation in the moonlight. It was true that she was marrying him for the sake of the baby—but it wasn't the whole truth.

She couldn't escape the thought that Flynn thought he was coming off second best to a shop. That she cared more about her shop than him.

And that wasn't true.

It might have been, once, but she'd done a lot of thinking lately, looking into her heart, as Lady Bea put it, and what she truly wanted, more than anything else in the world was for Flynn to love her, truly love her. As she loved him.

And the thing that she feared was that she'd fail him, let him down. Hurt him, as she feared she already had.

She wasn't the kind of wife he'd always wanted, but she was clever and hard-working, and she could do anything she put her mind to. She would work and learn and become the best wife to Flynn she could possibly be.

She'd had to fight for every single thing in her life, and dammit she was going to fight for Flynn too.

She sent a note around to Louisa Foster. And then made a list of what she had to do.

It took a few days, but when she'd done all she'd set out to do, she sent a note to Flynn, telling him that his gloves had arrived, and he could collect them at eight the following evening at the usual address.

And then she waited.

* * *

Her workers had all left for the day. Rain spattered fitfully against the window. It was gray and dreary outside. No sign of summer coming yet. She lit candles in their little attic room, and waited, rehearsing her speech in her head.

She straightened the bedclothes, nervously tidying, even though there was nothing out of place. Finally he came. He reached for her, but she skittered back, holding up her hands as if to ward him off.

"Sit down, Flynn. I have something I need to say to you."

He gave her a searching look, shrugged, then sat on the bed.

She took a deep breath. "I'm sorry—I know you probably think I've ruined your life, but—"

"You haven't—"

"Let me finish, please. It's hard enough to say what I want to tell you without you interruptin'."

"Very well. Go ahead then." He sat back on the bed, folded his arms and waited, giving her his full, blue-eyed, come-to-bed attention. Which of course only made it that much harder. But Daisy was determined to get through the speech she'd been rehearsing in her mind for days.

"You said that night in the country that you knew I was only marrying you because of the baby—and that's true—to a point. But I want you to know that if . . . if I was a different kind of person, someone like Lady Elizabeth maybe, I'd marry you like a shot, Flynn."

He frowned. "If you're tryin' to tell me you're one of them ladies of Llangollen, I won't believe you."

She made an impatient gesture. "No, I mean if I was a proper lady—*born* a lady, I mean, with perfect manners and a pretty way of speaking instead of soundin' like I belong with the barrow boys down the market—and I know I should, but—"

"You're talking nonsense, girl."

"Just let me explain, will you? And stop lookin' at me like that—you're makin' me get all tangled up." It had sounded so reasonable and simple in her head. "You said something that night that made me think you thought I wasn't happy about this marriage, that I didn't want to marry you."

"If I said that—"

"Hush! I do and I don't. The part of me that's selfish wants to marry you, the part of me that I would like to think is noble—but really it's just cowardly and afraid—that part doesn't."

"I prefer the selfish part."

"And I think you think that you come second in me affections to the shop."

He said nothing to that. And now she didn't know if that was because he did think that, or because he was finally not interrupting.

"So I've given away the shop."

"What? Given aw—"

She made a sharp gesture and he subsided, a peculiar look on his face. She continued, "If I'm going to be your wife, I'm going to do it properly, all the way. Society wives don't keep shops, and I don't want to embarrass you—and it would if you had guests who were also my customers. So it's gone—the shop. I hope you weren't counting on getting it when we marry, because it ain't mine anymore."

"Who did—?"

"Louisa, me silent partner. Now shush—I'm not finished." She took a deep breath, and said it, the thing she'd been afraid of saying all along. "I love you, Flynn. I really truly do—I'm not just saying it to please you—you know I'm a rotten liar."

His gaze softened. "I know." He reached for her.

"And I know you're bein' noble and—no, don't touch me, I'm not finished. I know I'm all wrong for you, but I *promise* you, Flynn, you won't regret it. I'm going to do everything I can to make me-*my*self into the kind of wife you can be proud of. I'll learn to behave like a proper lady—Lady Beatrice will help me. I'm going to stop swearing and learn good grammar, and—"

"Deliver baskets of food to me poor?"

She narrowed her eyes at him. "Don't you dare make a joke of this, Patrick Flynn. I'm dead serious here."

"You are, aren't you, ye daft wee besom." He leaned forward, tugged her forward and into his arms, and rolled with her on the bed.

"I'm not finished," she told him.

"Yes, you are. Now it's your turn to listen to me."

"But—"

He kissed her. "Ready to listen now?"

"I haven't expl—"

He kissed her again. "Keep talkin'. Every time you open your mouth, I'll kiss you."

She pressed her lips together and glowered at him. He wasn't taking any of this seriously.

"I've been a big eedjit in the way I handled this whole thing," he told her. "The first thing I should have told you, and didn't, was that I love you, Daisy-girl."

She looked up at him, her eyes wide.

"I love you with all my heart and soul. You're the other half of me, girl, don't you know that?" He kissed her, long and possessively, and it was a declaration and an affirmation, and if she didn't believe him at first, if she thought he was only saying it to be kind, the murmured words and endearments between kisses soothed at least some of the doubts.

Soon they were both trembling with need and with one accord they stripped off their clothes and fell back on the bed.

He reached for her, then hesitated. "Is it safe to do this? It won't hurt the baby, will it?"

"It's safe," she told him—she'd checked with Abby—and drew him down to her.

He made love to her then with a quiet intensity that brought tears to her eyes, murmuring endearments and repeating his declaration of love, and it was a forerunner—their own private vow-making. *With my body I thee worship.*

They climaxed together, their bodies in perfect harmony, and afterward lay in silence, curled together, listening to the light patter of rain against the overhead window, and the dripping of water in the pipes. Beyond their little haven, the huge metropolis of London rattled on, indifferent to the falling night, ever busy, ever changing.

He held her close, quietly, skin to skin down the length of their bodies, warm and replete, one hand stroking her almost absently. She felt worshiped, felt cherished. And loved.

She believed him when he said he loved her—he had affectionate ways, did Flynn—but she still knew she was the wrong kind of wife for him.

He could make a joke of it, pretend he didn't mind that she wasn't a proper lady, but *she* minded. He deserved the best, and she vowed to herself that he would get it.

She could do whatever she set her mind to. She would become the wife he needed.

"It's a funny thing, love," he said after a while. "I reckon I loved you all along, almost from the first, but I was so set on—"

"Marrying a fine lady."

"Exactly, that I couldn't see what was there, under me nose all the time. The sweetest, bravest, lovingest, prickliest, stubbornest girl in the world."

She wrinkled her nose. "Stubborn?"

He gave a huff of amusement and kissed her nose. "You are, darlin', but I even love that about you."

There was a long silence. She wasn't used to people saying "I love you"—not to her. Not meaning it the way he did. It made her feel so humble. So unworthy.

"I will become a proper lady, Flynn, I promise you."

He made a small exclamation and propped himself on one elbow to look at her. "Are you still on about that? For God's sake Daisy, I told you I love you—does that not mean anything to you?"

"It means *everything* to me," she said, her eyes filling with tears. "Which is why—"

He kissed her. "You're talkin' nonsense again. I don't want a perfect lady—I want *you*!"

Flynn looked into her wide, doubting eyes, and shook his head. She didn't really believe him—and who could blame her, the way he'd gone on about the finest lady in London. Fool that he'd been, prattling about perfect ladies when he'd had the perfect woman right in front of him all the time.

She wasn't a girl who trusted easily, his Daisy, and it wasn't surprising, the way she'd been treated all her life. As far as he could tell every single person she'd ever cared about had let her down—except for her sisters and Lady Bea and she'd only been with them for a year.

He had a lifetime in which he'd teach her different. But right now he had to make her understand.

Chapter Twenty

I cannot fix on the hour, or the spot, or the look or the words, which laid the foundation. It is too long ago. I was in the middle before I knew that I had begun.

—JANE AUSTEN, *PRIDE & PREJUDICE*

"Daisy, love, the way that old bitch from the brothel talked to you that time . . . it's no wonder you don't want to believe me. All your life she was runnin' you down, dragging you down, tellin' you you were rubbish, a joke, tryin' to make you less than you are. God, darlin', how you grew up with that and came out the other end so strong and sweet and decent—"

She made a small muffled sound of denial.

"Yes, you are. You're like . . ." He searched his mind for a way to make her understand. "You're like Damascus steel."

"Steel?" She pulled a doubtful face.

"Damascus steel is famous—the best quality steel ever. It's well-hammered in the making, tempered by fire and quenched in dragon's blood—that's you, growing up tough. Swords made of Damascus steel are the finest in the world."

She squinted up at him, as if wondering whether he was serious. "Gawd, Flynn. I reckon I know who the dragon was but really . . . You reckon I'm like one of them swords?"

"You are," he assured her. "Strong, beautiful, flexible, and wonderfully sharp. And greatly prized."

She snorted. "And here I was, thinking I was the sheath and you was the sword." Her hand moved to caress his "sword" and he laughed.

They made love again. But when it was over and they lay quietly, listening to the dripping of the rain in the pipes and the rattle of the carts over the cobbles, he knew he hadn't yet made her understand. That she'd turned it into a joke because it made her uncomfortable to think that she was good and fine and worthy of love.

"I can see I'm goin' to have to explain it, where I got that 'finest lady' notion from—or rather, where I think I got it from, for God only knows how some ideas get lodged in our brain."

He tucked her against him. "I told you about me mam and da', back in Ireland, and how it all ended."

She nodded.

"For years I tried not to think about them, tried not to remember. It was too painful." She slid her arms around him and hugged him, half draped across his chest, warm and soft. She didn't yet trust that he truly loved and wanted her, but she was a loving, generous little soul, his Daisy.

"Since I've been in London, I've been remembering more and more. Would you believe it was a blue teapot that started me thinkin'." He told her about the tea setting he'd seen in the shop window and how it had sparked a memory and how it had helped unravel all of his thinking about Lady Elizabeth.

"See, the first time I saw her, she was pourin' out tea for her guests, and somehow, it made me think she was the one."

She gave him an odd look. "You were goin' to marry her because of a teapot?"

He laughed. "Not exactly. It was what the teapot symbolized—and I didn't even know it meself, at the time. Until a certain girl's kiss brought me to me senses."

She kissed his chest and rubbed her cheek against him.

"Later I realized there was more to it than just that—things I'd forgotten, ideas that got somehow twisted up in me mind."

He told her how he remembered his father, during the good times, before the accident, saying he'd married the finest young lady in three counties. "And Mam would laugh and blush, and say, 'Only three counties, is it?' And Da would pull her onto his lap and say, 'The whole country, lass—I married the finest lass in all of Ireland.' And he'd kiss her.

"I was just a boy, but they said it often enough that I remember. But after the accident Da never pulled Mam onto his lap like that again."

There was a short silence. "Somehow, I tucked that memory away. Forgot it, but held onto it in some part of me. And over time, the memory hardened and changed, until there I was, a brash eedjit, tellin' everyone I was going to marry the finest young lady in London—and believin' it. And thinking that meant an earl's daughter, some kind of symbol of what I'd achieved with me life."

He looked at Daisy. "When instead, what I really wanted, deep down, was a woman like me Da had, a loving, warm-hearted woman, to share me bed and me life, and to raise a family with."

Her eyes were liquid with unshed tears.

"I didn't realize the right woman was there, right under me nose, until I'd kissed you, Daisy. And once I had . . . well . . ." He gave a rueful grin. "Served me right that I'd found the girl for me, but she didn't want me at all—only to use as her occasional plaything. It did terrible things to me self-esteem, so it did. But I like a challenge."

"You were never a plaything," she mumbled, embarrassed.

"You had all you ever needed, you said—your family, your shop, food in your belly and a man in your bed."

"I didn't mean any man, I meant you."

"And you never wanted children at all."

There was a short silence. "I know. It wasn't until I fell pregnant that I even thought about it. And when I did I was scared to bits. I still am. I don't know nothing about babies." She cupped her hand protectively over her belly. "But I realized I wanted her. Loved her."

Flynn covered her hand with his. "Her?"

She nodded. "And I want her to have all the things I never had—a mum, a dad, a home. I might never have wanted it, Flynn, but I'm going to be the best mother and wife I can be."

"I know, love. You never do anything half-hearted, do you?"

"What's the point of being half-hearted? If you want something, you have to go for it."

"My feelings exactly." Flynn dropped a kiss on her head. "So you think it's a girl?"

"Yeah, of course."

"Could be a boy."

She started at him and a faintly panicked look came into her eyes. "It can't be a boy. I don't know nuffin' about boys."

He smiled. "I do. There's two of us now, don't forget."

She stared at him frowning, and shook her head. "No, she's a girl. I know she is. With black curls and big blue eyes."

"Sounds grand to me."

"You won't mind if she's not a boy? An heir?"

He shook his head. "Whoever God sends us will be fine by me. I just want you and a family—you're what matters most."

Her eyes filled again. "I will learn to be a better—"

He rolled his eyes. "Oh, for God's sake, woman, will you not understand? I don't want you to learn *anything*! I want *you*, Daisy Chance, just exactly as you are—spiky, difficult, stubborn as hell, swearing, punching, loving—just exactly the way you are."

He glared down at her, frustrated by her persistent misunderstanding of what he wanted. "You're the woman I fell in love with. Why the hell would I then want you to become something different?"

She frowned up at him, puzzled. "I thought you were ambitious?"

"I am."

"Then you'll need a wife who's ambitious as well."

"So? You are ambitious."

"Well, I was for me shop, yes. But I don't have that any more, remember?"

He grimaced and gave her a cautious look. "Actually, no. I do."

She jerked her head back and stared at him. "*You* do? How? Did you find out—"

He grimaced, knowing she wasn't going to like what he said. But he had to say it. "*I'm* your silent partner, Daisy."

She blinked, then shook her head. "What are you talkin' about, Flynn? Louisa—"

"Is the widow of an old friend of mine."

She reared back, glaring at him, her eyes chips of anger. "She's *what*?"

He held up his hands in a peaceable gesture. "Now don't get cross with me, darlin—you were bein' so stubborn about taking me on as a partner, and when I bumped into Louisa, quite by accident, she told me she was at a loose end and finding society life a bit dull, after the life she and her husband led in the Far East. So I filled her in and gave her the money to invest in your business."

There was a long silence. She wasn't happy about it, he could see. He braced himself for a thump. It didn't come.

Her eyes still glittered with anger, but also betrayal. She lifted her chin. "You never did trust me to be able to do it on me own, did you?"

He sat up and grabbed her by the arms. "It wasn't that at all, darlin'. It was because you were wearin' yourself out, workin' all hours of the day and night, givin' yourself no fun at all and turning yourself into a pale wee shred of the girl I loved." He slid his hands up to cup her face gently. "I couldn't bear to see you like that, Daisy-girl, not when the solution was so simple."

She swallowed and pushed his hands away. "You lied to me, Flynn." She tried to hide the hurt in her voice, but it was fathoms deep.

He nodded. "I know. And I apologize. But I'm not sorry I did. I'd do the same again."

She frowned and opened her mouth to say something, but he jumped in first. "I had to lie to you—it was the only way. Because you couldn't bring yourself to trust me."

There was a short silence and he added, "I know I hurt your feelings, darlin', but think about where you'd be now, if I hadn't lied to you."

She thought about it. She wouldn't have her lovely shop,

she wouldn't have had that splendid opening, and half of London flocking to buy her things. She wouldn't have a bunch of girls working for her and making their own lives better, and she wouldn't have a friend like Louisa.

Most of all she wouldn't have had those glorious, beautiful private times with Flynn here in their own little attic love nest. She probably wouldn't have Flynn at all. Or the baby.

And at that thought her anger trickled away. "I was stubborn, wasn't I?"

"Just a little bit reluctant to mix business with friendship, I reckon—which isn't such a bad thing. And worried that I'd tramp all over your dream enterprise with me big clumsy feet, tellin' you what to do and sticking me nose in where it wasn't wanted."

She sighed. "That was partly it. But mostly it was because until you, there'd never been a man I *could* trust. I'm sorry, Flynn, I should have known better."

"Ah, don't be sorry, darlin'. It helped me to understand exactly why you were the perfect wife for me."

She frowned in puzzlement. "How?"

"You and me, darlin', are two halves of a whole. We're both ambitious, we neither of us care much for appearances—"

"Oy, I do care a lot about—"

"Not how-you-look appearances, but what-other-people-think-of-us appearances. If you cared more, you would have tried harder in those lady lessons of Lady Bea's."

She acknowledged that with a rueful nod.

"And if I'd married someone like Lady Elizabeth, I'd never be able to talk about the things that interest me—my latest ventures or new business possibilities—over the breakfast or dinner table."

"Vulgar," she said in an imitation of Lady Bea.

"That's right, or else she'd be endlessly polite—tolerating me vulgar ways, whereas you and I, we can talk about this stuff for hours." He pulled her closer. "Even when we're curled up in bed."

"Well, business is interesting."

"So it is. To both of us. And if you think I'm talkin'

rubbish, you'll tell me so, to my face, instead of hiding behind polite phrases, believing that what's on the surface is all that counts. Marrying some lord's daughter would have been the stupidest thing I could do. I'd be an outsider in me own house, and worse, I'd be bored. With you I'm never bored. We'll love and argue and love again."

He kissed her. She was starting to believe him now.

"So who will we get to run the shop?" she said after a while.

He gave her an odd look. "You, of course."

"*What?*" Daisy flashed him a look of complete surprise.

"You don't think I'm going to keep it meself, do you? What would I do with a ladies' dress shop? I'll sign it over to you now, if you like. Do you have a pen and paper?" He looked around for something to write on.

Daisy struggled to take it in. All these years she'd been worried about losing her business to some man—and she had!—and now he was handing it back to her like it was . . . like a handkerchief she'd misplaced.

"Don't worry, it can wait until after the wedding."

"But I thought—"

"I trust you, Flynn." She leaned forward and kissed him. "But I can't keep workin' at the shop. I'll be married, remember? Married ladies don't go out to work."

He raised his brows at her. "Do you want to give up the business you've worked so hard to achieve, then?"

"No, of course not, but I thought   "

"I wouldn't take your dream away from you, darlin'. If you want to continue running your shop, I don't see why you can't. We've got the money to hire all the help we need with the baby. As for what anyone else thinks, it's between you and me and nobody else."

He pulled her tight for a long warm hug. "Listen—can you hear that?"

She listened. "I don't hear nothin'"

"Yes, you do—the sound of London out there, still busy and tradin' and cheatin' and sellin' and buying, even though it's dark. It never sleeps, this city.

"The world is changing, darlin' and we're movin' right

along with it. But the toffs—most of them—aren't. They know things are changing, but they're not looking out and learning; they're resisting, closin' ranks, getting more and more exclusive, tryin' to keep people like you and me out.

"What they don't understand is, it's not about the past anymore, who your ancestors were, who knows the right fork to hold or any of that. It's not about London, or even England or the United Kingdom—it's about the world. And you and me, Daisy, we're citizens of the world. I've got a worldwide trading business and—"

"I've never been out of London except to visit me sisters' country homes."

"I'll take you to Venice on our honeymoon."

She shook her head. "No, the place is sinking, I heard. Damaris and Freddy were there just a few months ago."

He laughed.

She said, "But I see what you're gettin' at. The toffs still have a lot of influence, though."

"Yeah and we have plenty of friends. We don't need to play at being toffs—we'll just be ourselves, and know that the friends we have are real ones. And make sure this little one"—he patted her belly—"has the opportunities we never had, but doesn't fancy herself better than other people, just because she was born in a comfortable home."

She turned to him then. "I've been thinkin' about that— where we're going to live."

"Wherever you like."

She wrinkled her nose. "Wait until I've told you my idea—you might not like it." She explained.

He laughed. "Sounds like a grand plan to me, but it's not up to me, is it?"

"This looks ominous," Lady Beatrice observed as Daisy and Flynn were ushered into the drawing room by Featherby. "A deputation, is it?"

Daisy swallowed. "We got something to ask you, and before we tell you what it is, I want you to know that it was my idea, not Flynn's—in case you want to know who to blame."

"I see. And are you going to keep standing there, looming over me, with a face that might as well be heading for the guillotine, or will you sit, like civilized people?"

They sat side by side on the sofa facing her. "It's like this—" Daisy began.

"Show me your hands, gel," the old lady rapped.

Daisy and Flynn exchanged bemused glances, then Daisy extended her hands.

Lady Beatrice gave them a quick glance, snorted, then aimed her lorgnette at Flynn. "How long have you been betrothed? Notices in the papers, the banns being called and the gel *still* wears no betrothal ring?"

Flynn blinked. He looked at Daisy. "I'm sorry," he said, "it slipped my mind. I will of course—"

"It didn't slip his mind, he hasn't had a chance," Daisy said. "I wouldn't see him or speak to him before this."

The lorgnette raked over them, pausing a long moment at where Daisy was holding Flynn's hand under cover of her skirts. "But you are seeing and speaking now?"

"Yes, m'lady." Flynn grinned and put his arm around Daisy, bold and blatant as could be. Daisy tried not to smile but her grin broke out too.

The old lady sniffed and tried to look severe. "About time you sorted things out. Now, you will need a ring."

"Yes ma'am and I'll—"

"Featherby?"

"Milady." Featherby appeared as if from nowhere, produced a small box from his pocket and with a bow, handed it to the old lady.

Beside Flynn, Daisy gasped.

Lady Beatrice paused, turning the box between gnarled old fingers. "This might not suit, of course. You might prefer something flashier, more modern."

Daisy didn't say a word. Flynn glanced at her. She was pale and holding her breath. "Whatever Daisy wants."

The old lady nodded. "I don't know how much of our story

you know, Mr. Flynn. She's very loyal, our gel here, and not one to gossip, but when we first met, I was in a dire situation. Without going into details, I was waiting for death, alone and hopeless—until my dearest gels came into my life.

"I'd been robbed of all my valuables, or so I'd thought. Turns out they were paste, the lot of them, all except my rings, which I never took off, so my late husband was unable to get his hands on them. I thought they'd been stolen, but when we moved here, and dear Featherby and William dismantled my bed, they found them in a secret hollow in the bedpost that I'd had made a lifetime ago. I must have hidden my rings there and forgotten all about them. I'd been ill, you see."

She sighed reminiscently. "Four rings, four stones. I gave Abby the emerald, Damaris the sapphire, Jane the ruby and now I would very much like my dearest Daisy to have the diamond." She held out the box to Daisy.

She didn't move.

Flynn glanced down at her and saw she was blinking back tears.

"All my girls are precious to me, but this gel—as I hope you appreciate, Mr. Flynn—is as rare and precious and full of light as any diamond."

Flynn rose and took the little box from her. "Oh I appreciate it, milady. It's her that doesn't understand how precious she is, but I aim to change that."

"Good lad."

He returned, but instead of sitting, he knelt on one knee, opened the box, took out a gold ring containing the most superb diamond he'd ever seen, and said, "Daisy Chance, will you wear this diamond ring, not only as a betrothal ring and a pledge of my love, but also as a reminder of Lady Beatrice, your sisters, and all who love you?"

Her face crumpled, but she held out her hand, which was shaking like a leaf. He slipped the ring on, and it fit perfectly.

"Beautiful, dear boy, just beautiful," Lady Beatrice said, mopping her eyes with a wisp of lace. Behind her Featherby turned away to discreetly blow his nose, and out in the hall they could hear William blowing his nose in a bugle trumpet of emotion.

Tears streaming down her face, Daisy rose, hugged Flynn and hurried forward to hug and kiss Lady Beatrice. And then she hugged Featherby as well. And then turned to the doorway from which a smattering of applause came, growing louder as Lady Beatrice's staff crowded through the doorway to witness Daisy's moment and congratulate her. More than any of the other girls, she'd been one of their own.

"Champagne, Featherby," Lady Beatrice croaked when the fuss began to subside.

"At once, milady." He gestured and the crowd melted away.

Lady Beatrice blew her nose again. "Dear me, emotions, always so exhausting. The house is going to be dreadfully quiet without you, my dear."

Daisy reached for Flynn's hand. "That's what we come to talk to you about."

The old lady waved her crumpled shred of lace. "Go ahead, talk then."

"You know I never planned to get married," Daisy began, and hurried on before anyone could interrupt, "I always thought I'd live here with you for the rest of me life."

"You mean the rest of *my* life," the old lady said sardonically.

"*My* life," Daisy repeated obediently, then saw what the old lady was getting at. "Oh, yeah, I see what you mean—*your* life. I wasn't going to say that—I was bein' tactful. But since you've said it, yeah, I planned to keep you company for as long as you wanted and needed me."

"Very worthy of you, my dear, but I don't in the least begrudge you your happiness."

"Good, neither do I. But I thought . . . I wondered . . ."

"What Daisy is trying to say," Flynn interjected, "is that she'd very much like to go on living here, with you. We both would."

"We'd take the second floor," Daisy said. "If you didn't mind, that is."

The old lady sat very still. "With me? You want to live here, with me?"

"As a married couple, yes," Flynn said.

"You would do that?" she asked, clearly moved. "Live with an old lady?"

He grinned. "Not any old lady. Just an ageless, elegant, canny wee elf."

Daisy gave him an odd look. "She ain't an elf, stupid." She turned back to Lady Beatrice. "If you don't like the idea, of course, we won't. Flynn says he'll buy us the closest house available so I can pop in often and you won't have to miss me at all."

"Don't like the idea?" the old lady echoed.

"Because of the baby," Daisy said. "They make a lot of noise, I'm told."

"Live with a *baby*?" The old lady's face lit up. She turned to the doorway. "Did you hear that, Featherby, this house is going to have a baby in it, at long last." She blinked away tears and almost whispered, "All my life, I've wanted a baby."

Featherby beamed. "A baby?" He turned to William who was carrying in champagne and glasses. "We're going to have a baby, William. Living here, with us."

William's big ugly boxer's face split in a grin. "Congratulations, Miss Daisy. That'll make this house feel like a proper family home then, won't it?"

They drank toasts then—all five of them, including Featherby and William, who had been with them since the beginning. They drank to Daisy and Flynn, to the success of Daisy's shop, to the coming baby, and to Lady Beatrice, who, as Daisy pointed out, was going to become a great-aunt.

"A *great*-aunt? Nonsense!" the old lady declared. "I shall be a *splendid* aunt!"

Daisy laughed. "You are already!"

After Featherby and William had left, the old lady grew serious. "Now that you're getting married, I'm going to change my will," she told them. "I had planned to leave this house to Daisy."

"To me?"

"A woman should always have a home of her own. But between you and Mr. Flynn, I'm not worried about your future security—Max will ensure the marriage settlements provide handsomely for you."

"He won't need to," Flynn growled.

"I know, dear boy, but he likes doing that sort of thing and a nephew should be useful. But since Daisy's future is settled I'm going to write up a new will; when I die I intend to leave this house to Featherby and William."

Flynn frowned. They were good servants, but . . .

Daisy took his hand and started to explain but the old lady cut her off. "Featherby and William have been as much a part of this grand adventure as my dear gels. I shudder to think where we all might still be had they not come with you that first fateful day. And since then, Featherby has not only cared for me, he's made me the envy of the ton—did you know, Flynn, dear boy, half the aristocracy have been trying to steal Featherby from me, and he didn't so much as hint."

She gave a brisk nod of satisfaction. "Those two gentlemen tended me when I was at the lowest point of my life and never once turned a hair at what they were asked to do. They looked after me and my gels not simply as loyal servants, but almost as . . . family. And when I die—which I trust will be many years in the future—they will be elderly and in need of security. So as well as a pension, I will give them this house. You won't mind, will you, Daisy? The other gels all have their own homes already, but you—"

"Have a home here with you—the only home I've ever had—and I'll always have a home with Flynn and our baby, wherever we live. And I love this idea, Lady Bea. I never had a father, but Featherby and William have been like fathers to me—to all of us—and of course the other girls and I would always look after them, but it's so much better this way, something they've earned the right to, and not charity."

She hugged the old lady. "Do you know how much I love you? How much we all love you? And I'm so happy that you'll be here for my baby to grow up with. You can teach her all the things you've taught me—and no, I don't mean grammar and deportment, though I s'pose the poor little thing will have to learn that too."

The old lady sniffed. "Don't know as I've taught you very much at all."

"Oh, but you have—more than you know." Daisy's smile was blinding, and it took in Flynn as well as the old lady. "You'll teach her how to be a true lady—generous and kind and loyal and loving, in the heart, where it truly matters."

"Just like her mother," Flynn said softly. "The finest lady in London."

"Drat!" the old lady grumbled. "Got something in my eye again. Where's a wretched handkerchief when you need one?" Flynn handed her his.

Chapter Twenty-one

I have no notion of loving people by halves,
it is not my nature.

—JANE AUSTEN, *NORTHANGER ABBEY*

The first day of summer dawned fine, and miraculously, given the weather they'd been having recently, it stayed fine all day.

Carriages started arriving outside St. George's in Hanover Square, disgorging smart gentlemen who handed down elegantly dressed women in beautiful hats. A crowd of curious and hopeful onlookers gathered to watch. A society wedding always provided good entertainment. And possibly handfuls of pennies would be thrown.

Soon the church was crowded. It smelled of flowers, perfume, incense, beeswax and brass polish. Dappled lozenges of colored light lit the floor, sunshine through stained glass.

Inside the church, Flynn paced back and forth in front of the altar rail.

"Why so anxious? You've been through this three times," Max, his best man, observed in smug amusement. "My wedding, Freddy's and Janc's wedding just gone—you should be used to it by now."

"It didn't matter to me then," Flynn snapped and continued pacing. What if she'd changed her mind? What if she panicked, ran?

Freddy Hyphen-Hyphen grinned. "Nice to see someone else suffering, ain't it, Max?"

The music that had been playing quietly in the background now stopped and a firm, decisive chord announced a change. Flynn spun around and there she was, his bride, dressed in a soft cloud of white. She looked exquisite, so small and dainty and fragile, so strong and tough and prickly and perfect.

The music played and, walking on Featherby's arm, she started down the aisle towards him. She was nervous, he could see from the little frown of concentration between her brows, but the minute she saw him, her face lit up and she smiled.

He blinked. Her smile brightened the whole church. Her sisters followed her, but Flynn barely noticed. He had eyes only for Daisy.

She reached him and put out her hand, and he took it, the only thing that felt real—her small warm precious hand. Her hand in marriage.

In a daze he heard the minister begin, in a daze he repeated the vows, in a daze he slid the gold ring on her finger.

"You may kiss the bride."

They kissed, and Flynn started to breathe again. He'd done it, won the lady of his heart, Daisy Chance, now Daisy Flynn—the finest lady in London.

They walked back down the aisle again, well-wishers filled the church, waving and smiling and sobbing—the damp handkerchiefs were out in force—most of them for Daisy.

Did she see how she was loved? Not for any reason, no reason of birth or position, just because she was the dear, sweet girl she was.

Daisy walked back down the aisle in a blur. She was married. Flynn's arm was under her hand, strong and sure and warm. She lost track of the well-wishers who crowded around her, familiar faces, from the literary society, from her shop, friends of Flynn's and Max's and Freddy's.

The carriage awaited. She bade farewell to each of her

sisters, hugging them and sobbing, as if she was leaving them forever, not for a few weeks' honeymoon at the seaside—Flynn wanted her to see the real sea that he loved, not the stinky river, and was threatening to teach her to swim. She'd see about that.

She bade good-bye to Featherby and William, hugging them both.

Lastly she hugged Lady Beatrice, the old lady who'd changed her life.

"Don't see what you've got to cry about," the old lady grumbled, her own eyes red with weeping. "Got a fine husband there. All my gels have done exceptionally well in the husband department. But Daisy"—she leaned forward and said in a voice that no one else could hear—"for what it's worth I would trade every jewel, every lover I've ever had and ten years of my life—twenty—for what you have." She smiled and patted Daisy's cheek. "A man who loves you, just as you are, and a babe."

Flynn threw handfuls of silver coins into the crowd and they drove off in a shower of rose petals and rice and a clatter of noise from the things someone—probably Freddy— had tied to the back of the carriage.

They were spending the first night in a grand London hotel—the Pulteney, which the czar of Russia had graced with his presence. As the carriage bowled smartly through the streets, they fell quiet.

"Happy?" Flynn asked.

She nodded. "Happier than I ever believed possible. I love you so much, Flynn." She leaned against him, her heart full to bursting.

"I know darlin'—and I love you too."

After a moment she said, "So, did you notice?"

"Notice what?"

"What I'm wearin'."

He grinned. "You look beautiful, as always."

She rolled her eyes. "You didn't notice, did you?"

"I did. It's a beautiful dress."

She stuck her foot out and pulled the hem of her dress up so he could see them clearly.

He looked. Red shoes with a red and white rosette on the toe. "Are they . . . ?"

She nodded. "The ones you gave me. I wore them to our wedding—they're not exactly weddin' shoes, you know, but I wore them."

"Why?"

"For you. So I wouldn't limp down the aisle." She thumped his shoulder. "It's the first time I've worn them, and I didn't limp and you watched me all the way and now, you didn't even notice!"

He pulled her across his knees. "That's because, my little hedgehog, I was looking at you—the prettiest bride a man ever had—not checking how you walked." And he kissed her, hard.

"Are they comfortable?"

She nodded. "You were right—they do make it easier to walk."

"Good. So will you wear them again?"

"Maybe. For special occasions."

He frowned. "What kind of special occasion were you thinking of?"

She fiddled with his waistcoat buttons, suddenly shy. "Like when we waltz . . . or summat."

Flynn hugged her tightly, too moved to speak. And then he kissed her again because she was his wife and he loved her. "Have I told you lately how wonderful I think you are?" he murmured.

"You just called me a hedgehog—that's a compliment in Ireland, is it?"

"It is. The very finest of compliments."

His loving bride snorted. And then she kissed him.

Epilogue

I did not then know what it was to love.

—JANE AUSTEN, *SENSE AND SENSIBILITY*

"Have you got her safe?"

Daisy smiled at her husband. "Yes, Flynn, she's safe. I'm holding her good and tight."

"Not too tight, I hope." He cast the small white bundle in Daisy's arms an anxious look. "Is she warm enough?" At the sound of his deep voice, their baby opened her eyes and gurgled happily.

"She's warm as toast. Stop worryin'" Daisy loved the way her big tough husband fussed so over his tiny daughter.

"We should have waited. February is too cold. I don't know why she needs to be christened anyway."

"Oh, hush." The baby gazed solemnly up at her daddy from the depths of a soft white wrap. She had his blue, blue eyes. Beneath the tiny knitted cap lay a fuzz of dark hair. They'd be curls one day, Daisy knew. She was the most beautiful, perfect baby.

They entered the church and took their places in the pews nearest the font.

"Here, let me take her," Flynn said, and with a smile Daisy handed her daughter over. He tucked her in the crook of his arm, beaming down at the tiny scrap. "Ah, look at you watching everyone with those bonny blue eyes. You know everything that's going on, don't you darlin'? Such a clever girl," he crooned.

Daisy watched her husband and daughter, her heart so full she could barely breathe. She'd thought on her wedding day she could be no happier. But the good feelings just kept on growing.

Their family sat around them; Lady Bea, swathed in furs, proudly dandling the Davenham heir, her great-ncphew, Max and Abby's baby son, little Georgie.

Jane sat beside Lady Beatrice, making peekaboo eyes at the tiny boy who watched her with big eyes and gurgled happily. Beside Jane sat her tall husband, Zachary, the Earl of Wainfleet, dark as a gypsy and handsome as sin. Freddy and Damaris sat on the other side of Lady Beatrice, arm in arm.

All her sisters had made the journey from their country properties up to London to see her daughter christened. In the wettest February ever.

She slid her arm through Flynn's. She was so blessed.

Just eighteen months ago, she didn't know anyone here. She'd been all alone in the world, nobody to love and never dreaming anyone would ever love her. She didn't really believe in love then.

Now she had a family of her own, her very own husband and baby, as well as sisters, brothers-in-law, a beloved aunt and a nephew. As well as friends, good friends. And a shop.

It was—almost—more than one girl could handle.

The service passed in a blur until, "Will the godparents step forward?" said the minister, and Abby and Max stepped up. With ill-concealed reluctance Flynn handed his daughter over to Abby, but the baby made no fuss. She knew her aunty Abby.

Daisy was watching Lady Beatrice and her sisters. Her heart was too full to take in much of what the minister was saying. She was waiting for the naming part. She hadn't yet told them the baby's full name.

The minister took the baby from Abby's arms. She gazed up at him, calm and trusting.

"I baptize thee Beatrice Abigail Damaris Jane Kathleen Flynn, in the name of the Father, the Son and the Holy Spirit." He dipped the baby and dribbled water on her head.

Little Beattie Flynn opened her mouth and screamed the church down.

"That's my girl," Flynn said proudly.

Read on for a special excerpt from
the first Chance Sisters Romance

The Autumn Bride

Available now from Berkley!

Chapter One

*"Give a girl an education and introduce her properly into
the world, and ten to one but she has the means of settling
well, without further expense to anybody."*

—JANE AUSTEN, MANSFIELD PARK

London, August 1816

S he was running late. Abigail Chantry quickened her pace.
Her half day off, and though it was damp and squally
and cold outside, she'd taken herself off as usual to continue
her explorations of London.

Truth to tell, if her employers had lived in the bleakest, most
remote part of the Yorkshire moors, Abby would still have
removed herself from their vicinity on her fortnightly half day
off. Mrs. Mason believed a governess should be useful as well
as educational, and saw no reason why, on Miss Chantry's half
day, she should not do a little mending for her employer or,
better still, take the children with her on her outings.

What need did a governess, especially one who was
orphaned, after all, have for free time?

Miss Chantry did not agree. So, rain, hail or snow, she
absented herself from the Mason house the moment after
the clock in the hall chimed noon, returning a few minutes
before six to resume her duties.

Having spent most of her life in the country, Abby was

loving her forays into this enormous city, discovering all kinds of wonderful places. Last week she'd found a book-shop where the owner let her read to her heart's content without pressuring her to buy—only the secondhand books, of course, not the new ones whose pages had not yet been cut. She'd returned there today, and had become so lost in a story—*The Monk*, deliciously bloodcurdling—that now she was running late.

If she returned even one minute after six, Mr. Mason would dock her wages by a full day. It had happened before, and no amount of argument would budge him.

She turned the corner into the Masons' street and glanced up at the nearby clock tower. Oh, Lord, three minutes to go. Abby picked up speed.

"Abby Chantry?" A young woman, a maidservant by her garments, limped toward her with an uneven gait. She'd been waiting opposite the Masons' house.

Abby eyed her warily. "Yes?" Apart from her employers, Abby knew no one in London. And nobody here called her Abby.

"I got a message from your sister." She spoke with a rough London accent.

Her mouth was swollen and a large bruise darkened her cheek.

"My *sister*?" It wasn't possible. Jane was hundreds of miles away. She'd just left the Pillbury Home for the Daughters of Distressed Gentlewomen, near Cheltenham, to take up a po-sition as companion to a vicar's mother in Hereford.

"She told me where to find you. I'm Daisy." The girl took Abby's arm and tugged. "You gotta come with me. Jane's in trouble—bad trouble—and you gotta come now."

Abby hesitated. The girl's bruised and battered face didn't inspire confidence. The newspapers were full of the terrible crimes that took place in London: murders, white slavery, pickpockets and burglars. She'd even read about people hit over the head in a dark alley, stripped and left for dead, just for their clothing.

But Abby wore a dull gray homemade dress that practically

shouted "governess." She couldn't imagine anyone wanting to steal it. And she was thin, plain and clever, rather than pretty, which ruled out white slavers. She had no money or valuables and, apart from the Mason family, she knew no one in London, so could hardly inspire murder.

And this girl knew her name, *and* Jane's. And Abby's address. Abby glanced at the clock. A minute to six. But what did the loss of a day's wages matter when her little sister was in London and in trouble? Jane was not yet eighteen.

"All right, I'll come." She gave in to Daisy's tugging and they hurried down the street. "Where is my sister?"

"In a bad place," Daisy said cryptically, stumping rapidly along with an ungainly gait. Crippled or the result of the beating she'd received? Abby wondered. Whichever, it didn't seem to slow her down.

"What kind of bad place?"

Daisy didn't respond. She led Abby through a maze of streets, cutting down back alleys and leading her into an area Abby had never felt tempted to explore.

"What kind of bad place?" Abby repeated.

Daisy glanced at her sideways. "A broffel, miss!"

"A broff—" Abby broke off, horrified. "You mean a *brothel*?"

"That's what I said, miss, a broffel."

Abby stopped dead. "Then it can't be my sister; Jane would never enter a brothel." But even as she said it, she knew the truth. *Her baby sister was in a brothel.*

"Yeah, well, she didn't have no choice in the matter. She come 'ere straight from some orphanage in the country. Drugged, she was. She give me your address and arst me to get a message to you. And we ain't got much time, so hurry."

Numb with shock, and sick at the thought, Abby allowed herself to be led down side streets and alleyways. Jane was supposed to be in a vicarage in Hereford. How could she possibly have ended up in a London brothel? *Drugged, she was.* How?

They turned into a narrow street lined with shabby houses, and slowed.

"That's it." Daisy gestured to a tall house, a good deal smarter than the others, with a freshly painted black door and windows curtained in crimson fabric. The ground-story windows were unbarred, but the higher ones were all barred. To keep people in, rather than out. *She didn't have no choice.*

As she stared up, she saw a movement at one of the highest windows. A glimpse of golden hair, two palms pressed against the glass framing a young woman the image of Abby's mother.

Abby hadn't seen her sister for six years, but there was no doubt in her heart. *Jane!*

Someone pulled Jane back out of sight and closed the curtains.

Her sister was a prisoner in that house. Abby hurried across the street and started up the front stairs. Daisy grabbed her by the skirt and pulled her backward.

"No, miss!" Her voice held so much urgency it stopped Abby dead. "If you go in there arstin' questions now, it'll only make things worse. You might never see your sister again!"

"Then I'll fetch a constable or a magistrate to sort out this matter."

"Do that and for certain sure you'll never see your sister again. He—Mort—him who owns this place and all the girls in it now"—she jerked her chin toward the upstairs—"he pays blokes to warn him. Before any constable can get here your sister will be long gone."

Abby felt sick. "But what can I do? I must get her out of there."

"I told you, miss—we got a plan." The sound of carriage wheels rattling down the street made Daisy look around. She paled. "Oh, my gawd, that's Mort comin'! Go quick! If he catches me talkin' to anyone outside he'll give me another frashing! I'll meet you in the alley behind the house. Sixth house along. Big spiked gate. Go!" She gave Abby a shove and fled down the side steps to the basement area.

Abby, still in shock—Jane, in a brothel!—hurried away down the street, forcing herself not to look back, even when she heard the carriage draw to a halt outside the house with the black door.

She turned the corner and found the alley Daisy had described running behind the houses. It was narrow, gloomy and strewn with filth of all kinds, the cobbles slimy, the damp stench vile. Abby covered her nose and grimly picked her way along the lane. From time to time something squelched underfoot but she didn't look down. Whatever she'd stepped in, she didn't want to know. All that mattered was getting Jane out of that place.

She counted along the houses and came to the sixth, set behind a tall brick wall, the top of which was studded with shards of broken glass. A solid wooden gate was set into it, topped by a line of iron spikes.

The sinister row of spikes gleamed dully in the faint light. Ice slid slowly through her veins. With her dying breath Mama had made Abby promise to keep Jane safe, to keep them both safe. It hadn't been easy—Jane's beauty had always attracted attention, even when she was a little girl—but Abby had kept that promise.

Until now. Jane was imprisoned *in a brothel*. Abby raised a hand to her mouth and found it was shaking.

Her whole body was trembling.

How long had Jane been there? Abby tried to work it out, to recall what Jane had said in her last letter, but she couldn't. Over and over, the question pounded through her mind: How had Jane come to be in a brothel?

Abby shoved the fruitless question aside. She had to think, to plan what to do to get Jane free. What if Daisy didn't come? Abby would have no option but to fetch a constable.

Do that and for certain sure you'll never see your sister again. Abby shivered. She was entirely dependent on the goodwill—and ability—of a girl she'd never seen till a few minutes ago.

If constables and magistrates couldn't help, how could one small, crippled maidservant make a difference? And where was she?

The minutes crawled by.

Abby was almost ready to give up when she heard something on the other side of the gate. Her heart gave a leap of relief; then it occurred to her it could be anyone. She pressed back into the shadows and waited.

The gate cracked open an inch. "You still here, miss?" came a whisper.

"I'm here."

The girl poked her head out. "I got no time to explain, miss, but come back here in an hour with a warm cloak and some shoes."

"Shoes, but—"

"I was going to try and get your sister out now, but I can't while Mort's here. But he's goin' out again shortly."

She turned to leave, but Abby grabbed her arm. "Why? Why would you do this for us? For Jane and me?" It was obviously dangerous. Why would this girl—a stranger—take such a risk? Was she expecting payment? Abby would gladly give all she had to save her sister, but she didn't have much.

The girl shook her head. "'Cause it's wrong, what Mort's doing. It never used to be like this, stealing girls, keeping them locked up—" She broke off. "Look, I ain't got time to explain, miss, not so's you'd understand. You'll just have to trust me. Just be back here in an hour with a warm cloak and some shoes."

"Why?" Some kind of payment for services rendered?

"'Cause she hain't got nothin' to wear outside, of course." She jerked her chin at the filth in the alley. "You want her to walk through that in her bare feet? Now I gotta go." And with that the girl was gone, the gate shut behind her. Abby heard a bolt slide into place.

Numbly, Abby found her way back to the Masons' house. An hour.

A lot could happen in an hour.

"What time do you call this?"

Abby, her foot on the first stair, turned back. Mr. Mason stood in the hall entry, fob watch in hand, glowering. "You're late!"

"I know, and I'm sorry, Mr. Mason, but I only just learned that—"

"I shall have to deduct the full day from your wages, of course." He puffed his chest up like a particularly pleased toad.

"It was a family emergency—"

He snorted. "You have no family."

"I do, I have a sister, and she has come to London unexpectedly and—"

"No excuses, you know the rules."

"It's not an excuse. It's true, and I'm hoping . . . I was wondering . . ." She swallowed, belatedly realizing she should not have argued with him.

"What were you wondering, Miss Chantry?" Mrs. Mason swept down the staircase, dressed in a sumptuous puce silk dress, a feathered headdress and a cloak edged with fur. "Have you forgotten, Mr. Mason, we are to attend the opera this evening? I do not wish to be late."

"It's fashionable to be late," her husband responded.

"I realize that, my dear." Mrs. Mason's voice grated with sugarcoated irritation. "But we are going to be more than fashionably late—you don't even have your coat on."

The butler arrived in the hallway, heard the remark and went to fetch Mr. Mason's coat.

Mrs. Mason pulled on one long kid evening glove and glanced at Abby. "Well, what is it, Miss Chantry?"

Abby took a deep breath. The Masons were very strict about visitors of any kind. Abby was allowed none. "My younger sister is in London, ma'am, and I was wondering if she could stay with me, just for the night—"

The woman's well-plucked eyebrows rose. "Here? Don't be ridiculous. Of course not. Now come along, Mr. Mason—"

"But I haven't seen her for years. She's just left the orphanage and she's not quite eighteen. I can't let her stay in London on her own."

"That's not our concern." Mrs. Mason frowned into the looking glass and adjusted her headdress. "A stranger, sleeping in the same house as my precious babies?" She snorted.

"She's not a stranger; she's *my sister.*"

"It's out of the question." Mr. Mason allowed the butler to help him into his coat. "Blake, is the carriage here?"

The butler opened the door and peered outside. "It's just turning out of the mews, sir."

"And this is your last word?" Abby asked.

Mrs. Mason turned on her. "Why are you still loitering about? You heard my husband; the answer is no! Now get upstairs and attend to the children."

There was no point in arguing, so Abby went upstairs. She had no intention of obeying anyway.

She checked on the children, as she did every night. They were all fast asleep, looking like little angels, which they absolutely were not. The two older ones were full of mischief. Abby didn't care. She loved them anyway.

Susan, the toddler, was sleeping on her front with her bottom poking up as usual. Such a little darling. Abby gently turned her on her side and the little girl snuggled down, smiling to herself, still fast asleep. Abby tucked the covers around her.

These children were the joy and also the agony of her job. Abby loved them as if they were her own. She couldn't help herself—she knew it was foolish, and that one day they'd break her heart. She knew they'd be taken away from her, or she'd be sent away from them as if they'd outgrown her like a pair of old shoes.

It was heartbreak waiting to happen, loving other people's children.

She'd learned that hard lesson from the Taylors, her first position. Two years she'd been with them, loving the little ones with all her hungry heart. Not thinking ahead. Never even considering that one day she'd be dismissed and never see the children again.

They lived in Jamaica now.

She would lose the Mason children now too, but she would not—could not—leave her sister alone in a London hotel—not after what she'd been through. Even if she hadn't, if Jane had arrived in London unexpectedly, as she'd told the Masons, they had six years to catch up on; Jane had been a child of twelve when Abby saw her last.

Jane.

She bent and kissed each sleeping child and hurried out to collect the cloak and shoes for her sister, adding a shawl to the bundle, just in case.

G aslight had not yet reached the more sordid parts of the city. In the evening gloom the alleyway seemed more noisome and full of sinister shadows. Abby trod warily, counting the houses until she reached the high brick wall with the spiked wooden gate.

She stationed herself opposite the gate and waited, watching the windows like a hawk, noting every passing flicker of light, every shadow of movement. Was that Jane? Was that?

The time passed slowly. A distant clock chimed the hour. It was taking much longer than she'd expected. Had something gone wrong?

Something ran over her foot, a flicker of tiny damp claws and a slithery tail. She jumped, stifling a scream. She loathed rats.

She was concentrating so hard on the windows above that the scrape of the bolt on the gate opposite took her unawares and she jumped in fright.

The gate creaked open. A head peered out. "Abby?" A low whisper.

"Jane?"

A pale wraithlike shape slipped through the gap and then her sister was in her arms, clinging tightly, trembling, weeping and laughing. "Abby, oh, Abby!"

"Janey!" Tears blurred Abby's vision as she hugged her little sister. Not so little anymore, she realized. Jane was as tall as Abby now. She hugged her tighter. "Jane, dearest! Are you all right? How did you come to be in London? I thought Hereford—"

A hard little finger poked her in the ribs. "Oy! We're not

out of danger yet, y'know. Escape now, happy reunion later!" It was Daisy. "Now quick, where's them shoes?"

"Of course." Abby released Jane and as she stepped back her jaw dropped. Her sister was naked but for a thin chemise. "Good God, Jane, where are your clothes?" She pulled the cloak out and threw it around her shivering sister.

"It's to stop us leaving," Jane said between chattering teeth. "We can't go into the streets dressed like this."

Abby crouched to slip the shoes on Jane's cold feet, which were filthy from the alley. She wiped them clean as best she could with a handkerchief, her hands shaking with rage and distress. For her sister to be kept in such an indecent state, without even clothes to keep her covered! And in such cold weather!

"Put this on as well." She passed the shawl to Jane.

"No, Damaris can use it."

"Damaris?" Abby glanced up and saw another girl hovering uncertainly outside the gate, shivering, her arms wrapped around herself. She too was scantily clothed, but unlike Jane, this girl looked exactly like a woman out of a brothel.

She wore a thin red-and-gold gauzy wrapper that barely reached past her thighs. Her dark hair was piled high, spiked into place with two sticks. Her face—clearly painted—was a dead white oval. Her lips and cheeks were garishly rouged, her eyelids had been darkened and the line of her eyes was elongated at the corners.

"Damaris is my friend." Jane took Abby's shawl and tucked it around the shivering girl. "She's coming with us."

Abby frowned. Take this painted brothel creature with them?

Jane saw Abby's hesitation and put a protective arm around the other girl's shoulders. "She has to come with us, Abby. She saved me. I owe her everything."

"Come with us? But . . ." It was going to be difficult enough to smuggle Jane into the Mason residence, let alone this . . . this person.

"Damaris is the only reason I wasn't raped," Jane said urgently. "She has to come with us, Abby!"

Shocked, Abby stared at the garishly painted girl. *The*

only reason Jane wasn't raped? Suddenly she didn't care what Damaris looked like, how much paint she wore, how scandalous her clothing was, what her past was. Whatever she'd done before this moment, she'd saved Jane from rape.

Daisy shifted restlessly. "Goin' to stand around all night talkin'?"

It jolted Abby to her senses. "No, of course not. Here, Damaris." She unfastened her own cloak and wrapped the shivering girl in it. She tugged the hood up to conceal her face and hair.

Abby glanced down at Damaris's narrow feet, pale against the dark mud of the alley. "I don't have another pair of shoes, but here." She passed Damaris her mittens. "Put them on your feet. It's the best I can do."

"Thank you," Damaris said in a soft voice. "I don't mean to be a burden."

The girl's gratitude made Abby ashamed of her earlier hesitation. "You're not a burden," she lied. "You helped my sister and for that I owe you. Besides, I wouldn't want anyone to return to that horrid place." They would manage. Somehow.

She turned to Daisy. "I cannot thank you enough for what you've done. I have a little money. It's not much, but . . ." She proffered a small purse.

"I don't want your money!" Daisy stepped back, offended.

"But you risked so much—"

"I didn't do it for money. Anyway, I got me own money. Now, are you lot goin' or not?"

Abby stepped forward and hugged her. "Thank you, Daisy." Jane and Damaris hugged and thanked Daisy too; then, with whispered good-byes, they hurried down the alley.

Almost immediately Abby heard footsteps behind them. Had they been discovered? She whirled around. It was Daisy, carrying a small bundle.

"Are they Jane's belongings?"

Daisy clutched the bundle tightly against her chest. "No, it's me own bits. I'm getting out too."

"You?" Abby exclaimed. "But why?"

"Mort'll flay me alive when he finds out what I did." She

must have noticed Abby's hastily concealed dismay, because she added proudly, "Don't worry about me, miss; I can look after meself. Now hurry! They'll be out lookin' for them girls any minute now. Valuable property, they are."

Slip-sliding as fast as they could down the alley, the girls broke into a run as soon as they reached the street. They turned down the first corner, ran several blocks, turned another corner and kept running. When they had no more breath, they collapsed, panting, against some railings bordering a quiet garden.

A minute passed . . . two. . . . The only sound was their labored breathing. They watched the way they'd come, ready to flee at the first sign of any movement.

But no one came. Nobody was following them. They'd escaped.

"Right, I'll be off then," Daisy said gruffly when they'd caught their breath. "Good luck to you."

But Abby couldn't let her go like that. "Where will you go? Do you have family in London?"

"Nah, I'm a foundling." She shrugged. "But don't worry; I'll find somewhere." She went to push past them but Abby caught her by the sleeve.

"It's my fault you're in this situation—"

"Nah, I was going to leave anyway." Daisy pulled her arm out of Abby's grip.

"Abby!" Jane turned pleading eyes on her sister, but Abby didn't need any prompting. If she could take a painted prostitute under her wing, she certainly wasn't going to let this small heroine stump gallantly off into the night, alone and friendless. And bruised.

She took Daisy's hand in a firm grip. "You're coming with us, Daisy, for tonight at least. No, don't argue. After all you've done for us there's no way in the world I'm going to let you wander off in the dark with nowhere to go. Now come along; let's get Jane and Damaris into the warmth."

Anne Gracie is the award-winning author of the Chance Sisters Romances, which include *The Spring Bride*, *The Winter Bride* and *The Autumn Bride*. She spent her childhood and youth on the move. The gypsy life taught her that humor and love are universal languages and that favorite books can take you home, wherever you are. Anne started her first novel while backpacking solo around the world, writing by hand in notebooks. Since then, her books have been translated into more than sixteen languages, and include Japanese manga editions. As well as writing, Anne promotes adult literacy, flings balls for her dog, enjoys her tangled garden and keeps bees. Visit her online at www.annegracie.com.